ACCLAIM FOR E
BAN

D1205104

"E.K. Blair has created a complex puzzle. A woven mystery, dragging me deeper into its web of darkness and revenge, characters who have so many facets it's hard to know truth from fakery."
   —Pepper Winters, *USA Today Bestselling Author*

"*Bang* is a dark, twisted tale that will leave you reeling and begging for more. In the Black Lotus series, E.K. Blair has created a cast of intriguing characters that will forever lurk in the corners of your mind. One moment I despised their actions, the next I couldn't get enough. Hot. Suspenseful. This dark tale of thriller-meets-romantic-suspense is a do not miss!"
   —Aleatha Romig, *New York Times Bestselling Author*

"E.K. Blair's boldest, most daring work to date. Twisted and completely brilliant. You're in for a wild ride with this tale that's so beguiling and intriguing. There's suspense and steaminess, hopelessness and hope, romance and hate. It's simply damn good."
   —Vilma Gonzalez, *USA Today HEA blog*

"This is undoubtedly one of my favorite books to date. E.K. Blair took risks I have yet to see any author, indie or traditionally published, take. She found a way to fit a square peg into a round hole. *Bang* is sexy, lustful, and deceitful. I don't know what twisted, sick depths E.K. dug down to in order to find this story within her, but it is absolutely brilliant. Absolutely incredible!"
   —Denise Tung, *Flirty and Dirty Book Blog*

"There's so much we would love to say about just how disturbing, fascinating and riveting this story is. The concept and characters were a brave risk to take, however, what E.K. Blair achieved was thrilling and shocking. *Bang* was un-put-down-able and the end result was nothing short of brilliant! Standing ovation!"
   —Totally Booked

bang

THE BLACK LOTUS SERIES
BOOK ONE

e.k. blair

Bang
Copyright © 2014 by E. K. Blair

Cover Design by E.K. Blair

Editing by Lisa Christman, Adept Edits
https://www.facebook.com/adept.edits

Interior design by Angela McLaurin, Fictional Formats
https://www.facebook.com/FictionalFormats

Photography by Erik Schottstaedt

All rights reserved. No part of this book may be reproduced or transmitted in any form or by any means, electronic or mechanical, including photocopying, recording, or by any information storage and retrieval system, without permission in writing.

This is a work of fiction. Names, characters, places and incidents are the product of the author's imagination or are used fictitiously, and any resemblance to any actual persons, living or dead, events, or locales is entirely coincidental.

The author acknowledges the trademarked status and trademark owners of various products referenced in this work of fiction, which have been used without permission. The publication/use of these trademarks is not authorized, associated with, or sponsored by the trademark owner.

All rights reserved.

ISBN: 978-0-578-14180-0

For Cathy

Because life is not a fairytale,
but we all need that one person who keeps the dream alive.
You are that person for me.

"I'm afraid I can't explain myself.
Because I am not myself, you see?"

—Lewis Carroll

bang

preface

THEY SAY WHEN you take revenge against another you lose your innocence. But I'm not innocent. I haven't been for a very long time. My innocence was stolen from me. Taken was the life I was supposed to have. The soul I was born with. The ruby heart embedded in a life full of hopes and dreams. Gone. Vanished. I never even had a choice. I mourn that life. Mourn the what-ifs. But I'm done. I'm ready to take back what was always meant to be mine. Vengeance is what I seek to reclaim what was viciously ripped from me. So now? Now I plot. Now I take control. Now I don my crown of hatred.

one

(PRESENT)

"HONEY, ARE YOU almost ready?" my husband's voice calls from the other room.

I look at my reflection in the mirror as I slide in my pearl earring, whispering to myself, "Yes."

Straightening my posture and smoothing the slick fabric of my dress, I run my fingers through my long, red hair. A blanket of carmine. Loose waves falling over my bare shoulders. The coolness of the midnight blue silk that clings to the slight curves of my small frame. The stoic good wife. My husband, the beacon of my admiration, or so it seems.

"Stunning."

My eyes shift in the mirror to Bennett as he strolls into my closet and towards the island dresser where I stand. He drags my hair to the side, exposing my neck for his lips to land.

"Mmm," I hum at his touch before turning in his arms to adjust his black bowtie.

His eyes are pinned on me as I focus on his neck, and when I flick my attention up, he gives me a soft smile. I return it. He's striking with his strong bone structure, square jaw, and chestnut hair with the faint flecks of silver. A sign of his thirty-four years and his influential status. A mogul. Owner of the world's largest steel company. He is power. And I the recipient.

"Baldwin is ready with the car," he says before kissing my forehead.

I grab my purse and Bennett helps me with my coat before we take the elevator down. As we walk through the lobby of The Legacy, my home for the past three years, Bennett keeps his hand on the crest of my back, guiding me out into the night's bite of winter.

"Mr. Vanderwal," Baldwin, our driver and good friend to my husband for years, greets with a nod before turning his attention to me, "Mrs."

"Good evening," I say as I slip my hand in his, and he helps me into the back seat of the Land Rover.

Bennett slides in after me and takes my hand in his lap when Baldwin shuts the door and then hops in the front seat. 'Metamorphosis' by Glass, Bennett's favorite, swallows the silence and fills the car. Lifting my free hand up, I place it on the ice-cold window, feeling the dampness and chill as it seeps into my skin.

"I love the snow," I murmur, more to myself than to my husband, but he responds anyway.

"You say that every winter."

Turning to look at him and then down at our linked hands, I release a soft hum before he shifts and says, "So Richard said he stopped by this hotel the other day

4

and mentioned that it would be a good location to hold our New Year's Eve party this year."

"What's the name?"

"Lotus."

"Interesting," I note before asking, "This is McKinnon's new hotel, right?"

"His son's, actually. I've yet to meet him."

"Hmm."

Giving my hand a light squeeze, he questions, "What's that look for?"

"McKinnon can be, well . . ."

"An ass?"

I smile and agree, "Yes. I just never knew he had any children, that's all."

Driving through the Saturday evening traffic in the loop of Chicago, we finally pull up to the newly built boutique hotel that will cater to the city's elite. We tend to find ourselves at a monotonous number of events such as this. With Bennett's status, not only in this city, but worldwide, his presence is of an accord that is sought after for publicity and other reasons. But Bennett has found himself in several business dealings with Calum McKinnon over the years, so tonight's event wasn't one that we could skip out on.

When Baldwin opens the door and helps me down, I right myself and adjust my long dress before being led through the glass doors and inside the lobby of Lotus. While Bennett leaves my side to check our coats, I take in the decorum of guests and bite the inside of my cheek. I know I'm with the wealthiest man here, but my nerves tend to stain my gut, wondering if these people can see right through me.

I'm greeted with a glass of champagne and the eyes of a few women that serve on some of the charity boards that I sit on.

"You ready, honey?"

My husband wraps his arm around my hip and guides us over to the first of many interactions we will have. I gloss on my smile, raise my chin, and play the part. The part I have played since I met Bennett.

He's a loving husband, always has been. Firm in his business, but so very gentle with me, as if I'm breakable. Maybe I used to be, but not anymore. I'm as strong as they come. Weakness derives from the soul. Most everyone has one, which gives a woman like me leverage. Leverage to play people to my liking, and so I do.

"Nina!" I hear my name being drawn out by one of my *friends*.

"Jacqueline, don't you look lovely," I say as she leans in to kiss my cheek.

"Well, I can't even compete with you. Gorgeous as always," she says before turning her attention to Bennett and blushing as she says hello. I'm sure she just soaked her panties as well. She's a desperate flirt. Her husband is a sorry excuse for a man. But that husband is a business partner with Bennett, so I put up with his misogynistic bullshit and feel sorry for the twit that he married. She's been trying to get into my husband's pants since I first met her. I've never said a word because desperation is not something that Bennett is attracted to.

While Jacqueline flirts with my husband, I scan the room. Everyone dressed in their finest, drinking and socializing. I turn away from the mindless people and take in the sleek, modern design of the hotel. A minimalistic fitting but clearly bathed in money. As I float my gaze around the room, I land on a pair of eyes staring at me. Eyes that catch my interest. Standing in a small group, not paying attention to a single person around him, a man—a startlingly attractive man—is watching me. Even as I look at him from across the room, he doesn't divert his lock on me; he merely cocks a small grin before taking a sip out of his highball. When a slender blonde strokes his arm, the contact is lost. Impeccably dressed in a bespoke suit, he has a slightly uncaring look about him. His hair is styled loosely, as if he just ran his hands through the thick locks and said *fuck it*, and his defined jaw is covered in day-old stubble. But that suit . . . yeah, that suit is clearly covering a body that is well maintained. The lines and cuts hug his form, accentuating broad shoulders that V down to slender hips.

"Honey?"

Pulled away from my lingering eye, I turn to my husband's curious look and notice that Jacqueline is no longer by his side.

"What's got your attention?" he asks.

"Oh. I'm just taking everything in. This place is amazing, huh?"

"I was asking about the party, but I guess you were zoned out. So what do you think?"

"Yes, I agree. This would be a great venue and a nice change of scenery," I tell him, and when I do, I see *fuck it* guy approaching. He has an ease with his stride, and the other women in the room see it too.

"You must be Bennett," he says in a silky, rough Scottish brogue that's reminiscent of his father's accent as he reaches out his hand to my husband. "I'm Declan McKinnon. My father speaks very highly of you."

"Good to finally meet you, Declan. I haven't seen Cal here tonight," Bennett says as he shakes *fuck it* guy's hand, who now has a name.

"He's isn't here. He had to fly to Miami to take care of some business."

"That old bastard never stops moving, does he?" Bennett laughs and Declan joins, shaking his head, saying, "Sixty years old and still barking orders to anyone who will listen. Hell, even to those who won't."

When Declan looks over to me, my husband apologizes and says, "Declan, this is my wife, Nina."

Taking my hand, he leans in and kisses my cheek before pulling back and complimenting, "It's a pleasure. I couldn't help but take notice across the room earlier." Looking at Bennett, he adds, "You're a lucky man."

"I tell her that every day."

I wear my smile as a good wife should. I've been doing this for years, numb to the ridiculous accolades these men tend to throw around in their lame attempts at gentlemanly ways. I can see that Declan makes no attempts though. His shoulders are loose. He's relaxed.

"This place is quite an accomplishment. Congratulations," Bennett tells him.

"Thank you. It only took a few years off my life, but," he says as he takes in the surroundings, "she's exactly how I envisioned her," before bringing his eyes back to me.

This guy is outright flirting, and I'm surprised when it slides past Bennett as he continues in conversation.

"I was just telling Nina that your hotel would provide a perfect backdrop for our year-end party that we throw for our friends."

I butt in with a smirk, saying, "It's a once-a-year event where my husband releases the reins, allowing me to create an event to accentuate his financial power, simply to remind everyone who's on top. A penis extender, if you will, and he's due for his annual visit." I tease with a tender femininity that has the boys laughing in amusement at my tart words. I laugh along with them as I shoot my husband a flirty wink.

"She's got a sweet mouth on her," Declan says.

"You have no clue," Bennett responds as he looks down at me with his grin. "But despite what she says, she loves planning this yearly engagement, and I get a thrill out of watching her spend all of my hard-earned money. But we're in a bind because the venue we selected a few months back is now under renovation and the space won't be ready in time."

"When does this event take place?"

"It's a New Year's Eve ball," he answers.

"Sounds like that is doable," Declan says as he takes out a business card from inside his suit jacket, and instead of handing it to Bennett, he hands it to me, saying, "Since it seems you're the woman I'll be answering to, here are my contact numbers."

Taking the card from between his fingers, I watch as he turns and tells my husband, "I'll be sure to oversee the planning to ensure that Nina gets everything she requests."

"Looks like I'll be writing a big check this year," my husband jokes. "Well, Declan, it was great to finally put a face to the name, but if you'll excuse us, I'd like to show off my wife on the dance floor."

When Bennett leads us to the full dance floor and wraps me in his arms, I take the opportunity to peek over his shoulder to find Declan watching me intently. This guy makes no qualms about his interest, and a pang of elation thrums inside me as my husband slowly moves me with ease.

We continue to spend the evening mingling and visiting with friends and business associates before we retire for the evening and head back to The Legacy. Stepping off the elevator and into the penthouse that Bennett owned when I first met him four years ago, we walk through the darkened living room. The only light is from the moon that's casting its glow behind the snow-filled clouds outside the floor to ceiling windows that span across the two walls. I enter the master suite behind Bennett, and as I slip off my heels, I look up to see that he has already undone his bowtie and it hangs around the collar of his white tuxedo shirt, which he is now unbuttoning.

His eyes are rapt as they move down my body. I stand there as he slowly approaches and then slides his hands along the length of my sides until he finds himself on his knees in front of me. He runs his hands up my legs through the opening of the slit in my dress, and as soon as his fingers hit my panties, I turn it off.

The steel cage wraps around my heart and before my stomach can turn, I shut down.

Numb.

Vacant.

He drags my panties down my legs and I step out of them before I feel the warmth of his tongue when he slides it along the seam of my pussy, but I am able to keep myself from entertaining the slightest impulse of intimacy. I've been sleeping with my husband for years, but I refuse to allow the pleasure I lead him to believe I'm experiencing.

Why?

I'll tell you why.

Because I hate him.

He thinks, in this moment, that we're making love. His cock fills me slowly as I lie beneath him. Arms laced around his neck. Legs spread open wide, inviting him in deeper as he makes a meal out of my tits. He believes everything I want him to. He always has. But this is merely a game for me. A game he foolishly has fallen into. He never questions my love for him, and now my body writhes underneath his and moans in mock pleasure as he comes hard, jerking his hips into me, telling me how much he loves me, and I give his words right back.

"God, Bennett, I love you so much," I pant.

His head is nestled in the yoke of my neck as he tries to calm his breathing, and when he lifts up, I run my fingers through his hair and over his damp scalp as he looks into my eyes.

"You're so stunning like this."

"Like what?" I question softly.

"Sated."

Idiot.

two
(PRESENT)

ROLLING OVER IN bed, I find myself alone. Nothing new. Bennett's aftershave still lingers in the air, and when I freshen up and walk out into the open-concept living room, I see him sitting at the bar in the kitchen. He reads a file while drinking his coffee. Tying the sash of my silk robe around my waist, I approach him from behind, wrapping my arms around his shoulders, giving him a kiss.

"Good morning," he says with a grin, happy to see me.

"You're up early," I respond as I note his three-piece suit.

Setting the file down, he turns to pull me in between his legs. "I'm leaving for Dubai. Did you forget?"

"Of course not. But you don't leave for another few hours," I tell him and then drop my head, adding in mock sadness, "I wish you would stay."

Kissing my lips, he draws away and strokes his fingers through my long hair, combing it back. "It's only for a few days.

Plus, you'll be busy."

"Busy?"

"I need you to start getting everything lined up for the party. It's just over a month away and announcements need to go out soon. Richard isn't going with me, so he'll be around this week if you need anything."

Richard is Jacqueline's husband and Bennett's business partner. He has always rubbed me the wrong way, but I feign my liking for him merely for Bennett.

He wears an ascot for Chrissakes.

"Okay. Well, I'll do some work from here today and then call the hotel to set up a meeting."

As I walk over to fix a cup of hot tea, Bennett gets back to his work before he has to catch his flight. After a while, Baldwin takes his luggage down to the car while we say our goodbyes.

"I'm gonna miss you," I murmur, to which he responds, "Honey, you always say that."

Rubbing up against him, I cover his mouth with mine. "Because I always do."

He smiles.

I smile.

"Call me as soon as you land so that I know you're okay."

"I love you."

I follow him to the elevator and give him one last kiss before he leaves and then make my way to the study to work on the laptop. Getting myself comfortable, I open the lid and type *Declan McKinnon* into the search engine. Link after link floods the screen. I click on one and read:

Declan Alexander McKinnon
Born in Edinburgh, Scotland
Age: 31
Son of Calum McKinnon and the late Lillian McKinnon
MBA studies at The University of St. Andrews in Scotland

I continue to read about his various academic and business accomplishments and recognitions. I've met his father on several occasions and know that the family name is a well-respected one, so I can imagine the pressure on him to keep it as such.

Clicking over to the image search, hundreds of pictures of him grace the screen with a variety of women attached to his arm. Clearly he enjoys his bachelor status, but it seems he is new to the Chicago area.

Without pondering on him too much, I close the internet down and open Bennett's address book to begin working. Because of his notoriety, our extravagant annual event calls to the cravings of egos. For that alone, security and privacy are a necessity.

In lieu of my usual distaste for my husband, I must give him credit for being a self-made man. For building this multi-billion dollar company from the ground up and making the Vanderwal name something to be admired. A name that adorns me when my former was tarnished.

Once I have a rough guest list, I email it to Bennett for his lookover. Walking out of the study, Clara catches my eye. She's busy unloading groceries in the kitchen when I say, "I didn't hear you come in."

"Mrs. Vanderwal, hi," she says sweetly. "Your husband

insisted that I come in today since he's going away on business. Is he still here?"

"No, you missed him." Walking over, I step into the kitchen and start helping her put away the food.

"Stop fussing over this," she playfully scolds, and I smile at her when she shoos me out of the kitchen.

I never had a mom, and although Clara is an employee, she fills our home with a warmth that only a woman with a strong maternal sense can do.

"Would you like for me to fix you a cup of tea?"

"No, thank you. I had one earlier."

I take a seat at the bar as she asks, "You hungry?"

Shaking my head, I say, "I think I'm going to hang around here today. Bennett wants me to start working on the ball, so I figure I'll lie around and surf the internet for ideas."

"Is it that time already?"

"Mmm hmm."

"How fast the years go by. When you get to be my age, you better not blink. Ever," she says with a soft smile as she starts to pull out pans to cook.

I walk over to the windows and watch as the snow falls over the city. From up here on the seventy-first floor, I feel like a queen. I take a moment to enjoy the view before I get to work while Clara busies herself in the kitchen, preparing meals for the next few days. Time escapes me and before I know it, the sky is darkening and Clara is saying goodbye.

WHEN I WAKE up the next morning, I take my time getting ready. I wander over to the windows, and as I'm looking down on the busy traffic in the loop on this Monday morning, I take a sip of my tea and then hear my phone ring. I see it's Bennett and answer.

"Hey, honey," I say as I walk over to the sofa and take a seat.

"Hi. I tried calling when I landed yesterday."

"Sorry. I went to bed early."

"That taxing of a day, huh?" he jokes with light laughter.

"Yeah, something like that. Must be this constant snow we're having. Makes me lazy," I tell him. "So how is everything going?"

"Good. Just met with our new client and had a late lunch. I'm heading back to the hotel now to grab a shower before I have to wine and dine these bastards later tonight at dinner, but I wanted to catch you because I missed hearing your voice last night."

"You missed my voice, huh?"

"I missed more than your voice," he flirts.

Letting out a deep breath, I tell him, "I miss having you in bed with me. I'm always lonely without you here. This place is too quiet and too still."

"Didn't Clara stop by yesterday?" he asks.

"She did. You know, you don't have to mollycoddle me. I'm a big girl."

"I like to . . . what did you call it? *Mollycoddle?*" I can hear the chuckle in his voice when he says this, and I play right back in laughter, saying, "Yes. Mollycoddle. For such a worldly man, you should broaden your vocabulary."

"Is that so? Well, maybe when I get back I should show you just how expansive my vocabulary is."

I laugh. If there's one thing Bennett is not, it's a dirty talker, but I give him a flirtatious, "Hmm . . . maybe you should come home early."

"I wish. Although I *am* enjoying the warmer temperatures here. It's nice and sunny."

"If you're trying to make me jealous, it won't work. You know I love the cold and grey. Gives me a reason to cuddle up to your warmth every night."

"So what kept you warm last night?"

"Stuffing my stomach full of Clara's baked ziti and then huddling down deep in the blankets."

"Well, I'll be home soon enough to keep you warm, hun," he says in a smooth voice before asking, "So what's on your agenda today?"

"I was going to give the hotel a call to see if I can set up a meeting to look over the space again."

"We were just there."

"Yeah, but now I want to see it empty, without all of Chicago's upper crust loitering in it."

He laughs at me and then says, "Sweetheart, don't you forget that you are as upper crust as they get."

"And I only have you to thank for that, darling," I tease. "But seriously, I want to see what the space looks like empty and talk to management to find out if they have any new leads on vendors. I'd like to step out of the norm from what we've done the past couple of years."

"As long as it has your hand in it, it will be amazing. Everything you touch turns to perfection. Just look at me."

"Perfection, huh? Well, I can't argue with that ego of yours. I wouldn't change a thing about you."

"And I you," he compliments before saying, "The car just pulled up to the hotel, so I need to let you go."

"Okay. Try not to work too hard. I miss you."

"Miss you too, love. Have a good day."

We hang up and I let out a deep breath. Talking to him like that used to be difficult in the beginning, but now it's as natural as wanting to wipe dog shit off your shoe.

I walk into my closet to pull out the clutch I took to the party the other night. Opening it, I take out the business card that Declan gave me and walk back out to the living room to make the call.

"Lotus," a woman's voice purrs.

"Declan McKinnon, is he available?"

"And who shall I say is calling?"

"Nina Vanderwal."

She puts me on hold for a moment and when the line is picked up, she tells me, "Mr. McKinnon is finishing up a meeting. Would you like me to take a message?"

"Well, I don't want to disturb his schedule, but I will be organizing an event and would like to come see the main ballroom space and discuss vendors."

"Of course. Let me direct you over to our manager," she says before transferring me.

After a brief chat with the hotel manager, we set up a meeting an hour from now. Hanging up the phone, I call Baldwin to have the car ready to drive me over to the hotel. When he arrives, I'm ready as he helps me slip my coat on over my ivory silk top that's tucked into my tailored, black, wool pants.

"Are you ready?" Baldwin asks as I grab my purse.

"Ready."

We ride down on the elevator, and as we walk through the lobby, the car has already been pulled around out front.

"Watch your step," Baldwin says as I maneuver around the small ice patches in my high heels.

When I arrive at Lotus, I walk in and am greeted by the manager who is waiting for me. He leads me into the ballroom, and I take note of the space. The main seating area will easily accommodate the event, and there is an attached lounge that houses various cigars and liquors that are displayed around the dark mahogany room. The bar is broad and masculine, and the woodwork is quite impressive. It's a shame all this was hidden beneath the sea of people that was here at the grand opening. The setting is an intimate one despite the vast size of the room. The dance floor is situated down a small flight of stairs, setting it off from the dining room, creating a less hectic atmosphere for entertaining.

A familiar accent catches me off guard as I'm walking around and taking notes in my memo book.

"How does she look?" His brogue casts through the room, and when I turn to catch his eye, I ask, "Excuse me?"

Scanning the space, he clarifies, "The space, I mean. Looks different empty, doesn't it?"

Turning my head to admire the décor, I say, "Yes. I was just thinking about how much detail I failed to see the other night with all the people here."

He walks over to me, looking polished in his slacks and fitted button-up, sans suit jacket and tie, with a slight grin on his face, and reaches out for my hand and finally greets, "It's good to see you again, Nina."

The way my name is caressed by his accent is without a doubt sexy as hell.

As he brushes his lips over my knuckles, the stubble along his jaw grazing over the soft skin of my hand, I don't respond, but when he keeps his hold a beat too long, I pull away. His smirk remains, as if amused by my reaction.

He casually turns to the man that was showing me around and dismisses him. Turning back to me, he shoves his hands into the pockets of his slacks and asks, "So, what do you think?"

"I think my husband was right; it's the perfect place to host the party."

"Great. Did you need to look around anymore?"

"I think I've gotten my fill for the moment."

He seems humored by something, maybe me, and pulls his hands out of his pockets, placing one on my back as he leads me out of the room.

"Let's go to my office and discuss the details then."

We make our way into his office, and I stand in the center of the oversized room as he walks over to his desk, moving with a relaxed confidence, and grabs the laptop. He nods his head towards the leather couch, saying, "Please, have a seat."

I situate myself and open my planner, flipping through the pages to find my calendar, when I feel his eyes on me.

"Why are you looking at me like that?" I ask when I look up at him, feigning my annoyance.

"Where does one even buy a paper planner anymore?" he teases.

"Lots of places."

"I haven't seen one of those in years. You do know they make these things called tablets now."

Smiling at his banter, I say, "Yes. Every now and then I'm able to crawl out from under my rock to keep up to speed with modern technology, thank you."

He shakes his head and laughs as I watch his smile reach his green eyes and crinkle at the corners.

"Do you even own one?" he asks, still smirking at me.

"No."

He doesn't respond, but his unfaltering look pulls out my answer to his unspoken 'Why?'

"I like privacy. Technology disrupts that. I can burn paper and throw the ashes away as if it never existed. Untraceable." Giving the sly grin back to him, I add, "But you? Don't you think it's foolish that you're putting yourself out there? To be exposed?"

"Is this a riddle?"

I laugh, ignoring his question as I flip through my calendar and confirm, "You have December 31st open, correct?"

Sighing, he shifts and looks at his laptop, saying, "Yes."

"Great. Bennett likes to keep this event small, two hundred or so. Security is important to him—"

"You as well?" he interrupts and I soften my face, smile, and say, "Yes. Me, as well. As I was saying, guests will need to check in, so will your staff provide that amenity?"

"Anything you want."

We spend the next hour discussing ideas for setup and scheduling meetings with a few vendors for the next couple of weeks before I call to have Baldwin pick me up. Declan's well-bred manners sway to the salacious side with the way he kisses me when I leave, gripping my upper arms in his hands and dragging his lips along my cheek before pressing his lips on the shell of my ear, whispering, "Until next time."

three

(PRESENT)

DECLAN CALLED ME two days ago to confirm my meeting with the florist. He recommended the company located in Andersonville that his hotel uses to outfit the lobby, so I agreed. After discussing the masked ball theme with Bennett this morning, he gave me the green light, which made me happy. I can tell he misses me from our phone call—he wasn't quick to hang up—but he'll be returning from Dubai tomorrow evening. Despite his loneliness, he was happy to have acquired the production plant that he set out to buy from the nearly bankrupt company over there.

The drive to Andersonville takes longer than usual with the weather. Winters in Chicago are brutal to the city but a brutality that I enjoy. So as I ride in the backseat, I find myself watching the white snow hit the window and slowly melt to a drizzling cascade down the glass.

Arriving at Marguerite Gardens, I walk into the rustic shop.

Brick walls, weathered wooden floors, extravagant floral arrangements set atop the agrarian tables, and *him*. Standing there in charcoal slacks and a light blue button-up, he turns away from the woman he's speaking with and smiles as I walk over to him. Miffed.

"What are you doing here?"

"You made it," Declan announces quietly with what looks like irritation and drops a scant kiss to my hand when he takes it.

"I didn't know you'd be joining me."

"I promised your husband I would oversee everything to ensure you get exactly what you want. So here I am," he states, and then lowers his voice, "ensuring you get exactly what you want."

"Why do you do that?"

"Do what?"

"*That*," I say. "Your crass flirting."

"Do I make you uncomfortable?"

"Are you trying to make me uncomfortable?"

Completely ignoring my question, he turns around and calls out, "Betty, show us what you have."

The lady he was talking to when I walked in is now situated behind one of the tables.

Declan pulls a chair out for me, and as I take a seat, Betty greets me and says, "So I was informed that we are planning a New Year's Eve party. Do you already have an idea of what you'd like?"

"I believe we are firm on a masquerade theme. I was leaning towards dark oranges and whites."

Betty and I go through a couple of books, taking notes on flowers and arrangement styles while Declan remains quiet in the seat next to me. At the end of our meeting, we decide on various arrangements of rusty orange dahlias, mint and buttercup roses, antique hydrangeas, ranunculus, and aspidistra.

After Betty excuses herself to leave Declan and me, I pull out my phone to text for the car, but before I can start typing, he snatches it out of my hands and says, "I'm starving."

"Good to know," I snap—annoyed—and grab for my phone at the same time he pulls it away and out of reach. "Give me my phone."

"Have lunch with me."

"No, thank you," I say, making a mockery of my politeness.

Taking my hand and pulling me out of my seat as he stands, he says, "It wasn't a question."

His words come out clipped, almost angry, so I don't give him attitude when he picks up my coat and helps me put it on. I'm not sure what to think about this shift in his demeanor. Normally, he's light and flirty, but today he's quiet and stern.

The frigid wind nearly stings my skin when he leads me outside and walks us over to his black Mercedes sports car. Of course *he* would drive a luxury car like this. It fits the mysterious, sexy look about him. I slip down into the cold leather seat and watch as he walks around the front of the car before he opens his door and gets in.

"Where are we going?" I ask.

"Not telling." He says this with no interpretable body language as he pulls out of the parking lot.

"Why?"

"Because you argue too much."

Feeling like a scolded child with his tone, I want to defy him just to piss him off, but instead, I'll play his game. I'll give him the cooperation he wants.

It's time to start testing the waters.

The drive is short and quiet, and I'm surprised when he turns this luxury car into the lot at the Over Easy Café. I can't even hide the smile on my face at the contrast of this picture as he parks in front of the modest diner.

"Is something funny about this?" he asks when he shuts the car off.

Shooting my narrowed eyes at him, I say, "Your mood is really starting to scathe me. I don't know why you're so pissy, but I wish you'd just cut the shit," before opening my door and walking towards the building. When I look back, he's standing there with an almost proud grin on his face. *What the hell?* I can't figure out what this guy wants, sass or obedience.

Once inside, the place is busy with busboys clearing tables and people chatting loudly while eating. We are quickly served with coffee, and when I pick up the menu, Declan finally speaks, saying, "I figured you hadn't eaten in a place like this in a while, so I thought I would take you somewhere low-key. Don't worry; you'll like the food. Order the blueberry crunch pancakes."

His eyes are soft, as well as his voice, when he says this, and I ask, "Why are you suddenly being nice?"

"I'm cutting the shit. Take it while it lasts because I'm not a man who likes to take orders."

And now, I read him clearly.

With a smile, I give him a sliver of obedience when I say, "I'll have the blueberry crunch pancakes then."

After our waitress stops by to take our order and fantasize about riding Declan's cock, she giggles as she walks away.

"Do you get that a lot?" I ask. "Women feeding your ego as

you watch them blush in your presence."

"You always dissect everything like that?"

"You always avoid questions like that?"

Leaning his forearms on the table, he says, "No more than you do."

"You realize, unless we're discussing business, we talk in circles, right?"

"Okay then. No circles. Ask me a question," he prompts and then takes a sip of his coffee, waiting with curious eyes. Emerald ones rimmed with his dark lashes. I can't blame our waitress for her reaction. I wonder how many women go home after meeting him to fuck their fingers or vibrator before their pitiful husbands return from work.

Cleaning my thoughts, I ask the most innocent question I can think of, even though I already know the answer. "Where are you from?"

"That's your question?" he laughs, and when I glare at him, he swallows it and says, "Edinburgh."

"Scotland?"

"Do you know of another?"

Smartass.

"I thought you were cutting the shit and being nice," I say as I lean back and pick up my coffee mug.

"Momentary slip. My turn. How long have you been married?"

"A little over three years."

"How long have you been together?"

"Four years. And that was two questions," I lightly nag.

"I'm not good at following rules either," he says and then continues before giving me a chance to speak. "Sounds like a speedy path to the altar."

"What can I say? When Bennett wants something, he wastes no time in claiming it."

When our waitress returns, I watch as she nervously makes eyes with Declan while she serves our food. I laugh and he takes notice, shaking his head.

"See what I mean?" I ask after she walks off.

"Does that bother you?"

"Why would it bother me?" I question and pick up my fork to cut a piece of my pancake.

"Then why even mention it?"

"Circles, Declan. We're doing it again," I say and then take a bite of the granola-filled pancake as he watches.

"Okay, no circles. You have any kids?"

"No."

"Do you want kids?"

"I can't have kids, so it doesn't really matter what I want."

He takes a pause, not expecting that answer, and then asks, "Why can't you have kids?"

"That's none of your business," I tell him and then take another sip of coffee.

"Do you love him?"

Swallowing hard, I clarify, "My husband?"

"Yes."

He takes a bite of his eggs as I straighten my back and look him dead on. "Your assumption that there could be a possibility of more than one answer is offensive."

I notice the slight upward turn of the corner of his mouth, and he holds his stare for a beat before saying, "Funny how you chose not to answer that question, but instead, avoid."

"Of course I love him."

Lie.

"So he's it?"

I hesitate, making sure he takes notice, and then respond with a simple, "Yes," careful to ensure a slight tremble in my voice.

He catches my subtleties as he keeps his eyes pinned on me and I shift, playing uncomfortable, and I'm certain he buys it when he changes the subject. We spend the rest of our meal in idle chitchat about nothing in particular, and as we leave and walk towards his car, my foot hits a patch of ice, unsteadying my balance. Declan's hands are on me fast as I shuffle and land my back against the side of his car. He's close. Chest to chest. Foggy vapors escaping us with each breath. I don't speak or move away. I wonder if he's going to make a play, because I can tell he's thinking about it. But putting thoughts into action takes balls, and I'm hoping he has them.

In a low voice, he urges, "Push me away, Nina," as if he's testing me.

But I'm the one doing the testing; he just doesn't know it. So I respond with, "Why?"

"Because you love your husband."

Pushing my hands against him, I move him away from me as I say, annoyed, "I do love him."

As if no exchange was just made, he opens the door for me to get in.

When we pull onto the main street, he asks, "Where do you live?"

"Why?"

"Because I'm gonna drive you home," he says, turning his head to look at me.

"The Legacy."

The silence between us is noticeable, and I wonder what he's thinking about, but I don't dare ask. He doesn't allow my thoughts to overtake me when he turns on the stereo. I can tell he's using the music to distract himself as he keeps his eyes focused on the road. I'm granted no reprieve as I consider the thoughts that are scrolling through his head right now. But this part is out of my hands because I won't push. The fall has to come of his own accord. I'm merely the fuel that feeds the vehicle; he's the one driving it. And the destination is up to him.

When he pulls up to my building, he shifts the gear into park and looks over at me. He hasn't spoken for the whole drive, and he remains quiet. Wanting to calm any of the ill thoughts he may be having, I lean back against the seat and let out a sigh as I roll my head over to look at him.

Our eyes are locked, his hands still on the steering wheel, and then I say in a soft voice, free from any undertones, "I had a nice time with you." Declan nods, unconvinced, so I give him a little more to coax him, adding, "I don't have many friends."

When I say this, his hands drop slowly to his lap as he turns slightly towards me. He then asks, "What about those two hundred people on the guest list for the event you're planning?"

"If it weren't for Bennett, those people wouldn't give me a second glance. I wouldn't want them to though."

"Why not?"

"Because they're nothing like me."

"How so?"

Lowering my head to focus on my hands, I don't respond immediately.

"Tell me, Nina."

My eyes meet his when I say, with a faint shake of my head, "I guess I'm still trying to figure that out."

"And your husband?" he questions.

"He doesn't know this. He thinks I enjoy the lunch dates with the wives when I really loathe them."

"Then why even bother?"

Letting go of a deep breath, I say, "Because I want to make my husband happy."

He leans over, closer to me, resting his arm on the center console, and asks, "And what about you, Nina? Who wants to make you happy?"

"Bennett makes me happy," I state while his eyes search my face for hints of dishonesty, and I make sure to let a few slip through. Drifting eye contact for a quick second with a couple rapid blinks. Nodding my head as if trying to convince myself of the words. Giving him a small, feeble smile.

I know he buys it when he says with a gentle voice, "Liar."

He's confident in his accusation when I don't deny it, instead, lowering my head and then turning to look out the windshield.

"I should go." Looking over at him, he gives a nod before I open the door and step out.

Walking to the lobby doors, he calls out, "Nina." When I turn around, he's rolled down the passenger window and gives me back my earlier words. "I had a nice time with you too."

I reward him with a smile before walking away.

When I get inside, I drop my purse and coat on the dining

room table and call Baldwin to let him know I got a ride home with Declan and that I won't be needing him for the rest of the evening. I then walk over to inspect the kitchen and notice there is fresh fruit in the fridge that wasn't here this morning, letting me know that Clara has already been here and left.

Knowing there won't be anyone else coming or going, I waste no time pulling my coat back on and grabbing the keys to one of the cars before picking up my purse and heading back out.

When I pull out of the parking garage, I make my way to I-55 and start heading south to the one person who has always been there for me. It's been a few weeks since I last saw Pike, and I miss him. I allow myself the excitement of finally being able to see him—my best friend since I was eight years old.

I pull off the interstate and into the town of Justice before turning onto 79th and heading to the trailer park. When I pull up to the mobile home, I park the car, and take out the key I hide in the lipstick case in my purse. The bass of someone's car stereo rattles the windows, and when I unlock the door and step inside, I relax my shoulders, sigh, and walk straight into Pike's arms. I take his warmth, comfort, and everything else only he can offer as he holds me.

With my arms wrapped around him tightly, I breathe, "I've missed you."

"It's been nearly three weeks," he says as he pulls back to look at me, and when he does, I can see he isn't happy. "Where the fuck have you been, Elizabeth?"

four

(PAST)

"ELIZABETH," MY DADDY calls from outside my bedroom door. "Do you need help?"

I struggle against the glittery fabric of my princess dress, trying to find the opening of the sleeve to push my arm through. "No, Daddy," I call out in a heavy breath as I twist and wriggle my arm, finally finding the opening.

"Are you ready?"

I walk over to my toy box and pull out the pink plastic heels that match my sparkly dress. Putting them on, I walk over to my door and open it. I look up at my daddy, holding a small bunch of pink daisies.

"I never get tired of seeing that beautiful smile," he says before taking my hand and kissing the top of it. He then hands me the flowers. "For my princess."

"Thanks, Da—I mean, Prince."

"May I come into your castle?" he asks, and I grab his hand, pulling him into my bedroom—our pretend castle for the afternoon.

"Would you like some tea?" I ask as we walk towards my table by the window that my tea set is on.

"I would love some. My travel from the kingdom was quite long." I watch him sit down on the small chair and giggle as his knees hit his chest.

Daddy and I do this often, have our fairytale tea parties. I don't have a mommy or any brothers and sisters to play with, but that's okay because I get to have him all to myself. He has the prettiest blue eyes, but he tells me mine are prettier.

Setting down the flowers, I pick up the teakettle and pretend to pour him a cup while he eyes the plastic pastries, swirling his finger above them as he decides on the one that he wants.

"Daddy, just pick one."

His eyebrows shoot up in excitement when his hand lands on the yellow cupcake with sprinkles. "Ahh, this one looks delicious," he says before taking his make-believe bite and then licking his fingers.

I scrunch up my face, squealing, "Eww. Princes don't lick their fingers."

"They don't?"

"No. They use napkins."

He looks around, and says, "Well, I don't have a napkin, and I don't want to waste the icing on my fingers."

I exaggerate thinking, tapping my finger on my cheek, and then agree, "You're right. Okay, you can lick your fingers."

We sit in the sunlight of my room and have our fairytale

tea, talking about the flying horses we'll ride to the magical forest.

"Did I tell you about Carnegie, the caterpillar I met?" he asks.

"You met a caterpillar?"

"The last time I took my steed to the forest, I did. He had some berries he shared with me and then told me a secret," he says quietly as he sets down his teacup.

"What?!" I exclaim excitedly. "You met a *talking* caterpillar?"

"I did. Do you want to know what he told me?"

"Mmm hmm," I hum, nodding my head energetically.

"Well then, he told me he had been living in the magical forest for years, but that he was once a prince."

"Really? What happened?"

He folds his arms over the tops of his knees and leans his chest against them, saying in a secret whisper, "The kingdom's sorcerer cast a spell on him, turning him into a caterpillar."

"Oh no," I gasp. "Why?"

"Turns out, the king was upset because he told Carnegie to stop sneaking out of his room at night and stealing juice boxes from the fridge, so he had the sorcerer use his magic to turn him into a caterpillar."

"Daddy!"

He has a playful smile on his face. I know he's teasing me since he's been getting on to me about waking up and drinking juice boxes at night. Last night he scared me when he turned on the kitchen light and caught me drinking an apple juice.

"You're not gonna cast a spell on me, are you? I don't wanna be a caterpillar."

"Why not? I could introduce you to Carnegie."

"But I would miss you," I pout.

He reaches out his arms for me. "Come here, baby doll," he says as he turns in the small chair and stretches out his legs. Hoisting me up on his lap, he wraps his big arms around me and makes me giggle when he kisses the tip of my nose. "I'd never cast a spell on you and send you away. You're my little girl, you know that?"

"I thought I was a big girl now that I'm five."

"No matter how big you get, you'll always be my little girl. I love you more than anything."

"Anything? Even more than chocolate?"

I watch him laugh, big smile, lines at the corners of his eyes. "Even more than chocolate."

I place my hand on his cheek, prickly with his stubble, and tell him, "I love you more than chocolate too."

He pecks his lips to mine and then asks, "You wanna know what's sweeter than chocolate?"

"Uh huh."

Before I can leap off his lap, he starts playfully attacking my neck, tickling me as he blows raspberries and then plops us on the floor as I roll around, laughing and squealing. He doesn't stop until the doorbell rings. As I try and catch my breath from all the laughing, he sits up on his knees and orders, "Hop on."

I get off the floor and jump on his back, taking a piggyback ride all the way to the front door.

You've heard the saying, "Beware of what lies on the other side," right? Neither of us could have possibly imagined how our lives would be forever changed when he opened that door. I used to wish that someone would cast a spell on me, forever changing me into a caterpillar. I could've had a good life, living in the mythical forest with Carnegie. Spending our days searching for berries and floating aimlessly on the lily pads in the pond. But instead, I was about to find out the hard truth of life at the age of five. The truth they keep from you as a small child, allowing you to believe that the fairytales are real . . . but they aren't. And neither is magic.

"Cook County P.D.," is all I hear as men come charging into the house.

Chaos. Loud chaos.

"Daddy!" I scream, scared, panicked, clinging my arms around his neck like a vice when a man grabs for me. "DADDY!"

"It's okay, baby," I hear my dad say as another man is talking at the same time.

"You're under arrest."

I don't know what those words mean as ice cold fear runs through me, fisting my daddy's shirt in my hands, unwilling to let go of him.

"It's okay, baby. It's going to be okay," he keeps repeating, but his voice is different and I think he's scared too.

"You need to come with me," the man who's grabbing me says.

"No! Let go!"

I begin kicking my legs when I'm pried off my daddy's back, stretching his shirt because I have my hands clamped so tightly to the fabric as I'm being pulled away.

I see my daddy's eyes—blue eyes—as he turns to look at me. "It's okay," he says calmly, but I don't believe him. "Don't be scared. It's okay."

"No, Daddy!" I cry out as the tears fall. I hold on to his shirt until I am pulled so far back it pops out of my hands.

The moment I am no longer touching the man that sings to me at night, that puts my hair in pigtails, that dances with me while I stand on top of his feet, I'm whisked away. I see my prince drop to his knees as I watch over the man's shoulder who's carrying me away.

"DADDY!" I shriek, throat burning, as they clamp my daddy's hands together behind his back with something. His eyes stay on me, never once pausing as he says, over and over, "I love you, baby. I love you so much, baby girl."

And for the first time ever, I see my daddy cry before the door closes on him and he's gone.

"Let me go! DADDY! NO!" Kicking and swinging, I can't escape this man's hold on me.

"It's okay. Calm down, kiddo," he says, but I won't. I want my daddy.

The man sits down on my father's bed with me still in his arms, fighting. He continues to coax me to calm down, but my screaming and thrashing don't falter until I grow tired. My body is limp as I'm crumpled against his chest.

"Can you tell me your name?" he asks.

I don't speak.

A moment passes and then he says, "I'm Officer Harp. Michael Harp. I'm a policeman. You know what that is, don't you?"

I nod my head against his chest.

"Can you tell me your name?"

Still scared, my voice cracks when I tell him, "Elizabeth."

"Elizabeth. That's a nice name," he says. "I have a daughter whose middle name is Elizabeth. She's much older than you are though."

He continues to talk, but I don't pay attention to what he's saying. I'm so scared and all I want is my daddy. I close my eyes; I can see him on his knees crying. He was scared just like me.

After a while, the door opens and I lift my head to see a chubby woman walking in. I think I've seen her before but I can't remember where. As she gets closer, she says, "Your red hair is beautiful. Has anyone ever told you that?"

"Where's my daddy?"

"That's what I am here to talk to you about," she tells me. "Would you like to join me in the kitchen? We can get a snack or something to drink."

"Umm . . . O-okay," I mumble as the policeman sets me on the floor. When I follow the two of them out of the bedroom and into the kitchen, I look through the house to the front door, but nobody's there anymore.

"Why don't we have a seat?" the woman says, and I walk over to the table and sit down. "Do you want something to drink?"

I nod my head and she prompts, "Can you tell me what you want?"

"Juice box."

Looking over at the policeman, he opens the door to the pantry, and I say, "They're in the fridge."

He walks over, pops the straw in, and sets it in front of me before he leaves the room.

"Confusing day, huh?" she says as she folds her hands together on top of the table. "What's your name?"

"Barbara," she answers but it doesn't help me remember how I know her.

"When's my daddy coming back?"

She takes in a deep breath and then tells me, "That's what I'd like to talk to you about. Your father broke some pretty big rules and just like when you break a rule, what normally happens?"

"I get in trouble."

She nods her head and continues, "Well, your father is in trouble, and he won't be able to come home right now."

"What did he do?"

"I'm not quite sure just yet. But for now, you're going to come with me. I work for the Department of Children and Family Services, which means I'm going to find you a home with really nice people that you will stay with while your father is in trouble and can't be here with you, okay?"

"B-But, I don't want to leave."

"Unfortunately, I can't let you stay here alone. But you can bring some of your things with you. How does that sound?" She says this with a smile, but it doesn't help the churning of my stomach.

Quietly, I slip off of the chair and start walking to my room. I go over to the tea set that's on the table and pick up the pink daisies. My princess flowers. I sit down in the chair that he was sitting in and look over my shoulder to see Barbara walking into the room.

"Do you have a bag?"

I point to the closet and watch as she starts going through my dresser, packing up my clothes. She roams around, going back and forth between my bedroom and the bathroom as I clutch the flowers to my chest.

"You ready to go?" she asks when she steps back into the room, but I don't want to look at her because I don't want to go.

Staring out the window and up into the blue sky, I ask, "When can I come back?"

"I'm not sure," she responds. "Probably not for a while."

Out of the corner of my eye, I see her move across the room and kneel down beside me. As I turn to look at her, she says, "Don't worry. Everything's going to be okay." She looks down at the daisies. "Those are pretty flowers. Do you want to bring them with you?"

Leaving the house, we walk out to her car and I hop into the back seat. As I look out the window, I watch the policeman shut the front door to my house and lock some sort of black box onto the door handle.

"What's that?" I ask Barbara, who's sitting up front.

"What's what, dear?"

"That thing he put on the door."

She looks over to see what I'm talking about and responds, "It's just a lock since we don't have the keys," and then starts driving away while I hold tightly to my flowers.

five

(PAST)

IT'S BEEN THREE years since I was taken away from my home and placed in foster care. Three years since I've seen my dad. I was told he was trafficking guns to South America. I still don't understand everything, but then again, I'm just an eight-year-old kid. A ward of the state of Illinois. Three years and I miss my dad every day. No one will take me to go see him since he's over six hours away, serving his nine-year sentence in Menard Prison.

I sit in my room and wait on my caseworker, Barbara, to come pick me up to take me to my new home. Three years and I'm leaving my fifth home to go to my sixth. The first place I went was in the same town of Northbrook, where I'd lived. But after getting caught sneaking out of my bedroom window a few times during the night, they said they couldn't manage me, and so I left. The same thing has happened at each home I've lived in.

At first I was scared. I cried a lot. I missed my dad and

would scream for him, but he never came. I didn't understand then, but I do now. I'm not gonna get to see him until he gets out. I'll be fourteen years old. Fourteen is my new lucky number. I count everything in groups of fourteen just to remind myself that the time will come when I can see him again and we can go back to our life together in our nice house in our nice neighborhood. I miss his smile and the way he smelled. I can't explain it, but sometimes when I'd be at preschool, I can faintly remember lifting my shirt to inhale his scent when I was missing him. The smell of my dad.

Comfort.

Home.

When I hear the doorbell ring, I know it's time. I've been through several home switches before. You'd think I'd be scared, but I'm used to it now. So I grab my bags and head out to the front door. Barbara is standing there talking to Molly, the foster mom that doesn't want to deal with me anymore. They both turn as I approach and say *hi*.

"You ready, Elizabeth?" Barbara asks.

Nodding my head, I walk past Molly as she places her hand on my shoulder, saying, "Wait."

She kneels down to give me a hug, but I don't return it. I'm sad, but I don't cry; I just wanna leave, so when she lets go, that's what I do.

While I sit in the passenger seat, watching the buildings pass by as Barbara drives, she turns down the radio and says, "Talk to me, kid."

I hate when she calls me *kid*, like I'm not special enough for her to use my name. She only uses it when there are other people around, but alone, I'm *kid*.

"What do you mean?" I ask.

"I've found five good homes for you, and you've managed to get kicked out of every one of them. You keep me busy, you know that?"

I'm not sure if she really wants a response, so I stay quiet before she adds, "You can't keep sneaking out at night. What the hell are you doing out on the streets in the middle of the night anyway?"

"Nothing," I mutter just to say something to appease her. Truth is, I started sneaking out to see if I could find Carnegie. Sounds stupid now, but when I was five, I thought he'd be there, waiting for me to find him. So I would sneak out and walk around, hoping to stumble upon that magical forest. It never happened, and now I'm old enough to know fairytales aren't real, but I still sneak out and look for the forest anyway.

"Well, listen, I couldn't find a home to place you in around here, so you're gonna be in a different town. You're not gonna be seeing me anymore since I don't live there. I'm still going to handle your case, but Lucia will be your contact. She should be doing a visit with you later this week. But a piece of advice—stop causing issues or the next stop will be a group home."

"So I won't see you again?"

She looks over at me, saying, "Probably not, kid."

We've been in the car for almost two hours when we finally exit the highway.

"Welcome to Posen," Barbara says, and it isn't but a couple minutes later when she pulls into a rundown neighborhood.

Chain-link fences run alongside the cracked sidewalks. The homes are old and small, unlike the large brick house I lived in with my dad. Most of these homes have cars parked on their unkempt lawns, chipped paint, and everything about what I'm seeing brings on a well of tears. My stomach knots, and I turn to Barbara, saying, "I don't think I want to live here, Barb."

"Shoulda thought about that when I told you to stop sneaking out at night."

"I promise. I won't do it again. I'll say sorry to Molly," I beg, and when she pulls into the drive of a dirty, old, two-story house that looks like it's barely standing, I start crying. "Please. I don't wanna live here. I wanna go home."

She turns the car off and looks over at me. I feel like I'd do just about anything to convince her to turn the car around and take me back to Northbrook.

"I'm in a bind. You're eight years old with an unstable home history. Now this family has been fostering for years. They are currently fostering a boy a few years older than you," she tells me. "I talked to them just the other day. You'll have your very own room and will go to the same school as their other foster kid."

I keep my mouth shut and listen. I don't want to be here. I wanna run, just open this car door and run as fast as I can. I wonder if she'd be able to catch me.

"You listening?" she asks and refocuses my attention back to her.

I nod my head.

"Come on. I've got a long drive back," she says as she gets out of the car and opens the back door to grab my bags.

With a shaking hand, I open the door and follow her along the weathered driveway to the steps leading up to the front door. The rusted screen door squeaks loudly as she opens it and knocks a few times. I stand there, picking at my nails, praying to

God that no one opens the door. That this is all a big mistake and we're at the wrong house.

But it isn't a mistake, and someone does answer the door. A woman, dressed in a homely, long, denim skirt and a light purple sweater, opens the door. I stare at her as Barbara starts to talk. The woman doesn't look scary, but I still feel like bolting. She looks down at me and gives me a soft smile. Her ratty ponytail is attempting to tame her long, brown, frizzy hair.

Stepping aside, she invites us in, and the place smells like stale cigarette smoke. While she leads us through the small living room and back to the kitchen, the two of them continue to talk as I take everything in. Wood-paneled walls, brown carpet, mismatched furniture, and ducks everywhere. *Everywhere.* Ducks on pillows, wooden ducks, ceramic ducks, glass ducks. They line the book shelves, cover the tables, and when I look up, they are even on top of the kitchen cabinets.

"Elizabeth."

It takes me a second to realize that Barbara is saying my name, and when I look over at her, she gives me one of her fake smiles and says, "Mrs. Garrison says that your bedroom is upstairs."

"I hope you like purple," the woman says to me as I look at her purple top and then back up to her face when she says, "You're the first girl we've gotten, so I got a little carried away."

Barbara gives me an annoyed look, nodding her head to encourage me to talk.

"Yeah," I finally say. "Purple is nice."

She smiles and lays her hand over mine. I want to snatch it away, but I don't. I don't do anything that my mind is screaming I should. I just sit.

"Well then, why don't I help you up with your bags before I go?" Barbara says.

The three of us walk up the stairs as they creak beneath our feet and into the purple room. The walls match Mrs. Garrison's sweater, and I watch as she shows me the closet and then the Jack-and-Jill bathroom that adjoins to the other bedroom.

"This seems like a great room, huh?" Barbara says when she plops my bags down on top of the purple twin bed.

"Mmm hmm."

"Well, I have to get back on the road," she tells me, and when she does, I feel the tears hit my cheeks.

Suddenly, I've never felt more alone. Empty.

"There's no need to cry. You're gonna be fine. I know that change can be hard, but you'll be okay. Like I said, Lucia will be out to meet you in a few days, okay?"

"Okay." It's an auto-response because I'm far from okay.

With a light pat on my shoulder, Barbara leaves me behind, standing in the purple room with duck lady.

"Would you like me to help you unpack, dear?" she asks.

"I'll do it."

"Are you hungry? I could fix you a sandwich."

I look up at her through the remaining tears in my eyes and nod my head.

"Great. We normally always eat at the kitchen table, but I'll bring it up to you if you'd like."

"Okay," I say as I start unzipping my bags.

"Elizabeth," she calls from the hall, right outside the bedroom, "I hope you'll like it here. Carl, my husband, worked hard painting this room for you. He's out running a couple errands, but should be home shortly."

When I don't respond, she excuses herself and heads downstairs, leaving me alone to unpack. Next to the bed is a small window that looks out over the front of the house. All the houses are the same aside from the various colors of paint. Everything looks decayed here.

I take my time putting my clothes away and eventually eat the peanut butter sandwich that Bobbi brought me. She told me to call her that rather than Mrs. Garrison.

Aside from a small dresser, desk, and bulletin board, the room is pretty bare. When I walk into the bathroom, the sink counter is already occupied with the other kid's stuff. I wonder if he's like me, how old he is, and if he's nice. I feel like I need a friend more than ever right now. I'm so far from home and so alone.

A loud rumbling from outside calls my attention, and I walk over to look out the window. An old, grey, beat-up pickup truck pulls into the driveway. I watch as an older, fat guy gets out of the driver's seat and starts walking towards the house. Then the boy gets out, but I can't see what he looks like under his baseball cap.

I stay in my room and listen as they walk in, talk to each other, and then I hear the creaking of the stairs. Bobbi is the first one I see, followed by her husband.

"Elizabeth, how's the unpacking going?" she asks.

"Good," I say as I look at the man. He's got a big belly, stains on his shirt, and long, messy hair.

"That's good. This is Carl, my husband," she introduces.

"Elizabeth, is it?" he asks.

Nod.

"You settling in all right?"

Nod.

"You don't talk much, do you?"

Feeling like I need to say something, I mumble, "I'm just tired."

"Well, I'll leave you be then," he says. "Glad to have you here."

Bobbi smiles as Carl walks out and after she asks me how I'm doing and if I need anything, I lie and assure her that I'm fine. She closes the door behind her and as soon as she does, I see the light from the other bedroom flick on through the bathroom. I watch, and when I see the boy with the baseball cap, he turns to look at me.

"Hi," he says as he stands on his end of the bathroom.

"Hi."

Taking off his cap, he tosses it on his bed and runs his hand through his sweaty, dark brown, nearly black hair. He then walks through the bathroom and into my room, looking around.

"This color is sickening," he says, giving me my first real smile in a long time.

"I lied," I tell him. "I told her I like purple, but I don't."

"You been in the system long?"

"Three years."

"Nine for me. I just got here a couple weeks ago."

"Are they nice?" I ask.

He takes a seat on the bed next to me, and he smells like cigarette smoke and soap. "Bobbi hasn't been here much. She just got back in town from some crafting show she did."

"Crafting show?"

"Yeah, she makes wooden duck figurines and crap to sell at fairs, flea markets, and shit, so she's gone a lot. Carl works at the auto mechanic shop down the road." He pauses and then adds, "He drinks a lot."

I don't say anything, and we sit in silence for a moment before he asks, "How old are you?"

"Eight. You?"

"Eleven. Almost twelve. Name?"

"Elizabeth."

"You scared, Elizabeth?"

Looking over at him, I pull my knees to my chest, wrap my arms around them, and nod, whispering, "Yeah."

"It'll be okay. Promise."

I watch as a hint of a smile crosses his face and something about it tells me that I can believe him.

"I'm Pike, by the way."

Six
(PRESENT)

"WHERE THE FUCK have you been, Elizabeth?"

"I'm sorry," I say as Pike loosens his hold on me. "I haven't been able to get away, but I'm here now."

Pike takes a step back, raking one hand through his thick, choppy, dark hair and releases a rough breath through his nose.

"Pike, come on. Don't make me regret coming here. I only have tonight before Bennett comes back home."

"I'm just sick of living in this shithole while you're living your precious life in that fuckin' penthouse. It's been over three years," he bites and then falls back onto the couch.

Looking down at him, I try to soothe his irritation, "I know. I'm sorry, but you knew it would be like this. You knew this wouldn't work if we moved fast."

"Are you even working at it at all, Elizabeth? Because from where I'm standing, it seems you've gotten quite comfortable in your new life."

"Don't be a dick, Pike," I say, raising my voice at him. "You know me better than that. You know I hate that asshole with everything I am."

He leans forward, resting his elbows on his knees with his head dropped. Walking over to him, I sit down on the couch and start rubbing his hardened shoulder, muscles tense out of frustration.

"I'm sorry," he quietly says, and sits back, pulling me with him and holding me.

I need the contact, need his touch. I always have, so I linger in it for a moment with my arm slung around his waist. I hate being away from him, but I know he hates it more. I don't blame him. This is the shittiest place he's lived, but he's paying the owner of this trailer under the table to keep himself off the grid. He's still hustling to get by, and here I am, lying in his arms wearing a goddamn Hermés coat that probably costs more than this crap-hole he lives in.

"It's okay," I assure him. "I'm sorry you're stuck here, but it won't be forever."

"I'm beginning to wonder if it will."

I swing my legs across his lap so that he can cradle me to his chest, and when I get comfortable in this new position, I tell him, "I met someone."

"Yeah?"

"Yeah. I think he's interested."

"You said that about the others. What makes you think this one is different?" he questions.

"I don't know that he is, but it's worth a shot, right?"

He doesn't respond, and when I tilt my head back to look up at him, he locks eyes with me.

"I'm not giving up," I say. "I need you to know that. I'll do whatever it takes to get us that new beginning."

He kisses me, slipping his hand behind my head to hold me close. The familiar taste of his clove cigarettes comforts me the way a blanket would a child. He's my comfort. I've depended on him ever since I was a little girl. He's protected me as an eight-year-old child and continues to, even though I'm now a twenty-eight-year-old woman.

The rough warmth of his tongue slides along mine, slowly, as he pulls back, ending our kiss.

"So who's the unfortunate bastard?"

"His name's Declan McKinnon. Bennett and I were at an event of his when I first met him."

"What kind of event?" he asks.

"It was the opening of his hotel. He had a showy party with all the right names in attendance," I tell him. "I don't know much about him, but I do know that his father is a developer and has a long string of high-end hotels behind his name. I'm not sure how many Declan has his hands in, but that one for sure."

"He seems too high profile," he says as he shifts me off his lap and heads to the kitchen. "Beer?"

"Yeah."

He pops the caps then hands me a bottle when he sits back down next to me.

"I know he's not the ideal choice, and I wasn't even going to mess with him, but he's working with me on an event and we're spending a lot of time together. I dunno . . ." I take a sip of my beer, and then add, "Time will only tell, but I can already see the intrigue. But I just met him, so I'm still trying to figure him out."

"And what do you think so far?"

"I think he's the type of guy who likes to have control. But at the same time, he seems amused when I get snarky with him. I already planted the seed that I'm a person that might need to be saved." I laugh at the memory of being in his car just a couple hours ago. "I'm pretty sure he bought right into it. Stupid fool."

"Has he touched you yet?" he clips.

"No, Pike. I've known the guy for a week; you know I don't work that way. Men like to chase, so I'm gonna make him chase until he can't resist."

"You think he could possibly fall for you?"

"I'm hoping he does," I tell him.

"I do too. I'm sick of living like this, babe. You have no idea," he says as he clutches my face in his hands and looks me over. "Knowing that fuck has his hands on you . . ."

"I don't feel it."

"Don't lie to me."

"I'm not," I say, but I am. I try so hard to not feel Bennett's hands on me. I work at staving off any orgasm with him, and I hate myself when my body isn't strong enough to fight it and he makes me come. It happens every now and then and the bile that rises is a burning reminder of the weakness that still lives inside of me. A weakness I continue to try to kill off, but Pike would be pissed if he knew, so I lie, allowing him to believe that only he has that part of me. The part his eyes are telling me he wants right now.

"Tell me you hate him, Elizabeth," he grits as he crawls on top of me, pushing my back down on the couch.

"I hate him."

With a near growl, he crashes his mouth to mine, and the beer slips out of my hand, clanking against the floor. His tongue invades my mouth, hands grab locks of my hair, body pressing hard against mine. He takes over me, grinding his hard dick between my legs as I start fiddling with the buttons on his jeans. Once undone, I shove them down, past his hips, and he yanks mine down as well. We move quickly and carelessly. He sits back and jerks the pants off one of my legs.

"Show me your tits," he demands, looking down at me.

I pull my top off and unclasp my bra, tossing it aside, and his rough hands are on them quick. He then takes his cock and pulls off a couple hard pumps while he twists one of my nipples between his fingers, sending a shockwave straight to my belly.

"You want me to take it away?"

"Yes," I breathe.

"Say it. Tell me that you need me to take it away."

He continues his torturous attack on my nipple before releasing and moving to the other. Pike knows I need him to numb. He's always allowed me to use him like this. To numb the pain. Numb the past. Numb the present. Fucking Pike is my personal narcotic, and I'm long overdue for a hit. The words are near agony, when I give him what he loves to hear, "You're the only who can make it go away, Pike."

He lowers his head, sucking the abused bud into his mouth.

"Ohh, God, Pike. Fuck me. Just do it," I beg.

He quickly rips his shirt off, revealing the ink splayed across his chest and arms, before shoving my panties to the side and thrusting himself inside me. A volatile transgression as the sounds of our flesh slapping together fill the room. I grab his ass, urging him harder, and he gives it, pounding into me.

Closing my eyes, I drift away to where nothing exists but the pleasure that builds inside. His carnal grunts heat my ear with his breath as he buries his head in the crook of my neck. We fuck filthy, like animals. The denim of his jeans that are shoved below his ass chafe the backs of my thighs while we grind ourselves into each other, my butt off the couch as I meet his thrusts with my own. Greedy.

He grabs my hips as he sits back on his knees, bringing my pussy up to him when he starts slamming into me at a brutal pace.

"Fuck, Pike," I pant as I reach both my arms over my head and grip the arm of the couch.

The swell of his dick inside of me as he gets close causes an eruption of fire, singeing its way through my veins as he makes me come. I go rigid, tensing up to get the most out of the orgasm, grinding my clit against his pelvis. A few seconds later he crashes into me and stills, letting go of a guttural hiss, as he shoots his tranquilizing disease inside of me.

Collapsing his sweaty chest on top of mine, our labored breaths are heavy, and I'm pacified. For as long as I keep my eyes closed so I don't have to see the best friend that I just used, I'm okay.

Pike gives me a sick power that I crave. The power to take control, if even for a moment. Using him to clean me of the rot that contaminates me. And he gets off on being the one who can do that. To be the only person who can take it away, making my body a tomb. But now, as he slips his softening dick out from inside me, his warm cum running between my thighs when I sit up, I'm bathed in degradation, and he knows it. It's always the same.

He pulls me into his arms as he sits back after tugging his pants up. With his hand rubbing my back, I swallow hard as I attempt to control the feelings of shame.

"Why do you still feel this way?" he asks, knowing me all too well.

I don't respond. He's used to my silence after we have sex. What could I say that he doesn't already know? The thing is, I know Pike loves me in a way I don't share. He's my brother and my best friend. But to him, I'm more. He's never come right out and said it, but I know it anyway. It doesn't stop him from fucking other girls, but I know he needs it. Pike has a thing for sex; he likes a lot of it. More than the average person I would assume. It's never bothered me since I don't view sex much differently than one would toilet paper. Using it to wipe away the shit-stain of life, and when you feel clean, you flush it and walk away.

"You don't need to feel like this. I don't care that you use me in this way. I love you, so you can have it. If it makes you feel better, then just take it," he says. "I'd rather you let me do this for you than allowing someone else."

His words make it even worse, so I pull back and shift to slide my leg back into my pants. He watches as I grab the rest of my clothes and walk to the bathroom.

After I clean myself up and put my clothes back on, I walk out to see Pike wiping up the beer I spilled all over the floor.

"Sorry," I say as I stand there, and when he walks past me to throw away the wad of paper towels, he responds, "I don't care about the beer."

"I'm sorry for more than just the beer," I tell him. "I wish I could give you more money."

"I knew what I was signing up for. We both did. It's too risky, so just ignore my bullshit," he says as he walks back to the couch and motions for me to sit next to him. He pulls out a cigarette and lights it, taking in a long drag and then adding, "I just missed you," as the smoke drifts out of his mouth, forming a vaporous cloud in front of his face. "When will you be able to get back here again?"

"More often after the New Year. Bennett has a busy travel schedule, and I'm sure it's gonna be even busier now."

"Why's that?"

"He just bought another production plant earlier this week in Dubai, so I imagine he'll be going back to oversee the new outfit on the place and get it up and running," I explain.

"That's good for us," he laughs and I join him.

"My thoughts exactly," I say through a thick smile that I let wane when I ask, "How've you been?"

"You know how it is. Nothing has changed for me," he tells me. Pike has always found a way to skate by, pulling small cons and such. But he makes most of his money selling drugs. I used to as well. When we got out of the system, we lived with one of his friends that Pike worked for, dealing drugs. Pike was the middleman, putting himself on the street to sell product and made a decent amount of money doing so.

"You need anything?"

"For you to get your head on straight with this one."

"I've got my head on straight, Pike." I hate when he talks to me like that. Like I don't know what the hell I'm doing when I'm the one pulling the biggest con here, putting his skills in the sewer. "My focus has never wavered. But I need you to trust me. I know what I'm doing."

"Just be careful. Hands clean, remember?"

I nod and then grab the remote to turn on the TV. We spend the next few hours hanging out like we used to, but before it gets too late, I know I have to leave and head back into the city.

"With the holidays coming up, don't get mad if I can't get away, okay? I'll try, but until January, it'll be hard."

"I get it. Don't do anything stupid trying to come see me," he says as we stand up and walk to the door.

I grab my coat and slip it on, then turn to give him a long hug. It's hard to leave him, knowing he's here in the shit-hole. He's the only family I have and to not have any contact with him is scary for me since I know how easily family can be taken away. So with my cheek pressed to his chest, I take in his scent and hold on to it while he runs the fingers from both of his hands through my hair and down to my face. Cupping my jaw, he angles me to look up at him. His brown eyes are intense when he asks, "Hard as steel?"

"Yeah," I breathe.

He taught me, at an early age, how to live without emotions. How to wrap that steel cage around my heart, always telling me that no one can ever hurt you if you can't feel. So I don't. Outside of Pike, there's no one I'll give that to because emotions are what make people weak. And I can't afford to make that slip. The heart is a weapon—a self-inflicting weapon—that if not trained properly, can destroy a person.

Seven

(PRESENT)

I WATCH AS Bennett moves around the bedroom, getting dressed in his three-piece suit to go in to the office for the day. He arrived late a couple nights ago and as I presumed, his schedule is now packed with travel after the purchase he just made. Even though he's home now, he's been living at the office before he heads out again at the end of this week.

The chill in the air is getting to me, and I sink down into the bed and further under the covers.

"Do you need me to adjust the thermostat?" Bennett asks me as he nears my side of the bed.

"Are you not cold?"

He sits on the mattress beside me, leans down to kiss my nose, and then smiles.

"What?" I ask as he pulls away.

"Your nose is cold. Come here."

I sit up, and he wraps me in his arms in an attempt to warm

me up. Slipping my arms around his waist, under his suit coat, I curl into him.

"I missed this," I breathe. "Having you—here—with me."

"I know. I missed it too," he says, moving back to look into my eyes. "You can always come with me, you know? You don't have to be alone."

"I know, but Declan has already scheduled appointments out with vendors for the party. I'll be busy for the next few weeks."

"How did your visit with the florist go the other day?" he asks.

Running my hand along his silk tie, I tell him, "It went well. I think we got nearly everything picked out."

"Good."

He combs his fingers through my hair and leans in to kiss me. Slow and soft, taking his time. Bennett tends to be overly affectionate after he returns from a trip, and I never deny him, so I shift up to my knees and hold his face in my hands. When he grips my hips, clutching onto the satin of my slip gown, I take over his mouth, urging him on. He pulls me down atop his lap, and his growing cock presses against me as I grind my hips into him.

"God, baby. I can't get enough of you," he mumbles against my neck, between his gentle kisses.

"You want me?"

"I always want you," he tells me. "But you're gonna make me late. I've got a meeting."

Grinning at him, I say, "I'll be fast," before slipping off his lap and onto my knees on the floor beside the bed. Quickly working my hands, I undo his slacks and yank them down. And as he sits on the edge of the bed, I wrap my lips around his dick and suck him off while he moans my name.

Once fully satisfied, he kisses me deeply when I walk him to the door before he leaves.

"I hate that I have to leave when all I want is to make love to you all day."

The ringing of my cell interrupts us, and he waits while I grab it off the kitchen counter and answer.

"Hello?"

"Nina, it's Declan."

"Hi."

"I was wondering if you could stop by the hotel later today. Betty, from Marguerite Gardens, is having a few arrangements delivered for you to look at," he says.

"Um . . . sure. That shouldn't be a problem at all. What time would be good?"

"They should be delivered by noon."

"Okay, I'll swing by later then," I tell him before we hang up.

"Who was that?" Bennett asks when I walk back over to him.

"Declan. The florist is sending over some sample arrangements for me to look at later today, so I'll just take one of the cars to the hotel if Baldwin is going to be with you."

"You sure?"

Lifting up on my toes, I give him a little kiss. "I'm sure."

"I'll call you when I leave the office. How about I take you out for a nice dinner at Everest tonight?"

"Sounds perfect," I say with a smile.

He runs his thumb down my lips and then gives my chin a

little pinch, saying, "Have a good day, okay?"

"You too."

As soon as he leaves, I walk into the kitchen to put the kettle on the stove, and while I wait for it to boil, I look over to the dining room table. The extravagant vase of purple roses that Bennett gave me when he got home last night sits in the center of the table. The sight causes a physical reaction inside of me. A twisting in my gut as I grit my teeth. I hate purple. I told him it was my favorite though, so when he gives me flowers, his way of showering me with affection, it only reminds me of everything I hate. Purple walls flash in my mind, and it only reinforces my steel wall. Bennett is everything a husband should be, so it was essential that I create fissures within him. Purple flowers being one of them.

The squealing whistle of the kettle snaps me out of the purple and into the present. I fix my tea and make my way into the bedroom to get ready for the day. Knowing I'm going to be seeing Declan, I want to look nice, so I set my mug down on the center island in my closet and start sorting through my clothes. Selecting a simple black shift dress, I pair it with patent black heels and my white, wool, knee-length coat.

After a slow morning getting ready and taking a phone call from Jacqueline to schedule a lunch date with the girls, I grab my purse and head down to the parking garage. It takes a while to get to the hotel with the hectic lunch traffic in the loop, but when I arrive, the valet takes my car and I make my way back to Declan's office.

When I approach his door, I can hear his voice on the other side. He sounds angry, barking orders with whoever he must be on the phone with because it's only Declan's voice I hear. I wait, and when I notice the conversation has ended, I give the door a couple light taps.

"Come in," he calls.

Opening the door, his focus is on his laptop and nothing else as he's clicking away at the keyboard.

"Bad time?" I question hesitantly, and when he hears my voice, he flicks his eyes my way and swivels his chair away from his computer to face me. "I can come back."

"No," he simply states as he stands up and walks towards me, taking me by the elbow and turning me to walk with him. "This way."

His snippy attitude the other day at the florist was irritating, but for some reason, right now, it doesn't have that effect on me, figuring that whoever he was just speaking to is the culprit of his mood, and not me. I follow him out of his office and down to an opulent private dining room that's currently free of people. He opens the double-etched glass doors and leads me into the dark room, dimly lit by the sparse chandeliers. Towards the back of the dining space, there is a secluded table that's covered in burnt orange and white flowers with dark, rich greenery. Some accented with spiral grapevines and others darkened with blackened moss.

Declan still has a hold on my arm when we walk over to the table.

"I'm impressed," I say, and it's then that he releases me. When I look at him, I notice his jaw flex as he grinds his teeth. His focus is on the table and not me, so it's with a soft voice, I speak. "Declan?" Looking over at me, I ask, "Are you sure this isn't a bad time? I can go."

He relaxes his face and runs his hand behind his neck and

down along his lightly stubbled jaw. Releasing a sigh, he says, "Stay."

Nodding my head, I turn away and take a step over to the arrangements and begin studying each one. There are five, each ornate and exquisitely put together. The designs unique and exactly what I had in mind.

I still when I feel Declan's fingers graze the sides of my neck, and as I turn my head to see him standing right behind me, he moves his hands to the collar of my coat, and starts to slip it off my shoulders. Adjusting myself, I allow him to take my coat and watch as he lays it across the back of a chair.

"Thanks," I murmur.

"What do you think?"

Keeping my eyes on him, I don't answer immediately. I want the contact to see how he responds. It doesn't take long for a sexy grin to cross his face.

"They're perfect. I'm not sure how to pick one over the other."

"So take them all," he says.

"Take them all?"

"Why not? Who says you have to choose?"

"Isn't there always a choice?" I ask with an undertone that states we're talking about more than just flowers.

"Not when you're a Vanderwal."

With superficial offense, I say, "Is that what you think? That because of my name I simply take what I want?" He quirks a brow without saying anything, and I add, "Is that what *you* do? Because correct me if I'm wrong, but the McKinnon name sure isn't one that people are not aware of."

"Are we talking personal or business?" he questions.

"Business is personal when it belongs to you, and last time I checked, it's your name that robes this hotel."

He walks over to one of the other tables and takes a seat. Leaning back and resting one of his arms on the table, he says, "Yes. I take what I want."

I stay put, standing by the flowers, and question, "In which case?"

"In all cases. Now stop standing there and sit with me."

"Is this you taking?"

With a smile that he plays so well, he says, "Are you up for grabs?"

"No," I state curtly. "And these games you tend to enjoy playing with me are getting old, and frankly, I don't enjoy being toyed with as if I'm here solely for your entertainment. So again, cut the shit, Declan." I grab my coat and start walking towards the door, hoping he makes the move I'm goading him into.

His hand grips the top of mine as soon as it hits the door handle, and I freeze, keeping my head down.

"Don't go," he says, and I remain silent as he continues to speak. "You're not a toy, Nina, and I apologize if I made you feel that way."

"So what is this?"

"This is me, simply wanting to get to know you," he says, and when I look at him, he adds, "You say you don't have friends, right?"

Turning my head away from him to avoid eye contact, he says, "Everyone deserves a friend, Nina. Even you."

"And you think you're gonna fill that void?" I ask, looking back at him. "What makes you think I need that?"

"Tell me then, who do you talk to about the things you

can't with your husband?"

I pull my hand out from under his and move to face him. "Who do *you* talk to?"

Silence.

"You expect me to just put myself out there when I don't know anything about you? And what do you give me in return, huh?" I question.

"The same," he answers. "So let's start now. Before you knocked on my door a few minutes ago, I was on the phone with my father. He was being a fuckin' knob as always, ridiculing me for decisions I'm making that he doesn't have a say in, and it drives him crazy to not hold the power in this situation. So there you go, my father's a bastard to me."

His eyes are sharp as he says this, the intensity prevalent, and I feel like I just made progress. But I don't want him pissed right now, so I break the tension, and make him smile when I tease, "A fuckin' *knob*? Is this some Scottish insult you guys throw around because I've never heard anyone call someone a *knob* before?"

"Yeah, darling, it is, but if you prefer something more authentic, I can call him a fannybawbag, but then to the random American, I'd probably just sound like a pussy."

I laugh at his statement, but let it fall off my lips as I look down at my feet and quiet myself.

"What is it, Nina?" he asks, taking note of my shift in mood. When I don't immediately respond, he takes my hand, holding it in his as he walks me over to a table and we sit down. "Tell me something about you."

"I don't know what you're wanting."

"Anything. Just give me a piece," he says, but when he sees

me hesitate, he offers, "Tell me why you don't have any friends."

I release a breath, giving him what I know he wants to hear. "Because I'm not from this world. I'm not like those women, and . . ." I stall, taking a moment before adding in a hushed voice, "I'm afraid they'll judge me, so I rather they just fear me because it's easier that way." When I say the words, the truth that lies within them surprises me.

"So you hide?"

"I suppose."

"Are you lonely?"

"Do I seem lonely?" I question.

"In this moment? Yes."

Deflecting, I turn it on him, asking, "And what about you? Are you lonely?"

"I moved here from New York when we broke ground on this place. I've been so wrapped up with getting everything fit for opening, so yeah, I've become lonely."

"When did you leave Scotland?" I ask.

"I used to spend my summers here in the States when I was in university back home. I'd come here and work for my father, learning the ins and outs of the business, but I didn't officially pack up and leave until after I graduated with my master's," he tells me. "That was seven years ago."

"Do you miss it?"

"Scotland?"

With a nod of my head, he answers flatly, "Yes," before asking, "Where are you from?"

"Kansas."

"What brought you out here?"

I shift in my seat, marking my discomfort with answering,

but before I can speak, my cell rings from inside my purse that's lying on the table. Picking it up, I see it's Bennett, and answer the call.

"Bennett, hi," I say so Declan knows who I'm talking to.

"Just checking in. My meeting wrapped up a lot earlier than I expected, and I was hoping to see you," he says sweetly.

"You just saw me."

"So is this your way of saying you're too busy?"

"No, I'm never too busy for you. Are you still at the office?" I ask as I cast a quick glance over at Declan and see the irritation in his eyes.

Good. Get jealous.

"Yeah. Are you hungry? I can have something delivered."

"That sounds great, honey," I tell him, playing up the sweetness just to pluck on Declan's nerves, and I can tell it's working by the tensed muscles in his neck and his set jaw. "I'm on my way now, okay?"

"All right. I love you."

"Love you too."

Looking at Declan, I tell him, "I have to go meet Bennett."

"Yeah, I heard," he says, clipping his words.

I run my hand over his clenched fist that rests on the table, and say, "Thanks."

"For what?"

"Talking to me." Staring into his eyes, I tell him again, "Thank you," so he can hear the sincerity in my words.

His hand relaxes under mine, and he flips it so that he's now holding mine, and with a smile, says, "Let me walk you out."

As he helps me with my coat, I finally feel like I've found

the match I've been looking for. There have been a few men before Declan, but none that ever gave me the promise I feel he may have, so I let him hold on to my hand for a moment longer than I should as he walks me out to the valet who is waiting with my car.

I slip into the driver's seat and Declan peers down, reminding me, "Friday is your appointment with the caterer. Four o'clock."

"I've got it on my calendar."

"You mean that paper calendar that doesn't provide you with notifications or reminder alerts?" he teases.

Laughing at his dig, I say, "Yeah, that one. But apparently that's all I need since you tend to do the reminding for me."

"I'll see you Friday then?"

"You'll see me Friday," I affirm before he closes my door, and I start driving over to the Willis Tower to meet my husband for a late lunch, all the while, feeling optimistic for the first time in a long time.

eight

(PAST)

I SIT BY myself on the front steps of the school, waiting for Pike to meet me so that we can go home. He's in trouble with one of his teachers again and has detention, so I take the hour to get all my tears out so that he doesn't see me cry. Apparently I've lost track of time when I hear the metal doors bang open and pop my head up to see Pike walking down the steps. Quickly, I wipe my face, but he sees the tears anyway.

"Why're you crying?" he asks, but I don't say anything as I stand up and shrug my backpack on over my shoulders. "Elizabeth? What happened?"

"Nothing. Can we go now?"

"No. Not until you tell me why you're upset."

Hanging my head down, I kick a couple pebbles on the sidewalk, telling him, "The kids in my class make fun of me."

"What did they say?" he asks in a hard voice.

"Doesn't matter," I tell him. I've been at this school for a few months now. Long enough to hit a growth spurt and no longer fit into the clothes my last foster family bought me, so now I'm stuck wearing clothes that Bobbi gets from thrift stores, and the other kids pick on me for the way I look.

"It matters to me," he states, and when I look up at him, I say, "They call me names. Saying I look like I get my clothes from a garbage can." I can feel the tears fall again as I continue, "They call me names to my face and then whisper and laugh at me."

"Those kids are ass wipes."

"I have no friends, Pike," I say, crying. "I'm all alone, and I wanna go home. I miss my dad, and I wanna go home."

In a second, he has me in his arms, and I wet his shirt with my tears. Every night I pray to a God I'm not sure even exists that I'll wake up from this nightmare, but I'm still here. I'm almost nine years old and I haven't seen my dad, heard his voice, felt his hugs—nothing—in nearly four years. I have a case worker who has only seen me twice since I've been here, and both times I cry and beg for her to take me to my dad, but she won't. He's too far away. I'm starting to believe that I'll never get him back because waiting until I'm fourteen seems like forever.

"I'm sorry," Pike eventually says as we stand on the sidewalk hugging. "But you're not alone. You have me."

He's right. He's the only one I have, but he's a twelve-year-old boy, and next year he'll be at the middle school, leaving me here alone. Alone with kids that don't like me.

When he draws back and looks down at me, I cringe at the greenish tint left over from the black eye Carl gave him the other day. I learned fast that when Bobbi is around, Carl is semi-pleasant, but the moment she leaves, he starts drinking. I try to hide and be invisible when he drinks because he's scary to be around. He yells a lot, and if Pike and I make too much noise, he gets really mad and usually hits us.

My first slap came a week after I got here. Bobbi left for the weekend and Carl was downstairs watching TV while I was upstairs. I found a radio on the top shelf of the closet in my room and was standing on a chair to get it down, but I slipped, causing the chair to tip over and the radio to crash to the floor. Carl busted through my door and saw the broken radio. Before I knew what was happening, he had yanked me up by the arm and slapped me across the face. The burning sting held to the skin of my cheek as I cried into my pillow afterward.

Pike and I take our time walking home, but when we get to our street, Bobbi's car is gone, and only Carl's truck is in front of the house. My stomach sinks. It's the weekend, so I'm sure it'll just be the three of us. Bobbi never tells us when she's leaving, but lately, it seems to be all the time. She's never home anymore.

"Just go straight to your room," Pike tells me as we walk to the front door. "I'll grab you a snack and bring it up."

"Okay."

But that wouldn't happen. Instead, I was about to be introduced to a black hole that would claim another piece of my faith in human decency.

"Where the hell have you kids been?" Carl yells at us when we walk in, and the gravel in his voice makes me cling to Pike's arm in fear.

"I had detention. I told Elizabeth to wait for me so she wouldn't have to walk home alone," Pike explains.

"You think I have all the goddamn time in the world to be wondering where you shits are?" he shouts and then grabs Pike by his shirt, ripping him out from my hold on his arm and shoving him away from me. He then gets in my face, stinking of beer and cigarettes.

"And you . . ." he spits as I start to cry, which does nothing but piss him off even more. "Fuck! Why are you always fuckin' crying? I'm not gonna spend another weekend here with you listening to this shit." When he lifts his dirty shirt and starts to unbuckle his belt, the chills of fear run rampant, spiking through my veins.

Pike bolts off the floor and goes after Carl, but it only takes one hit to knock Pike back, and Carl has his hand locked around my wrist as I scream and thrash. Suddenly, he has me lifted off the ground with a firm hold around my waist.

"Let me go!" I scream. "Stop! Let me go!"

I hear a crash, and when I look up through my tears, I see I've kicked over a couple of Bobbi's ducks and have broken them.

"You little shit!" he yells, but it's blended with Pike's screams as well, and I panic. Sheer panic.

Screaming, crying, kicking, and the next thing I know, I'm being shoved into the small hallway closet. Carl throws me hard against the floor and then pulls me up by my wrists, using his belt to tie me up to the lower garment bar. Everything is a chaotic blur. Everyone is yelling, and the terror in my body is making it hard for me to breathe through my shrieking cries for help. I hear Pike, and I hold on to his voice when Carl's fist smashes into my face.

SLAM.

LOCK.

Darkness.

"No! Let me out!" I cry. "Pike, help me! Let me out! Please!"

I can hear the beating Pike is getting now. Grunting. Heaving. Screaming. I twist and yank my wrists, trying to free myself, but the leather is biting into my skin, and I'm only hurting myself. The side of my face where he hit me pulses in beats of hot pain, and I fall onto my bottom with my arms pulled above my head and cry. I cry for what feels like years in the darkness.

My body grows tired and weak. Arms cold and tingly. I stand up, wedging myself between the wall and the garment rod, and I can feel the warmth flowing back through my arms to my hands. I try wriggling my fingers around to grab on to the strap of leather, but it's too dark to see anything and my fingers are too small. What would I do anyway? Unstrap myself and walk out of here? Carl would kill me, so what's the point in trying?

I listen to the faint sound of the TV in the living room as my head starts to droop. I'm so sleepy, but my arms hurt too bad when I sit, and I can't sleep standing up. Not sure what to do, I remain wedged against the wall while I keep jerking out of sleep when my head falls. My mind is a haze. I try resting myself in the corner, but can't find any comfortable position. Soon enough, I hear the sounds of the TV shut off and listen as Carl walks out of the room.

Oh my God. He's not gonna let me out.

Tears fall, burning my skin on the way down my face, and I can only assume that Carl split my skin when he punched me, but nothing can stop them from falling down my cheeks.

WAKING UP, MY arms are freezing. I must have fallen because I'm now sitting on the floor. I have no idea if it's night or day, and the urge to go to the bathroom is overwhelming. When I stand up to relieve the pain in my arms, I press my legs together to keep myself from peeing. I begin to cry, wondering what I'm supposed to do, but in that very moment, I hear Pike on the other side of the door.

"Elizabeth?" he whispers.

"Pike?" I whimper.

"Shh. Carl is sleeping."

Trying to choke back my cries to stay quiet, I strain my words, "Please, Pike. Get me out."

"I can't," he says. "The lock on this door works from the inside."

"What?"

"Without the key, it can only be unlocked from inside," he tells me.

"He's got my hands tied. I can't move, and I can't see anything," I say, beginning to panic, and he hears it.

"Don't cry, okay? I'm here," he tries assuring me.

My body begins to twitch as I clamp my legs tighter. "Pike?"

"Yeah?"

"I have to pee," I tell him. "Really bad."

"Fuck," I hear in a muffled voice.

It's then the pain and urgency take over, and I feel the

warmth seep out, spreading through the fabric of my pants and trickling down my leg. Mortified. Embarrassed. I slip to the floor and begin weeping as quietly as I can.

"Are you okay?" he asks, but I don't answer, I just continue to cry.

PIKE STAYED WITH me on the other side of the door for hours last night, talking to me, trying to keep me company. I must have fallen asleep again because I don't remember him leaving. The TV is now on, so I know Carl is awake. My stomach has been growling, but I'm too scared to call out to him.

The time passes slowly, and I try to keep myself distracted by daydreaming, pretending I'm anywhere but here. I imagine I'm with my father, and we're riding together on his white steed he used to tell me he had when we would play make-believe. We ride through the countryside and find ourselves in that magical forest. Carnegie is there, and we go hunting for berries. Some berries give us special powers, and some are just delicious to eat. When rain falls, we hunt for mushroom tops to hide under until the storm passes, and we meet fairy butterflies that fill the air with glitter as they fly.

My thoughts get interrupted often with the pain that surges through my hands and arms. I'm so tired but can't find a way to get any real sleep, and now with my stomach knotting up from hunger, I find myself constantly shifting from sitting to standing.

"ELIZABETH?"

Pike's voice brings me out of a light sleep, and I try to bend and flex my wrists as the leather cuts into my skin. "What time is it?" I ask.

"It's Saturday night. Almost midnight," he tells me.

"I'm hungry."

"Hold on."

I move to my feet to soothe my arms. I feel so gross with my pants soaked in my own pee. It stinks, and I know Carl is going to be pissed whenever he decides to let me out, which hopefully will be tomorrow since I have school on Monday. Plus, Bobbi should be coming home soon. At least I hope she is.

I hear Pike sliding something under the door. I lower to my knees, but didn't think this through, because my hands are bound.

"Pike, I can't get whatever you slipped under the door."

"Shit. I'm sorry, I didn't even think," he whispers. "Is there any way you can lean your head down to get it with your mouth?"

"No. The bar is too high."

"Use your foot and try to push it back out," he instructs. "I don't want Carl to know I was trying to sneak you food."

I shuffle my foot around, but can't feel anything, so I just start sliding it against the floor and towards the door, hoping by chance I get it out. After a second, I hear, "Got it."

"What was it?"

"Just a tortilla," he says. "I heard Carl talking to Bobbi. She's gonna be home tomorrow afternoon."

"I feel sick."

"What's going on?"

"I'm just so tired and hungry," I tell him. "My arms hurt really bad. He's got his belt pulled so tight around my wrists."

"He's a sick fuck."

"Pike?"

"Yeah?"

"Please don't leave me. You're all I have." The tears return, and I let them come without fighting it. I feel so hopeless.

"I'm not leaving you. You're my sister. We're not blood, but you're my sister." His words hit my heart, knowing he's all the family I have. "Did I ever tell you about the time I fell off the roof at my last foster home?"

"No."

I sit back down and listen as Pike tells me story after story. He even tells me about his mom, that she was a drug addict and that's how he wound up in foster care when he was only two years old. Hours pass and he never stops talking to me, keeping me company until I drift off into a fit of restless sleep.

WHEN I HEAR someone messing with the door handle, I swiftly move to my feet, wedging against the wall. Light pierces my eyes, and I immediately close them.

"What the fuck is that smell?" Carl snarls as I slowly try to open my eyes against the stabbing light.

His hands start undoing the belt around my wrists. You'd think I'd be happy to be getting out of this closet, but I'm so tired that all I feel is numb.

"Did you piss yourself?" he asks with anger, and when I nod my head, he yells, "You better clean this shit up."

The belt is finally off, and my hands are free. I grip my one wrist in my hand and stand there, scared to move, until he tells me to get out. Before I can go upstairs, he makes me clean the floor where I had been going to the bathroom. I finally look at my wrists to see they're covered in blood from the broken skin where the leather was cutting into me.

When I get upstairs, Pike is sitting on my bed, but I'm too embarrassed, so I ignore him and go straight to the bathroom, shutting the door, and stripping out of my soiled clothes. Before I get into the shower, I look in the mirror to see the black eye Carl gave me. I step into the spray of water and fall apart.

After I finish my shower, I wrap up in a towel and go back into my room. Pike is still on my bed, so I grab some clothes and go back to the bathroom to get dressed. Coming out, I finally look at the bruises on his face as he reaches his hand out. I walk over to the bed, take it, and let him pull me down and hold me. I stay in his arms, the only comfort I feel life has to offer me right now, and close my eyes.

I was locked in that closet for two days with nothing— nothing but Pike, who snuck down each night to talk to me through the door so that I wouldn't be alone. Knowing that he would do that for me makes me want to hug him harder, so I do.

"Thank you," I mumble against his chest.

"What for?"

"Staying with me at night."

"Like I said, no matter what, you're my sister," he says, and I respond with, "And you're my brother."

nine

(PRESENT)

BENNETT LEAVES TODAY to go back to Dubai to start an overhaul on the production plant, gutting it and replacing everything with the same equipment that is used at the other plant he has here in the States. When I told him that I was meeting with the caterers today, he had his assistant call and hold his plane so he could go with me. The idea of having him and Declan in the same room causes my nerves to go a bit haywire. Especially when I just saw Declan for coffee yesterday.

He continues to press me about Bennett, and I'm confident with my performance as he seems to be under the assumption I'm not all that happy and that I'm only keeping up the façade for the sake of appearance. But I don't want there to be any awkward exchanges today when we meet up with him at his hotel, so this is where it turns tricky. I'd like to keep both men apart from each other, so the added fact that Bennett is linked with Cal, Declan's father, isn't optimal. It was never in my plan to target a man like Declan, but so far, he's the one that has taken the bait. I just need to be careful with handling this situation. One little slip could be disastrous, and I've invested too much time to make a fatal error.

"Are you ready, honey?" Bennett asks as he walks into the living room where I'm sitting.

I stand, straighten my pencil skirt, and walk over to him. "Yes. I just need to grab my coat."

"We'll drive so that you'll have the car with you when you leave. Baldwin will pick me up to take me to the airport."

"I hope it wasn't too much trouble to delay the charter," I say as I slip on my coat and grab my purse.

"No trouble at all. I just hate that I have to be gone again with it being so close to Christmas."

We leave the apartment and head down on the elevator.

"By the way," he says. "I spoke with my parents. They want us over Christmas Eve for a dinner party they're hosting."

I cringe inside at the thought of spending time with those assholes, but I smile anyway, saying, "Okay. I've been meaning to call your mother, I've just been a little scattered with everything else going. And now you're leaving again."

He takes my face in his hands and kisses my cheek. "It's only temporary."

"I know."

"It'll be busy for a while, but once everything is up and running, it'll slow back down."

The elevator opens and we make our way to the parking garage. We take the Land Rover, and when we pull out, we're greeted by more snow.

"It's supposed to get bad later," Bennett says.

"I'll be sure to get home before it does."

"I can hire another driver if you need me to."

Cocking my head at him, I smile, saying, "I survived before without a driver, Bennett. I'll be fine."

Baldwin will be accompanying Bennett on his trip this time, so he won't be around to drive me. One less person I have to worry about.

"With me gone so much and this brutal winter we've been having, it worries me knowing you're driving around in this mess."

Laying my hand on his thigh, I assure him, "I'll be fine. You worry too much."

He takes my hand in his, kissing my knuckles, and says, "I just don't want anything to happen to you. I can't help but worry when I'll be a world away."

I lace my fingers with his and relish in the fact that this new purchase will have him so far away for a longer span of time, allowing me to work on Declan. It couldn't be a better situation. With Bennett and Baldwin gone, I'll be able to come and go as I please without having to explain.

When we pull up to Lotus, the valet opens my door and helps me out.

"Watch your step, miss."

"Thank you," I say before Bennett walks around to take my hand and lead me inside.

I show him to the private dining room that Declan had the flowers in earlier this week, and when we walk in, Declan is there talking to the chef.

"Nina," he says with a smile, and my nerves float to the top of my stomach. He takes my hand, giving me a chaste kiss on the cheek, and then greets my husband. "Bennett," he says with a firm handshake. "It's good to see you again."

"I hear my wife is keeping you busy."

"She knows what she likes," Declan chuckles and Bennett joins him. "But she hasn't fired me, so I guess I'm doing something right."

"Don't get too high on yourself just yet," I add with the sass I know Bennett loves but, at times, can irritate the hell out of Declan. He takes it well, never losing his grin. I want to make him jealous, but it's a fine line with Bennett here, so I'll make sure to gauge Declan's body language and not push him too far.

Declan introduces us to Marco, the chef I'm considering for the party, and we then take a seat at one of the tables.

"So, Bennett, Nina tells me you've been slammed with work lately."

"That's a massive understatement, and to be happening this time of year is less than ideal," Bennett says and then reaches over to hold my hand that's resting on the table. "Fortunately for me, I have an understanding wife."

Just as I give him a smile, we are presented with a sculpted Caprese salad.

"So how did you get into steel production?" Declan asks, and I remain quiet as they talk.

"At the time, I was acquiring and renovating vacant buildings when I came across a manufacturing plant that was going bankrupt. I was able to purchase it at a bargain, keeping the owner from going into insolvency. I flipped the place, and next thing I knew, we were up and running, gaining a solid client base."

"From the ground up," Declan states.

"Just like your father," Bennett adds.

I watch Declan's jaw flex as he grinds his teeth. He takes a sip of his wine and then says, "You two must be proud of yourselves," with a condescending tone, possibly taking Bennett's remark as a stab against the fact that Declan is, in a sense, riding on his father's coattails by going into the family business. But I know Bennett, and no such suggestion was meant on his part.

Bennett notes Declan's insinuation, and deflects, turning to me, asking, "Are you going to see Jacqueline tomorrow? I thought Richard mentioned something to me about it."

"Mmm hmm." I wipe my mouth, and add, "The girls want to make a day at Neiman's, and I need to find a dress for the party."

"I thought you couldn't stand them," Declan butts in, and I immediately heat in anger that not only is he being grossly inappropriate in exploiting something *he thought* I was revealing in confidence to a friend, but I also don't need him raising any red flags with Bennett.

I widen my eyes, letting him know he crossed a line, when Bennett questions, confused, "You don't like them?"

"Um, no. I mean . . . Declan just meant that . . ." *fuck*, "Well, I voiced to Declan that sometimes they can be a tad overbearing. That's all." Looking into his eyes, I have to wonder if he's upset that I would reveal something like that to Declan. Something that has nothing to do with the business we are supposed to be conducting while we're together, so I cover myself, adding, "I had run into one of Jacqueline's friends at the florist when Declan and I were there. She was being a little snippy, so I loosely made that statement to him. I possibly spoke out of frustration. I like the girls, but you know how it can be when you get us all in one room."

He buys it, saying, "I'll never pretend to understand the mind of a woman," with light laughter, and I smile with him.

"Me neither," I tease. "And I'm one of them." Taking my fork and stabbing a basil leaf, I mumble with a grin, "Snarky bitches," before taking a bite.

Bennett laughs at my crudeness as I give Declan a disapproving glare.

We get halfway through the second course with building tension from Declan when Bennett gets a call from Richard that he has to take. He excuses himself and steps outside of the room, walking down the hall, and when he's out of sight, I turn and snap, "Your games aren't funny. I was under the assumption that the few pieces I gave you, pieces *you* asked for, would remain private and not for you to use when you felt someone was stepping on your dick."

He leans to the side, grabs the arm of my chair, and abruptly yanks it towards him, quietly gritting, "Your smart mouth is unbecoming, Nina, so watch how you speak to me. And no one *steps on my dick*, especially your husband—the man you say you love but doesn't seem to know shit about you."

"You think you're cute?"

"Do I look like a man who gives a shit about being cute?"

Narrowing my eyes, I tell him, "You look like a man who's jealous, but you shouldn't even be going there with me."

"Why's that?"

"Because I'm a married woman, and your juvenile accusations are insulting. You don't know anything about my husband and what he does or doesn't know about me."

"You're a liar," he accuses.

"Excuse me?"

He leans in closer, mere inches away from my face, and says, "I think you like making me jealous. Am I right?"

In a soft voice that I make sure comes out shaky, I respond simply, "No."

"I don't believe you."

"What do you want from me?"

"Bullshit aside?"

"Bullshit aside, Declan. What do you want?"

His eyes are near daggers when he answers, "You."

Perfect answer, idiot.

I stand up, throwing my napkin on the table and turn to go find Bennett, although I have no intentions of leaving this room, and Declan doesn't fail when he grabs my arm and jerks me around, pulling me flush against him. He looks down at me, and I shift my eyes away.

"Look at me," he demands, and when I don't he grabs my chin and pulls it around to face him. "I said look at me, Nina."

"You're an ass."

"And you've got a filthy mouth," he says before taking a taste, sealing his lips with mine. He isn't gentle, and his stubble grazes roughly against me as he wraps his hand around the back of my neck. His grip on me is firm, and I make sure he feels me respond to him for a brief moment when I move my lips with his before forcefully pushing him away.

His grin is arrogant as he takes a step back, putting distance between us.

"What do you think you're doing?" I bite harshly.

"Testing you."

"You're an insolent prick."

"Then why did you kiss me back?" he questions. "Don't lie to me either because I felt it."

"You didn't feel anything, and neither did I." Walking back over to the table, I pull my chair back and sit down, saying as I keep my eyes forward, "Don't ever do that again."

Seconds later, Declan returns to his seat in front of me, and with perfect timing, Bennett comes back in. This situation is bordering on dangerous, so I'm relieved when Bennett says, "I apologize about that, but it seems I'm going to have to leave earlier than expected."

"What?" I ask.

"I'm sorry, honey. The charter is ready to go. There was miscommunication about the reschedule, and we have to head out."

"Now?"

He holds his hand out to me, and I take it as I stand up. "Declan," he says when he turns to look at Declan who is now standing as well. "Sorry to run like this. It was good seeing you again."

Declan doesn't speak, but instead gives him a curt nod as they shake hands.

"If you'll excuse us for a moment," Bennett says as he wraps his arm around my shoulders and starts leading us out. Looking over my shoulder, I watch as Declan remains standing, keeping his eyes on us as we walk out of the room.

God, he's so transparent.

I walk with Bennett to the lobby, and when he stops in front of the doors, I play the sad wife. Slipping my arms around his waist, I lay my head on his chest and hold on to him.

"I don't want you to go."

His lips fall on the top of my head, giving a kiss, and then he responds, "I know. I'll get back here as soon as I can."

I look up at him, and he takes my lips, the lips that Declan just had, and he kisses me. Long, slow, soft. He keeps the connection for a moment before pulling away and looking down at me. "You're so beautiful."

"Don't."

"Don't what?" he questions.

"Say sweet things that'll make me miss you even more."

He smiles, and when I glance out the front, I see Baldwin pulling up. With a heavy sigh, I turn back to Bennett as he says, "I've gotta go."

"Okay," I respond with hesitation as I nod my head.

"I'll call you as soon as I get there," he tells me and then teases, "Use this time to buy me lots of Christmas gifts."

"I'll spoil you rotten," I laugh.

"You already spoil me rotten."

With one more kiss, we say goodbye, and I watch as the car pulls away, happy that he's finally gone.

ten
(PRESENT)

WITH MY HUSBAND on his way to the airport to spend the next
two weeks on the other side of the world, I get my game face on
and head back to Declan, who's still in the dining room.

"What was that about?" he questions when I walk back in
and sit down.

"Just saying goodbye."

"Are you sad?"

Shifting in my seat, I say, "Can we not talk about this?"

Declan doesn't push his questions anymore, staying quiet
for the most part, aside from safe chitchat as we finish our meal.
We discuss the catering and visit with Marco for a while, and
after I hire him to cater the party, we open a bottle of wine while
we spend a lengthy amount of time selecting the menu offerings.
Once business is handled and the foods are selected, Marco
excuses himself and I follow Declan to the lobby to have the
valet pull my car around.

"Oh no," I breathe as I look out front. "How long were we talking with Marco?" It's a white out with snow falling hard and already piling high, making it impossible for me to leave.

"A few hours," Declan responds. "You can't drive in this, Nina."

"No, I know," I say and then shake my head, adding, "It's just . . . I told Bennett I would leave before the storm hit."

"We lost track of time. Nobody's fault. You can stay here."

"I don't have anything with me," I say and Declan lets out a quiet laugh. "What?"

"Nina, you're standing in one of the most exclusive hotels in the city. I'll get you whatever you need."

"Anything?"

Smiling at me, he says, "Come on," as he leads me back to his office. He then gets on the phone telling whoever is on the other end to prepare a penthouse suite with all amenities and to bring him the key.

When he hangs up, I tell him, "You didn't have to do that. I don't need the penthouse."

"You'll be next to me. This way you won't be tempted to sneak out and play in the elevators," he jokes as if I'm some teenager.

"Next to you?" I question.

"I occupy one of the penthouses."

"You live here?"

"No," he replies. "I have a loft in River North, but I house a room here as well for when I'm too tired to drive home, or in this case, get stuck in a blizzard."

"River North? I would've thought you lived here in the loop."

"Too pretentious for me. No offense."

"Says the man who drives a pretentious car," I tease with a smile, and suddenly, all the tension and frustration from earlier seems to let up as we lightly poke fun at each other.

"Well, I can't argue the car, but it's nice to leave the loop at the end of the day and escape to a place that's a bit more low-key."

He says this and I think back to the breakfast diner he took me to the other week. Declan definitely looks the part and has the name that follows, but I wonder how much of it is really him. River North is full of wealth these days, but he's right, it's not pretentious.

After a while, when one of the staff delivers my room key, I follow Declan as he shows me to my room. Only two suites occupy the top floor, which is only accessible by the occupants—Declan and myself.

"This is you," he says as he walks me over to the left side of the elevator banks.

"Thank you."

"I'm on the other side," he tells me. "So if you need anything . . ."

"I'll be fine," I assure.

"Dinner later?"

"I'm pretty full from Marco's meal," I say. "I think I'll make it an early night."

As I turn to unlock the door, he adds, "Like I said, if you need anything, let me know."

"Night, Declan," I say and then walk into the room, letting the door shut behind me.

Looking around, the walls are solid floor to ceiling windows showcasing the twinkling lights of the city that's now covered in a blanket of snow. The space is large, with an open-concept living room, dining room, and kitchen. All of which are furnished in sleek upholstery and rich leather. I note the fireplace that is situated in a smaller sitting area that's set off from the rest of the room in a sunken section a couple steps down. I make my way into the bedroom that's lined with the same panoramic windows. I lay my coat and purse down on the plush white linens and go into the bathroom. I laugh at the extremities Declan's staff went to when I see every toiletry you could possibly need, plus a two-piece set of pajamas folded inside a shopping bag from Roslyn Boutique. Picking them up, I note the designer. The length that this hotel went to is no doubt a simple favor to myself. Lotus is known for its exclusivity and privacy for its patrons. Not anyone can just walk in and book a room.

After settling in, changing into the pajamas, and making a cup of hot tea, I sit on the floor with my legs crossed, knees pressed against the cold window as I watch the snow fall down on the city below. I think about how to use this night to my advantage with Declan. I know I should find my way to his room, and start to go through a variety of reasons for why I would go knocking on his door.

Time passes as I get lost in thought, and when I look over to the clock sitting on one of the end tables, it reads 10:23 pm. Setting my mug on the floor beside me, my mind drifts to Pike, and I can't help the guilt that passes through as I think about him in that cold, dilapidated trailer while I'm sitting on top of the city. The click of a door steers me away from Pike, and when I turn to look over my shoulder, I see Declan.

"What are you doing on the floor in the dark?" he asks as

he walks across the large living room towards me.

"Do you make it a habit of breaking in to your guests' hotel rooms?"

With a grin, he says, "Technically, I didn't break in." He holds up a key card before dropping it on the coffee table when he walks past it.

"You could have knocked."

He steps next to me as I sit on the floor, and I have to tilt my head back to look up at him. He stands with his hands in the pockets of his slacks as he looks out the window.

"I love the snow," he murmurs, and without thinking, I agree, "I do too."

He looks down at me, his face shadowed in the darkened room. "Are you okay?" he asks, concerned for some reason.

"Why?"

"Because I come to check on you and you're on the floor pressed up against the window without a single light on. Seems sad."

I turn my attention back to the city below when I respond, "I like watching the snow fall."

He sits down next to me, his knee touching mine. I allow a few moments of silence to pass before saying, "Thank you."

"For?"

"The room," I tell him. "It's beautiful."

"It's just a room, Nina," he says, downplaying the scale of his hotel as he keeps his focus on the snow.

"Lotus," I say, acknowledging the name of the hotel. "Interesting choice. Why Lotus?"

"There's something about a beautiful, nearly flawless flower, emerging from muddled water."

"Hmm." I pause before stating, "Self-reflection," inferring that the meaning strikes a chord with himself.

Tilting his head to look at me, his breath feathering my cheek, he says, "Is this you trying to dissect me?"

"Is there something lying beneath that I should be looking for?"

"Everyone has something beneath that they're hiding." He peers into me. At least that's what he wants me to believe, but I'm not permeable. I soften anyway, giving him the sense that he's actually having an effect on me. I blink a few times and shift myself, cueing him that I'm nervous, and then he asks, "So what is it? Tell me what you think you've found."

Taking in a deep breath, I release it with my theory. "You have a distaste for the business that owns your name."

He doesn't move, and I add, "Or maybe your distaste is for your father."

"Interesting. Why bring him up?"

I smile and say, "Come on. We've both met the man. He's a bastard; you said it yourself the other day."

Declan laughs under his breath, saying "You're not delicate with your words, are you?"

"Did I give you the impression that I'm delicate?"

With a soft hum, he gives me an inquisitive look, and then asks, "What about *your* father?"

He catches me slightly off guard. A pinprick in the one soft spot that I've never been able to harden.

You want to know my weakness?

Well, there it is.

I miss my father.

Shifting the focus, I redirect, saying, "We're not talking about me, remember?"

"Of course."

"Do you even get along with him?"

"As well as anyone else does," he answers.

"That's a very political answer."

With his hand, he brushes my cheek slightly as he takes a lock of my hair and tucks it behind my ear, saying, "Whether or not you're in politics, everything is political. We all save face for others to perceive us in the best light. Nothing is real until you break down the walls and reveal the ugliness."

"Ugliness," I repeat as I look at him.

"The truest part of a person is always the ugliest. And with your evasiveness, I would bet that you're pretty damn ugly beneath all that gloss."

He keeps a straight face as he says this, and the truth behind his words irritates me. I know I'm ugly. Uglier than most. I'm tarnished and decrepit, but I'll be damned if I ever let him or anyone else see the wretched heart that beats inside of me.

"You're an asshole," I bite.

"Baby, I've been called a lot worse, so if you're trying to offend me, you'll have to do better than that."

With a glare, I say, "I don't get you and your insults. I thought you wanted to be my friend."

He moves in closer to me, and with a low voice, murmurs, "I don't want to be your friend, Nina."

Taking a hard swallow, I feign nervousness, whispering, "You should go," as he continues to move himself toward me, and then over me, forcing me to lie back on the floor with both his hands braced on either side of me. "Declan, this is wrong," I breathe.

"Why?"

"You know why."

"Tell me you love your husband," his voice taunting.

"I love my husband."

"Tell me you don't want me," he says, eyes pinned to mine.

"I don't want you."

My breathing increases and grows heavy when he lowers himself onto his elbow and starts running his one hand down the center of my sternum, between my breasts, adding quietly, "Tell me you're not lying to me."

"I'm not lying to you."

Then, with his legs intertwined with mine, he slips his hand down my pants, under my panties, parting the lips of my pussy and dragging his finger through my heat. He smiles cagily down at me when he feels how wet I am and then quickly removes his hand, bringing it to my lips and shoving his finger into my mouth, telling me, "Taste your lies, Nina."

His breath bathes me with his words, and I give in, allowing my tongue, for a brief and noticeable moment, to wrap around his finger, giving him the obedience I know he craves, but inside, I'm mortified and disgusted. I hate that my body would react this way—growing wet for this man. Pulling away and jerking my head to the side, I don't look at him, but soon feel his nose gliding along my exposed neck, hearing him inhale my scent.

"Declan . . ."

"Hmm . . .?"

I roll my head back, and look straight up at him. "Get the fuck off of me."

When he doesn't move right away, I fist my hands, and flip the switch on him, weakly slamming them against his chest, allowing the look of guilt to wash over my face. "Get off of me now, Declan."

He moves back and sits on his heels as I rise off of my back and scoot away from him, muttering, "Please, just go. Just leave me alone."

"Nina . . ."

"You can't do this to me. I'm not *that* person."

He reaches out for me, saying, with apology in his voice, "I don't want to upset you; you just make it hard for me to control myself when I'm around you."

"Why are you doing this?"

"Because I like you. Because I know you're not happy. I can see you hiding, and I don't want you to do that around me."

"I'm not hiding," I affirm sternly.

"Okay then," he releases in frustration. "You want me to accept that when we both know it's a lie?"

"I'm not hiding," I repeat, and with that, he stands and walks away and out the door.

Fucking, Christ!

A part of me wants to squeal in victory, knowing I've got this guy by the balls, and the other part feels like it needs a drink because he's so goddamn deluged with intensity. I've come across a few guys in the past year, but none have shown this level of interest. They all fizzled before anything could ever get started, so the elation that I feel with Declan gives me the power I need to move forward.

I NOW FIND myself tossing and turning in bed, unable to sleep because my mind won't seem to quiet down. It's past one in the morning when I decide the night with Declan isn't over just yet. He wants to believe that I'm lying to him about my contentment with Bennett, so I'll give him reason enough to confirm his assumption. Throwing the covers off of me, I walk through the room and out the door. This floor is private, so I go ahead and walk past the elevator bank and down to Declan's room. Standing in front of his door, I take a deep breath, and allow my mind to go to a place that'll put me in the state I need to be in when he opens the door and looks at me. He needs to believe I'm harboring a deep pain inside, so I drift back twenty-three years. I'm being ripped out of my father's arms, watching him fall to his knees as he's cuffed. I can see the tears falling down his face, and when I feel my cheeks heat in the pain, the tears puddle in my eyes. I knock.

Lights.

Camera.

Action.

The door opens, and I look up to see Declan standing in nothing but a pair of pajama bottoms that hang on his narrow hips that angle down from his broad, sculpted chest. My tears are heavy, but they don't spill over. He takes one step towards me and pulls me into his arms, his cheek pressed to the top of my head, holding me tight. No words are spoken when he brings me inside his room and shuts the door.

I keep my arms around his waist as he walks me back to his room and over to his bed. Cradling my face in his hands, I look up at him, and his eyes are noticeably worried.

"Stay."

With a nod of my head, he pulls the sheets back, and I crawl into his warm bed. He follows, scooping me into his arms. His body pressed against mine, my head resting on his chest, I take the comfort I need in this moment. My mind isn't with Declan or Bennett or this whole fucked up scenario, it's with my dad. I opened that gate for one second to trick Declan and now I'm five years old—scared and lost.

The first tear drops, and I fucking hate that I'm exposing this weakness. It's one thing to manufacture pain for the sake of deception, but my father is very much real, and it hurts. I don't want to think too much, so as Declan comforts me from what he believes is Bennett, I take the consoling for my father.

Neither of us says a word as I silently fight to contain the few weeps that break free, all the while Declan's hold is firm and strong around me. I weave my legs with his and eventually allow myself to drift to sleep.

eleven

(PRESENT)

STANDING IN FRONT of the windows, I look down and watch as the snowplows make their way through the city, clearing the streets. I left Declan's room early this morning while he was still sleeping. I wanted to build the mystery and chase, and waking up in his arms would make it too easy for him, and from what I've learned about men, easy leads to a shallow investment. I need Declan to be fully immerged if I have any chance at this working out, so I quietly slipped out of his room.

I laugh when I hear the knock on my door since last night he took it upon himself to just barge in on me with no warning. But it isn't Declan standing on the other side; it's room service.

"Mr. McKinnon ordered breakfast for you this morning," he says as he wheels in a white-clothed cart with a French press and a platter of fresh fruit and crullers.

"When was this request made?" I ask.

"Maybe an hour or so ago, Mrs. Vanderwal," he says. "May I pour you a cup?"

"No, thanks."

"Would you like anything else?"

"It seems Mr. McKinnon has covered all his bases this morning. Thank you though," I tell him before he turns to leave. The pit of my stomach pinches and this display should please me, but instead, irritation swarms. I should have never connected to his comfort last night. It was a foolish move on my part, and now I'm pissed at myself.

I leave the food and coffee and head to the shower to clean up. Not having any other clothes besides what I wore yesterday and the pajamas, I slip back into my dress and press a little powder on my face from the compact in my purse and then dry my hair.

Bennett calls in the late morning, worried about me getting stuck in the storm yesterday, but I assure him that I'm fine and should be home later today now that the city streets have been plowed. We talk for a while, and when I hear another knock, it's then that we say our goodbyes and hang up.

As I open the door, Declan walks right in, looking more put together than me in his tailored suit, white button-up left open at the neck, and no tie.

"What, no breaking and entering today?" I say, my words laced with the remaining irritation from earlier.

"I left the key on your coffee table last night," he responds as he walks over to the food cart. "You haven't touched anything."

"I don't need you catering to me, assuming you know what I like to eat or that it's your right to even make assumptions about me," I snap while I walk into the kitchen to put the kettle on.

"So, we're back to steely-bitch Nina?"

Turning to look at him, I say, "I'm going to have a cup of tea and then I'd like my car to be ready so I can go home."

"It's still snowing."

"The plows already came through."

He walks over to the kitchen and stands by the bar, asking, "What happened to you this morning? I woke up and you were gone."

"Your ego bruised?" I say with a condescending grin that pisses him off.

Rounding the bar, he backs me against the countertop, and hisses, "Now it's time for *you* to cut the shit." The kettle starts to squeal, and before I can turn to get it, he reaches over and slams it on the other burner, startling me, and flips the knob off. Caging me in with his arms, his tone is hard when he says, "Your games are starting to piss me off, and I don't like being played."

"And what about your games, Declan? The ones you've been playing since the night I met you?"

"Did I not apologize to you?" he questions. "Don't forget that *you* came to *me* last night."

"Moment of weakness. Won't happen again. So if you were hoping—"

"God, you're fucking aggravating."

"The feeling's mutual," I say as I move to push him back, and when he keeps his stance and doesn't budge, I bark, "Let me out."

"No."

Pushing my hands against his hardened chest, I get pissed.

"I'm serious, Declan. Back up!"

"No."

"Let me go!"

"Not until you stop bullshitting me. Stop lying, and tell me why you came to me last night."

Pressing my chest against his, I narrow my eyes, saying, "I already told you. Moment of weakness."

He grabs me above the elbows, biting down hard before saying, "And I told you not to lie."

I fist my hands, jerking my body away from him, and he lets go of me. He stays back while I walk across the room, putting space between us, and go over to the windows.

"You think I get off on encroaching on a married woman?" he asks.

Wrapping my arms around myself, I keep my back to him.

"You think I'm an asshole?" he continues. "Join the club. I'm a fucking ass, but I can't help how you make me feel when you're around."

I can feel the heat of him as he moves in behind me. His hands find my shoulders, and he gently tugs to turn me to face him, but I cast my eyes downward.

"Tell me I'm not alone here, or tell me I am because the moment I think I can read you, you flip on me." When I look up at him, his eyes hold hope in my response. "Tell me why you came to me last night."

"Because . . ." I begin, but let it linger.

"Tell me."

"Because I didn't want to be alone."

"Why?"

"Declan . . ." I hesitate.

"Why, Nina?"

Lowering my head, my voice cracks perfectly when I say, "Because I'm lonely." He runs his hands from my shoulders, up my neck, and to my cheeks, angling me up to him. As I look into his eyes, I add, "Whether he's here or not, I'm lonely."

"And when *I'm* here?" he questions.

"I don't feel so alone."

He releases a breath and drops his forehead to mine as I grip my hands around his wrists.

"I'm sorry," he says. "I was a dick to you yesterday."

"I wasn't very nice either."

He lifts his head, telling me, "Don't leave. Stay. Let me make it up to you."

"I can't. I need to go home."

"Why?"

With a light laugh, I say, "Well, for one, I need to change into some clean clothes."

"So go home and change. I'll pick you up."

"What are we gonna do?" I ask.

"When's the last time you had any fun?" I shrug my shoulders and he says, "So let's have some fun."

A COUPLE HOURS later, I'm back home. Declan called a little bit ago, saying he was on his way and to be sure I was dressed warm. So I've made sure to comply since the temperatures are no less than frigid as the snow continues to fall.

When the doorman calls to let me know Declan is here, I

grab my wool coat, scarf, gloves, and knit hat. I see Declan standing in the lobby as the elevator doors open, and it's the first time I've seen him dressed down in a pair of dark wash jeans and grey sweater under his black wool coat. He looks sharp, and when he turns towards me, his smile grows.

"You ready?" he asks as we walk towards each other.

"I'm not sure," I respond warily. "I don't know what we're doing."

"Come on."

I follow him out the front doors and see his car parked along the street, but he leads me in the opposite direction.

"We're not driving?"

"No."

I slip on my ivory knit hat and wrap my scarf a couple more times around my neck while he watches with a smile and then holds his hand out for me. I don't take it at the risk of someone seeing me, so when I begin to walk, he places his hand on the small of my back as he leads us across the street to Millennium Park.

"You know it's closed, right?" I ask when he leads us to the ice rink. "The snow's too thick."

"It's closed for everyone in the city, but you."

"What?"

"Mr. McKinnon," a young man greets as we approach the rink.

"Walter, thanks for doing this," Declan says as they shake hands.

"Any time, man," he responds and then looks at me, asking, "You ready?"

"We're skating?"

Declan laughs, and Walter says, "That's the deal we made. You ever been?"

Slightly embarrassed, I tell him, "Actually . . . no. I haven't."

"Never?" Declan asks, and when I shake my head, he says, "But you live here in the park." When I shrug my shoulders, he jokes, "This oughta be fun," and I smile at his mischievous grin.

After we grab our skates, Walter opens the gate to the rink, and I grab ahold of the metal railing as Declan steps out onto the ice with ease.

"Take my hand," he instructs, seeing my nervousness.

"This is embarrassing," I tell him.

"Good."

"Good?"

"You're always so uptight, Nina," he says. "Come on, take my hand."

"I'm gonna fall on my ass."

He glides over to me, holding out both of his hands, and tells me, "Let go of the railing and take my hands."

Placing one hand in his, I step onto the ice before letting go of the railing and giving him my other hand. It doesn't take but a second before my balance falters, and I fall into his chest. He grips my waist, laughing, and says, "Relax. You're too stiff."

"It's freezing out here, and you've got me on ice. I can't relax," I grumble.

"Stop bitching." He then takes my hands again and begins skating backwards while gliding me forward. "Try moving your feet."

"Uh uh. I'll fall."

With a grin on his face, he asks, "Why are you so stubborn?"

"Are you serious? I could ask you the same question."

"Just for today, why don't you try trusting me?"

As he continues to hold my hands and pull me around the rink while he skates backwards with total control, I question, "Is that what you like? Having someone that just obeys you and never voices their opinion?"

"No, Nina. It's not about obeying, it's about trusting; something I don't think you do too easily."

"Trust can be costly," I argue.

"Or it can be comforting."

He keeps his eyes steady on me when I finally give in, and with a sigh, agree, "Okay, fine. One day."

His smile is cocky, and I shake my head at him, asking, "How did you get the rink to open for us?"

"Walter did some work for me at the hotel during construction. So I called him, slipped him a few bills, and here we are."

"Is everything that easy for you?"

"No," he says with a piercing look. "Some things I have to work for."

He says this and I drop my eyes to cut the tension building, and when I do, I lose my balance, tripping over my toes. I grab on to his coat as I fall hard on my hip, pulling him down with me. He hovers over me, laughing, while I'm flat on my back.

"My ass is getting wet," I say as I try to sit up, but he doesn't allow me with his body lying on top of mine.

His fingers run through my hair, and he murmurs, "Your red hair is beautiful with the snow in it."

A shiver runs through me from the chill of the ice, and he moves away, getting steady on his feet before helping me up.

"You done?"

I give him a nod, and he helps me off the ice and over to a bench. When we sit down, he pulls my feet onto his lap and starts to untie the laces on my skates. Slipping them off my feet, he runs his thumbs firmly up the arch of my foot, kneading along the way before repeating the same on my other foot. I watch him as he does this, and he never pulls his attention away from my eyes. The adoration he exudes is palpable, and it's a shame that it's wasted on someone like me, but I'll take it and use it to my benefit.

We get our shoes on and thank Walter before we rush back towards my building. Walking over to his car, he pulls his keys out and opens the passenger door.

"Get in."

"Where are we going?"

"It's my one day for you to trust me," he says. "Get in."

I move past him and slip down into the leather seat of his Mercedes before he closes the door. When he gets in, he starts the car and pulls out onto the scarce streets of the city. I keep quiet during the drive as we head north on Michigan Avenue towards River North. Looking over at him, he turns his head to me, questioning, "What?"

"Are you taking me to your place?"

He shoots me a wink, and when I open my mouth to speak, he shuts me down, reminding, "One day, Nina."

Turning into the building's garage on Superior, we head inside and onto the elevator. He slips a key into the punch pad before hitting P.

"You nervous about being here?" he asks as we ascend to the top floor.

"Should I be?"

Stepping over to me, he takes my hand as the doors slide open, and we step off the elevator and into an impressive living space. He has the whole top floor to himself, and as I look across the massive living room with multiple bucket accents in the vaulted ceiling, I note the architectural detailing of the modern design. Near solid glass walls that look out over the city, and against the far wall, an enormous Archlinea chef's kitchen.

Noticing the stainless steel staircase, I ask, "What's up there?"

"A private rooftop deck."

"This place is amazing," I say as I step further into the loft. For as impressive and spacious as it is, it's warm and comfortable, a feeling I appreciate because it's so far from how my place feels.

"Coffee?" he asks.

"Please." Taking off my coat and scarf, I lay my things on one of the couches and walk over to the couch that's closest to the large walk-in fireplace.

Declan soon joins me, handing me a mug and then turning the fireplace on before sitting next to me.

"How long have you lived here?"

"Since I moved to Chicago around two years ago."

"It's a big place for just one person."

"Says the woman who lives in the penthouse of The Legacy," he remarks with a smirk, and I laugh.

"That was my husband's place since before I met him," I defend.

"You like it there?"

"I've grown to," I answer. "It's only me there most of the

time with Bennett working and traveling so much."

He doesn't respond as he takes a sip of his coffee and then sets it down on the end table. Turning to me, he says, "I want to know about you."

"What do you wanna know?"

"What did you study in college? Did you work before you married? I want to know who you are aside from his wife," he says as he angles his body to face me.

I cradle the mug in my hands, drawing in the heat, and answer, "I was studying Art History at the University of Kansas when my parents died during my third year."

"How did they die?" he asks. He doesn't respond the way most people do when you mention death. He never says *I'm sorry*, apologizing for something he had nothing to do with, and I appreciate that, even though I'm feeding him lies.

"Tornado came through and landed on top of the house I grew up in. They were found under the rubble a few days after," I tell him. "I was an only child, so when I found out they had been pulling loans and a second mortgage on the house to pay my college tuition, there was no money. I had to drop my enrollment for the next semester and never went back."

"What did you do?"

Bringing my legs up and folding them in front of me, I respond, "I was all alone, so I did what I had to do to get by. I worked various jobs to barely meet my rent and pay my bills."

"So how did you wind up here in Chicago?" he asks.

"After a few years, I was just depressed and going nowhere. All my friends had since graduated and were moving on with their lives while I was stuck. I needed a change, so I packed up what little I had and drove here. No reason, really," I say. "I had just enough money to put a deposit down on a small studio apartment and got a job with a catering company. I used to work these fancy parties, and as stupid as it sounds, even though I was nothing but the help, I used to pretend that I was part of that world. The part that didn't have a care in the world, being able to wear pretty dresses and drink expensive champagne. A world I would never be a part of until I was hired to work a party for Bennett Vanderwal."

"That's how you met him?"

"Pathetic, huh? Kinda makes me look like a gold digger, but it wasn't like that at all," I tell him. "For the first time in a long time, I didn't feel so lost. And when he looked at me, he didn't see the poor girl from Kansas who ran to escape her miserable life."

I tell Declan this lie and the look on his face is that of sorrow, but the life he feels bad about me having is a life I would've done almost anything to have. God, if he knew the truth about how I grew up, he'd run. It's not a story anyone in their right mind would ever want to hear. It's the type of story that people want to believe doesn't really exist because it's too hard to stomach. It's too dark of a place for people to even consider being reality.

"And now?"

Looking down at my mug, I watch the ribbons of steam float off the coffee and dissolve in the air when I answer with false trepidation, "And now I realize that I *am* that poor girl who ran. The girl he never saw me as. It's like I woke up one day and suddenly realized that I don't really fit in to all of this. That I'm no longer sure of my place in this world."

Declan moves to take the mug out of my hands and sets it

down on the table as he closes the space between us. Taking my hands in his, he asks, "Do you love him?"

With diffidence, I nod my head, murmuring, "Yes."

When he cocks his head in question, I add, "He loves me. He takes care of me."

"But you feel alone," he states.

"Don't."

"Don't what?"

"Make me speak badly of him," I respond.

"I don't want that. All I want is for you to speak honestly to me."

"That's what I'm doing, but . . ." Dropping my head, I hesitate, and he urges, "But . . .?"

"It feels wrong to talk to you like this."

"Did it feel wrong when you were in bed with me last night?" he questions.

"Yes."

His voice is low and intent, asking, "When did it feel wrong? When you got into my bed or when you snuck out of it?"

I take a moment and swallow hard before answering, "When I snuck out."

His hand finds its way into my hair, threading through the tresses, and then he guides it to my cheek with his other hand still holding mine. With a faint voice, he says, "I want to kiss you right now."

Reaching my hand up to the one he has on my face, I hold on to his wrist, close my eyes, and weakly plead, "Don't."

"Why?"

"Because I don't want you to."

"Why?"

I open my eyes to him and say, "Because it's wrong."

"Then why doesn't it feel that way?"

"Maybe it doesn't now, but eventually it will."

He drops his hand from me and sits back. I hold him off because right now he's merely hungry and I need him starving—ravenous. I need him to fall hard for me. Harder than I believe he's capable of right now. So I'll keep him at bay for a bit longer because it seems to be working.

twelve

(PRESENT)

BENNETT CONTINUES TO call me every day to check in as usual. He misses me. Nothing new. Let him miss me. Let Declan miss me too. Both men, eating out of the palm of my deceitful hand. Mortal puppets. Foolish puppets.

The drive to Justice is a long one because of all the snow on the roads. From the scenic display of Christmas in the city, to the muted slum of the ghetto—I miss Pike no matter where I am. I take my key when I park my car and let myself in. The sounds of a woman moaning, almost theatrically, filter through the trailer from the bedroom. The squeaking metal from the bedframe composes the rhythm at which Pike fucks her. The curdling inside my gut is sickening, and I go back out to my car to wait for the chick to leave.

If you think I'm jealous, you're wrong. I don't care who Pike fucks. I don't care who anyone fucks. To me, sex is disgusting. It's a means to an end. If you're not miserable, I don't see the point. My body used to reject the act, rousing me to vomit afterward. Hell, sometimes I would throw up during sex. I've been able to sequester the nausea, but the dirtiness of the act remains.

With Bennett, I've become numb and vacant when we have sex. I used to be overcome with hatred when he'd find his way inside of me, but I shut that off quickly, and now the illusion that what we have isn't just sex, but making love, is one that he has never questioned.

Yeah, I'm a good actress.

I watch as the snow collects on the windshield, and with the screech of a door, I turn to the trailer to see a pathetic-looking woman walking down the steps with her ratty, purple fur coat wrapped around her. She probably thinks she looks trendy, but she just looks like a skank.

When she gets into her rusted Buick, I turn to see Pike standing, arms braced on the sides of the door frame, pants unbuttoned, no shirt, and tattoos on full display. He smiles as he looks at me, and when I get out of the car, he asks, "Been here long?"

"Not too long."

He steps aside as I walk in, and the door slams shut.

"I didn't expect to see you so soon."

"Bennett's out of town. Will be for another week," I explain and set my coat and purse down on the edge of the couch.

He lights a cigarette, and when he takes a drag, I step over and hug him. He folds me in his arms and I get a whiff of perfume. Pushing back from him, he questions, "What is it?"

"I can smell her cheap drug store perfume on you."

He laughs at me and shakes his head. "What's got you so pissy?"

Sighing, I turn to walk over to the couch, and as I sit, I release a heavy breath, saying, "I'm just tired."

"I guess," he mumbles when he joins me on the couch. "So, how's it going with the guy?"

"Declan? Good. Really good."

"Where are you at with him?" he asks.

"I'm working him," I say. "He's jealous of Bennett."

"That's it? Come on, Elizabeth, clue me in."

"We've been spending time together. What do you want me to say? He likes me; it's evident. We spent the day together yesterday."

"What did you guys do?"

"He took me ice-skating," I say with a slip of a smile, and his face contorts before he snaps, "What the fuck?"

"What?" My voice is pitchy with defense.

"You're shitting me, right? You're out ice-skating like a goddamn kid when you're supposed to be seducing this ass wipe. And while you're off screwing around, I'm living in this shitfest."

His tone sparks my temper. Standing up, I turn to look down at him, and piss my words, saying, "Fuck you, Pike. You don't know shit about what I'm doing, so just sit tight, fuck the trash that walks in here, and let me handle myself."

"Handle yourself?" he sneers. "Tick tock, tick tock."

"You wanna speed this shit up? You're tired of waiting? Then hire one of your thuggish street friends to take care of it and spare me my own time," I lash out.

"You're taking too much of that time."

Walking across the room, I clench my hands at my sides

and take a deep breath before turning back to him. "Just remember that we *both* agreed to keep our hands clean in this. We hire someone, we have a direct link to our plan. The deal was that we would never speak the words, that we would simply goad a person into it. You think you could do a better job?"

He stubs his cigarette out in the tray on the coffee table and then stands, saying, "Not unless they prefer dick over pussy."

"God, Pike," I seethe as I fist my hair, and when I drop my hands to my sides, I tell him, "I'm so sick of fighting with you. It's all we seem to do lately, and I'm done with it."

"Perks of an older brother," he says with a pompous smile.

Mumbling under my breath, "I guess," I grip my hands on my hips and look over at him.

He stands there staring at me, and I can't help but laugh at his demeanor, full of ego. "You really do drive me crazy," I tell him.

"I know."

With a shake of my head, I add, "And you need to stop doubting me. It pisses me off."

"I know," he repeats with surrender. "Come here."

With a childish groan, I make my way over to him and stubbornly take his hug, and then tease, "Seriously, her cheap perfume is making my nose burn."

"You're so high and mighty now, huh? Don't forget where you come from."

"How could I?"

We stand there for a long while as I get the comfort from him that I've been missing since the last time I saw him before I finally speak again. "I have a good feeling about him, Pike."

"Hmm."

"He's already falling. He doesn't hide it well."

"I worry about you," he says, and I lean my head back to look at him, questioning, "Why?"

"Because I know how hard it is on you being with Bennett. I worry about how it's going to affect you when you start adding this other guy in."

I know that Pike is genuine in his feelings for me. We're family, and I get that he worries. He always has. But I remind him, "Hard as steel, right?"

With a nod of his head, he keeps his arm around my shoulders as we walk back to his bedroom. It's routine at this point—our sex. We do it every time I come and see him, reminding me of the one person I can trust in this world, the one person who has always taken care of me.

His pants are still unbuttoned, so with a tug, he drops them to his ankles and steps out. I lie back on the bed—the bed he just fucked another girl in, but I couldn't care less. My body is entirely worthless, so I give it freely without much thought. Undoing my pants, I watch as he pumps his dick a couple times, and when he reaches to check if I'm ready, he feels how dry I am. I want the sex with him, but most of the time, I struggle to get wet. It didn't seem to be a problem when Declan felt me up the other night, but more often than not, I need a little help.

Pike pushes my knees wider and spits his saliva on me, wetting me, and runs his fingers through my folds to spread it. When I give him a nod, he holds himself and pushes inside of me. Pinching my eyes shut, I grip my arms around him as he fucks me, clearing my head and wiping away the stains of Bennett, and now, Declan.

RETURNING HOME, CLARA is in the kitchen cooking. I unwrap the scarf from around my neck and walk over to the kitchen to greet her.

"Clara, hi," I say as I look on the stove to see what she's making.

"There you are. I feel like we keep missing each other."

"Smells good," I say, eyeing the skillet of beef stroganoff.

With a warm smile, she responds, "I figured you could use some comfort food with the nasty winter we've been having."

I open the fridge to pull out ginger soda, saying, "It's perfect. I haven't eaten all day, actually."

Turning to me, she spots my drink and asks, "Is your stomach upset?"

"A little."

I always tend to feel a little queasy after my visits with Pike. The after sex blues followed by the upsetting goodbye. It tends to have this effect on my stomach when I leave, turning back into the emotionless machine I've been forced to become ever since I was a little kid.

"There's a package from Mr. Vanderwal in the living room. It was delivered earlier today when you were out," she says, and when I walk over, I see the large, white box wrapped in a gold satin ribbon.

My stomach churns, and I down another gulp of my ginger soda.

I pick up the lightweight box and untie the ribbon, letting it drop to the sides. Inside lies a masquerade mask. Black, laser-cut metal, which gives it an almost evil, seductive feel. The black, double-faced satin ties hang as I pick it up out of the box. It's probably more perfect than anything I could have found on my own and that annoys me, the fact that he can be so good at nearly all he does. I look in the box for a note, but there isn't one, so I turn and ask Clara, "Was there a note or anything with this?"

"No, dear," she answers over her shoulder from the kitchen and then my cell rings.

Cringing when I see who the caller is, I answer with charm, "Jacqueline, hello."

"Where have you been?" She's huffy in her question.

"What do you mean?"

"Neiman's? Shopping? Yesterday?"

I completely let it slip from my mind that I was supposed to meet the girls yesterday. I was so distracted with spending the night at the hotel and then hanging out with Declan that it didn't occur to me that instead of being with him, I should have been at Neiman's.

"I'm so sorry; I must have forgotten. You're not upset with me, are you?"

"I'm not, but Catherine was running her mouth about how you've been acting like a bitch towards her."

And this is the shit I hate about these women. I have absolutely nothing in common with any one of them. They have way too much time on their hands that they seem to enjoy filling with petty drama. They're all spoiled and entitled, yet I'm forced to grin and bear it, and so I respond, "I don't even speak to Catherine outside of when we're all together."

"Exactly. She thinks that you think you're better than her."

I am. As sick as I may be, I'm still better than the shallow depths of them.

"Jacqueline, you know I don't enjoy the gossip, so if there isn't anything else, I should get going."

"I was hoping we could get together soon. It's been a while—the gathering at Lotus, I believe," she says.

"Of course. I'll check my calendar and call you," I reply before we say our goodbyes.

Walking over to Clara, I smile as she moves around the kitchen. I wonder for a moment what my life would have been like if I'd had a mom. For one, I wouldn't have ever gone into foster care after my father's arrest. I never met my mom. I don't know anything about what happened to her since the only one who could have explained it to me was my father, and I was so young when he went to prison.

I've seen a few pictures to know I got my red hair from her. She wore it in a short bob, where mine is long with just a hint of waves. She was pretty. I used to imagine her living with my dad and me when I was tied up in that closet. She'd smile and kiss my father while I cringed but secretly loved watching them like that. She would hold me at night, rocking me while my dad sang to me. He always sang to me at night. I'll never forget the sound of his voice as I would fall asleep.

The top of my nose tingles at the thought of him, and I don't even realize how tight I have my teeth clamped shut when Clara asks, "Are you okay?"

Unlocking my teeth to answer, an ache shoots through my gums at the release. "Will you stay for dinner?"

Her warm smile penetrates my mournful thoughts, and I

smile back at her when she says, "I'd love to." She turns to pull a couple plates down as she inquires, "Now tell me, what did that lovely husband of yours send you?"

"A very beautiful mask for the masquerade."

"Have you gotten a dress yet?"

She fixes our plates as we begin to talk about all the details of the party I've been working on. We eat and talk and laugh, and for a moment, I pretend she's my mom.

But only for a moment.

thirteen

(PAST)

TOMORROW'S MY BIRTHDAY. You'd think I'd be excited about turning ten years old, but it's just another reminder that life isn't going to get any better. I used to go to bed at night thinking that tomorrow would be a new day, a hopeful wish on stars. But stars don't grant wishes. I've lived in this house with Pike for almost two years, and I now know that tomorrow is nothing but a repeat of the day before and stars are nothing but burning rocks.

I wonder if I'll even be let out of this closet for my birthday. Unlikely. This is where I have spent nearly every weekend since the day Carl first tied me up a year and a half ago. When I told Bobbi what had happened, her response was, "Well, what did you do to provoke him?" Yeah, turns out, she doesn't give a shit about me or Pike. We're nothing more than her paycheck. A means to get by, to pay her bills and put food on the table, food I rarely get to eat since I'm always locked up with my hands bound.

I feel like I live in the dark more than I do the light. Pike sneaks down every night to talk to me. There's not been a single night that he hasn't spent with me outside of this door. I quickly learned to train myself to sleep during the days so that I could be awake when Pike would visit me. I didn't ever want to be alone and without him.

Carl likes to slap me around before tying me to the garment rod, and there is now a padlock on the outside of the door. I'd tell my caseworker, but I'm terrified of losing Pike. And there's no guarantee that the next home would be any better; at least here, I have my brother. So when my crappy-ass caseworker does decide to show up, which is about once every few months, I keep my mouth shut.

Shifting up to my feet, I allow the blood to drain back down my arms. I pee as I wait on Pike. The filth of spending days peeing on myself doesn't even faze me anymore. It used to embarrass me, but now, it's second nature.

"Elizabeth," I hear Pike whisper, and I'm relieved that I finally have him here with me—my distraction.

"Hey."

"Are you okay?"

"I don't even know why you still ask me that question," I reply.

"Sorry," he says. "Happy birthday. It's after midnight, so it's officially your birthday."

"Wish me a happy birthday when I turn fourteen," I tell him.

"Just four more years."

"It feels more like four hundred," I say in defeat. I'm starting to feel like I'm never going to escape this hell and see my dad. I don't believe life can be that good.

"Well, it's not four hundred, it's only four," Pike tells me.

I situate myself back onto the floor with my hands bound above my head, and ask, "Since it's my birthday, can I pick the game tonight?"

"Go for it."

"Umm . . . how about food, but it has to be junk food," I say. Pike and I play alphabet games with each other. One of us will pick a theme and whatever letter our words ends with has to be the beginning letter to the word the other person has to come up with. If you can't think of a word, you lose. It was Pike's idea to start playing these games. I used to just sit and cry when he would come to me at night, so this was his way of keeping my mind occupied.

"Okay, junk food," he starts. "AirHeads."

"Swedish Fish."

"Happy Meal."

"That's not a food, Pike. It's a meal," I laugh.

He tries defending his play, saying, "Yeah, and what is a meal made of? Food."

"But it's not an actual food because you can choose what you want in it."

"Yeah, but no matter what you choose, it's still junk."

Pike is nothing but serious in his argument, which makes me laugh. Our connection with one another is strong. He's everything a brother should be: protective, caring, annoying, and everything else I could have imagined a sibling would be.

"Uh uh. You can't use that as a game play," I tell him.

I can hear the irritation in his sigh before he says, "Fine. Ho Hos."

"Those are so good."

With a chuckle, he agrees, "I know."

We continue with the game, and eventually, I win, making sure I rub it in since he's beaten me the last two times we've played.

After a while, Pike has to go back to his room and I'm alone once more. Resting my head back against the wall, I shut my eyes and try to relax enough to at least drift a little, if not actually fall asleep.

I startle awake when light hits me. Opening my eyes, I quickly clamp them back shut from the pain of being in the dark for the past three days. Who knew light could be so painful? But it is. It always takes a couple hours for my eyes to adjust.

I can smell Carl along with the stench of my urine, and I'm shocked when he starts to unlatch the leather belt he uses to bind me. He has holes poked all the way down so that he can fasten me tightly and not have to worry about me working my hands free. My arms are like noodles as they fall to my sides. Warmth slowly flows back into my hands, and the tingling begins to run through the length of my lifeless limbs.

"God, you smell like shit, kid," he grumbles, and I crawl to my knees, squinting to find the bottle of bleach he keeps stored in the corner of the closet. It's now routine, that as soon as I'm untied, I'm to clean the floor with bleach.

When I get upstairs, I head into the shower to wash myself. I didn't think I'd be getting out until tomorrow, so I'm determined to stay quiet and invisible so that Carl doesn't change his mind and toss me back into that black hole again.

After I'm cleaned up, I return to my bedroom to see Pike lying in my bed. He's always here to comfort me when I get out of the closet. Walking over to him, I crawl into his arms and let him hold me.

"I have something for you," he whispers, and when I lift my head from his chest, I ask, "What is it?"

"A birthday present."

I let my head fall back down on him and sigh, "You shouldn't have bothered."

"Well, I did, so be polite and pretend you're happy."

Sitting up, I cross my legs as Pike quickly runs into his room and then returns with a plastic grocery sack. He hands it to me and sits back down on my bed. Inside is a doll with bright red hair made out of yarn. A smile finds its way to my lips, and he says, "Her hair reminded me of you."

No doubt, Pike stole this from some store, but I don't care. This will be the only gift I get this birthday, and I love him for giving it to me since there are very few things I can call my own.

"I love you, Pike," I say, looking at him as he sits there with an almost worried expression when he asks, "You don't think it's stupid?"

"No. It's perfect, and I love it."

He reaches out to hug me, and I cuddle into his embrace with the doll pressed between us as he says, "I just didn't want you to be sad today."

"I'm sad every day, but it would be worse if I didn't have you."

"Pike!" we hear Carl yell from downstairs. "Get down here."

My stomach twists when I see Pike's face go to stone. He hates the man as much as I do.

"One sec."

e.k. blair

When Pike sits up, I ask, "Did you do something?" wondering why Carl sounds so pissed.

"Does he need a reason?" is all he says when he sulks out of my room, and I feel sick when I follow him out and stand at the top of the stairs as he walks down.

Carl grips the back of Pike's neck and tugs him in close, saying, "Basement, you little shit."

His head drops, and when Carl opens the door that leads to the basement, Pike descends down the stairs. I hate that he's always down there. He told me that Carl takes him there to knock him around, and I hate that I can't do anything to protect him. Every time he goes to the basement, I just sit and wait for him to return, and when he does, he won't even look at me. It's like he's mad at me. I asked him once if he was, but he swore that he could never be upset with me. It's so different with us, because when I'm let out of the closet, Pike is always there to hold me. But when Pike comes up from the basement, he wants nothing to do with me. He avoids me and hides in his room. It's awful when all I want to do is hug him to make him feel better like he does for me, but he won't let me.

I lie on my bed, slip on my headphones, and hold my new doll while I listen to music, trying to drown out the pain that fills my chest. Closing my eyes, I eventually grow tired and start to nod off when, suddenly, my doll is snatched out of my arms. Opening my eyes, I see Carl hovering over me. As I slip off my headphones, he snarls, "Get your ass in the basement."

Too scared to even question him, I trail behind him as fear chills my body. When he opens the door to the basement, my legs shake beneath me as I step down the stairs. I've never been down here before, and the panic has never been so fierce when I see Pike standing in nothing but a pair of boxers, his clothes crumpled on the floor next to him.

The look on Pike's face scares me. He's never looked at me like this, like he's scared too. But Pike is never scared. I stand a few feet away from him and nervously turn my head back and see a dirty mattress lying on the cement floor. Turning back to Pike, my eyes wide, my heart pounding, my tears pricking, I hear Carl ask, "How old are you today?"

I face him as he sits in a metal folding chair that sits in the corner.

In a weak voice that trembles, I answer, "Umm . . . t-ten."

He doesn't respond, only slowly nods his head and takes a long moment before adding, "You scared?"

I take a quick look at Pike, whose eyes are pinned to the floor, and then back at Carl and nod yes.

His next words changed my life forever. It was my tenth birthday, and I was old enough to know better than to believe in fairytales. I knew that Prince Charming, flying steeds, and talking caterpillars didn't really exist, but what happened next made me realize that monsters did. And I just so happened to be living with one.

A

Real

Life

Monster.

With a low, stern voice, his demand comes. "Take your clothes off."

My heart slams down into the pit of my stomach as my body shivers. I'm frozen. I can't respond, so I just stand there. The air is still until Carl repeats harder, "Take your clothes off. All of them."

I snap my head over to Pike, and he's now looking straight at me. I know I should be terrified by the tears on his cheeks and the look of sorrow in his eyes. Without even blinking, I feel my own tears roll out effortlessly. Shaking my head in confusion, Pike gives me a nod that tells me I need to obey.

My jittery hands slowly go to the hem of my shirt, and when I grip the fabric, a pained cry rips out from my constricted throat. It echoes off the concrete walls and floor. Pinching my eyes shut, I slip my shirt off and over my head and then hold it over my chest, even though I haven't grown breasts yet.

"Pants," he orders.

I don't look at him. My eyes remain closed as I unzip my jeans and push them down my legs and step out, still clinging the shirt to me.

"Drop it."

The ice in his voice frightens me, so I open my fingers and let it drop to the ground.

"Good girl," he says and I can hear the smile that wears his words. "Now your underwear."

God, if you're real, please help me.

Stepping out of my underwear, I attempt to cover myself with my arms and hands as I stand there. And when I finally open my eyes, that's when Carl speaks.

"Have you ever seen a dick before?" he asks as he opens his fly and tugs his pants down. His is the first I have ever seen and my throat burns with the bile that creeps up.

"You ever touched one before?"

My tears are heavy, and I can't hold back the sobs any more, pleading, "Please don't hurt me. I'll do anything."

"Anything?"

My cries are loud when he makes his demand, "This is what I want. You're gonna let Pike fuck you while I watch. You do that for me, I won't lay a hand on you."

I shake my head vigorously, not understanding what he means, and when I look over at Pike, he stands for a moment before taking the two steps towards me, quietly saying in a choked voice, "You don't want him touching you."

My head won't stop shaking, and I can't stop crying as I try to stammer out, "I d-don't know what he w-wants."

He releases a defeated sigh when he tells me, "He wants us to have sex." When he reads my confusion, he asks, "You know what that is?"

"I th-think so. I mean . . . I d-don't, umm . . . ." I can't get my words out through the terror that's stabbing me from the inside. I've heard of sex. I know of sex. I just don't understand what it is exactly.

"On the mattress!" Carl's voice booms, causing me to startle.

In a hushed voice, Pike begs, "Please don't be scared of me," as he takes my hand and walks us over to the stained mattress on the floor.

"Lie on your back," he says, all his words in whispers so that only I can hear. He takes off his underwear before lying on top of me and my helpless cries fill the room. He lowers his mouth to my ear and quietly talks to me, saying, "It's gonna be okay. Don't even look at him. You don't have to look at me, but please promise me you won't look at him."

I nod my head against the side of his head so that he can feel my response.

His last words to me before I lose every last piece of hope that somehow life will be okay are, "I'm so sorry, Elizabeth."

fourteen
(PAST)

MY LIFE CONTINUES to be a wasteland. It's simply pointless to even try to see the good in anything anymore. I'm now twelve years old. The only hope I've been clinging to is that in two years, I'll get my dad back. But that hope turned to ash and dust when my caseworker stopped by yesterday.

"Only two more years," I said, and with a confused look, she asked, "What happens in two years?"

"I get my dad back," I told her. "I can go home."

She seemed annoyed when she shook her head and sighed, "That's not how it works."

"What do you mean?"

"The state terminated his rights to you. When he gets out, you don't get to go back home. He's not allowed to have any contact with you."

My face heated in pure white anger when she added, "This is your home—here—with Carl and Bobbi."

135

I walked away from her at that point. The hopelessness and defeat were too much for me to hide and I didn't want her to see me upset. She's a piece of shit, this world is a piece of shit, my life is a piece of shit. I used to pray to God to help me, but he never did, so he's a piece of shit too, leaving me in this nightmare. Me—living in the darkness, bound up with leather belts, scars imbedding their home in the frail skin of my wrists. Me—humiliated and degraded—having sex with my brother while Carl beats off as if we're his own personal porn show. It's my living hell.

I used to cry all the time after being forced to have sex with my brother, the horror that started on my tenth birthday. When it was over that first time, I locked myself in my room, screaming and crying into my pillow. I'll never forget that day; it's burned its memory inside of me. A day that I truly felt my innocence being stripped away.

Putting my clothes back on, Carl laughs at me and I run up the stairs and into my bedroom, locking the door behind me. I feel disgusting and when I fall onto the bed, I take the red-headed doll Pike gave me earlier and with all the force I have, throw it against the wall, releasing a violent sob as I do. I can't stop the tears or the ache that fills me. I'm nothing but tears and snot and drool—ugly—and the salts from my eyes eventually start making the skin of my cheeks sting. My body wears out, after first being tied up in the closet for the past three days, and now the depth of my breakdown. With swollen eyes, I'm finally unshackled from this misery as I drift off into my dreams.

When I wake up, Pike is sitting in bed next to me. I look up at him as his back rests against the headboard. His eyes are sad and bloodshot, and I'm mortified. I can't even look at him. I don't want him to see me, so I close my eyes and roll over, away from him.

His voice is soft and strained when he says to my back, "I'm so sorry."

I cry. It only takes a second for this heavy weighted pain to claim me—to own me. My body heaves in an unsteady rhythm, and he doesn't touch me like he normally does when I cry.

Time passes as my cries weaken into shallow whimpers that hiccup out of me, and then he speaks again, "Please look at me. Tell me you don't hate me."

I shake my head, keeping my body turned away from him when I feel him scoot down and lie behind me. His head presses against my back, and I hear him sniff before he starts talking to me quietly, making his confessions. "You're not alone. I haven't been telling you the truth. Carl doesn't just hit me when I'm down in the basement with him." He chokes back a whimper, and when I hear it, the tightening in my throat becomes painful. "He makes me do sick things to him." His voice cuts off; he's crying, and I can't stand it. I roll over and his eyes are shut, but his hands find my face as he rests them on my cheeks.

When his eyes open, he says, "Please don't hate me. Don't let him destroy what we have. Don't give him that power to rip us apart from each other." He takes in a shaky breath. "You tell me all the time that I'm all you have, but it goes both ways. I have nothing but you. You're my only family, Elizabeth. Please don't let him take you away from me."

Wrapping my arms around his back, I bury my face in his neck as we both cry together. In this world, a world I'm beginning to learn is a cold and dark place, I fear being alone. I need Pike, and knowing that he needs me too, pushes me to finally speak. I never thought I'd be saying these things, but suddenly I become an open book when I start blubbering against the damp skin of his neck.

"I don't hate you; I love you. But you hurt me. It hurt really bad."

"I'm sorry."

"And now I'm sad and scared and embarrassed and so alone."

"I am too," he admits.

"I'm scared I'm gonna lose you."

"I won't ever leave. I swear."

Pike never has left my side. Even though we don't attend the same school, he has planted himself in my life as a threat to others. I still get teased, but not as much. The summer is nearing an end, and I'm going to be at the middle school this year with Pike at the high school. I wish I could be with him. The only times I feel even a remote amount of relief from the never-ending suffering is when I'm with him. Somehow, he makes it possible for me to breathe in this clandestine world the two of us live in.

If anyone knew that Pike and I were having sex, they would freak, but to us, it's become just another facet of our lives. It used to scare me, used to make me cry, but I've learned to numb myself down in that basement. We have sex long enough for Carl to get off and then we escape to our rooms. Bobbi knows what goes on down there, but she chooses to ignore it as she makes her cheap-ass crafts and collects her stupid ducks.

I'm ready to go back to school because it means I don't have to constantly live in that God-forsaken closet. Now that I'll be back in school, I know I'll only have to go into the blackness on the weekends. I'd endure almost anything to keep Pike, so I've never mentioned a word of what goes on inside of that house for fear that I'd be taken away—away from Pike. If I didn't have him, I'd have no one, and no guarantee that I wouldn't be placed in another abusive home, only to find myself all alone. So I stay, and my silence eats away at the little bits of goodness that are left in me.

I'VE BEEN IN bed all day with a bad stomachache. I've been tossing and turning, trying to distract myself from the pain by listening to my music, but I'm miserable. I jerk up and sit when I feel something warm between my legs. Rushing to the bathroom, I cringe when I see blood on my underwear. I sit on the toilet, pee, and then clean myself, wadding a handful of toilet paper up and shoving it in the crotch of the clean pair of underwear I put on. Embarrassed, I know I need to get some money to go to the drug store, but there's only one person to ask, and I really don't want to. With my hand on his bathroom door handle that leads into his bedroom, I close my eyes and swallow an awkward breath as I rotate the knob and wait for the click.

Peeking in, he's lying on his bed, reading a sports magazine.

Timidly, I quietly call out, "Umm . . . Pike?"

He looks up at me as he lowers the magazine to his chest. "What's up?"

With my head down, I stammer, "I . . . umm, I need a few dollars."

"I just gave you money the other day," he complains.

"I know, but I . . ." I briefly look up at him and then move my eyes away when I let him know, against the heat of my face, mumbling, "I think . . . I think I just started my period."

"Oh," he responds, caught off guard with what I just told him. "Umm, yeah. I mean, sure," he rattles as he gets off the bed and walks over to his dresser.

God, this is so embarrassing.

"How much?"

"I don't . . . I don't know."

When I see his feet appear next to me, I hesitantly look up at him. He hands me a ten-dollar bill and asks, "Want me to walk with you?"

I shake my head and then duck back into the bathroom.

When I return from the store, I shove the bag of maxi pads in my dresser and then go set Pike's change next to his sink. I really don't think I can face him right now. My stomach still hurts, so I decide to crawl back into bed. I close my eyes and roll to the side when I hear Pike walk into the bathroom.

"You okay?" he asks.

"Mmm hmm."

"Is that what the stomachache is all about?"

I really wish he would stop asking so many questions. He has no idea how much I just want to disappear right now, but I answer anyway, saying, "I don't know," because I honestly have no clue. Bobbi wouldn't sign the permission slip for the sex ed the fifth graders went to last year, and I have nobody to talk to, so his guess is as good as mine.

The bed dips, and when I look over my shoulder, he's lying down, reading the same magazine from earlier. I turn my head back and smile at the fact that, no matter what, he's always here for me.

After a while, a couple of Pike's buddies stop by. He hops in their car and takes off for a while, leaving me at the house all by myself. I go down and rummage around the kitchen. I fix myself a sandwich, and when I sit down to eat it, I hear the screen door squeak open and then slam shut. Leaning over in my chair, I see Carl. He's so gross with his greasy shirt that's barely covering his fat, pot-bellied stomach. I sit back and continue eating as he strolls in and grabs a beer from the fridge.

"Where's your brother?" he asks before taking a swig.

"Don't know. He left with a couple friends."

Not wanting to be in the same room as him, I shove the rest of the sandwich in my mouth and rush upstairs. It's then that I hear Pike return, and when he gets upstairs, I go to his room and watch as he pulls out a wad of money and shoves it in his dresser.

"Where'd you get that money?"

"Shh, I don't want anyone knowing I have this, okay?"

Lowering my voice, I ask again, "How did you get it?"

"I've been working for a few months, trying to save money so that I'm not on the streets when I turn eighteen."

"Working? You were gone for thirty minutes."

He comes to stand in front of me and whispers, "If I tell you, you can't say anything to anyone."

"Pike, I don't talk to anyone but you."

"I've been running drugs for a guy I know."

My eyes widen, and I ask, "What do you mean *running*?"

"Selling," he states.

"Are you crazy? What if you get caught?"

"I'm not gonna get caught. Relax."

"What are the two of you doing up there?" Carl hollers from downstairs.

"Nothing," Pike shouts.

"Good, then get your fucking asses down to the basement."

"Fuuuck," Pike sighs and then holds my hand.

For a moment, I feel the drowning of my heart, but this is

nothing new. We are down in that basement at least once a week, if not more. Pike has really helped me learn how to numb myself from what goes on down there, so I take in a deep breath and hold it for a second before slowly releasing it.

"You okay?" he asks, and when I nod, he gives my hand a soft squeeze before we make our way down.

I never know what Carl will have us do, so when I get down there, my stomach turns at the thought of me being on my period. Pulling back on Pike's hand, he turns to me, but before I can mutter anything, Carl speaks.

"Clothes off and fuck her on the bed," he barks at Pike.

He lets go of my hand and starts to strip while I remain standing, not wanting to do this while I'm bleeding.

"I said *clothes off!*"

"I-I . . ."

Pike looks at me, and I start to shake my head quickly, not wanting this to happen, and he gives me an urging eye.

"What the fuck is going on?" Carl yells as he stands in front of me.

I'm scared as hell when I open my mouth and stammer, "P-please, I . . . I started my period."

The hungry grin that grows on his face is sickening. He takes a few steps back, and then asks, "You're bleeding?"

I give him a nod.

"Okay then," he says as he sits down on the chair. "Take off your clothes and lay on the bed."

"What?" I breathe out.

"Don't worry, Pike's gonna fuck you in the ass."

"What?!" Pike's voice is that of shock, and I begin to panic.

My hands turn jittery and I start apologizing, "No. I'm s-sorry. It's fine, we can have sex."

"I like my idea better, now take off your fucking clothes and get on your hands and knees."

"What the fuck? I can't do that," Pike says as I start removing my clothes.

It's as if my blood is running dry because all I feel is cold ice running through me. I swallow hard, and then terror floods through when Carl lurches out of the chair and grabs Pike by the neck, seething, "The way you shits are trying to defy me right now is pissing me the fuck off."

Pike grunts loudly when Carl's fist hammers into his jaw, nearly knocking him over.

"Do what I fucking tell you or she's gonna get locked in the closet for the rest of the week after I beat the shit out of both of you!"

My legs are jelly, barely able to support me on my knees as I prop myself up on my hands. Suddenly, I forget how to go numb, and my body begins to quiver as I start crying, scared of what's about to happen.

I let my head hang down as I feel Pike behind me. Nothing happens though. All I can hear is his heavy breathing. I stay in this position for a while longer and eventually turn my head to see Pike stroking his penis with an almost pained look on his face. He then lets go of himself and puffs out a heavy breath, saying, "I can't do this. I can't even get hard."

Sitting back on my heels, I feel relieved, but that feeling is immediately snatched away, and sheer horror invades when Carl growls angrily. He knocks over his chair when he stands, metal clanking against the concrete, and suddenly the flow of life stops.

Slow motion.

Carl walks straight towards me, yanking his belt out from the loops of his pants. My heart goes frigid, pounding in solid hard beats that vibrate through my whole body. Pounding so hard I can hear it. His eyes are filled with a murderous glare, and Pike's screams penetrate me as he charges Carl and slams his fist into the side of his face.

I can't breathe, but somehow I'm screaming when Carl turns and knocks Pike straight to the ground with one single punch, followed by ruthless kicks to his side. Pike writhes in agony as he heaves, "Don't you fuckin' touch her!" over and over and over until his voice is no longer audible and his eyes glaze over.

When Carl looks back at me, he unzips his pants and adrenaline kicks in. I'm on my feet fast, bolting to the stairs. After a couple steps, I'm brought to my knees as a piercing sting slices through my back.

THWACK!

A shrill wail rips out of me, and I look over my shoulder just in time to see the leather belt he's holding come flying down at me.

THWACK!

Arching my back in pure agony, I scream out as tears spring from my eyes. The leather belt bites my flesh again and again before he forces me on all fours, pushes my face down to the cold cement, and rapes me from behind.

fifteen

(PAST)

AFTER CARL'S ATTACK, Pike doesn't come into my room for a while. All I want to do is die, just put myself out of this misery. I don't even know how to understand what just happened down there. It all came so fast, and I've never experienced that much pain in my life. The pain in my back seemed to disappear when he started raping the one part of my body I never expected.

And now, I lay on my stomach with my face buried into my pillow as I try to muffle my sobs. My top is still off because of the stinging of my back. I'm too scared to look at it to see what he's done to me.

"Oh my God," I faintly hear through my cries, and when I lift my head, I see Pike looking down at me. He's horrified, but I don't ask why because I'm so humiliated.

He kneels beside my bed with a painful groan and lays his hand on my arm, stroking it with his trembling thumb. The side of his face is swollen and badly bruised.

"Tell me what I can do." His voice is worried and his eyes are nothing but a display of his pity.

I can't even think about speaking as my tears soak into my pillow.

He takes my hand, folds his fingers through mine, and holds it tightly, and the touch alone makes me cry harder.

"I'm so fucking sorry," he says with his eyes welled with tears.

My hand is clenched around his and I don't let go for a long time. Eventually, Pike kisses my knuckles, and moves to stand.

"I'll be right back," he says and then goes into the bathroom. When he returns, he's holding a wet towel. "I don't want to hurt you, but your back is covered in dried blood. Just lay still, okay?"

I nod as he gently lays the warm, wet towel on my back. My muscles cinch up, and I whimper as my flesh stings. He presses his hand down on the towel, and I cry out, "Oww."

"I'm sorry."

"W-what does it look like?" I ask, but also scared to know.

"You have a couple nasty gashes and a lot of welts."

"It hurts."

He sighs and holds my hand as he carefully starts cleaning the blood off my back.

"One day, I promise you, that fucker is gonna pay for this," he grits out and all I can do is nod my head as I start thinking about what it would feel like to kill him.

How sick am I? A twelve-year-old girl fantasizing about killing someone.

What's happening to me?

A FEW WEEKS have passed and school has started back up. Carl hasn't touched me since that day, but it was only three days later when I was back in the basement, forced into giving Pike a blowjob. Afterwards, I was tied up in the closet and left there for another two days.

Pike and I now sit out on the curb in front of the house. Bobbi is inside watching TV and Carl is still at work. Summer is coming to an end and the smell of autumn is in the air. You know that smell, the smell of death. I don't know why, but I love it. Leaves falling to their grave on the chilled, damp streets, eventually to be covered in ice and snow when winter hits.

I listen to Pike as he rambles on about some girl who's an upper classman at his school that keeps following him around. It doesn't surprise me. I've always thought Pike was cute, and now that he's almost sixteen, he's even cuter, not that I have a crush on him or anything; it's just a fact. But nobody knows how pathetic the two of us are. Sometimes I get curious as to how someone would react if they knew. I mean, could you imagine that girl asking Pike to tell her something about himself, and his response was, *I'm almost sixteen, and, oh yeah, I have sex with my twelve-year-old sister.* Yeah, people would definitely think we're sick.

"Isn't that your caseworker's car?" Pike questions, and when I turn to look down the street, sure enough, it's Lucia's car.

"What's she doing here?" I can't stand my caseworker. She only stops by to check in on me a few times a year, so the fact that she was just here a month ago makes me a little anxious.

She pulls her car along the curb as Pike and I stand.

"What are you two doing out here?" she asks, and Pike tells her in a shit-mocking tone, "Oh, you know, just enjoying the lush scenery of this picture-perfect neighborhood that you thought would provide a nice backdrop for a wholesome upbringing."

Lucia sends Pike a glare before saying, "You mind giving Elizabeth and I a moment to speak?"

"I'll be in my room," he tells me as he heads inside the house, leaving Lucia and me standing on the front lawn.

"Why don't we have a seat?" she suggests, and we walk over to the front porch steps.

"What are you doing here?"

"I got some news that I needed to come talk to you about."

"Am I being moved?" I ask, nervous of her response because I can't live without Pike. The thought alone pricks my eyes with tears.

"No. It's about your dad," she says.

Pulling on that one tiny piece of hope in my heart that I've been able to hang on to, I ask, "Is he getting out early? Will I be able to see him?"

She shakes her head, and when I see her face drop, she takes that hope right along with it, saying, "I'm sorry. Your father's dead."

And that's the moment when you realize that hopes and dreams are as fucked up as the fairytales.

I drop my head and watch my tears drop like heavy weights to the dirty concrete below my feet. They spread and seep into the porous ground where I'm sure they'll find their home in hell.

But they won't be alone for long because my heart feels unbearably heavy too, like it could drop right out of me at any moment.

I wanna scream. I wanna kick and hit something. I wanna stomp my feet like a toddler and throw the most soul-ripping tantrum a girl my age could, yelling at the world and to anyone who'll listen how I hate all of them. I want to scream so hard that blood comes out. I wanna do it all, but I don't. It's a war inside me, but I hide it well. What's the point of exposing it? It's not like it's going to make a difference. No one is coming to rescue me. So instead, I sit on these steps and quietly cry.

I have a million questions swarming, finally asking, "How?"

"It seems there was a fight that broke out with some of the inmates and your father was stabbed. The place went on lockdown and by the time the guards were able to get to him, it was too late."

"Why? I mean, I-I . . ." I can barely speak as the sobs start breaking through my façade, causing my body to wrack in heaving tremors. "Are you sure it was him? I mean, what if they made a mistake?"

"There's no mistake, Elizabeth," she says softly. "I'm so sorry."

"But I don't have any other family. I mean, w-what happens n-now?"

"Nothing changes."

Glaring over at her, I say, "Everything changes." I turn my head back down and begin crying, covering my eyes with my hands. The instinct to run is fierce, but I have nowhere to go, and that pisses me off. I don't wanna be stuck here. I don't want this life. All I want is my dad. So with that, I stand and spit my words at my worthless caseworker, "I fucking hate you! I hate everything about you! You don't give a shit about me or my dad! You're just a stupid bitch!" I go inside the house, slamming the door as hard as I can behind me and run upstairs. But I don't go to my room; I go to Pike's. I'm loud, bawling like a baby when I walk in. He immediately pops off the bed and is in front of me in a second, asking, "What's wrong? What happened?"

Falling into his chest, he bands his arms tightly around me while I release the most wretched sobs of my life. I fist his shirt in my hands so tightly it feels as if I could break my own fingers, but I like the pain. I need the pain. I need something— anything—to distract me from the most unbearable pain of all.

It can't be real.

He can't really be dead.

He just can't be.

"Elizabeth," Pike says, and I feel like I'm gonna throw up the emptiness that fills me because if he's gone, I'm gone.

I don't even realize we've walked across the room until I open my eyes and we're lying down.

"What did she say?" he asks.

"I hate her, Pike. I hate everyone," I choke out around the pain.

"Tell me."

My words hurt as they come out, "M-my dad. She said he's dead, Pike. That someone stabbed him, and he died." Saying the words cuts deep, and the hold that Pike has on me suddenly becomes a thousand times stronger.

"Shit," he murmurs under his breath before I cry, "It isn't true. It can't be."

Hearing it from Lucia, I felt numb, but now, with Pike—

my safety—the emotions overpower me. I'm drowning and I can't breathe. All I can do is scream and cry, and so I do, just like a helpless baby, never letting go of my grip on Pike's shirt. It's as if his shirt is my lifeline, and if I let go, I'll free-fall into nothingness.

And now I lie here, crumbling into a million pieces. I'll never be whole again. I'll never forgive the world for this.

I want my dad.

Now.

I want the rough whiskers of his face scratching me when he gives kisses, I want his smooth voice singing to me again, I want his touch, his hold, his love, his healing, his smile, stories, tickles, laughs, eyes, hands, smell—everything. I wanna be saved.

I want my prince.

Pike tucks me under his chin, kissing the top of my head every now and then. Eventually the noise in the room begins to fade as I tire and quiet down. My body feels so heavy and my head pounds, making it hurt to open my eyes. Pike continuously runs his hand up and down my back in an attempt to soothe me, but nothing can dull this agony.

Into the quiet room, I whisper, "Do you ever think about dying?"

"Sometimes," he responds softly.

"Does it scare you?"

"No. You?"

"Not anymore," I tell him, and then ask, "Do you think my dad was scared?"

"No," he says without any hesitation.

"How do you know?"

"Because, if he's dead, then he'll always get to be with you.

Knowing he'd finally get to see you again, I doubt he was scared."

His words bring on a slew of silent tears that soak into his shirt. "It's not fair, Pike."

"No, it's not. You deserve everything that's good in this world, and I swear to you that I will fight to give you that. One day, when we're out of this mess, I'll find a way to make you happy."

"I don't believe in happiness," I weep. "I don't believe in anything anymore."

He brushes my hair back and scoots down to look me in the eyes. "Believe in *me*."

His dark eyes are stern, and I realize, that in this moment, he's my only chance at survival. Pike has always done his best to protect me; he's always cared about me. From the first day I got here, he's been my brother. It was instant. And now, I have no other choice but to believe in everything he says because he's my only constant.

When he leans in and kisses my forehead, I don't even think when I nuzzle in and kiss his neck. He keeps his lips on my forehead and doesn't move, but his hands find my cheeks as he holds me close. Before I know it, his lips are on mine in an unmoving kiss. I grip on to his wrists, and in a blur, in an unnoticeable moment, our mouths move together.

I've never kissed Pike before—never even thought about it—but somehow, this feels right. He's the first boy I've ever kissed. We've been having sex for two years, so you wouldn't think kissing him would feel like anything at all, but it does. Out of nowhere, he's taken my mind away from everything bad as I focus on only him. It's like I can finally breathe.

Rolling on top of me, he reaches back to take his shirt off, and I sit up to remove mine as well. When we're stripped down to nothing, he pulls the sheets over us, and I'm tucked in warm with him. Everything about this feels different than the hundreds of times we've done this before. It's always cold and dirty, with Carl watching us the whole time.

"Don't go there," Pike says, knocking me from my thoughts.

"Where?"

"Don't think about him. He has nothing to do with this. We're not on that mattress down there; we're here in my bed. You're safe."

"Just us?" I ask.

"Just us," he says as he pushes himself inside of me, and for the first time, I find the magic that I gave up believing in. It turns out Pike had it all along, because in this moment, I don't feel any more pain or hurt.

It's just us, and I'm safe.

sixteen
(PAST)

MY TEETH CHATTER as I walk home from school. I wound up getting in trouble for fighting a girl who was making fun of me today, landing me in afterschool suspension for the next two weeks. Pike has been working more and more, so we haven't been walking home together much lately, and he refuses to let me tag along with him. He says he doesn't want me getting mixed up with his friends, but he always makes sure he's home before Carl gets there so I won't be alone with him.

Life hasn't changed that much. I'm fourteen—a little taller, filling out more, my hair has grown a few more waves than it used to have, and I have more scars on my wrists. It looks like I've been trying to slit them, but six years of being belted up in a tiny closet will do that to you. I hide them well though, wearing long sleeves that fall past my wrists that I often tug further down.

Since learning about my dad's death two years ago, I've

grown pretty numb to everything around me. I feel like a living, breathing machine most of the time. I'm able to turn myself off and on pretty easily. For the most part, I'm in off mode, frozen and void. I only allow Pike to see me on. He's my only release, the only one I show my true self to. Since that afternoon, the afternoon I learned that I would never see my father again, Pike and I have continued to sleep together, privately, in his bed. I've found myself becoming selfish with him, using him to take away all the bad. It's so hard to explain, but when I'm with him like that, I feel like I'm washed clean. Once I realized what I was doing, I was honest and told him. The guilt was overpowering me, and when I explained my feelings to him, I thought he'd be mad, but he wasn't. He told me to take whatever I needed to take from him. I still feel the guilt though. The shame of using him so selfishly eats at me after we're done and I grow quiet, often crying. Pike soothes me as best as he can, holding me, assuring me that it's okay—that everything's okay.

I'm a mess, but that's to be expected with the harsh introduction I received to this crazy, fucked up life. I'm fourteen—too young to be this bitter and angry. For a while, when I would see a child with their parent, I'd wish for that parent to die. I wanted every kid to feel the pain I was feeling because it wasn't fair to me.

Life's cruel, and I'm its bitch.

I'm Carl's bitch too. Lately he's been fucking me, wanting Pike to watch. He made me promise to never look at Carl, so I always keep my eyes locked on Pike's no matter who I'm fucking that day.

My first orgasm came about a year ago. Carl was jerking off in the corner while Pike and I were having sex. It had never

155

happened before, so when what was always such a sickening act turned into pleasure, it scared the crap out of me. I couldn't face Pike afterwards; I was too ashamed. When I finally unlocked my bathroom door a few hours later, he came in and talked to me about it. It was humiliating, having my brother explain to me what had happened. He told me it was a natural part of sex, but I didn't like it. It made me feel dirty and embarrassed. And now, knowing it could happen again, I fight hard to prevent it. Pike knows this, so when we're alone in his bed, he tries to get off fast so that he doesn't accidentally make me feel it again. It's weird, because I like having sex with Pike when we're alone, but at the same time, it scares me because I don't want it to feel good—it shouldn't feel good. But I want to be with him because it's with him that I don't feel the misery and the ugliness. He takes it all away, and even if it's only for a moment, I feel free.

When I turn the corner, I see Pike sitting on the curb smoking a cigarette. "Pike!" I shout from down the street, and he looks over to me then stands up.

"Where the hell have you been?" he asks, pissed.

"I got in a fight and now I have afterschool suspension."

Taking a drag from his cigarette, the smoke drifts lazily out of his mouth when he gets all big-brother-protective, saying, "Tell me what happened."

"That girl I've been telling you about, you know, the one who's been making my life hell? She just kept running her mouth in the cafeteria, calling me names. I couldn't take it anymore, so I lost it."

"What'd you do?"

"She was sitting at the end of the same table as me, so I chucked my apple at her and it hit her in the head. Before I knew it, we were out of our seats and I had her on the ground."

"No shit?" he says with a mild, pleased grin on his face. "Well, I don't see a mark on you, so I take it you won?"

"It wasn't a competition, Pike," I say, still feeling like the loser the kids at school tell me I am.

"What's wrong? You kicked her ass; you should feel good."

"You're such a boy," I sigh, dropping my head. When he drapes his arm around my shoulder, I add, "I hate it there. I have no friends."

"They're bitches, Elizabeth. Young, stupid bitches."

"*I'm* young and stupid."

Pike tosses his cigarette before we walk inside the house. "Young, yes. Stupid, no," he says as we go upstairs. "You only have a couple months left there. Next year, you'll be with me again."

"Right," I scoff. "You'll be a senior and I'll be the freshman freak."

He plops down on the bed, folding his arms behind his head, responding, "Nothing about you says *freak*. Trust me. Those girls are just jealous because you're prettier than them."

His words heat my neck, but at the same time fill something inside of me. The last time anyone ever said I was pretty, I was five, and it came from my dad. He would always tell me I was beautiful and pretty, saying I had the most gorgeous red hair. Looks are shallow, I know that, but I didn't realize how much I needed to hear that until just now.

"What's wrong?" he asks, noticing the sadness behind my eyes. "Come here."

I walk over and sit down next to him.

"What's wrong?" he repeats.

"I feel ugly inside," I admit.

"Don't," he states as he sits up next to me. "There's nothing about you that's ugly."

"Really, Pike?" I question with ridicule.

Annoyed with my tone, he defends, "Nobody knows us. Nobody knows. It's you allowing what other people might think or say that makes you feel that way."

"It's what I feel, Pike," I argue in a pitched voice.

"You have the power to change that. How you feel is how you *allow* yourself to feel."

"So, it's my fault? My fault that I feel this way?"

"Feel sad. Feel angry. Hate whoever you want. Blame whoever you want, but don't, for one second, think that you're any less than what you are. You're not ugly or dirty or whatever else you're thinking." His tone is hard and stern when he says this, but in an instant, he softens it, saying, "There isn't anything I wouldn't do for you. You still believe in me?"

I nod.

"Good. Because it won't always be like this."

"No?"

"No."

"Tell me, Pike. What's it gonna be like? Tell me the fairytale," I voice with a slip of mockery.

"I'm gonna make you believe in the fairytale again."

I laugh softly at his determined words, and he smiles at me.

We spend the next hour goofing around and getting our homework done. Carl got home a while ago, but he hasn't said a word to us, which is a relief, and now the smells of food cooking fill the house. Bobbi hardly ever cooks. More like never.

"You think we're gonna get any of that?" Pike asks,

referring to whatever it is she's making in the kitchen.

"Doubtful," I respond with a roll of my eyes, and we both smile at each other.

"Pike," Bobbi calls from downstairs after the doorbell rings.

"Be back," he says.

I stay on his bed, and when I hear the front door shut, I turn to look out the window to see Pike and his caseworker on the front lawn talking. Whatever is being said, Pike is visibly pissed, raking a strong hand through his hair. His muffled yells are distorted and I can't make out what he's saying. When he turns his head and looks up to the window, my stomach drops hard. The expression on his face tells me I should be worried, and I am. I jump off the bed when he walks back to the house. He runs up the stairs, meeting me at the door. With his hands on my shoulders, he pushes me back into the room and closes the door behind him.

"What's going on?" I question as the panic rises.

Looking down, he shakes his head, and then pulls me tightly in his arms, hugging me.

And now I'm freaking out.

"Pike, what's happening? You're scaring me."

"I'm so sorry," he says, and I know it's bad. He only says that when something bad is about to happen. He doesn't let go of me as we stand there, holding on to each other.

I didn't think life could get any worse for me, but it could—and it would. I've always battled with the idea of hope. Hope had always failed me, but for some reason, I kept holding on to a tiny piece of it. I was scared to know what the world would be like if I didn't have it. But Pike's next words to me would stab me from the inside—white horror—filling me with the blood of life's harsh reality. A reality that would spit its gritty words in my face, telling me, "Hope is for the ignorant, little girl. Give it up."

Taking his arms from around me, he cups my cheeks, takes out the knife, and stabs me to the core with his words.

"You're gonna be okay, Elizabeth."

My whole body shakes, my voice trembling in confusion, "What?"

Pressing his forehead against mine, I hold his wrists in a death grip as he says, "I'm leaving."

He just siphoned all the air from my lungs with those two words, and I turn cold, shaking my head vigorously against his.

"I have to go. They're placing me in a group home."

"No."

"I'm so sorry," he painfully breathes.

"No." My word, a wretched plea.

Pike presses a hard kiss to my forehead, and I cry out, "No!" as his back shakes against my hands. "No!"

"It's done. Apparently Carl made a call. He wants me out."

"Don't go. You can't go."

"I don't have a choice," he says, and when he pulls back, I see the fear in his eyes, and I know it's all for me. We both know what'll happen without him here. I'll be all alone for Carl to do with as he pleases.

"You can't leave me here. You can't leave me with him," I desperately plea.

He takes a step back, fisting his hair, gritting under his breath, "Fuuuuck." He paces as I stand in shock, crying. Eventually, he turns back to me and affirms, "Fourteen is still gonna be your year. Your dad won't be coming back for you, but I will."

"Don't do that," I tell him. "Don't you dare give me hope."

His eyes are burning, dark coals when he says, "I swear to you. I'll give you that fairytale. Let me age out. I'll come back for you."

"A year? Pike, don't leave me here with him for a year!"

"We can't run away now. Think about it—two of us go missing—it's too risky. But just one—you—we could get away. Less than one year, you'll be free from here. One year alone and out at fourteen; you can do it," he tells me while I cry in fear of what life is going to be like without him. "You're so fucking strong," he asserts. "I *will* come back for you."

I sling my arms around his neck, and continue to beg him not to leave me. I'm terrified I'll never see him again, my only friend, my only family—my brother. Who's going to protect me?

"I have to pack," he whispers.

"Now?"

"My caseworker is downstairs waiting on me."

"Oh my God," I mutter to myself. I can't believe this is happening. My heart feels like a wrecking ball inside my chest, pounding away at my pathetic life. I wander over to Pike's bed and sit down, gripping the edge of the mattress with my hands, and watch as he starts shoving clothes into his duffle bag. The tears simply fall from my eyes with no effort. I lost my dad with the faith that I would see him again, and now I'm losing Pike with the knowledge that life doesn't guarantee you anything, no matter how badly you want it.

Once his bag is zipped, he kneels down in front of me with his hands on my knees. He's a blurry vision, muddled through the tears that separate us. "You're all I have," he says. "You're it. I won't lose you, and you won't lose me."

"Please." It's a vague plea—a plea for anything, really.

"I need you to listen to me, okay?" He takes his thumbs and wipes the tears from my eyes. "*Really* listen to me."

I nod.

"I'm with you," he assures. "When you're in that closet, I'm with you. When you're in that basement, I'm with you. I'm always with you, okay? But I need you to make me a promise. I need you to promise me that you'll turn yourself off. Just shut it off. He can't hurt you if you don't feel. The people who get hurt in life are the ones who allow themselves to feel."

My tears grow heavy, plunking to their death in a free-fall, landing on my knees. Looking down at him, without much thought, I kiss him. We've never kissed outside of his bed when we're having sex, but I kiss him now because I don't know what else to do. He holds me tight, kissing me back as I cry against his lips, refusing to let go of him.

When our mouths part, he looks into my eyes, saying, "I love you."

"I love you too."

He stands, grabs his bag, and promises, "I'll come back for you."

And just like that, as if I ever had a choice in the matter, my brother, my only lifeline, walks away from me.

And I'm all alone.

Seventeen

(PAST)

I DON'T NEED to tell you what happened next.

You already know.

Life without Pike was worse than the swamps of hell. Alone. Desolate. A life no one wants to believe is real—but is. I became dark inside. No. That's not true. I became colorless. You couldn't have painted a portrait of me because I no longer existed. To exist, you have to have life and I was merely a robot—a machine—tell me what you wanted and I'd do it, paralyzed to emotions and consequences.

Fuck you, life.

I hate you.

The moment Pike walked out the door, Bobbi came up to my room. I was crying, begging her to use the phone when the threat came. She told me that she knew about Pike and I having sex, and if I told anyone or attempted to leave, she would tell Social Services and I would be placed under mental evaluation in a state hospital. She also told me that Pike would be arrested and sent to jail for statutory rape of a minor since seventeen is the legal age of consent in the state of Illinois. So that was it; I kept my mouth shut.

I haven't heard from Pike since he left a little over three months ago. He's gone, probably happier, and left me to fend for myself. I don't blame him. *Run away, Pike. Run far from me and this life.* I've come to accept that he wouldn't be coming back for me. I had my first freak out after the first month, missing him, wondering if it was all a lie and whether I'd ever see him again. That first month was really the only time he would have been able to see me. I was still in school, but as soon as summer hit, I was rarely let out of the closet. No longer did I have Pike to talk me through the nights; I had no one.

School started up again last week. I was so anxious, nervous to see Pike now that we would both be in high school. Would he grab me and hug me, or would he look right through me as if I no longer existed? But I didn't have to worry so much because he wasn't there. I searched the halls and then wound up going to the office only to find out that he transferred to another school. They wouldn't tell me where though. Walking out of the office that day, I thought to myself, *Maybe this is where you give up, Elizabeth. Maybe this is where you realize life's fate for you. Maybe this is where you finally stop fighting for something that was never meant to be.*

That was last week, and I still haven't made any decisions about those thoughts. And so I resume my mechanical life. Wake up, go to school, go home, be fucked by my greasy, fat foster dad, shower, homework, bed. Bed is always a variable; it's either bed or leather restraints and locked in the closet. Despite the disgust, I'm hyperaware of my appearance. I've been lucky so far to avoid the puberty pimples; my skin is soft and flawless from the neck up. Beneath my clothes is a different story—various colors of new and healing bruises, welts, and cuts. My wrists look like I've had a few failed suicide attempts. My red hair is bright and full of lazy, loose waves that fall past my slender shoulders. My face, it deceives everyone because no one would ever guess the horror that lives beneath. But no matter how ugly I feel, I try to take care of myself.

When the final bell rings, I shove my books into my backpack and walk through the halls. I have no friends here; maybe it's my fault, or maybe it's theirs. I keep to myself. I never speak unless called on by a teacher, and even with that, I never say more than necessary. My grades are good, not that I have any aspirations after I graduate. I'm sure I'll be flipping burgers somewhere or turning tricks, giving out blowjobs depending on how much money I want to make.

Cynical?

Yeah, I am.

I move slowly, letting everyone pass, bumping into me as they rush out of this school and into their freedom. But this is my freedom—here at school and away from home. So I take my time, and when I finally walk out the metal double doors, I tighten my coat around me and start heading home. Before I can make it off school grounds, a black, vintage Mustang pulls alongside me, and I think I'm imagining things when I hear his familiar voice.

"Elizabeth, thank God."

Pike gets out of the car and has me in his arms fast. The comfort is overwhelming, and it doesn't take long before I'm weeping into his shirt.

"Fuck, I've missed you," he breathes in my hair, and I nod

against his chest. "Are you okay?"

I pull back and look up at him, ignoring his question, asking, "Where have you been?"

"I didn't know how to find you. I tried sneaking by the house a few times this summer, but you were never there."

"I was there," I tell him. "He kept me locked up for most of the summer. He knew about us . . . that we were . . . you know. It pissed him off and he said that's why he got rid of you."

"Shit."

And then the crying starts as I deflate and say, "I thought you gave up on me."

"Never."

He then turns to the car, and when I peek around him, I see the driver. He's older, maybe in his twenties, with tattoos down his arms.

"Come with me. We can talk," Pike says as he looks back at me.

"Can't be gone long. Carl normally gets home around five."

"Don't worry. I'll have you back in time," he tells me and then opens the door to crawl into the back seat before holding his hand out for me. "This is Matt, by the way," Pike introduces, "He's a good buddy of mine."

"Hey," Matt says, giving me a nod in the rearview mirror before pulling back out onto the street.

"Hey." My voice, barely a whisper when Pike pulls me into his arms.

"Talk to me."

I keep my eyes on Matt, not wanting to speak in front of this stranger.

"Don't worry about him," Pike tells me. "He's cool."

"I was scared I would never see you again," I admit quietly.

"I told you to believe in me. I'm not leaving you. The place I'm staying has strict rules. Basically school and then back by eight o'clock curfew."

"What's it like?" I ask. "The group home, I mean."

"It's okay. You're not there, so I spend most of my time worrying about you."

"This cool, man?" Matt says when he pulls into the back lot of a rundown strip mall.

"Yeah. Just give us an hour," Pike tells him as he parks the car and then gets out.

"Where's he going?"

"Just giving us some alone time. I want to talk to you. I wanna know if you're okay."

I shake my head and a few tears slip out. "It's awful, Pike. It's so bad."

"You're gonna be okay."

I shake my head again.

"I know you don't see it, but you're a strong girl. You *will* be okay."

"He does horrible things to me. Things he never did before," I reveal. He cradles me to his chest and kisses the top of my head as I hold on to him, adding, "And now you're not there to take it away."

Moving my head up to him, he kisses me, resting his lips on mine and I go soft in his hold. He shifts and moves over me, lying me down on my back against the cold leather seat.

"What are you doing?" I mumble against his kisses.

"Taking it away."

"But your friend . . ."

With his hand on the button of my pants, he says, "He won't be back for a while." He pops the button, looking down at me, and then asks, "Is this okay?"

I nod as I murmur, "Yes. Just take it away."

And he does, right there in the back seat of his friend's car. Pike cleans me of the past three months, fading away all the filth Carl left behind and covers it with the goodness of himself.

PIKE HAS CONTINUED to pick me up after school for the past seven months, but only once or twice a week. He's mostly with Matt, but every now and then, Matt loans him his car and Pike and I can be alone. I love those times. I found out that Pike and Matt work together, running drugs on the street. After I met him, it didn't take long for Matt to question Pike about fucking a fourteen-year-old in the back of his car every week. I had never seen Pike so pissed and defensive, threatening Matt that he'd knock the shit out of him if he ever questioned him again.

Matt is slime and gives me the creeps. He eyes me constantly, like he's waiting for his chance to get into my pants as well. I don't say anything to Pike about it, but I don't trust the guy.

Every time I see Pike, he has a new tattoo. I hate that he's marking himself up so much. Kinda like, with each tattoo, he's taking away a piece of the Pike I know and replacing it with a new Pike—a Pike I only get to see once a week in the back seat of that Mustang while we have sex. We don't have a lot of time to talk, so it feels as if I pretty much use him to escape. It's overwhelming now, the emotions afterward. I've started crying a lot when we're done. It worries Pike. He tries to talk to me, and I've tried explaining how it's starting to make me feel guilty, but he assures me it's okay. So after sex, I cry and Pike holds me, doing what he can to make me feel better.

But Pike hasn't come around in two weeks. He told me to give him time to sort out his plans for when he turns eighteen, and I've been trying to be patient. His birthday was last week, and I've been on pins and needles, anxious to get the hell away from Carl and Bobbi. Carl has been getting more violent with me lately, punching me during sex and spitting in my face. He fisted me across my face last night, giving me a black eye before tossing me on my stomach and taking me from behind. He doesn't do that all too often, only when he's really pissed about something. But last night got really bad, and he lost control. I kept my mouth shut and let my mind drift as far away as it could, waiting for it all to be over. He still has that same mattress. It's now stained in blood, vomit, sweat, and Carl's urine.

This is why I'm so anxious for Pike to come get me.

So after I apply more ointment to the split skin of my black eye, I sit on my bed and stare out the window, looking for Matt's black Mustang. Soon I grow tired as I peer into the darkness outside. Disappointed, I sulk down under my covers and stare at the purple walls for a few minutes before turning out the light and drifting off to sleep.

A weight on my arm causes my eyes to pop open. Startled in the blackness, my heart pounding, I hear a soothing, "Shh."

"Pike?" I whisper as I sit up and reach out for him.

His hand runs down my cheek as he softly breathes, "You still believe in me?"

"Yes."

Pike tosses the sheets off of me, and the adrenaline kicks in. Like a million bees swarming in my chest, my heart pumps as Pike and I move fast, tossing my clothes and few belongings into a bag. Everything blurs in a speedy haze, and I almost feel like I'm going to be sick. My stomach is in knots with fear and excitement that I'm seconds away from being free from the hell I have been living for the past six years.

When Pike zips the bag and throws it over his shoulder, he takes my hand in his. I can see his smile grow in the shadows of the moonlight, and I can't help myself when I lean in and kiss him, giving him every piece of my heart for this gift he's giving me. My fairytale, rescuing me from the evil monster that lurks in the dungeon.

"I love you so much, Pike."

"I love you too," he quietly murmurs. "You ready?"

"Yeah."

With my hand in his, he walks me over to the window he'd crawled in and slips out before helping me out. We teeter along the roof to the edge where Pike tosses the bag down to Matt who is waiting on the front lawn. He quickly runs to the car, tossing the bag in while Pike jumps off the roof and into the grass below. You'd think I'd be scared to jump, but I would jump ten stories down into a pile of varmints if it meant escaping from here. So when Pike holds his arms out, I jump, leaping into whatever life awaits me on the other side.

Once in the car, Matt drives us away as I stare back at that shitty, white house that has kept me caged since I was eight. I've spent nearly half my life locked in that tiny closet and forced down into that basement. The car finally turns, and when the house vanishes, I fall into Pike's chest and begin sobbing like a baby.

Free. Relieved. Saved.

Pike swore fourteen was still going to be my year. I wanted to believe him, but I always doubted. Nothing has ever worked out for me, nothing until now. My cries are loud, but nobody speaks, and eventually, after time passes, I curl up in Pike's lap and close my eyes while Matt continues to drive into the night.

eighteen
(PRESENT)

CHRISTMAS HAS PASSED and Bennett has been home for the past couple of weeks. With the holidays, time has been consumed, leaving little interaction with Declan. We did meet up for coffee before Bennett returned from Dubai. The encounter was more pleasant than our usual tension. We just talked, and he told me about living in Scotland and falling into his father's business. I almost feel bad for manipulating him so much—almost. My purpose is clear, and no one will stand in the way of me righting the wrong.

To appease Jacqueline, I agreed to meet up with her for lunch with a couple of the other girls. So when Baldwin drops me off at Le Sardine, a local French bistro in the west loop, I see the girls already sitting at one of the white, linen-covered tables.

"There she is," Jacqueline says as I approach and take a seat.

"Sorry I'm late. I had to take a few calls."

"Are you all set for New Year's Eve?" Marcia asks as I take a sip of the water that's set for me.

"I believe so. I'm just happy Bennett is here. A part of me was worried he'd have to go back out of town."

"Please. He'd never miss this event, or a chance to show you off," Jacqueline says. "The man is crazy about you. I'm a little jealous."

Who is she kidding? Jacqueline is innately jealous and does a shit job at covering her attraction to my husband, but I give a charming smile, responding with, "I'm just happy he's back home."

Marcia's attention goes to the front of the restaurant, and when I turn to see what's caught her eye, I tense for just a moment.

"He is so fuckable," she says under her breath, causing Jacqueline to blurt out, "Marcia! My God."

"What?" she defends. "Look at him and tell me you wouldn't let him do things to you."

I watch as Declan talks to the hostess as Jacqueline responds, "You're married."

"I don't care. It's worth the risk, right?"

"Ask Nina."

Turning my attention back, I question, "Ask me what?"

"About *him*," Jacqueline says as she nods her head towards Declan.

"What makes you think I know anything?"

"Don't be coy. He owns the hotel you're planning the party at," she states.

"Doesn't mean I know him personally," I defend. "But

from what I do know, he seems like a nice man." As I say this, Declan catches my eye, and with a slight smile, walks back towards the kitchen. Scooting my chair out, I politely excuse myself, saying, "With that being said, I'll be right back."

"Where are you going?" Marcia asks.

"To go say hello," I tell her as I drop my napkin on the table and walk to the back of the restaurant.

When he turns to see me, I smile, and slide up next to him along the cold granite countertop that divides the dining room from the kitchen. "You following me?" I question with flirtation.

"Do you want me to follow you?"

Taking a pause, I turn on my game and respond, "Maybe."

His smile meets his eyes.

"I haven't heard from you in a while," I say.

"I figured you were busy with family affairs. Didn't know you were wanting to hear from me," he says, flirting right back.

"I enjoyed our coffee date," I tell him. "I like talking to you. Just missed it, that's all."

"Is that all you missed?"

"Declan," I softly nag.

"Yeah, I know. You're married."

Needing to break him, I softly whisper, "I miss spending time with you."

His eyes hesitate for a second, and then he grips my elbow, causing me to instinctively look over my shoulder to see that, for the moment, the girls aren't looking at us. Declan quickly pulls me back to a private hallway that leads to the restrooms.

"What are you doing?" I ask and tug against his hold, but he has me pinned against a wall before I can say anything else.

His face is close to mine as we stare at each other. My heart pounds in fear that someone will see us, and he reads my anxiety, saying, "No one can see us."

"What are you doing?" I ask again.

"What are *you* doing?"

"Nothing."

"You're flirting with me, Nina. You're leading me on."

"I'm not."

His eyes roll down to my mouth, and then he speaks in a soft, guttural tone, saying, "Don't fucking lie to me."

"I don't know what you want me to say," I whisper.

"What are you feeling?" he questions, pressing his body into mine, pushing my back flat against the wall. "Tell me what you're feeling . . ."

Pressing.

". . . right . . ."

Closer.

". . . now."

"I love my husband."

"Is that you telling me or you trying to convince yourself?"

Releasing a fractured breath, I see the darkness in his eyes, and I make my move, saying, "I don't know."

His hand comes to meet my neck, almost forcefully, wrapping his fingers and thumb around its slender form, pinning my head back to the wall in a possessive, yet soft, chokehold. Taking a moment, he simply looks into my eyes and I finally see the hunger before he kisses me, sucking the breath straight from my womb. Lips crashing, heavy breaths, all the while, keeping me in his firm grip. His aggressiveness spurs me to grab on to his dress shirt, clenching the crisp fabric in my hands while he takes over. Sinking his tongue into my mouth, I taste the ice of his breath, or maybe it's my soul I taste. I lure him in further as I slide my tongue along his, and when I do this, he quietly growls into my mouth, causing a slight vibration between us.

Abruptly, he pulls away, keeping his powerful hand around my neck as he takes a step back. He stares; he doesn't speak, he just stares, examining my reaction. But my reaction is calculated, pulled straight from my playbook.

Quaking, aroused breaths.

Making the rise and fall of my chest visible to him.

Letting out an erotic but nervous hum.

Relaxing my muscles and sinking into the hold he has on me.

"Say it," he demands.

I shake my head, denying his request, and when I do, the tips of his fingers increase the pressure around my neck.

"Tell me how you feel," he urges.

I quicken my breathing and am able to push the deceit out in the form of a tear. Slowly spilling over, I feel the wetness linger down my cheek, but before it drips off my jaw, Declan's tongue licks it away. The tender touch surprises me, and when I drop my head, he finally releases his hold on me and cradles my face, tilting it up to look at him.

His eyes soften, and I give him the words I know he wants, saying quietly, "I don't know what the word is for what I feel for you, but I feel it."

"Do you want it?"

With slight mock-hesitation, it's game on when I respond, "Yes."

The corner of his mouth lifts, and this time, he's gentle when he moves me to kiss him. His lips are soft as they press into mine, but he keeps it short, and then says, "Come to the hotel after you're done here."

"Okay," I answer without any question, and then he's gone, walking away from me. I take a moment to compose myself before returning to the table, and when I walk back out into the restaurant, I do a quick glance and notice that Declan has already left.

"And where were you?" Marcia asks with gossipy intent.

"Restroom."

"With?" she presses.

Narrowing my eyes, I tell her, "You're insinuations are vastly inappropriate and offensive. If you're wanting dirty gossip, you're going to have to find it elsewhere."

"I'm sorry. I wasn't trying to insinuate anything," she says, back-stepping.

I pick up the menu, mind still on Declan, while Jacqueline and Marcia fall back into whatever conversation they were having before I returned. We spend the rest of our lunch in idle chitchat, and then Jacqueline goes on her usual rants about our other so-called friends. I sit, playing along, nodding my head to feign my interest in what's being said.

After the bill is paid, we exchange cheek kisses before leaving. Baldwin is parked out front, waiting on me, and when he opens the car door, he asks, "Good lunch?"

"Lovely," I respond sarcastically, and when he gets into the front seat, he looks at me through the rearview mirror with a pondering look that I have to smile at and then admit, "Okay, maybe lovely isn't the right word."

He laughs and pulls out into traffic.

"I need to stop by Lotus before we go home. Seems my

signature is needed on a few invoices and I want to see that the room is set up properly."

"Of course."

Pulling up to the hotel, I get out of the car and walk in, heading straight back to Declan's office. He sits behind his desk, and when I step in, he stands up, saying, "Close the door."

I do.

He strides right up to me, takes my face in his hands, and kisses me, never breaking his fluid movements. Slipping my arms around him, I kiss him back. Excitement rushes through me, or maybe it's the adrenaline of finally knowing this is happening. The plan that Pike and I set out to accomplish over four years ago. All this time, and finally, it's happening. I want to throw myself at Declan, but I have to be smart, remember the game, and not lose focus of what I need to do. So I control the endorphins and pull away.

"What is it?" he questions.

"I'm just . . ."

"Just what?"

Taking a moment, I respond, "Scared."

"Of me?"

I shake my head with his hands still on my face, holding me.

"Of this?"

"Yes." With a drop of my head, I lay my forehead against his chest, adding, "I'm married. I don't know what I'm doing."

"You're married, yes. But are you happy?"

Looking up into his eyes, I say, "I'm not sure what I am. All I know is that this feels good. You feel good."

The intensity in his eyes reveals the pleasure he's taking in my candid words, and I take advantage when I slip my hand around the back of his neck and pull his lips down to mine, showing him that it's him I want—because truth be told, he *is* what I want, what I need.

"Come see me," he says when we break our connection.

"When?"

"Tonight."

"I can't. I have a dinner," I tell him.

"I want you to come see me."

Taking a step back, out of his hold, I hesitate, saying, "I don't know."

His jaw twitches in what I can assume is frustration or anger. "Don't waver, Nina."

"That's so easy for you to say, isn't it?" I nearly snap. "Because you're not the one who is about to fall into a situation that will turn you into a person who acts in Machiavellian schemes. I am."

"I am too. I know what I want. And even if it comes with the manipulation right now, I still want it."

"I don't know," I say in a heavy sigh. "I'm not that kind of person, Declan. I'm faithful and good. This—kissing you—it's already hurting me. But . . ."

"Say it," he demands.

"But it's already filling something in me I didn't know was even empty until you. I just . . . I just need a little time to think about this."

"I'm not a patient man, Nina."

"I know. But please, just . . ."

He steps to me, gripping my arms tightly in his hands, and says, "We both know what you want here. You're lying to yourself right now if you say it's Bennett or else you wouldn't have come here."

"Stop."

"No."

Tugging my arms away, his grip tightens and I see the beginnings of a smirk.

"Declan, stop. Let go."

"No," he says in a hardened voice. "I don't play games, and this is you, playing with me."

"I'm not playing, Declan. This isn't a game; this is my life, a life I've made with my husband, and right now, I'm really confused. Just let me think," I tell him.

His hands let go of me and he walks to the door, opening it. I watch him, trying to read past his glare as he states, "Then go think," before he silently dismisses me from the room.

I don't worry too much about the fact that I just pissed him off. All is fair in love and war, right? So I straighten myself and walk to the door, stopping to look at him with soft eyes, and then leave. This will never work properly if I go to him; he needs to come to me. So I'll make him jealous. I'll make him attack.

nineteen

(PRESENT)

RETURNING HOME FROM running a few last minute errands before the party tonight, I hear the annoying chuckle of Richard, Bennett's business partner, coming from the office. I toss my shopping bags on the dining room table before heading into the kitchen.

"Honey, is that you?" Bennett calls out from across the house.

"Yes, dear."

I grab a bottle of chilled Chardonnay from the wine fridge and begin opening it as the boys round the corner. Smiling up at Bennett as he moves in behind me, I turn my head so that he can take a kiss.

"What are the two of you discussing?" I ask.

"Just a couple of merger opportunities, that's all."

Setting the bottle down, I respond, "I didn't know you were interested in something like that."

"We're not," Richard blurts out. "We're not entertaining any of the offers."

I turn to face Bennett, and he doesn't even seem to acknowledge Richard as his eyes are focused on me with a slight smile. It isn't until I raise up on my toes to give my husband a kiss that Richard speaks again, saying, "Jacqueline mentioned you girls having lunch yesterday. Said you had the attention of another man."

He's such an asshole.

"Who?" Bennett asks.

"Declan," I tell him and then step away to face Richard, adding, "He's the owner of the hotel the party is being held at tonight, but I'm sure that small detail was left out of whatever gossip was being slung around about me. I'm sure you're well aware of maintaining good graces with people you do business with, am I right?"

"No need to get defensive, honey," Bennett says.

"Not defensive, just cankered with offhanded suggestions," I defend while eyeing Richard.

His wink peeves me as he says, "Well, you know how women can be."

Mustering up the most gracious smile I can, I say, "As charming as this little interaction has been, you must excuse me while I get ready for the party." I turn to Bennett, give him a kiss along his jaw, and whisper suggestively, "Join me in the bathroom," before walking away and saying to Richard, "I look forward to seeing both you and your wife tonight."

Whatever Jacqueline's intentions were when she decided to tell her husband about my run-in with Declan, I know I need to play it off as nothing to Bennett and be on my best behavior tonight so that he isn't the least bit tipped off about what I'm doing. So when he walks into the bathroom after a few minutes, I turn to face him, and silently strip off my clothes as he watches. His growing erection is noticeable through his slacks as I sit myself up on the sink counter and spread my legs open, inviting him to take what he wants.

I watch him loosen his tie, and when he starts working the buttons on his shirt, I lick my fingers and drag them down to my clit, rubbing soft circles. I think about anything but Bennett, working hard in my imagination, attempting to get myself wet. Leaning my head back against the mirror, I prop my feet up on the ledge and close my eyes. When the vision of Declan hovering over me with his hand inside my panties in his hotel the other night flashes in my head, my eyes pop open.

Fuck. I can't think about him.

In an instant, Bennett is crouched down in front of me, hands spreading me open wider before dipping his tongue inside me. I continue massaging myself as he laps me up like I'm the only one who can quench his thirst. He sickens me, and as soon as I feel the swirl of hate manifest, I turn every part of me off and simply go through the movements I know he likes. I'm a well-oiled machine at this point, flawless in my performance.

He has no idea that I'm the poison in his bones, making my home in his soul. I've crept under his skin, and he never suspected a thing other than everything I've wanted him to, but he's made my life a hell, and payback is a wicked bitch that comes in the form of me. I'm the devil seeped within the cracks of him. What he doesn't know is that it's because of him that I am what I am, and he's fallen into the cobwebs of my lies like a fool. I guess I should love him for that, because when he least suspects it, he's going to give me everything I've been seeking—vengeance.

"WOULD YOU MIND zipping me up?" I call out to Bennett from inside my closet.

I stand in front of my floor-length framed mirror that rests against one of the walls. The strapless black satin gown is adorned with a scattered crystal beaded bodice that fades down into the slim, silky black skirt that falls to the floor. When Bennett walks up from behind, his smile is wide when he catches the zipper and slowly drags it up the center of my back.

"You're beautiful," he tells me before dropping kisses along my bare shoulder.

"Bennett, that tickles," I giggle as I shimmy away. I look at his reflection in the mirror as he laughs and then ask, "Can you help tie my sash?"

Looking down at the wide, burnt orange, satin sash that's draped around my waist and down my hips, he shakes his head, holding the two ends and says, "What do I do with this?"

"For such a smart boy, you think you could manage a simple tie," I tease. Giving a wink, I straighten my posture and instruct, "Just a loose knot. I'd like it to hang slack a little below my waist."

As he works the fabric, my mind goes back to Declan. I haven't spoken to him since yesterday, but I know he'll be at the party tonight. He's growing impatient with me, which is good, but just as before when Bennett and Declan were together, my nerves are heightened. I don't mind if Bennett suspects that I might be having an affair, but to have him suspicious this early on could be fatal. I need to make sure that Bennett is none the wiser and to simply assume that through the time spent together planning this event, we have become nothing more than friends and that the only intimacy I crave is that of my husband.

"How's that?" he asks as he steps away.

I turn and look over my shoulder at the back of my dress and smile. "It's perfect. Thank you."

He wraps his arms around me and draws me in close. He's clad in his black tux and bowtie—classic Bennett. Looking into his eyes, I softly sigh and relax in his embrace, whispering, "I miss you."

"You have me, honey. I'm right here."

"For now. But I still miss you, like I can never get close enough to you for it to be enough," I tell him, my words nothing but maladies for my liking.

"God, do you have any clue what that does to me?"

"Hmm . . . tell me."

"If I tell you, I'm going to unknot that sash and peel this gown off of you."

My smile grows, and he kisses the corner of my mouth, always careful not to smudge my lipgloss. We spend a few moments holding each other before we slip on our coats and head down to the car.

When we pull up to the hotel, Baldwin parks in front and Bennett grabs the box with my mask. He opens it and pulls out the black, laser-cut metal mask and says, "Where did you find this? It's really unique."

His comment catches me off guard because I assumed it

was a gift from him, but then it dawns on me that the reason there was no card or note was because it's from Declan.

"Oh," I say, taking a second before lying, "I found it online and ordered it."

"Come here," he says as he leans in. Gently placing it on my face, he loops the ribbon behind my head and secures it in a bow.

I can't believe Declan did this and never said anything. "Does it look okay?" I ask.

"You're perfect."

I hold out my hand for his mask—a golden etched mask with large contrasting burnt orange and deep red swirls of flame. When I have it tied in place, I softly press my lips to his.

"Let's go," he says. "I want everyone to see how beautiful you look tonight."

Laughing at his words, I remark, "Arm candy?"

"You're so much more than candy."

He takes my hand as we walk in, fashionably late, to the already busy room. I stop for a moment to take everything in: the dark room is flanked with fire-burning rustic lanterns lining the walls, lavish orange and red flowers and greenery filling the tables, people dressed in their finest gowns and tuxes, and masks that reflect the theme—devils, harlequins, studded black leather, and of course my own black metal mask.

"I didn't think you could top yourself, but this is amazing, honey," Bennett tells me.

The room is busy with friends, my husband's colleagues, waiters serving various drinks and hors d'oeuvres, the band playing, and people dancing and mingling.

"Shall we?" Bennett says as he leads me into the dark, fire-lit room.

It isn't long before we are mixed in with the crowd and greeting our guests. I quickly snatch a flute of champagne off a silver tray. Taking a sip, I hear Jacqueline from behind me, "Nina, I'm impressed."

When I turn to face her, I respond, "You say that as if you had doubts." My words come out a little tart, but she doesn't seem to take offense.

"Never. You always put on the best events," she says. "You look amazing, by the way. I love the orange."

"Thank you. I had the pleasure of seeing your husband earlier today. Seems he and my husband couldn't take a day off from business."

"Boys will be boys," she says, and then adds with a smirk, "Especially when it comes to money and slinging their power around."

We both laugh at the honesty of her statement when I feel Bennett's arm wrap around my shoulder. "What are you girls laughing about?"

"Do you really need to ask?" I tease.

"Do you think you could pull yourself away from gossiping about me so that I can take you for a spin on the dance floor?"

"But talking about the quandaries of the men in our lives is so much fun," I mock with a grin.

"I can only imagine," he states before giving Jacqueline a nod and complimenting, "You look lovely this evening, Jacqueline."

"As do you, Bennett," her response laced in her usual

flirtation. "If you'll excuse me, I should probably go find Richard."

When she walks away, Bennett leads us down to the crowded dance floor, and I finally spot Declan out of the corner of my eye. He stands in a small group, looking sharp in a black tux, but with no tie and the top couple buttons open. His eyes are covered in a gold and black diamond checkered harlequin mask, but I know it's him by the day-old stubble on his strong jaw. When Bennett holds me close, I watch Declan over his shoulder as we move around the dance floor. His eyes finally find mine at the same time a slinky brunette slides up next to him and he wraps his arms around her waist. His eyes never stray from mine as she whispers something into his ear and I see the smile grow on his face, pleased by whatever she's saying.

My stomach coils, not from jealousy, because I don't get jealous, but from the fear of knowing that I could've fucked myself by playing too hard to get with him. Maybe I read him wrong and the push and pull act I've been playing with him was more of a turn off than a turn on. Or maybe he's just trying to make me jealous to get me to finally make a move with him. No matter which of the two scenarios it may be, I only have one option in this and that's to play him at his own game.

So as Declan flirts with the woman on his arm, eyes still pinned to mine, I let my eyes fall shut as I run my nose along Bennett's jaw until my lips meet his in a tender kiss. With one hand behind his neck, I bury my fingers in his hair as I continue to kiss him.

Drawing back slightly, Bennett runs his knuckles down my cheek with soft eyes before he pulls me back into his arms. When I look over to Declan, he isn't paying me any attention;

instead, he's sipping on whatever is in his double old-fashioned as he grazes his fingers slowly up and down the woman's bare arm.

The thick cloud of defeat begins to wash over me and not even the best actress in the world could stave off the mood shift that flicks inside of my stomach. It's a sick feeling that chokes me in a painful clench of knowing that this may not ever happen for me. That more years of my life were spent wasted on a quest that will come to naught.

I spend the next couple of hours focusing on Bennett, trying to distract me from myself, swallowing down the shit mood, but it still manifests in my gut—a never-ending reminder. But no one is wise to my inner-workings as we stroll through the room, visiting, toasting to the new year that is upon us, laughing, drinking, smiling, bragging, complimenting, faking . . .

And then I become the biggest fake of all when Bennett spots Declan and calls out for him.

"Bennett," he drawls in his ever-present brogue. "Good to see you again."

"Same here. This is quite an event."

"Well, you and I both know it's only because of Nina here," he says as he gives me an approving nod.

With a hint of a smile, I loop my arm through Bennett's as I return the nod.

"Catherine," he says to his date, "I'd like you to meet Mr. Vanderwal and his *wife*, Nina."

I can't ignore the needle he uses to stab the word *wife*, but I keep myself in check as I extend my hand to her for a gracious shake.

"It's a pleasure," I say.

"This is a wonderful party."

"Well, I'm glad you're enjoying yourself," I tell her and then turn to Bennett. Reaching up to affectionately cup his cheek, I excuse myself, saying, "Do you think I could get a few minutes? I'm a little warm and not feeling too well."

"Are you okay?"

"I'll be fine. I just need a little breather. I'll be back shortly," I tell him and then give him a loving kiss in front of Declan, taking my time in an indecent display of affection. Lucky for me, I know Bennett, and he loves to make a show out of me, so I use that with the intent of making myself somehow feel better about this colossal failure I've created.

The emptiness inside of me swells as I make my way out of the room and down the hall towards Declan's office where I know there's a private bathroom. I just need to be alone to pull myself together from the swarming thoughts that are flooding my head right now.

Another knife in a faltered dream.

I walk over to the large, leather ottoman that sits in the center of the plush powder room. Heat creeps its way up my neck as thoughts of Pike enter, and I reach back to pull the ribbon loose on my mask. The cool air meets my skin as I drop the mask to the floor. I allow myself this rare moment of weakness as I sit here, but it's interrupted when I hear the door open and look over my shoulder to see Declan.

I don't speak as I watch him lock the door behind him. And then he faces me. His jaw is set tight as he takes his mask off, giving me a clear view of his darkened eyes, nearly black.

"I'm done with the fucking games here," he barks as he walks over to me.

I stay quiet, slightly confused about this situation, as he continues, "You, making a spectacle in front of me with that man we both know you're not happy with. Is this you trying to make me jealous?"

He stands over me, looking down, when I snap, "I should be asking you the same question."

"Shut your mouth, Nina," he demands sternly.

He's pissed—jealous.

I'm suddenly revived, but the games are over. I'll give him exactly what I know he wants, my submission to his demanding request. He startles me when he abruptly grabs ahold of my arms and forcefully yanks me up to my feet and spins me around in his arms so that we're both facing the mirror. With one hand clenched around my arm, his other grabs my jaw, forcing me to look at our reflection.

"Look at me."

I do.

"You want me?"

Nerves crash inside of me, accelerating my breathing, but I don't respond.

"Answer me!"

"Yes." My voice, hoarse in its attempt to speak.

"Say it," he snaps as he releases my face and slips his hand down to my throat, gripping it firmly, forcing my head back. "Say it!"

"I want you."

As soon as the words are out, he pushes me down quickly, and before I know it, he has my dress lifted, exposing my backside. My hands grab on to the edge of the sink to brace myself as he yanks my panties to the side.

e.k. blair

"Look at me," he instructs in a hard voice, and I do as he says, lifting my head to meet his eyes in the mirror. "I don't have a soft touch, Nina."

I nod my head and see him nodding as well in our mutual understanding of his words as he unhooks his belt and begins to unfasten his slacks. I shut down, taking my mind far away from what's about to happen.

"Stick your ass out for me."

I do, and without any warning, he slams inside of me, locking our bodies, causing a pained whimper to bleed out from my lips. With his hands on my hips, he hunches his shoulders over me, pinning me over the sink as he thrusts his cock in me over and over in a pounding feat of control, and I give it to him as I hold on tightly.

"Look at me," he snarls in my ear. His eyes are hooded in primal need as I watch him fuck me from behind. I fight the heat that I can feel boiling inside of me, grinding my teeth as I try to ignore the slapping of his balls against my clit with each volatile thrust. But unlike Bennett, Declan forces me to stay in the moment with him when he says, "Tell me how bad you want me."

I quickly shake my head, not wanting to speak.

"Tell me, Nina."

"Mmm mmm."

My denial is punished in an erotic agony that shoots through my core and up my spine when Declan painfully pinches my clit between his fingers, causing me to scream out and jerk my body away from him, but he bands his one arm around my waist, locking me still in his hold. He doesn't let up as he hisses in my ear, "Tell me," never once faltering as he continues to pump in and out of me.

"Please," I shriek as tears prick the back of my eyes when he pinches harder, pulling on my most sensitive part. My head drops as I release another pained cry before finally giving him the words, "I want you."

"Louder!"

"I want you. Please." My words, more a plea than anything else, spur him to go harder, pounding inside of me at a violent pace. His assault erupts quickly as he comes, spurting his hot sperm inside of me with a powerful grunt.

I stand there, legs quivering beneath me while Declan has his face buried in my neck. His dick is still rock hard inside of me when he finally lifts his head, but I keep mine down, confused about what just happened. Wondering if that was him wanting me as his or if that was nothing more than a punishment for playing games with him.

When he pulls out of me, he drops my dress down, covering me up. His breaths are labored, as are mine, and when I right myself, I catch a glimpse of him shoving his dick inside of his pants, and then I look away.

"Don't do that," he says, and I turn around to face him. "Don't look away from me."

I don't say anything because I have no clue what to say in this moment, but he breaks the silence after his shirt is tucked in and his belt is buckled. Taking a couple steps towards me, I grip the edge of the sink as he scolds, "Don't ever try to make me jealous again, do you hear me?"

"Yes," I murmur.

"Now go back to your husband, but don't you forget whose cum is inside of you right now," he says before taking my chin between his fingers and giving me a hard kiss, then turning and walking out of the bathroom, leaving me standing here, a fucked up mess.

I turn around and look at myself in the mirror, working quickly to pull myself together before returning to the party. Taking in a few slow, deep breaths to calm my racing heart, I smooth my hair and blot the sweat from my forehead with a towel. I don't have time to think about what just happened because I've been in here for long enough, and I need to get back to Bennett. I give myself another glance over to make sure everything is in place before I pick my mask up from the floor and walk out.

When I make my way back to the party, I scan the room for Declan but he's nowhere to be seen.

"You feeling better?" Bennett asks, causing me to jump. "Are you okay?"

"Yeah, you just snuck up on me," I breathe.

His eyes roam over my face before he asks, "Why did you take your mask off?"

"I was hot," I tell him. "Would you put it back on for me?"

When I hand it over to him, I turn around, and as he's tying it back on, I spot Declan's date, but she's alone. Taking one more look over the room, I still don't see him.

"There," he says and then wraps his arm around my shoulder. "Let's go find a quiet spot and sit down for a little bit."

"I'm fine. Really," I assure. "Dance with me."

He smiles and we spend the rest of the evening dancing and enjoying our night. After the countdown to midnight, we ring in the New Year with champagne toasts and lots of kissing, but with Declan nowhere in sight, it seems he must have ditched the party after fucking me in the bathroom. It isn't until we get home that I lie in bed and replay everything that happened with Declan. Putting all the pieces of him together, I'm fairly certain that what happened was him staking his claim, albeit in a primitive and territorial fashion.

With Bennett going to Miami in a couple of days, I plan to lay low and focus my attention on him before I seek out Declan. That is, if he doesn't seek me out first.

twenty
(PRESENT)

"Honey."

"Yeah?" I say as I grab a few more dress shirts from Bennett's closet and walk back out into the bedroom to pack them in his garment bag.

"I wanted to talk to you about Baldwin. I'll need to continue taking him with me for my trips to Dubai. I just want to make sure you're okay with that."

"We discussed this before, and I told you I'm fine. But why do you need to take him with you?" I ask.

"The laws there are strict, and I like having him to keep an eye on everything," he explains. "It's just safer that I'm not alone."

After zipping up his bag, I walk over to him and ask as I wrap my arms around his waist, "Should I be more worried about you?"

"No. I don't want you to worry about a thing, which is why

Baldwin will be traveling with me."

"Just you saying that already has me worried."

"It's just, last I was there, a situation arose with a couple who shared a cab that was staying at the same hotel as me. It made me realize how much I didn't know about the laws there," he tells me and then leads me over to one of the chairs that sit next to the windows.

"What happened?" I ask as he takes a seat and pulls me down on his lap.

"They were friends sharing a cab and they got arrested. According to the driver, they were holding hands and kissed, which I found out was against the law unless you're married. The bellman who brought my bags to the room told me that they would most likely go to prison for the indiscretion. So, I just want the added security measures around me while I'm there on the jobsite, that's all."

Shaking my head, I remark, "That's crazy."

"I know I had mentioned you coming with me, but I don't think that would be a good idea. I'd worry too much, so I think it's best that you stay put here, where I know you're safe." He runs his hand through my hair, adding, "I wouldn't know what to do with myself if anything ever happened to you."

"Baby, nothing's going to happen to me. I'll stay here and wait for you," I tell him and then add with a smile, "impatiently."

He laughs and brings me in for a kiss.

"So what are your plans for the next few days while I'm gone?" he questions.

"I need to stop by the Tribune Tower to meet with Mr. Bernstein about that social piece I was approached about writing."

"Did you decide to do it then?"

"I think so. I mean, it'll be great exposure for the charities we work with. I figured we could use this opportunity to get the word out about some of the smaller foundations we are affiliated with," I explain. "I know I'm not a writer or anything, but I can try, right?"

"I'm proud of you, you know that? Plus, you'll have an editor, but I have no doubt that you're fully capable of writing a great article."

"Well, the least it will do is keep me busy while you're gone."

"Three days. It's only three days," he says with a grin.

"Yeah. Three days and then you leave a few days after that," I tell him with a soft poke to his ribs, which causes him to laugh and nuzzle his head into the crook of my neck, giving me a couple nips.

We continue to talk and be close until Baldwin calls with the car, and Bennett and I say our goodbyes for the next few days while he's in Miami on business. Once he's gone, I go to check my phone, wondering if Declan has tried contacting me, but I have no new messages. It's been several days since the incident in the bathroom at the New Year's Eve party, and I haven't had any contact with him since. But now that Bennett is gone, I make the decision to drive over to his loft.

I distract myself when Clara comes over, helping her in the kitchen, preparing meals for the week. We share a glass of wine, and I fill her in on the party and we talk about her daughter's wedding that is coming up in a few months. When everything is prepped, labeled, and placed in the freezer, she says goodnight and I take a quick shower to freshen up.

I dress casually, leaving my thick, red hair in loose waves and dabbing on a touch of makeup. I prep myself on the drive over to River North with how I plan on approaching Declan, needing to play heavily on his emotions to pull him into what he will assume is just your everyday affair. So I listen to a few songs that aid me in my doleful mood, and as I pull up to Declan's building a little after nine, I breathe a sigh of relief when I look up to the very top to see the lights on in his place.

Giving myself a last look in the rearview mirror, I walk into the building and buzz for Declan on the intercom.

"Who is it?" his voice questions through the speaker.

"It's me," I say softly.

I have to wait a few silent moments before his voice responds, "I'll be right down."

Since you need a card to get to his floor, I wait for him by the elevator. When it finally opens, and Declan steps out towards me, I do as I planned and simply stand there, staring at him, willing the tears to bathe my eyes, until he finally speaks, "What are you doing here?"

With a subtle shrug of my shoulders, my voice trembles when I respond, "I don't know."

He closes the space between us, cupping my cheeks in his hands, but I don't give him a chance to say anything when my vision blurs with unshed tears and I weakly say, "I want to be mad at you. For what you did the other night. But . . . for some reason I can't bring myself to hate you." My head falls to his chest, and he holds me tight in his arms when I add, "I just . . . I'm scared, but I want to be here with you."

He presses his lips to the top of my head, and with me tucked in his arms, he moves us to the elevator and holds me the whole way up to his loft. When the doors open, he leads me across the room and over to the same couch we sat on the other week, next to the already burning fireplace. I curl up next to him, resting my head on his shoulder when he finally breaks the silence, saying, "The last thing I want is for you to hate me, Nina."

"Then what was that in the bathroom?"

"Me."

Lifting my head, I see the creases in his forehead, but his look is solid when he says, "I won't apologize."

With a faint nod of my head, I whisper, "Okay."

"Like I told you, I don't have the softest touch. I don't want you to mistake that for a lack of feeling, because I won't deny that I already feel strongly about you."

"I'm scared."

"I know," he states softly.

"Do you?"

His thumb runs along my cheekbone when he says, "I won't ever do anything to hurt you."

"But . . . Bennett . . ."

"He doesn't need to know anything until you're ready to say something. He doesn't exist here, here in my home. It's just you and me," he tells me before his lips touch mine in a soft kiss. A very un-Declan-like kiss. He's gentle, and when I reach up to touch his face, he grabs my wrist in his hand and hoists me on top of his lap. My legs straddle his hips, and his erection is evident as it presses between my legs.

His hands quickly find my breasts, and he squeezes them achingly hard as I sink my fingers into his hair, fisting it in my hands. When I tug at the roots, he growls in my mouth and lifts up my top. I raise my arms in an invitation, which he accepts as he pulls off my sweater. And in a fluid movement, he stands up with my body clung to his, legs wrapped around his hips, and he walks us down the hall and into his master suite.

The room is dark, lit only by the lights of the city below. My back falls against the soft bedding when he lays us down. His mouth is all over me, dragging down my neck, over the swell of my breasts, to the dip of my navel. He unhooks my pants and slips them off my legs, along with my shoes. I look up at him as he stands over me, peering down as I lie here in my bra and panties. Slowly, he starts working the buttons on his shirt before tossing it across the room. His shoulders and arms are roped in muscle. His smooth chest is nothing but hardened, accentuated slabs that define his broad build and narrow to a deep-cut V, sinking down into his pants.

He starts to undo his leather belt, and when he slips it from the loops of his slacks, he grips it firmly in both of his hands as if he's about to make use of it. Suddenly I run cold, and ask hesitantly as I sit up, "What're you gonna do?"

"Don't ask me questions, Nina."

My eyes lock on the leather belt, and I begin to feel nauseous at the thought of it, at the thought of being tied up in a closet for days, at the thought of being beaten and the snapping of leather as it slices into the skin of my back, at the thought of being choked with a leather belt while forced to suck my foster dad's dick. I can't tear my eyes away from the tight hold he has on his belt and the spiraled veins in his arms. All I can hear is the pounding of my heart in my ears, and I take a hard swallow.

"Look at me," he says, and I can't hide the fear that I'm sure is splayed across my face. "I meant what I said, I'll never hurt you, but I'm not like most guys."

I nod. I don't know what else to do because I can't lose him when I've finally come this far.

"I like control. Do you understand what that means?" he questions in an even tone as I shift my attention to his eyes.

"I don't want you to hurt me."

He steps between my legs and touches my face. "This isn't about pain, Nina. This is about trust. Do you trust me?"

I don't trust anyone, but I give him the word anyway. "Yes."

"Do you?"

"Yes."

"Good girl."

Those two words, I've heard them so many times from that piece of shit, Carl. He'd always say them to me when I would make him come. No one has ever said those words to me since him, until right now. And I know this is going to destroy me, but what other choice do I have? So I play the part and give him a soft smile when all I want to do is vomit.

"God, you're so beautiful," he breathes and then leans down to kiss me, sliding his tongue past my lips, tasting me deeply. He reaches around and unclasps my bra with ease. It's then that he kneels between my thighs, running his hands over my knees and up my legs while he sucks my pert nipple into his hot mouth. His tongue swirls around before he bares his teeth, pulling more of my breast into his mouth and biting down, making me whimper as his teeth sink in to the supple flesh.

In a quick move, he thrusts my legs wide open and drops his head to my center, taking my pussy in his mouth, licking me through the lace of my panties and then grazing his teeth along

bong

my mound as he pulls away to take a lingering look before standing up.

"Do you have any idea how sweet you taste or what it's like for me to look at you like this?"

"Declan," I sigh at the same time he tells me, "Lie back."

I do as he instructs and he takes my hip, flipping me over onto my stomach. In forceful movements, he grabs my arms, bringing them behind my back, and I feel the cool leather binding around them, above my elbows, in a painful restraint. With a sharp jerk of the belt, my shoulder blades pinch together, and all the slack disappears as the leather bites into my skin in an unrelenting vice, which there is no getting out of as he loops the belt and then fastens it. My heart trills in my throat, and my heavy breathing is prevalent. But it's when I begin releasing panicked noises into the sheets that a ribbon of breath heats my ear as he presses his lips to its shell and gives me a quiet, "Shhh, baby. Trust me."

He brushes my hair back as I lie there with the side of my face resting on the bed. I give him a nod, but everything in me is telling me that this is going to be too much. And then he's off the bed, grabbing my hips and lifting my ass up in the air, propping me on my knees with my chest still on the mattress. He yanks my panties down to my knees, and then his hands spread my ass open before his mouth is on my bare pussy. The wetness of his tongue gently laps over my clit while his hands roughly squeeze my butt, and when he wraps his lips around my nub and sucks, he brings a hard hand down, smacking my ass. I yelp in pain, lying there like some animal, helpless at the hands of someone else, and I'm taken back to the fucking basement I never wanted to think about, but I'm there, on that filthy mattress being humiliated by my foster dad.

My eyes squeeze shut, and I will every ounce of effort to disengage, to think about anything other than what's happening, but Declan makes it impossible when he slips his tongue inside of my pussy as he drags his fingers along the crease of my ass, forcing me to tense up. He then takes that hand, reaches under me, and grabs my breast, pinching my nipple between his fingers as he continues to fuck me with his mouth. I try to focus on the ache in my arms, but he grasps my attention when he takes his mouth off my pussy, grabs ahold of the belt, and pulls me back, lifting my chest off the bed, so that I'm now sitting on my heels. Turning my head to him, he offers me his mouth, saying, "Taste yourself," and then kisses me, caressing my tongue with his.

I want to scream for him to stop because I don't want to be doing this with him, but I don't. I force myself to think about what I'm using him for, what I need him to do for me. The words *you can do this, you can do this* repeat over and over in my head, but there's an intensity with Declan that I haven't experienced with a man before. It's easy to shut down with Bennett, but Declan has a power that keeps me in the moment, making the escape near impossible.

Pulling away from our kiss, he says, "Tell me what you want. Ask for it."

"I want you," I lie.

"What do you want me to do?"

"Fuck me."

"Ask me," he demands and the request irks the shit out of me, but I swallow the irritation.

"Will you please fuck me, Declan?"

Rounding his hand over my butt and down between my

legs, he sinks his finger inside of my pussy, asking, "You want it here?" with his face pressed to the side of mine, his chest against my back.

"Yes."

"I want to hear you say it," he requests, and I just wish he would stop fucking talking so I can at least attempt to go numb.

"Please, Declan. Just fuck me. I want you inside of me. I want to feel you in my pussy. I want all of you filling me up," I tell him, giving him all the words I feel he wants to hear so that we can get this over with.

And with that, I hear his pants hit the floor from behind me as I sit on my knees, waiting for his next move, and then it comes.

His hand grabs a fist of my hair as he shoves my face back down into the mattress. Letting go, he widens my knees, ass up, and then gives my pussy one last lick before he buries himself balls deep into my core, forcing me to slip forward on the bed. He quickly grabs my wrists that are stationed at the small of my back and holds them firmly with one hand while the other fists the belt.

I turn my head face down in the bed, and do what I can to disengage, but his voice keeps penetrating me as he talks, forcing me to tell him that I want him, that I want this, that I like this, that it feels good. I can't escape. I'm in the moment. I'm never in the moment, but right now, I'm in the goddamn moment, and the churning of my stomach begins to rouse into a disgusting rumble of bile I pray stays down.

"Let go, Nina. Stop fighting me," he says, as if he knows I'm trying with everything I have not to come. My body is so tense; I'm an idiot to think he can't feel it. He'll know if I fake it, but I keep fighting anyway. "Don't fight me," he hisses, his accent thickening as his desire grows. He then reaches around, dragging the wetness up to my clit, and starts massaging in slow, torturous circles. He has no idea he's destroying everything inside of me.

I hold my breath and bite down hard. I can't deny him what he's demanding. He'll ask too many questions, questions I can't ever answer for him, so I give in and allow him to give me the repulsive pleasure I hate to feel. It builds along with the bile, and when his cock swells inside of me with his oncoming release, I break. And out of nowhere, he makes a tender gesture when he laces his fingers with mine and holds my hand while I come. The orgasm takes over my body in ripples of fiery explosions that shoot through every inch of me. I can't suppress the moans that rip out of me, humiliating me, and then they're joined with Declan's as his orgasm mirrors mine. The feel of his cock throbbing inside of me as my walls spasm around him prolongs the release I wish would stop, but it quakes through me, holding me hostage to the man behind me. Our hands locked tightly together the whole time, as if he knows how hard this is for me and this is his way of offering a gentle support.

A second later, he lets go of me, and with fast hands, releases his belt from my arms, and they drop lifelessly to the bed as his body collapses on top of mine. I can't look at him. I can't even open my eyes. As my orgasm fades away, the pleasure between my legs remains as a reminder as to what just happened. I have to pull my shit together—fast—as Declan shifts to my side and brings me into his arms.

I tuck my knees up, and when I do, he cradles me in his hold, humming into my ear. I focus on his sounds to calm my racing heart and queasy gut. Taking in slow, deep breaths, I wonder how I'm going to get through sex with him again. I'm too exposed—too alive—too hot—too ripe—too present. I want to cry, but I don't, so I lay my head on Declan's chest and selfishly take the comfort he's offering because I don't have any other options here. He holds me, soothing me with the lull of his hums as I listen to his steadying heartbeat.

"Talk to me," he requests.

"I don't feel like talking."

"I need you to talk to me. Tell me why you were fighting me."

"I wasn't," I try to deny.

Turning on his side to face me, he wraps his hand behind my knee and drapes my leg over his hip, bringing us closer, when he says, "I felt you, Nina. I need you to talk to me. Did I scare you?"

Yes.

"No."

"Did I hurt you?"

Yes.

"No."

"Then what?" he asks softly with worry etched in the lines of his face.

Trying to relieve whatever is running through his head, I wrap my arms around his neck, hug him close, and tell him, "You're just really intense, and I guess . . . yeah . . . maybe you scared me a little."

"I'm sorry," he says, shifting his forehead to rest against mine. "Look at me."

When I open my eyes, his are peering into mine, noses together, so close.

"I *never* want to scare you. I *never* want to hurt you. I only want to be close with you, but this is the only way I know how to be."

"You don't have to apologize for who you are," I faintly breathe. "This. Being here in your arms. I've never felt more safe. So just hold me, okay?"

And he does, for a long time, while I try to get my head straight. We just hold each other, and then after a while, he takes my hand, and licks my palm before kissing it and then presses it to his chest.

"You consume me, you know that?"

I shake my head, saying, "I assumed I annoy you most of the time."

"You do," he laughs. "Your smart mouth irritates me, but it's also something I love about you. You don't take my shit, and I like that. But at the same time, I need you to be able to take my shit. I'm demanding and stubborn; that's not something I'm willing to change because I thrive on control."

"Why?"

He releases a deep breath, telling me, "Let's not talk about why. Not tonight."

"One day?"

"One day, darling," he says as he pulls me in closer to his naked body. "Can you stay with me tonight?"

"Mmm hmm. Bennett's in Miami for a few days. I'm yours until he gets back."

Leaning his head back to look me dead on, his voice is acid when he says, "No."

"No?"

"You're mine regardless of where he is. Here or not. I don't play well with others."

I hesitate for a second and then say, "It's not that simple. He's not like he appears, Declan."

"What does that mean?"

"It's just . . . It's not easy."

When he shakes his head in confusion, I repeat on a hush, "It's just not that easy."

His lips lightly brush over mine in a sweeping kiss, and I can taste the ice of his breath when he whispers, "I don't expect anything with you to be easy, but that's not enough to stop me from having you."

And with those words, I kiss him, allowing him to feast on my sugary poison. He may have a power over me in bed, one that will no doubt cause me suffering, but in the end, I'll take the pain because I know I'll be able to destroy him enough to save myself, to give me everything that was stolen from me when I was five years old.

twenty-one

(PRESENT)

WAKING UP IN Declan's bed the following day was peaceful. Peaceful in every morbid way. His hands were all over me while his face made its home between my legs before he pulled me on top of his lap. He had my arms crossed behind my back while he held each of my hands, locking my arms from moving as I fucked him. And again, he held my hands while I came. If I'm being honest, I feel like I need that support from him, because what he makes me feel during sex is sheer torment and anxiety. I don't want sex to feel good. It shouldn't feel good. But he doesn't give me any other choice, so I lied to him, telling him that Clara was going to be at my place and that I needed to be there so she wouldn't worry or question my whereabouts. I just needed to get away from him.

As soon as I get home, I take a scalding hot shower, washing every part of me, but nothing can clean me the way Pike can. I feel myself breaking and stop the fight long enough to let it out. Never in my life have I ever wanted to feel what Declan makes me feel. As images from last night and this morning run through my head, the tears surface as my stomach convulses in bubbles of putrid disgust. Unable to hold it down, I quickly step out of the shower, fall to my knees over the toilet, and vomit uncontrollably. It's a painful mixture of saliva, puke, and tears. Visions of Declan, Carl, leather, flesh, cum, that filthy mattress, the smell of that basement, the smell of Declan, my vicious hate for Bennett, my loneliness of missing Pike, my father's headstone. Everything consumes me. I hear it, smell it, see it, feel it, and then another forceful expulsion barrels its way up my throat and into the toilet.

In this moment, I hate my life. I hate everything about this shithole of a life I so desperately want to free myself from. Sobs achingly rip out of me, and as I fall back onto the cold slate floor, I lie there, wet and naked, the smell of my vomit filling the room. And when I close my eyes, I see my dad.

"Princess, what are you doing?" he mumbles in a sleepy voice as I crawl under the covers with him.

"I'm scared."

He helps me pull the blanket over myself and then cuddles me in his arms, saying, "Nothing will ever hurt you. I'll always protect you. Now, tell me what scared you."

"I can't remember. I just woke up and I was scared."

"Bad dream?"

I nod my head against his chest and snuggle underneath the covers of his bed, asking, "Can I sleep with you tonight, Daddy?"

"You don't want to go back to your own bed?"

"No. I just want you."

His large arms band around me tighter. "How can I say no to that?" he says and then kisses my forehead, the stubble on his face pricking my skin, causing me to giggle.

"Daddy! That tickles," I squeal and as soon as the words are out, he's laughing and nuzzling his face in my neck, pretending to eat me. The both of us laugh loudly in the dark room, rolling around his big bed.

I start pinching his sides, and he rolls onto his back with a huge smile and chuckles, "You win. You win. I give up."

"You never give up," I tell him, and he responds, "Sometimes a man needs to know when to let a lady a win. Now give me a kiss right here."

He points to his cheek as he speaks, and I lean in and kiss his unshaven face, feeling the prickling pokes on the soft skin of my lips.

"Come here," he says, and I lie back down in his arms as he kisses the top of my head. "Close your eyes now. There's nothing to be scared of. I'll never let anyone hurt you. You're always going to be safe."

"I love you, Daddy."

"I love you so much more, Princess. Come find me in your dreams."

The vision fades and I roll to my side, curling into a ball, and cry for all the things he promised me that never happened. I was never safe, and this world hurt me beyond what I ever thought a human could be hurt. All because of Bennett. And now I lie here in his bathroom, our bathroom. He's my husband. We share a home, a bed, a life. I knew what I was doing when I embedded myself into his world, but after what just happened with Declan, I wanna run. Run so far that I never have to look back and remember any of this. Run all the way back in time. Back to Northbrook, back to the house I used to live in, through the front door, into my bedroom where my father still waits for me at my little table, with pink daisies, to join him for our princess tea party. Maybe if I cry hard enough, the world will take pity on me, shift off its axis and make all my dreams come true.

I want my daddy.

After all these years, I just want my daddy.

A COUPLE HOURS pass, and I now sit in the living room as I watch another snow-filled day. My body aches, and I'm tired after my meltdown. I know better than to let those feelings bleed through. It's been a long time since I've cried like that and allowed myself to feel sorry for the life I wound up with. So now I sit here and gain control as the fire ignites inside of me. The fire I let fizzle out earlier. I feel its embers in the molten heat of my veins. A resurgence of what I'm doing here. This is about regaining what was stolen from me. Taking back what was mine to be had before my father was ripped away from me and murdered in prison. I can handle Declan; I just had a moment of weakness last night, but now, I have rectified that steel wall.

Fuck Declan.

Fuck Bennett.

This is about righting the wrong.

This is revenge, and I'm ready.

Without wasting any more time, I grab my coat and keys and head down to the garage to go to Justice. I need to see Pike.

When I pull up to his trailer, I see Matt's car. I'll never forget that night when Pike crawled through my bedroom window in the middle of the night. Matt was there too. Pike held me while I cried for hours in the back seat of Matt's car as he drove us to northern Illinois where he had rented a rundown apartment with Pike. The three of us lived together for a few years until Pike and I got a place of our own.

I never went back to school. I was a runaway, but I didn't let that define me as a complete failure. Pike gave me money to buy a few home schooling kits that got me through high school. Doing it on my own doesn't take away from the fact that I'm just as knowledgeable as any other graduate, diploma or not. I've always loved school and learning new things. I would look through the course catalogues from the local university and buy the textbooks for the classes I was interested in and read them on my own. Pike has always teased me, but I wasn't going to let the reality that I was a high school dropout plague me.

Until I was of age, I couldn't risk getting a job either, so I helped Pike, weighing and bagging the product Matt would bring in. Because of the people they dealt with, I was always by Pike's side. It was safer running the streets with him than to be left alone in the apartment.

But I've never liked Matt despite Pike's friendship with him. I had to fight him off a few times when he would get drunk and try to get into my pants. But it was him that stood by my side on that fateful night, the night he and Pike gave me one of the greatest gifts I could've asked for. Matt and Pike gave me payback in the form of death. The first stroke of revenge as the both of them stood by my side as I lit the match, killing both Carl and Bobbi in the ink of night. I was only fifteen when I discovered the sweet taste of vengeance as their pleading screams were engulfed in the flames of hell.

So to see him here, now, irritates me because no matter how much I dislike him, I'll always be indebted for that one precious gift he allowed me. And when I shut off the car and walk inside, Matt sneers, knowing everything about what I'm doing with Bennett, "Well, well, well, what drug in the shit-stain on high society living?"

"It's an amazing thing to see."

"What is?" he asks.

"The way your vocabulary has matured through the years," I give him as I slip off my coat and then look over to Pike, saying, "I need to talk to you."

"Dude, get lost," he tells Matt.

"What the fuck?"

"Don't start that shit, you know Elizabeth has a hard enough time getting out here to see me," he tells Matt as he stands up and walks over to me.

I give Pike a hug and watch as Matt grabs his coat and starts heading for the door. "Call me when she leaves."

"Yeah, man. Talk to you later."

Matt looks back over his shoulder at me when he gets to the door and then leaves. I wrap my arms more tightly around Pike and nearly smother him.

"Whoa. What's going on?" he says as he holds me.

"I really missed you," I tell him thickly.

"Is everything okay? Did something happen?" he asks as then we walk over to the couch and sit down.

"I fucked Declan last night."

The concern on Pike's face isn't surprising. Aside from Carl, Pike is the only guy I've ever had sex with, until Bennett. But Bennett is nothing compared to Declan.

"Shit," he sighs. "Are you okay?"

"He tied me up with his belt," I reveal to him.

"What the fuck?"

"It's how he is. He's forceful. He actually fucked me at the New Year's party. That was the first time. It was a dirty fuck in a bathroom."

"Wait. Go back," he says, confused.

"I was trying to make him jealous at the party, apparently it worked. He followed me into the bathroom and we had sex. I didn't see him or talk to him until I went to his place yesterday. Bennett is in Miami, so I wound up spending the night with Declan. Sex with him is awful. It's impossible to drown out what's going on because he's so demanding throughout. I left this morning to go home because I was feeling disgusted."

"Come here," he breathes as he tugs me into his arms. We sit for a moment and then he asks, "So what are you thinking?"

"I can't walk away. He's the right guy, I know it."

"How can you be sure?"

Shaking my head, I say, "I don't know. I just feel it. I can't explain; it's just how I feel."

"I don't know," he says, doubting my words.

Feeling a little annoyed, I question, "What?"

"Do you think he's capable?"

"That's not a question anyone can really answer, but yeah, I think he could be."

"What if he finds out?"

"He won't."

Eyeing me, he presses, "Don't be so sure about that. Confidence is a dangerous thing to have."

Turning out of his arms, I sit back and exhaust, "Fine. What if he finds out? I don't know, Pike. What would it matter? No crime would've been committed."

"What about Bennett? If Declan finds out or isn't capable, are you going to be able to do it?"

I laugh in frustration, turn to face Pike, and say, "The way you doubt me makes you look stupid. I love my father, and he paid the ultimate price when he was murdered." With a stern look, I seethe, "If you don't think I'm capable, you don't know me."

"I do know you. Better than anyone else. But we're talking about killing someone, Elizabeth."

"I know what we're talking about, Pike. I've been living this game for four years. I share a bed with that son of a bitch," I snap.

Pike rakes his hands through his hair, exasperated, and says on a heavy breath as he leans back, "I know. God, I know. It's just, it's been such a long time. You just kinda get used to the life you're living, you know?"

"Yeah," I say softly. "I know. It's the same for me, but I guess I'm a little more distracted than you are, considering my role. But I feel it's finally happening. This is what we still want, right?"

"I promised you I would do whatever it took to make your life better. I'm not changing my mind on that. That fucker is gonna pay for what he did to your life."

Nodding my head, my smile grows at the thought of paying Bennett back for all the shit that has happened to me. For the death of my father, for all the destruction he and his parents caused. I'll revel in the only thing that will remain after Bennett is gone—money and power. Ruining Declan's life along the way to my salvation is something that's simply unavoidable if Pike and I want to keep our hands clean in this. So that's it; we move forward with the plan.

This is the moment Pike and I have been waiting years for. We take the evening to discuss plans and timing, and agree that I'll come back in a few days after Bennett leaves for Dubai. After we talk, Pike cleanses me, and then I'm back on the road. Back to gain my retribution.

twenty-two
(PRESENT)

AFTER MY MEETING with Mr. Bernstein at Chicago Magazine this afternoon, I've been working on the social piece that they want to publish next month in the February issue. The magazine is featuring a few "It" couples for their Valentine's edition, and wanted to highlight Bennett and me by having me write the piece myself. I was instructed to write about how we keep the spark alive while noting the many pots we have our fingers in, such as the charities and foundations we work with and support. Bennett seemed excited when I called him a couple hours ago to tell him about the details of the piece and my meeting with Mr. Bernstein and the editor that was assigned to me.

When I wrap up my work, I start getting ready. Declan finally caved and texted me after a mere twenty-four hours. It didn't surprise me he couldn't wait any longer. The text was short and clipped, straight to the point, and I agreed to stop by. Although I'm nervous about sex with Declan again, I try to focus my attention on other things, but it still lingers in the back of my mind. After I'm dressed, I head out and drive to Declan's place. When the elevator opens, he's already wearing a smile as he steps out, holding his key card out for me.

"Here," he says.

"What's this for?"

"To save me the hassle of having to come down here to get you every time you want to come by. Take it."

With a flirtatious smile, I say, "So, I'm a hassle?"

"You? Never."

As we ride up in the elevator, he steps in front of me, pushing me up against the mirrored wall, and kisses me. With his hands around my neck, he controls every movement of the kiss as his tongue parts my lips so that he can take more. Our bodies are pressed together, and the heat of him overcomes me, so that when he finally pulls back, I feel a little flushed.

"Missed you," he states as he looks down at me.

"Did you?"

"Always."

He takes my hand when the doors open, and I can smell food cooking in the kitchen. I follow him as he leads me to the bar and pulls out a stool for me.

"What's all this?" I ask as I take a seat.

"Dinner."

"You cook?" I ask with a smirk as he grabs a bottle of wine and begins to pour me a glass of Pinot Noir.

"Why do you look so surprised?"

Shaking my head, I take a small sip before saying, "I guess I don't really know much about you, so I'm sure there's a lot about you that'll surprise me."

He smiles at my words as he walks into the kitchen and begins chopping a few vegetables.

"What are you making us?"

"Champagne almond chicken, roasted vegetables, and new potatoes."

"Sounds amazing," I tell him as I continue to sip my wine and watch him move with ease around his kitchen. "Who taught you how to cook?"

"My mum. I can remember back to when I was little and she used to drag a chair in front of the stove for me to stand on. I would watch her and help her when she needed something stirred up. Eventually she started having me crack eggs and doing other simple tasks," he tells me as he scoops the veggies up and drops them into a steel bowl. "And as I got older, she and I would cook these elaborate meals."

"She sounds like a wonderful mom."

"She was."

"Was?" I ask, and when I do, he looks up at me, and says, "Another day," the same words he used when I asked him why he needed to control everything.

"What about you?" he asks me. "Do you like cooking?"

"I never learned."

"Your mum never taught you?" he questions.

I shake my head, knowing the truth of never having a mom, but Declan only knows of the lies I've told him about my family, so I tell him, "No. She worked a lot and wasn't around much. I do like to watch Clara cook when she comes over to prepare meals. Every now and then she lets me help out, but not often. I pretty much do what your mom allowed you to do on that chair. I only stir things and sniff around."

I watch the creases deepen at the corners of Declan's eyes when he looks at me and laughs.

"I've asked Bennett to cut back on her schedule, that I'd like to do more around the house, but he refuses. Clara has worked for him for a long time, and he likes knowing she's there."

Declan looks at me for a few moments when I stop talking, and then finally breaks the silence when he says, "Come here," and motions for me to join him.

"Why?" I ask suspiciously.

"Because I'm going to teach you how to cook, darling."

I smile, hop off the barstool, and walk over to join him. He reaches over and grabs a head of garlic, setting it on top of the chopping block, and then hands me a knife.

"I roasted that earlier. Garlic is always better when you roast it beforehand," he explains as I look at him and nod. "Peel off two cloves and then lay the knife flat on top."

I do as he says, plucking off a couple cloves. Declan stands behind me and holds his hands over mine, laying the knife flat on top of one of the cloves, and then grabbing the wrist of my other arm.

"Now, make a fist and slam it on top of the knife to mash the garlic," he instructs.

With his hand on my wrist, I make a fist and bang it down on the knife, smashing the garlic beneath.

"Perfect," he murmurs over my ear. "Do the same thing with the other clove."

He keeps his hands on mine as I repeat the process. He then helps me prepare the sauce for the chicken, toasting the almonds and chopping up the shallots and mushrooms. Once

I've poured in the champagne, he helps me line the dish with the chicken and pour the sauce over top.

"Would you turn the oven on? It'll automatically set at 350, so just put it on bake."

"Okay," I say as I walk over to the oven and turn it on.

I watch Declan finish up, and when the oven beeps, he slides in the dish and sets the timer for thirty minutes.

"What are you smiling at?" he asks as he steps in front of me.

"You."

"Why's that?"

Reaching out to wrap my arms around his waist, I tell him, "I like you like this," my words coming from a place of honesty.

"Like what?" he questions as he steps even closer, running his hands through my hair and tilting my head up to him.

"Just like this. You, laid back in your jeans and t-shirt, teaching me to do something new. I like sweet Declan," I say softly as I peer up into his emerald eyes.

"You're saying I'm not always sweet?"

I begin to laugh and then respond, "Most of the time you're an asshole."

His head falls back in a burst of laughter, and the sound causes me to laugh harder. His smile is wide when he looks back down, giving my words back to me, admitting, "I like you like this too."

"I'm afraid to even ask," I tease.

"Don't ever be afraid," he says before adding, "You're soft. You don't show it often, but when you do, I like it."

His words immediately straighten my face as he runs his

hand down my cheek, telling me, "I like it when you're soft with me."

"It's not easy for me."

"I know, but I want that from you."

He's oblivious to the fact that I intend on using his words to create the perfect venom to bite him with. So with a gentle nod of understanding, I slip my arms around his neck as he dips his head to kiss me. His hands grip my ass and he pulls me off the floor and into his arms. Looping my legs around him, he takes me over to the couch and sits us down with me on top of him. We continue to kiss, his taste of need spilling into my mouth. Hard, fast, soft, slow, licking, biting, sucking, it's all there in the heat of him as time falters in the moment. But we both snap our heads back when the fire alarm sets off and the smell of burning food takes center stage.

"Fuck," Declan breathes in mild amusement as he looks over my shoulder, and when I turn to see the smoke-filled kitchen, I jump off his lap and rush over to find pillowed clouds of smoke billowing from the oven.

"Shit!" I squeak out and immediately open the oven door, only to be blinded by the rushing mound of smoke.

Declan moves next to me and reaches in with oven mitts to pull out the black, charred chicken. My look of mortification for somehow ruining dinner is contrasted by his laughter, which ticks me off. He tosses the dish on top of the stove and then runs over to open a few of the sliding glass doors to air the place out and then goes to shut off the screeching smoke alarm.

"What did I do wrong?" I ask when he returns to the kitchen, and when I see he's still laughing, I snap, "Cut the shit and stop laughing at me."

He leans over the stove, looking at the oven setting. "Shit, Nina," he chuckles.

"What?" I huff.

"You turned the oven to broil instead of bake."

Embarrassment builds inside of me, and I don't say anything as I back up to the counter behind me and stare across at the meal I incinerated.

"Well," he says when he turns to face me. "Looks like you weren't kidding when you said you couldn't cook."

"I'm so sorry, Declan."

"Don't be. It's fine," he assures, running his hands down the length of my arms.

"Stop."

"Stop what?"

"Grinning at me like that. It's embarrassing."

"Why?" he questions. "Because you're not perfect?"

I narrow my eyes at him, saying, "There are things I can cook perfectly."

"Is that so? Now you've piqued my interest."

"Out!" I demand as I start pushing against him. "I'll fix this. Just give me a few minutes."

He turns back, saying sweetly, "You don't have to fix anything. All the delivery menus are in the drawer by the fridge."

"No. You've given me something to prove to you, so I'm going to prove it," I tell him. "Just . . . get rid of the charred chicken please."

"Okay then," he chuckles, and when his dinner is disposed of, I start rummaging around the kitchen to find the few items I need.

Truth is, I was honest with him. I have no idea how to

cook. Once Pike and I were on our own, we barely had enough money to pay rent in the gutter apartments we lived in. Hell, half the time we would wind up being evicted. We scraped by our whole lives, finding liquor to be a better investment than affording a safe place to live. At least when you're drunk, you can escape the realities of life.

So as I stand over the pan on the stove with a spatula in my hand, I look over my shoulder to see Declan closing the sliding doors. I'd be lying to myself if I said I wasn't attracted to him, because I am. It's a shame we couldn't have met in a different lifetime, but to dwell on the never-be's is nothing but an endless path of disappointment because this *is* the only life in which we will meet.

Plating our dinner, one of the few things I can cook, I walk over to the dining room table and set the plates down.

"Would you grab the wine?" I call out to Declan, and when he walks over to the table with the bottle, I smile up at him as he looks at his plate and laughs.

His eyes flick to mine, noting, "You look extremely proud of yourself, and I haven't even tasted it yet."

"Because I know there's no way you're not going to like it," I remark as he takes his seat and places the napkin in his lap.

"From the girl who teased me about taking her to the Over Easy Café," he says as he picks up the grilled cheese and takes a bite. I take a sip of my wine, and then he finally admits, "Best grilled cheese of my life."

We both laugh as I pick up my sandwich and begin eating with him. It's been a long time since I've felt comfortable like this. It's different with Pike, probably because he knows every disgusting piece of me, but Declan looks at me as if I'm something clean and good. It's all a lie, but for the moment, the lie makes me feel happy and maybe a little bit whole. So we sit here, in his multi-million dollar penthouse and enjoy our dinner of grilled cheese and Pinot Noir.

After dinner, I help Declan with the dishes. We clean the kitchen up, and when everything is back in place, I notice the burnt smell still lingering. Taking a lock of my hair, I sniff it while Declan watches.

"What are you doing?" he asks.

"My hair, it reeks of smoke."

"What about mine?" he says, walking over to me and ducking his head down.

Running my fingers through his thick hair, I tell him, "Yeah, yours does too."

He then takes my hand and leads me down the hall and into his bedroom. Flicking on one of the lamps, he walks us into the large bathroom, which houses a massive, marbled, doorless shower with a large, seamless pane of glass on one side. His and hers sinks line two of the walls in dark cabinetry with tailored, white, apron-front sinks. And along the wall of windows is an extra-large, sleek, rectangular jacuzzi tub that is sunken down. The room is modern and masculine, just like the rest of the loft.

Focusing back on Declan, he's running a bath, and when he turns to me, he stands in the middle of the room.

"Take off your clothes, Nina."

"A bath?" I question.

He reaches over his head, pulls off his shirt, and tosses it aside, saying, "Yeah, a bath," as he walks over to me and grabs the hem of my top. "Lift your arms."

He removes my shirt and then slips my pants down my

legs. I hold on to his shoulder as I step out, and with him knelt before me, I look at him as he slowly drags my panties down. When he has them off of me, he runs his hands up my legs to the center of my tiny V. With one hand sliding up between my legs, he splays it over my pussy and lower belly, holding it in place as he looks into my eyes. "So beautiful."

His accent fucks those two words. No one has ever looked at me the way he does, and it spurs an awkwardness inside of me because if he only knew what this body has been through, he'd be repulsed by the sight.

After we take off the rest of our clothes, he holds my hand as I step down into the tub filled with hot water. When Declan gets in, I situate myself between his legs, resting my back against his chest as I lie back into him. His arms wrap and cross around my breasts as he holds me close, and the warmth of both him and the water take me over. Releasing a heavy sigh, I close my eyes, and sink further into his hold as my body relaxes.

"Tell me what you're thinking," he murmurs from behind me.

"Mmm."

His chest vibrates in silent laughter before saying, "That's all I get? *Mmm?*"

"I'm relaxing."

He drags my hair off my one shoulder and starts kissing my damp neck, pressing his lips into my sensitive skin, causing me to shiver with goosebumps, which I know appeases him when he quietly chuckles.

We remain like this for a while, just taking in the warmth of the bath, nearly melting into each other.

"Should I be worried?" Declan says, breaking the long span of silence.

"About what?" I ask, my eyes still closed as I rest the side of my face against his chest.

"That I've been fucking you without a condom."

"I told you before, I can't get pregnant," I remind him.

He remains silent for a moment before responding, "Tell me why."

Taking in a deep breath, I shift up and slightly turn to the side so I can look at him when I say, "I have stage three endometriosis."

"I don't . . ." he begins with confusion written all over his face, so I explain, "It's basically where you have abnormal cell growth outside of the uterus. So the chances of me getting pregnant are pretty much non-existent."

"Baby, I'm . . ." he starts, shaking his head, and he's clearly more uncomfortable about it than I am. "When did you find this out?"

"In my early twenties," I tell him. "I started having painful periods around that time. They became worse and worse until the pain got so bad that I was taken to the hospital because I didn't know what else to do. They started running a bunch of tests and after a few months they finally figured out what was wrong."

"Is there anything they can do?"

"No. When you have it, you have it. There's no cure or anything."

"And the pain?" he questions with apparent concern.

"I've experimented with a few hormone treatments for pain, but the side effects were pretty bad, so I had to stop. I only take prescription pain pills, but it doesn't help that much."

He runs his fingers through my hair and then cradles his other hand to my face when he says, "God, baby, I'm sorry. I don't know what to say."

"It's fine," I try assuring him. "This isn't anything new to me. I've known this for years. It's okay."

"Do you want children?"

Shrugging my shoulders, I respond, "Does it even matter what I want? I mean, it's not like life is giving me a choice here."

"Of course it matters."

"I won't ever be a mom, so there's no point in tossing dead wishes into the air." I've done enough of that. I can remember Pike sitting next to me when the doctor told me that I wouldn't be able to have children. It was never anything I had even thought about until he told me that I couldn't. I cried for days while Pike held me. As if I was mourning the death of something that never was mine to lose. But that was over six years ago, and I've come to the realization that I'd probably be a shitty mom anyway. What would I be able to give a child? Before marrying Bennett, Pike and I survived by dealing drugs and barely scraping by. It's not a life I want, so why the hell would I want it for my kid?

"You can still be a mum, you know?" Declan says, his words coming out gently.

Not wanting to be rude and completely shut him out, I give him a weak grin and softly request, "Can we talk about something else please?"

"I'm sorry."

"It's okay. It's just not something I talk about often, so . . ."

"You don't have to say anything else," he assures before giving me a kiss and wrapping me back up in his arms.

twenty-three

(PRESENT)

I ENDED UP leaving Declan the other night after our bath. Bennett was returning from Miami the following day and I wanted to be home in case he arrived early. I've been careful about my communication with Declan while my husband is home. We talk mostly through email because those are easily deleted unlike phone records that are logged and recorded. I would prefer to not even send emails, but Declan insists on talking to me throughout the day.

While Bennett is in the shower, I sit in the study to find that I already have an email waiting for me.

FROM: D. McKinnon
TO: Nina Vanderwal
SENT: Jan. 10, 1:23pm
SUBJECT: Want You

When does he leave? I want to see you.

-D

I quickly reply while I still hear the water running from Bennett's shower.

FROM: Nina Vanderwal
TO: D. McKinnon
SENT: Jan. 10, 1:58pm
SUBJECT: Re: Want You

Some people find it polite to start with a greeting, even if it's as small as a simple 'Hello.' But to answer your question, he leaves around 3:30pm.

-Nina

His response is almost immediate.

FROM: D. McKinnon
TO: Nina Vanderwal
SENT: Jan. 10, 2:00pm
SUBJECT: Greeting as suggested- HELLO.

Meet me at the hotel?

-D

FROM: Nina Vanderwal
TO: D. McKinnon
SENT: Jan. 10, 2:01pm
SUBJECT: Re: Greeting as suggested- HELLO.

We need to work on your social etiquette.
Greetings in the subject line are rude as well. I
can be there at 4:00pm.

-Nina

FROM: D. McKinnon
TO: Nina Vanderwal
SENT: Jan. 10, 2:04pm
SUBJECT: Etiquette Reject

4:00 then. Come to my room. I'll leave an elevator
key for you at the front desk.

-D

FROM: Nina Vanderwal
TO: D. McKinnon
SENT: Jan. 10, 2:05pm
SUBJECT: Cheap

Why do I feel like a prostitute or worse, a booty
call?

-Nina

FROM: D. McKinnon
TO: Nina Vanderwal
SENT: Jan. 10, 2:06pm
SUBJECT: Cheap?

Booty call? What the hell is that? Regardless, you know damn well you are so much more than either of those. But I'm not going to sweeten it up for you; I need you, and I'm growing impatient and harder with each minute I don't have your body all over mine. 4:00!!

-D

I laugh at the realization that he doesn't pick up on the American slang as I delete the emails from my inbox and then delete out of my trash. Closing the laptop lid, I make my way into the bedroom where Bennett is walking out of the bathroom, covered in only a towel. I smile as I walk over to his suitcase.

"What's that smirk all about?" he questions as he approaches.

"You."

"What about me?"

"Walking around here wet, wearing only a towel, is a mean thing to do to your wife," I tease.

"Why's that?"

"Because you're leaving me for a couple of weeks, and this is the lasting vision you're giving me."

"And what about what I gave you a couple hours ago?" he says, referring to the long sex session we had earlier.

"That will give me something to think about when I'm lying in bed at night . . . lonely."

"You better call me when you're feeling lonely," he says

suggestively, sparking me to laugh.

"Stop that. You need to go get ready before you start running late," I nag. "I'll finish packing for you."

"Whatever you say, boss," he jokes before kissing me chastely and then walking back into the bathroom.

I gather the rest of his things from his closet and make sure he has everything he needs packed up. Bennett and Baldwin will be in Dubai for the next two weeks, along with Richard. They will be working on hiring a team while the renovations are still underway. I shifted around Clara's schedule to allow myself more freedom to come and go without her eyes on me.

When Bennett finally comes out of the bathroom about a half hour later, I decide to give him a proper good wife farewell. Maybe it's my conscience weighing on me, or maybe it's knowing I want to keep him from getting suspicious of me, but no matter what, I need to do whatever I can to make him think that what we have together is solid. So as I walk towards him, I reach under my arm and start unzipping the side zipper of my dress. He stays put, staring at me as I stroll across the room. When I'm standing in front of him, he slips his hands under the straps on my shoulders and allows the dress to fall to the floor around my feet.

"I just want you," I tell him, "One more time before you go."

"However many times you need, I'll give it to you."

And he does. Maybe I'm overcompensating, but I feel it's needed as we lose all track of time. Once I've led him to believe that I'm fully sated, we pull ourselves together and regroup. I take a glance at the clock to see it's already four and that I should be at Declan's hotel. When Baldwin walks in to help

Bennett with his luggage, I grab my coat from the closet and slip it on.

"Where are you headed?" Bennett asks, and I quickly lie, "I told Marcia I would meet her for a coffee when you left. But now you've made me late," I flirt with a wink.

"I believe you made *me* late, Mrs. Vanderwal."

"Are you complaining?"

"Not at all, and please feel free to make me even later if it suits you."

I catch Baldwin smiling as he overhears our conversation and turn to Bennett, accusing, "You're a perv."

"Only for you," he laughs. "I'm going to miss you."

We say our goodbyes on the elevator down to the lobby. Bennett seems genuinely sad to be leaving me while I'm anxious to get to Declan, knowing I'm running really late. I keep it hidden though as I take my time playing the loving wife who's already missing her husband who hasn't even left yet. But when he does, and we exchange our gentle kisses, Bennett walks out to the car where Baldwin is waiting and I head down to the parking garage.

When I arrive at Lotus, I leave my car with the valet before walking in and picking up the keycard Declan left for me at the front desk. As I step out onto the top floor, I use the keycard to let myself in to Declan's penthouse room.

"Where the fuck have you been?" he immediately shouts when I walk in, and the gravel in his voice startles me.

"I'm sorry."

"Where have you been for the past hour?"

He stands across the room as he barks his words at me. Wearing a tailored suit and tie, he looks powerful in his firm stance, and his narrowed eyes and clamped jaw are evidence that he's beyond pissed.

"Declan, I'm sorry," I say softly. "Bennett was running late and didn't leave until now. I got here as soon as I could."

He begins to make his way over to me, hands clenched in fists to his sides, stating, "I don't like not knowing where you are. You say four o'clock, you better be in front of me at four o'clock."

I open my mouth to speak, but nothing comes out. If I argue, I'm just gonna piss him off even more. His hand comes out to grip me under my chin. With his face hovering over mine, he admits, "I was worried something happened to you."

"I'm s-sorry," I breathe.

Dropping his forehead to mine, he closes his eyes for a moment as he takes in a deep intake of air through his nose. My body jumps when his fingers suddenly pierce into my jaw, and I can feel every bit of tension in his body as he opens his eyes and takes a small step back with my face still in his grip. His eyes are venomous, causing my heart to pound as a small whimper sounds from my throat.

"His smell is all over you," he seethes in disgust.

"I-I . . ."

"Did you fuck him before you came here?" his voice grinds out from his clenched jaw, but I don't lie when I whisper on a shaky breath, "Yes."

His hand falls from my chin as he looks at me in pure anger.

"On the bed," he barks. "And take that fucking dress off, I don't want to smell him when I'm fucking you."

"Declan, please."

"Get on the fucking bed! NOW!"

The bite to his words has me in a panic, worrying about what he's going to do, but I don't hesitate when I start moving across the room and into the bedroom. Quickly removing my dress, I sit on the edge of the bed and wait in the darkness for Declan. It takes him a while, but eventually he appears in the doorway. His shirt is now off, and his slacks hang on his hips with his belt clutched in one hand. The sour taste of bile burns the back of my throat, and I close my eyes, begging, "Declan, please."

"Don't talk, Nina."

I keep my eyes closed out of fear and urge on the disconnect, willing the fire of revenge to consume me so Declan won't have this power over me. I know he's right in front of me; I can feel the heat of him soaking into my skin.

"I'm not stupid to think you wouldn't have sex with that man, but I expect you to come to me clean, do you understand?"

With a quick nod of my head, he snaps, "Answer me!"

"Yes."

"Open your eyes, and answer me."

When I open my eyes, I notice the strained muscles in his arms and shoulders as I murmur, "Yes."

"Were you trying to make me jealous?"

"No," I quickly blurt out in defense. "I didn't . . . I didn't think, Declan. I'm sorry."

He moves to sit down next to me, saying, "I'm going to punish you now. Not because I want to hurt you, but because I don't want you to forget."

"Please," I say as I shake my head, and when he looks at me, it's dejection that I see in his eyes.

"I don't ever want to smell him on you again."

"I promise."

"Lay your chest across my lap," he instructs in an even voice.

I reach my hand over, placing it on his knee, giving it a soft squeeze, before obeying his request and laying myself across his thighs. When I close my eyes, I hear the clank of his metal belt buckle as it hits the floor, and in a few movements, he takes his tie out of his pants pocket, and wraps my wrists in the cool silk, knotting the fabric tightly.

His hand begins to caress my exposed ass in nothing but a lace thong, and then his hand is gone. Tensing up, I wait for the impending strike, and when it finally comes in a merciless slap against my flesh, I yelp out in a bleeding squeal as the pain radiates through my skin.

In the next second comes another vicious blow as he grunts with force.

And another.

Another.

Smack.

Smack.

Smack.

"Aaagh," I cry out in fiery pain. The sting of his firm hand hitting me chokes me up with each punishing slap. My arms strain against his silk tie, and his hands grab my hips, throwing me forcefully on my back, landing in the center of the bed. Smiling cagily at me, exultant in debasing me. Like a raging animal, he rips my panties down my legs, forces my thighs open, and strikes my pussy with an excruciating slap.

I scream out in pain as tears spring to my eyes. His soft

tongue is immediately on my now burning flesh, licking me in a slow lap over my seam. The contrast of his touches has a maniacal effect on me, evoking vulnerable whimpers. I feel everything he's doing, but I'm also outside of my body, no longer in control of any part of me. Emotions take over—fear, pleasure, pain, satisfaction, sadness, comfort. They conflict and collide in a volatile war inside of me, taking me over as I fall powerless to Declan, lying here as he kisses and licks through my folds the same way he does my mouth. He then slips his hand under my back, finding my hand and holding it tightly as my mind begins to swirl in a kaleidoscope of colors and lights, and I give in to the goodness of it all, losing myself as he wraps his mouth around the sensitive bundle of nerves while he pumps his finger inside of me.

To ward off the pleasure in his touch is a doomed feat as I lie here, restrained, weak to everything he's giving me until I feel the wet heat between my legs as I crash into fragments of pure warmth as it trills through my core and down my limbs. A glittering fire sparking inside of my veins, taking my body captive as I writhe under his touch, our hands clenched together.

All I can think in this moment is that this man is obscene.

He doesn't give me a chance to gather all the pieces he just broke me into when he jerks me up and pushes me to sit on my heels as he stands on his knees before me. Fisting my hair in each of his hands, he yanks my head back, looks down at me, demanding, "Suck my cock with that sweet mouth of yours," before forcing my head down, but I take him willingly into my mouth. He doesn't give me any control as he tugs my hair, bobbing me up and down the length of him. I begin to fight his demanding ways, pushing my head back against his hands, wanting to move more slowly, but he's much stronger than me with my hands bound behind my back.

"Don't fight me, Nina," he grunts, but I want to. I want to fight him and he feels it, yelling in scolding grit, "Yield to me!"

But I don't and he pulls my hair harder, biting on his sulfurous voice, "Yield to it. Trust me, baby."

The whisper of his pleading demands seep out through the cracks of his words. He doesn't know I hear it, but I do, and something about it makes me turn it over to him, giving him the control he so desperately needs for some reason. He moves me along the heat of his large cock as I let my tongue glide along the silky smooth flesh. The sounds spurring from him are nothing but primal lust, and when I feel him thicken in my mouth, he throws me back on the bed, straddles his knees on either side of me, pulling off a couple of hard pumps, right before he shoots his cum onto my stomach and tits. His eyes are pinned to mine as he spreads himself on me while he continues to jerk himself off. I watch him—he's beautifully brutal with his merciless touch.

He keeps my arms tied behind me as he lies down next to me and pulls me into his hold, hugging me against his strong body. I'm completely vulnerable to him, naked and restrained, but I'm not scared. He punished me, yes, but he'd never really hurt me. He keeps telling me to trust him, and I can at least trust knowing that I'm safe with him, so with my hands bound, my body goes limp, molding to his as he holds on to me.

We lie there together, his cum drying on my skin, as he combs his fingers through my hair, saying, "I only want to smell myself on you," before he reaches behind me and unknots his tie.

As soon as my hands are free, I sling my arms around his neck, needing the comfort and not quite knowing how to react after what just happened between us. He cradles the back of my head, pressing his lips to my ear, whispering, "I've got you, darling." And when I nod my head against his as I cling to him, he strengthens his hold on me as he breathes into my skin, "I adore you."

My emotions are all over the place, and I don't know what to do with the feelings that overcome me. It's a sickening delight. I hate that he enjoys this with me, that he looks at me the way he does. But I really hate that I can't escape with him. He doesn't allow me that freedom and it scares the shit out of me. My heart continues to race as I lie here, and he feels it, keeping me close to him and giving me a soft, "Shhh," in my ear. He holds me in his arms in a nurturing way, but Declan is far more primal than nurturing, yet somehow he's able to blur those lines in moments like this.

"I missed you," he eventually tells me.

"I missed you too," I sigh. "But he's gone, so I'm all yours."

"I don't just want you to be mine when he's gone, Nina. I want it all the time."

"It's complicated, but I'm here with you, and I just want you now. No Bennett, please," I urge.

Declan moves to kiss me, keeping his touches soft and affectionate, as we slowly move together. And with his lips against mine, he mumbles, "How are you feeling? Did I hurt you?"

"No."

"I need you to know that I will always protect you," he

says, his words reminiscent of my father's when I was younger, and when I pull away to look in Declan's eyes, I can see the truth behind them.

"I know," I tell him. "Trust comes hard for me, but I'm trying."

"Love that."

I smile at my manipulations as they come so easily with him. It's like I don't even have to think or try; I just speak and he's putty in my hands. Eventually we fall asleep before waking a couple hours later. Declan orders up some food, and I lie, telling him that I need to be home because Bennett wanted to video chat later and he would know if I wasn't at our place. Declan is frustrated but we agree that we will get together tomorrow and spend these next two weeks together as much as possible. Truth is, I have to go to Pike tonight.

Before I leave, Declan installs an app on my cell phone that will allow us to text without anything being tracked by phone records. His possessive ways make me laugh, but I'm curious to know why he is the way that he is.

twenty-four

(PRESENT)

IT'S NEARING MIDNIGHT and my stomach is in knots when I pull up to Pike's trailer. I turn the car off and sit for a moment; the sounds of the sharp wind blowing over the snow-covered ground fill the silence. My nerves keep multiplying the longer I sit here. I've known that this day would eventually come, but the realness that it's finally here pangs in my gut.

When I get out of the car and walk inside the trailer, Pike doesn't say a word when he comes over to me. My face is stone as I stand there.

"Hey," he says in a gentle voice.

"Hey."

"So . . .?"

"So . . ." I begin and then tell him with a nod, "This is it."

"Are you sure?"

"Yes."

Pike places his hands hesitantly along my jaw, asking, "So we're doing this?"

"Yes." My voice trembles, but I muster up my strength, resisting all the emotions I feel swarming around the two of us.

"Are you scared?"

I nod my head, giving him my honest answer through my hardened façade, and he nods along with me, letting me know I'm not alone, but we both know it's up to me to pull this off.

"Don't be scared. Remember what we're doing this for," he tells me, his eyes burning with intensity. "This is for your father. This is for you and everything you were stripped of. You wanted a new life; we're almost there, Elizabeth. Can you taste it? The fairytale?"

"Yeah," I breathe.

"So we fight the monsters first," he says and then softly presses his lips to mine, and when he pulls away, I slip off my coat and toss it aside before looking up at Pike, swallowing hard, telling him, "I'm ready."

"Say it again."

"I'm ready."

"Close your eyes," he instructs, and I do.

I stand here and feel the warmth of Pike's hand brush down the side of my cheek as he whispers to me, "This is for you," before taking his comforting hand away.

My heart crashes inside my chest as I wait, and then it comes, Pike's hard fist barreling into the side of my face and over my eye. A blast of pain singeing across my cheek and down my nose as my body collapses to the floor. Pike then grabs ahold of my wrist, moving my hand that's covering my eye away from my face and hammers down another powerful fist across my cheek. My screams are strained as I cry them out, and Pike instantly covers my body with his, holding me in his arms and cradling my head against his chest as I cry in agony. My face is hot, tingling as I feel the immediate swelling.

Pike continues to hold me, rocking me back and forth, reminding me over and over why we are doing this, but he doesn't need to convince me; I know why I'm doing this. As my tears dry, the pounding of an oncoming headache dulls out the piercing throbs down my face.

I don't even need to say anything when Pike picks me up off the floor and carries me to his bed.

"I'll be right back," he says and then walks out of the room, only to return a few moments later with a glass of water and two Tylenol. "Here. Take these."

Swallowing the pills, I set the glass down and lay my head back on the pillows.

"How bad does it hurt?" Pike asks.

"I have a really bad headache."

"Your eye?"

"It all hurts, but it's okay. I don't want you to feel bad or apologize," I tell him as he lies down next to me. "How does it look?" I ask.

He reaches out to touch the tender skin, and I flinch back at the pain.

"Sorry," he mutters. "It's really swollen and pink right now. It's starting to bruise. You'll have a nasty black eye for sure by the time you wake up tomorrow."

I nod and can't help the evil smile that creeps along my lips and then turns into laughter. Pike hesitates before allowing his smile to appear, and when I see it, I roll onto my back as my laughter grows louder. Clutching my belly, I feel deranged, like somehow I'm on top of the world, celebrating our devilish game, and basking in the glory of my growing black eye.

The past few years have been spent bonding a marriage to look like nothing other than a happy couple who is completely devoted and in love with one another. It seemed as if getting to this point of destruction would never come, but here it is in the grasp of our fingertips. And now the emotions of stress, loneliness, doubt, and determination come to fruition as they spill out of me in this crazy display of morbid laughter.

When we start to calm down and compose ourselves, I roll over to face Pike, asking, "Am I crazy?"

"Aren't we all a little crazy?"

Smiling, I say, "A simple *no* would suffice."

"No."

I straighten my expression, and when Pike turns his head to look at me, I remind him, "I love you."

"I know you do."

"No," I say. "You've never wavered on me. After all these years, you've always been my constant, from the moment we met when I was eight years old. You're the best brother anyone could ever have, and I really love you."

Turning on his side, his fingers feather along my swollen cheekbone as he leans in and kisses me, running his tongue along my bottom lip. I pull him in closer, tangling my legs with his as he shifts on top of me. We begin to undress each other, and I'm ready to take what only Pike has been able to give me. Moving my naked body with his, I reach down to grab his hardened dick and then guide it inside of me. And finally, I'm able to escape from everything around me.

WAKING UP IN my bed the next morning, the side of my face throbs in heated rhythm with my heartbeat. I haven't put ice on it to help with the swelling because I need it to look as bad as possible. I know Pike felt like shit last night after hitting me the way he did—the way he had to—but I tried assuring him that I'm okay.

As I walk across the room and into the bathroom, I look at my reflection in the mirror. Pike was right, there's a nasty black and blue bruise around my eye and along the crest of my cheek. I reach up to touch the swollen flesh and wince. The bruise is tender and the side of my face looks horrific.

It's perfect.

I go ahead and take a quick shower and get dressed, slipping on a pair of jeans and a long cashmere sweater, dabbing on just a light touch of powder and lipgloss. The chime of my phone comes as I expected with Declan's text.

Miss you.

I type my response.

Miss you too.

Come to my place. I need to touch you.

My devious smile grows while I type out my next text.

I can't. I'm not feeling well.

You okay?

Just sick.

I'll come pick you up and bring you here.

He responds just as I predicted, so I continue to goad him to me with my replies.

Thanks, but I'm just going to stay here today.

You avoiding me?

No. I just don't feel good.

Then let me take care of you.

As I'm typing out my next text, the phone begins ringing in my hand, displaying Declan's name on the screen.

"Why are you calling me?" I ask when I answer.

"Why are you avoiding me?"

"I'm not. I told you; I'm not feeling well."

"So instead of lying in your bed, lie in my bed. I'm coming to pick you up. Pack a bag," he insists in a calm tone, but I resist, telling him, "Declan, no."

He lets go of a sigh and then questions, "What's going on?"

I pause, and with an uneven voice, lacking confidence, I murmur, "Nothing. Just . . . just nothing."

"You're lying to me."

"Declan, please."

"I'm on my way," he snaps, hanging up before I can respond.

He'll be here shortly, and I've no time to waste getting excited. I have to look the part, so I focus my attention on the one thing that always destroys me—my dad. I sit on one of the couches in the living room, stare out at the grey, snow-filled day, and let my mind drift to him, to my childhood, to everything that hurts me. I think about pink daisies, and the feel of my father's whiskers poking me with his kisses. And then I think about the first time I went to his grave, coming face to face with the reality that he was really dead.

After a while, I'm not even thinking about Declan. I'm solely consumed with pain and sadness as I cry into my hands. My throat knots as the misery takes over, but the jerk of reality comes when the house phone rings, and I know Declan is here.

"Hello?" I say when I answer the call.

"Mrs. Vanderwal, this is Manuel. I have a Mr. McKinnon here to see you."

"Um, yes. Go ahead and send him up, please."

"Will do. Good day, miss."

I hang up the phone as a few more tears seep out, and I let them linger on my skin as I wait for the knock, and when it comes, I look at my splotchy face, bloodshot eyes, and bruises in the hallway mirror before walking over, ducking my head down, and slowly inching the door open, saying, "Declan, you shouldn't be here."

"Let me in, Nina."

Turning my face away from him, I walk into the living

room as he follows from behind.

"What's going on?" he questions, and when I don't respond, he grabs my arm and turns me around. "Fucking Christ," he says with a horrified look on his face when he sees my black eye. "What the hell happened?"

Covering my face with my hands, I begin to cry again. It's easy to do with my current state of mind. He doesn't miss a beat when he pulls me into his arms and holds me while I quietly weep, wetting his shirt with my tears.

"Darling, what happened?"

"Bennett was here when I got home last night," I lie.

Gripping my shoulders, he pulls away to look down at me, his eyes filled with venom when he asks, "He did this?"

The tears drip off my chin, and I slowly nod as I watch his face turn to pure rage, his grip on my arms tightening.

"I'm gonna fucking kill that bastard," he growls. "Go pack your bags. You're coming with me."

"Declan—"

"Now, Nina. I can't even fuckin' think straight. Go pack your shit. You're not staying here," he snaps, and I don't say anything else when I turn to walk into my bedroom and to my closet. I begin to quickly pack my bags, and as I walk back out, Declan is pacing the room. When he looks up at me, he rushes over, takes the bags out of my hands, and tucks me under his arm.

"Where's your coat?" he quietly asks, and when I point to the foyer closet, he wastes no time. He pulls out my coat, slips it over my arms, and then hands me my purse. I quickly put my sunglasses on before we walk out the door.

He doesn't speak as we take the elevator down and head

outside to his car. He tosses the bags in the trunk and then we are on our way to his place. His grip on the steering wheel is firm, knuckles white, muscles flexed. With his focus on the road, I watch his jaw clenching as he grinds his teeth.

When we finally make it to his place, his silence remains as we walk into his loft. With my hand in his, he leads me back to his bedroom. Tossing my bags onto the floor, he sits me down on his bed and gently removes my sunglasses. His eyes look over my face, examining my swollen cheek and black eye. I flinch when he touches it, and he whispers a quick apology before reaffirming, "I'm serious, Nina. I want to kill him for doing this to you."

"It's not that bad," I mumble as I drop my head.

"Have you fuckin' seen your face?! It's pretty fuckin' bad!" He takes a moment and a few deep breaths before softening his voice, "I'm sorry. I don't want to yell at you. Just . . . Why don't you lie down? I'll be right back, okay?"

"Okay."

Declan leaves the room, and when he returns with an ice pack, he takes a seat next to me on the bed where I'm lying down and gently places it over the side of my face. Wincing at the contact, I close my eyes and place my hand over his as he holds it in place.

"Tell me what happened," he whispers as he looks down at me.

"When I got home last night, he was there. I had told him that I was spending the afternoon with a friend, but he found out I was lying and delayed his flight until early this morning," I explain, and when a few tears seep out and roll down my temples, I continue, "He was mad, and just . . ."

"Hit you?"

I nod, and he asks, "He's done this before?"

When I nod again I see the muscles in his neck strain. Sitting up, I lean back against the headboard and begin to cry, telling him, "I'm so scared, Declan. If he ever found out about us, I don't—"

"He won't find out," he jumps in.

"He could."

"He won't."

"He's not what people think."

"How long has this been going on?" he asks.

"Shortly after we married. It didn't start out so bad, but now . . ."

"Come here," he says as he shifts to my side and drapes his arm around me, drawing me into his hold. He kisses the top of my head before saying, "I can't let you go back to him."

"I have to."

"You don't have to do anything, Nina."

"It's not that simple. I'm terrified of what he'll do because he's capable of anything," I tell him as the remaining tears roll down my face. "This black eye is minor compared to . . ."

"To what? Christ, Nina, it looks like someone beat the shit out of you with a fucking bat. You have no idea what I want to do to that fucker right now. Just thinking about him having his hands on you is paralyzing."

The rage in his voice is unyielding, and his eyes are dilated in fury.

"I'm sorry. I didn't want you to see—"

"*You*? The *real* you?" He closes his eyes for a second, pinching the bridge of his nose, and then looks at me with sincerity. "Don't ever hide from me. Not a single goddamn thing."

I don't respond, but he isn't waiting for me to when he wraps his arm around my waist and shifts us down into the sheets. My eyes close as he drops delicate kisses on my battered cheek and over my eye. With his lips against my skin, he breathes his words, saying, "It kills me to know this about you."

"I don't want you to hurt for me."

"I'll always hurt for you. I *want* to hurt for you, to take it away from you so that I can bear it for the both of us," he whispers and then seals his lips with mine in a passionate kiss. But he can't take my pain away. Nobody can. Pike tries, but it never lasts longer than a brief moment. My pain is threaded within the fibers of my existence. Here to stay. A reminder that we all come in different forms of decrepit.

Declan drags his lips away from mine, saying, "Open your eyes."

Blinking them open, I stare up into his green emeralds when he tells me, "Leave him."

"It's not that simple."

"Leave him."

"It's not easy like that," I say, needing him to understand that I can't just walk away, but he moves past my words, telling me, "I don't want easy. I want *you*."

"I . . ."

"Tell me what you feel for me," he says as he parts my legs and settles himself between my thighs.

"I don't know if there's a word for it, because it's strong, but it can't be love."

"Why not?" he says, his cock growing harder with each word spoken.

"Because I've only known you a couple of months. It's crazy to think about how much I already feel for you. I feel crazy for having the feelings I have for you."

"Why?"

"Because I hardly know you."

"You know me," he states as he rocks his hips, pressing his erection into me.

"Do I?"

"I adore you. Do you need to know anything else?"

My breathing grows unsteady as he continues to grind himself against me.

"Open up to me. Tell me how you feel. Give me the words," he insists.

"I don't know," I release on a staggered voice.

"You do. You're just scared."

"Let me be scared then," I request, but he turns it down, saying, "I won't ever let you be scared, baby."

He reaches back and pulls off his shirt before sitting on his haunches and telling me, "Undo my pants."

Sitting up, I slip the leather strap of his belt out of the buckle, and unzip his slacks. He watches me as I reach my hand inside of his boxers and take his stiff cock in my hand, curving my fingers around the thick shaft. Without taking our eyes away from each other, I begin to stroke along the velvet smooth skin sheathing his rock hard erection. When his breathing begins to falter, he grabs ahold of the end of his belt and pulls it free from his pants.

"Take your hands off me and put them above your head."

I lie down on my back and place my hands where I was told. He pulls my top off and unclasps my bra, tossing it to the floor before lacing his belt through the slats in the headboard, tying my wrists together, and securing them in an unrelenting bind.

"Tell me how you feel right now."

As we look deeply into each other, I reveal softly, "Safe," and there's a part of me that doesn't believe that word is a lie.

"Say it again."

"Safe."

Leaning down, he brushes his soft lips along my bruises. "Always." He then begins running his warm lips down between my breasts, taking them both in his hands when he peers up to me. "Always safe with me."

twenty-five

THE SHOCK OF cold touching my skin jolts me awake.

"It's just me, darling," Declan soothes as he presses an ice pack to my cheek. "I didn't want to wake you, but your bruises look to be swelling."

I stare up at him as he takes care of me and just watch as he examines my face.

"You okay?"

"Sleepy," I mumble as I move to sit up.

Declan releases a soft growl when the sheet drops to my waist, exposing my naked breasts.

"You're obscene," I tease with a grin and then pull the sheet up to cover me, but he yanks it away.

"Don't cover yourself; you're too beautiful."

"What about you? You expect me to be naked while you're fully clothed?" I argue weakly with a smile.

Dropping the ice pack onto the pillow, he stands beside the

bed and looks down at me, saying, "You want me naked?" and when I nod, biting my lip, he tells me, "Then undress me."

"Now, not only are you obscene, but obnoxious."

"You love it," he states with a devious smirk.

"Mmm . . . maybe."

"Say it. Tell me you love it," he urges.

"No," I squeak out in laughter, and with a stern tone, he retorts, "Don't ever tell me no."

"No," I repeat with a flirty wink.

He crawls back into bed and over the top of me with a sexy growl. "Bad girl."

"I thought I was a good girl?"

"Only when you listen well," he responds as he lies next to me. "Come closer. Wrap yourself on me."

And I do, rolling over, draping my arm across his chest and wrapping my leg around him as he bands his arms around me.

"You feel so good like this," he releases on a heavy sigh.

"Like what?"

"Covering me like you want me."

"You think I want you?"

"I can't seem to figure out what you want," he exhales. "I hate that you won't let me inside your head."

I don't respond to his statement as we continue to hold each other, and after a while, he breaks the silence, saying, "Why do you hide yourself from me?"

"Does it look like I'm hiding from you?" I tease with a grin as I lie here naked.

With a straight face, he lays his hand over my heart and says, "You're hiding *this* from me."

"How do you know that?"

"Because I can see glimpses of it at times. Of whatever pain is inside. Do you ever let yourself feel that? The pain?"

"Why would anyone want to feel pain?" I whisper. "Showing that exposes vulnerability, and vulnerability is your soul's weakness."

"People are weak, Nina. It's just fact."

"I don't want to be weak."

"You're only human," he says. "You bleed like everyone else, but you hide it."

"And what about you? You like to control nearly every facet of your life. You wouldn't do that if you weren't attempting to bury something."

"You're right," he willingly admits. "I need control to deal with pain, but trust me when I tell you this, I *feel* that pain. I can temper it, but it's always there." And then he hits my one tender spot when he asks, "You miss your parents?" and everything inside of me runs towards my dad.

"Yeah," I whisper on a pained breath as I feel my father's presence ache inside of my chest. And when the tears prick and my nose tingles, I close my eyes.

Declan sees right through me though. "Open your eyes."

But I don't.

I keep them closed, saying with honesty, "You want me to show you my pain, but I don't know how to do that," and when I open my eyes, the tears spill out.

"You're doing it right now."

Pointing at my dampened cheeks, I state, "This is weakness."

With his hands cradling my head, he contradicts my words,

saying, "This . . . this is strength," before licking the salt of my pain.

I hold on to his wrists as he rests his head against mine in this soft moment. I feel like I use Declan so much for this, for this comfort I've never really had before. He gives it in a way that's different from Pike, and it feels good. Peaceful. I know my time is limited with Declan, so I might as well take what I can while I have him.

And in an unusual reaction for me, I reach down to the hem of his shirt and lift it up, peeling it away and dropping it to the floor. He takes my face in his large hands again and holds me still as he looks down at me, and I swear he can see inside of me.

I begin to unbutton his pants, and when he's finally naked with me, he drops his head to my chest, grazing the stubble of his jaw lightly over my nipple. The friction is replaced with the smooth softness of his tongue. I feel it between my legs when he sucks the pert bud into his mouth as he continues to caress me with his tongue.

His touches are soft, not like his usual display of dominance over me, and in this moment, I need the softness. So as I nestle my fingers into his thick hair, I move his head to look up at me and breathe, "Don't tie me up. Not this time."

He's never *not* restrained me or been forceful in his touch, so when he gives me a nod, I'm a bit surprised. This is the first time he's allowed me to touch him during sex, and in this moment of uncharacteristic fragility, I let my hands wander along the deep cut lines of his muscular body as it hovers over mine. We move at a relaxed pace, his hand skimming over every curve of my body.

When he positions himself between my legs, he holds his

cock in his hand and runs the head of it up through my folds to my clit and slowly back down, saying, "I'm gonna make your heart beat," as he pushes himself inside of me, filling me entirely as my eyes fall shut.

He fucks me with slow, deepening strokes. There's no friction, no tension. It's just the two of us moving in this tender rhythm.

"Open your eyes. Connect with me."

I do, and he never takes his focus away from me. He's never felt so real as he does right now, in this very moment. The collusion on my part festers guilt inside of me, but it shouldn't. I shouldn't be this live wire that I am right now, gripping on to the broad knots of muscle that run along his arms. I shouldn't be feeling the pleasure that he's slowly building to fruition inside of me. I shouldn't be allowing him to do this to me, allowing me to do this to myself. It's too ripe, too much life.

I'm getting lost between reality and fantasy, and I need to pull pack. I didn't think Declan would be able to drive me so high like he's doing, moving as slowly as he is, so I close my eyes in a weak attempt to fight it away. To fight away the foreign emotions that are brewing inside.

You will not feel.

You will not feel.

You will not feel.

"Oh, God," I moan without any filter of control.

"Let yourself go with me," he urges when he takes my hand in his, lacing his fingers with mine as I begin to tremble into a shattering explosion of colorless light.

Clinging my free arm around him, he never lets go of my hand. Holding him tightly against me, my body writhes and bows up into his as I ride out the wave of ecstasy, coming hard around his cock. When I look up at him, I see the grimace in his face as he continues to move inside of me and then pulls out.

"What are you doing?" I ask, knowing he didn't come.

He lies on top of me, bracing himself on his elbows with his face over mine.

"Why?" I breathe out on an uneven whisper.

"Because that was for you."

Don't let yourself feel.

Don't let yourself feel.

My cycle of words slowly dies inside of my tightening chest. The thickness of my throat makes it hard and painful to breathe, and I know he sees it when he gently squeezes my hand that he's still holding and says, "Don't hide. If you need to cry, it's okay."

Immediately, with his words, the liquid heat fills my eyes, blurring my vision of his face into a prismatic swirling of watercolors before they finally spill out and run down the sides of my face. He rolls us to our sides, never letting go of my hand, as I quietly weep into the warmth of his skin.

We stay in bed for most of the morning. Declan cooks us a late breakfast while I take a shower and get ready. The smell of eggs is in the air when I walk into the living area and over to Declan who's standing over the stove.

"Smells good," I say as I slide up next to him and watch as he folds the egg of the omelet over a mixture of tomatoes and spinach.

"You hungry?"

"Starved," I answer before he leans down to give me a kiss filled with eagerness as his tongue invades my mouth. He doesn't stop fucking my mouth with his until the scent of burning egg wafts through the air.

"Fuck," he says, pulling the pan off the stove and onto the unlit burner, making me laugh as I move over and start opening and closing cabinets. "What are you looking for?"

"A mug."

He walks over, opening the door to one of the cabinets and pulls down a mug for me, saying, "There's coffee in the French press," as he nods to the glass carafe on the counter.

"Thanks, but I prefer tea in the mornings."

He smiles, and then gets the kettle on for me. While I wait for it to boil, I spot my purse lying on the foyer table, and when I pull my cell out, I have two missed calls from Bennett. When I look at the time, I count the hours and realize that it's a little after eight in the evening for him. It's not like me to miss his calls, but with this new turn of events, my mind has been elsewhere.

Knowing I have to call him and check in, I walk back over to the kitchen with my cell in my hand.

"I need to make a call. Would you mind if I stepped out?" I ask gently, careful not to rock the boat too much.

But he doesn't give it a second thought when he responds, "Of course. My office is down that hall across the room," as he points in the opposite direction of where his bedroom is.

"Thanks. I won't be too long."

Walking into his office, it's nearly as large as his massive bedroom, with rich, wooden bookshelves that line the back wall and up to the ceiling. His desk sits in the middle of the room. A dignified piece of mahogany accented by a large, leather chair with antique brass nailhead trim. I don't sit at his desk, perching instead on the tufted black leather Chesterfield sofa that sits over by the bookshelves. I take in the musk of rich leather and look around. Everything in this room is covered in Declan's masculinity.

I quickly swipe the screen of my phone and call Bennett. He picks up, immediately saying, "Honey, I've been worried."

"I'm so sorry. My phone was on silent and in my purse."

"What have you been doing all morning?"

"Writing. I've been working on that article," I lie. "Seems I'm not a natural. I've been cooped up in the office and lost track of time. I'm sorry I missed your call and made you worry."

"I don't want you to apologize. It's fine. I just miss you, that's all," he says sweetly, not even questioning my deceit. Knowing how fooled I have both of these men makes me smile, and I play into the good feelings, returning the sweetness, "I miss you too. Tell me about your day."

"I had to fire a couple men on the project. It's been stressful."

"What happened?"

"Deadlines weren't being met by the contractor, oversights to code specifications, and other issues I'd rather not discuss right now," he explains, the note of frustration and exhaustion evident in his voice.

"I wish I was there. I'm sorry you had such a rough day. Is there anything I can do on my end to help you with anything?"

"Just tell me how much you love me."

"Bennett . . ." I say, leaving his name lingering between us.

"What, honey?" he murmurs softly.

"I miss you, and I love you so much. I hate it when you're not here, when I don't have you next to me. It's . . ." I trail off when I realize Declan is standing in the double door entry to the room. His scowl is murderous as he glares at me from across the room, causing my spine to straighten as I sit up. He's irate, there's no doubt, but I'm playing my ace at this point. To one man, I'm his loving and devoted wife. And to the other, I'm an abused woman who's trapped in a marriage to a terribly violent and powerful man.

Bennett pulls me back to him when he picks up my lost words and questions, "It's what, honey?"

With my eyes on Declan, I answer my husband, "It's lonely," and my words aren't taken well by Declan as I watch his jaw grind and then set.

"I feel it too," he responds as I drop my head to avoid Declan's scowl.

Needing to end the call before Declan loses his shit on me, I say, "Honey, can we talk later?"

"Yeah, no problem. I'm actually in the car with Baldwin. We are meeting the project manager and one of his architects for dinner."

"Okay, well, I hope you have a good evening. I'll call you later tonight before I go to bed."

"I love you."

With my head still down, I return his words, "I love you too, Bennett."

When I hang up, I slowly raise my eyes to see Declan walking towards me. He stands in front of me as I look up at him, but he doesn't sit, he just exudes his authority while staring down at me, jaw still locked.

"Dec—"

"Don't talk," he snaps, cutting me off, but I don't take his order when I state softly, "He's still my husband."

"And those words you said to him?"

"They're just words," I whisper in a mock cowardly tone.

"You miss him?" he asks, keeping his words clipped and tight.

"No."

"You love him?"

"No."

"Are you lonely?"

"No," I tell him firmly.

His tension looms as he stands here, unmoving as time passes in silence. He eventually breaks it when his rough voice admits, "I want to punish you for calling that dickfuck in my home, but . . ."

His voice trails as he closes his eyes and puffs out a hard breath through his nose, his lips pressed firmly together. I give him a moment and then he slowly shakes his head as he drops down to his knees in front of me. His hands grip my hips and his head falls to my knees before he looks up, but he isn't looking into my eyes; he's looking at my bruises.

I open my mouth to speak at the same time he does, but I let him go first.

"You have no idea how hard it is for me to keep my shit under control, knowing what's going on. And then finding you in here, talking to *him* . . . I wanna throw my fist into the fucking wall." He takes his hand and cups the side of my tender face. "But then I look at this," he says, referring to the bruises, "and I'm afraid I'll scare you."

"I don't scare that easily," I breathe.

"I think you lie about that. I think you want me to believe

that. Maybe even *you* want to believe that, but it's all a lie. It's you . . . trying to convince yourself."

I take a hard swallow, nervous, that even through all my shit, he seems to read me pretty damn well. As much as I want to deny what he's saying, if you cut me deep enough, I believe there's truth to how he sees me. I hate that about him.

"I want you," he states matter-of-factly, and I nod. "I can't refute my feelings, even though a part of me wants to because I know I can't have you, but I want you. I want to have you, I want you mine, I want to own you."

Closing my eyes, I rest my forehead against his as my body slacks forward. Declan holds me, adding, "I want all of you, and it fucking hurts to know I can't have that. But I don't want to stay away from you either."

"I don't know what to do because . . ."

"What, baby?"

I draw my head back slightly to look at him when I explain, "There's a reason we got married so quickly. I didn't see it at the time, but . . . shortly after we were married I saw his obsession with me." I urge on the emotion when I feel the constricting of my throat. My words strain as I say, "He'll never let me go. And if he knew about you, he'd ruin you. He's powerful enough to do that."

"Let him ruin me."

"But it's me," I tell him on shaky words.

He peers his worried eyes into me, and I choke back a faint whimper, when he asks, "What are you afraid of?"

I take a pause before finally speaking the words that bring a flare of protectiveness to his eyes.

"He'll kill me."

twenty-six
(PRESENT)

DECLAN WAS BEYOND furious about me coming back home yesterday. I've spent the better part of the last two weeks staying at his place, only coming home a couple of times when I knew Clara would be here. I made my case to him though, making it clear that it has to be this way and that Bennett could never know about us. Spending as much time together as we have been, I see Declan falling hard for me. He's honest about how he feels about me and us and makes no apologies about it. For a man who exercises his power and authority, not only with me but with nearly everyone I see him come in contact with, he masks a vulnerability that I can see him trying to hide.

The bruises on my face were pretty much nonexistent when Bennett arrived home this morning. We spent hours in bed together, making up for the two weeks he was away. He wasn't happy when I had to leave to drop off my article that I was able to finish on the days Declan went to work, leaving me with nothing but time while I hid out at his place. It's not like I could really go out with my face looking as bad as it did. But Bennett understood, and even suggested that I take a little time for myself since he was starting to feel the jet lag of the nine-hour time difference from Dubai.

While Bennett's at home, Baldwin takes me over to North Michigan Avenue where I spend most of the day strolling in and out of the various stores, doing some much-needed shopping. I stop by Neiman's to pick out a few dress shirts for Bennett and a couple of ties. Before calling Baldwin to return with the car, I decide to make one last stop. Bearing the single digit temperatures outside, I loop my scarf a couple of times around my neck and head down to La Perla.

I learned while staying with Declan that he has an affinity for lingerie. Since I need to continue to draw him in deeper, I'll do whatever I can. When I walk in, my stomach instantly rumbles. Being in stores like this makes me feel dirty and gross. Always has. I know I have a fucked up sense of sexuality; I'm not blind to the effects my childhood has on me. Just thinking about adorning a body that I find repulsive—a body that has no value to me—disgusts me. But this isn't for me or my liking, it's for Declan's.

Browsing through the insanely expensive selection of silks and laces, I pick out a few silk culottes that are embellished with hand-embroidered lace. For as kinky as Declan is in the bedroom, he prefers when I wear things delicate and feminine, so I'm sure he'll like these French knickers. I add a few pairs of lace panties and bras before a sales lady approaches, offering, "Would you like for me to start you a fitting room?"

"No. I'd like to go ahead and purchase these," I tell her,

feeling like I need to get out of here before my mounting nausea suffocates me.

After I make my purchases and shove the ivory bag down into my larger Neiman's one, I text Baldwin for the car and tell him to meet me at the Starbucks that's down the street. The last thing I need is for him to know I was buying lingerie.

Baldwin is noticeably quiet as he drives the few minutes it takes to get back home. When I get off the elevator, I'm surprised to see Jacqueline with her baby on her hip walking through my living room.

"Jacqueline, what a pleasant surprise," I greet as she approaches me with Bennett striding along behind her.

"Well, Richard would rather sleep and let me take care of his business than doing it himself," she says, and when Bennett kisses my cheek and takes the shopping bags from my hands, he explains, "I needed to sign off on a few files Richard had that need to be faxed off ASAP."

"I see," I mumble, and then turn to Jacqueline and her son. "He's growing fast."

"I know. It's amazing, isn't it?"

"I suppose," I respond, not caring to discuss the charms of motherhood.

"Well, I better get going. Richard is going to be hungry when he wakes, so . . ."

That guy is such a lazy bastard. Always has been. He treats Jacqueline more as a servant to his needs than a wife. Pitiful woman puts up with it too, but that's her choice.

"It's a shame you can't stay longer. I've been so tied up lately, but we should see about a lunch date," I say, pretending I truly care about our plastic friendship.

"That sounds great. I'll call you," she replies and then looks to Bennett, saying, "I'm sorry Richard couldn't come himself."

"No worries, Jacqueline. We will see you later," he says as he walks her to the door to see her out.

They exchange goodbyes and then Bennett is back to me, taking me in his arms. "Did you have a good time shopping?"

"I did. Have you been working this whole time?"

"No. She just stopped by a few minutes ago," he tells me. "I took a short nap and unpacked."

"You? Unpacked?" I tease. "I'm impressed."

"So little faith in me," he responds with laughter and then dips his head to kiss me. "By the way, Cal made a call to my office while I was gone. Seems he heard about the refitting in Dubai and is curious about investment options."

"Oh," I remark, wondering if Declan knows his father is interested in investing with Bennett's company.

"He wants a meeting, but isn't able to get out of New York because of his tight schedule, so I'm going to fly out there for a few days. I want you to come with me."

"Of course. When would that be?"

"In a couple of weeks. I have to run back down to Miami for a few days beforehand."

"Miami?" I question, letting him see my frustration. "I didn't see that on your schedule."

"The realtor called while you were shopping. We finally came to negotiations on the property sale."

"Finally."

Bennett has a number of properties, a beachfront in Miami being one of them. He's had it for years, but since I've known him, he's never used it. Although he travels there for business, he stays in hotels since the house is out of the way.

"So . . . New York?"

Smiling, I respond, "Sounds perfect. Hopefully it's not all business; I'd like to be able to have some time with just you."

"I'll make sure of it, but for now, I've made reservations for dinner tonight."

"I better go get cleaned up then. I think I'll go soak in a hot bath for a while."

"Want company?" he asks in a smooth tone, and I nod before kissing his jaw.

We spend the rest of the day together, and after an extravagant meal, we head home and it isn't long before Bennett crashes from not only the rich food, but the time change as well. I lie there in bed next to him and simply stare. I faintly remember him as a child. His face is clear to me only because I've seen plenty of his childhood pictures at his parents' house.

He sleeps peacefully as I recall playing with him in my backyard. I don't remember much, but he used to push me on my swing set. I would tell him to push me higher, push me into the clouds, and he would give me a giant push and then run under the swing as I went up. One time he didn't make it, and I came crashing down on him. He said it didn't hurt him, but I could tell that it did.

We were never good friends, just neighbors who would sometimes play together if we were both outside at the same time. He was older and already in elementary school. Soon after I started kindergarten, I was taken away and never saw him again. That was until Pike found him several years ago. When I saw him again, he had just turned thirty. Nothing about him looked the same to me, not until his mother showed me some old photo albums. That's when I started remembering more of our time together as young kids.

And now I lie here, thinking about the part he played in the nightmare that became my life and the hate begins to fester. I want to kill him. But more than that, I want to make him suffer. I want to yell and scream, tell him who I really am. Tell him how he ruined my life, and how because of him, my father is now dead. I want him to know the destruction he caused for opening his foolish mouth. It takes a lot of effort not to clench my fist right now and beat the living fuck out of his face.

Suddenly, a muted glow casts along the ceiling and I turn my head to see there's a notification on my cell phone. Rolling over, I look to see Declan has sent me a text. I grab the phone and quietly slip out of bed to make my way to the other side of the apartment and into the office before reading his text.

Miss you.

I sit down at the desk and type back.

Same here.

Are you okay? I can't stop worrying about you. I fucking hate it.

I'm fine. You don't need to worry about me.

Don't ever tell me not to worry.

When I notice it's after two in the morning, I respond.

Why are you up so late?

I told you. I can't stop thinking about you and if you're okay. I got used to having you in my bed and now all I can picture is you lying next to him.

I don't know what to say. What do you want me to say?

That you feel what I feel.

I do.

Tell me.

I _____ you.

What does that mean?

There's not a single word I can think of that could properly describe how I feel about you, but I feel it and it's powerful.

So you _____ me, huh?

Yeah.

I _____ you too. I want to see you. Tomorrow.

Okay. I can get away during the day.

Come to 31st Street Harbor. Dock-K. Slip-47.

You have a boat?

Yes. What time can you be there?

10am.

10am. Don't be late.

I shake my head at his need for control and grin as I message him back.

Trust me, I won't. My ass and pussy are both still mad at you.

Ass, maybe, but there is no way your pussy could still be mad with the number of orgasms I have given it since.

You think so?

I know so. I'm getting hard just thinking about your divine pussy wrapped snug around my cock.

His crass words come as no surprise to me. Declan has a filthy mouth that he's let loose a few times. He's so blunt and honest in bed, never feeling the need to be modest with his words in any fashion.

Mmmm.

I'm serious. I have to control my thoughts because as soon as I think about you I get rock hard.

I'll be sure to take extra special care of you tomorrow. I can't have you walking around like that. The women already stare at you as it is, fantasizing about riding that cock.

Nobody is riding this but you.

I laugh and give him a taste of his possessive words and type my response.

MY cock!

Fuck. You're killing me. I'm going to bury it so deep inside of you tomorrow.

I'm not going to want to let you go. I already miss you terribly.

Love that. My girl.

Your girl.

It takes him a while to respond as I sit here in the darkened room until he finally sends his next text.

Did you fuck him today?

Declan, you can't ask me that.

Make sure you're clean and don't fuck him before you come see me tomorrow.

His request makes his jealousy crystal clear. I'll tell him whatever makes him feel better, but I won't stop fucking Bennett. I have to keep my charade up with him too.

Please don't treat me like that.

I'm serious. I'll lose my shit if I smell him on you.

You won't. Now stop being a dick and be nice to me.

Getting feisty?

I shake my head with a smile.

Always feisty.

I know. We need to work on that.

I'm not subservient!!!

You could be. ;)

Now you're just trying to get a rise out of me. I get your little game, McKinnon. Push me till I defy you so that you can get your jollies by 'teaching me a lesson.'

You've got me all figured out, don't you?

Does that bother you? That I can read you?

No. I love that you can read me. Now I just have to figure out how to read you.

Hmm…Maybe I like being a mystery.

I think we both know that I can see past your walls pretty well. Hide all you want, darling, but I'll always find you.

You think so?

I know so. When I want something, I do what it takes to get it.

So, McKinnon, tell me. What is it that you want?

You. You already know that, but I like that you asked me anyway just so you could get the affirmation you were apparently seeking, which tells me all I need to know.

And what's that?

That you want me too.

Possibly.

Don't be coy. You don't need to play that game with me because you already have my full interest. I get that you're scared, but you don't need to be with me.

You sure about that?

There's no doubt. What about you?

I take a moment and think about how I want to respond to his question. I don't want to be too blunt and just say *yes*.

I'm afraid.

Of what?

Afraid that you'll hurt me.

Never.

Don't say never because you're very capable.

If you're afraid, I'll hold you.

And what if I freak out?

I'll hold you tighter.

It's now that I realize I have a huge smile splayed across my face that has been there for most of this conversation. Regardless of the truth as to what is going on, Declan is fun to talk to. He always has been. Despite the evil I'm playing and the lies I've told him, I feel like I have a friend. I'm playing him just as I am with Bennett, but I despise Bennett whereas Declan was never a person I had any disparaging feelings towards. The only fault is that he's the unlucky bastard that fell for me.

You better have a good grip.

No one will ever hold you tighter.

I could stay up all night talking to you, but I have a date tomorrow morning that I cannot be late for.

Why's that?

This time, I opt for sweet words over the flirty, tart ones I typically use with him.

He tends to worry about me when I run late. He gets upset. But I really like this guy, so I want to be sure that I'm rested and on time so that he knows I care about him enough to not cause him worry.

I adore you.

I _____ you.

10am?

10am. Night.

Night, darling.

When I make my way back into the bedroom, Bennett is

still in the same position, sound asleep. It only takes a second for my ill feelings to return, so when I slip into bed, I roll to the side so I don't have to look at him. And with my thoughts returning to the conversation I just had with Declan, I quickly ease myself to sleep.

twenty-seven

(PRESENT)

"DID YOU HAVE any trouble finding it?" Declan asks as I step aboard his luxury performance yacht.

"Dock K. Slip 47. Just where you said she'd be," I say with a shiver as the biting wind gusts off the water.

"Let's go inside."

I follow Declan into the saloon that's fitted with a white, linen sofa and chairs that surround a large, wooden table.

"Quick tour?" he suggests as he takes my hand, and I give him an agreeing smile as he leads me through the galley and down the stairs. After showing me the starboard cabin and en-suite, along with the guest cabin and bathroom, he leads me down to the owner's stateroom and master en-suite. The room is sleek with rich, cherry wood, a small seating area to the side, and a large bed in the center.

Declan doesn't waste a second when he turns me in his arms and kisses me. Relaxing into the kiss, I let him move me to his liking, and when he finally pulls his tongue out of my mouth, I grin.

"What's so funny?"

With jest, I say, "No conversation?"

Running his hands possessively down my neck and over my tits, he squeezes them in his hands before responding, "We'll talk after I've had my cock inside you."

He then grabs my hips, lifts me up, and tosses me on the bed. He climbs on top of me and between my legs with a breathy groan as I grab his face and kiss him again. Our lips crash, and we're a blur of quick moving hands, fumbling off each other's clothes. When he slips my shift dress over my head, tossing it aside, I know my shopping trip was worth it when his eyes flare as he takes in my French knickers and matching bra.

With both of us up on our knees, he pauses as his eyes roam over me, taking me in. It's awkward to have a man look at me the way Declan does, with intense want and desire.

"Do you have any idea how beautiful you are?" he says softly, taking his hands and slowly running them down my ribs and stopping on my hips where he gently tugs the silk of my panties.

"Stop," I whisper, wanting to deny his words.

"Stop what?"

"When you say things like that . . ." I start, dropping my head to break the intense eye contact, "it makes me uncomfortable." I look back up into his eyes, adding, "I don't know how to respond."

"I don't need any response, darling. But you shouldn't be uncomfortable, not with me. I love looking at you. I love the way you look naked, your flawless, milky skin," he says as he starts to slowly move his hands over me. "Your perfect tits," he continues, unclasping my bra and slipping it down my arms. "Your pink nipples. It fucking makes me so hard when I see them tighten up just for me." And then he covers my one bud with his mouth, sucking it in and swirling his tongue around before moving over to my other breast to do the same.

I run my fingers through his silky hair, and he lays me back. He begins to lightly trail the tips of his fingers down, over the swell of my breasts, and along the very sensitive skin of my abdomen, sending a shiver up my body.

"And then there's this," he says smooth and low as he hooks his fingers under the waist of my panties and slips them off. "Open your legs for me."

I do, spreading them apart and exposing my bare pussy to him. As he watches me, he releases a guttural moan. He sits between my legs, and with his hands on my knees, taking in the sight of me, he says, "Touch yourself."

Wetting my finger in my mouth, I keep my eyes on him as I reach down and slip it between my lips, dragging my slick arousal up to my clit and begin rubbing slow circles. I watch as Declan's eyes dilate in molten, black lust. He shifts to remove his bottoms and then moves back between my bent knees before he takes himself in his hand and begins pumping his thick cock over me. The sight alone causes me to grow even wetter, which surprises me. I've always struggled in the past, but with Declan it's different. My body always responds to him, even when I try to fight it.

"Dip your finger inside and give me a taste," he demands, and I do, sinking my finger inside the heat of my pussy and then reaching up to offer it to him. He grabs ahold of my wrist and lowers his head, sucking my finger into his mouth. "Fuck, I need you."

He leans over and grabs his discarded necktie.

"Do you trust me?" he asks as he looks down at me and I give him a nod.

I'm used to Declan's need to restrain and control me. There's only been that one time we had sex when I asked him not to that he didn't, but that's been the only time.

"Say it."

"I trust you, Declan," I tell him as he wraps the tie around my head, covering my eyes in a makeshift blindfold.

"Lift your head," he whispers and then knots it in place, leaving me in darkness.

It's now that I feel my heart begin to race. After spending most of my childhood locked in a darkened closet, I have been claustrophobic. I hear movement, and feel Declan getting off the bed, only to return a few seconds later.

"I'm going to tie you up, okay?" he says and I can feel the heat of his body above me as I lie here. He takes my hands and holds them together as I feel a prickly, coarse rope being looped around my wrists. As he continues to secure my wrists and tie me to the headboard, he tells me, "This is a natural fiber rope. It's all I have, so if you fight the restraint you'll hurt yourself. Understand?"

"Yes," I respond and when he's done I try adjusting my wrists, only to have the coarse fibers poke into my skin.

"I'll be right back," he says and then the bed shifts, followed by the click of the door closing.

He's gone, and the darkness begins to consume me. The only noise I can hear is the lapping of the water against the boat.

My wrists begin to rub against the brittle rope as I shift around. My breathing picks up, but soon becomes labored with my increasing heartbeat. Suddenly, I feel the room caving in on me, swallowing me up as the air grows thick. I plant my feet flat on the bed; I can't seem to sit still anymore. And then I smell it. That familiar smell of Carl's cigarettes.

"Declan?" I murmur, but all I hear now is the muffled TV on the other side of the closet door. Confusion begins to swarm, and my head grows unbearably turbulent with the increasing smell of cigarettes.

Fear and confusion take over when I realize I'm naked. Carl has never locked me up naked before, and I begin jerking my hands, trying to break free. My entire body goes numb and tingly as I start thrashing around, desperate to find light and escape. Nothing feels real as my head floats, and I hear the echoes of screaming. The pressure of the walls caving in on me is so heavy, collapsing on my chest. I struggle to breathe, yanking and jerking, doing everything I can in my sheer panic to get loose.

Someone grabs my hands, and light filters in. Opening my eyes, I realize the pressure on my chest is a man and the screams are coming from me. Tugging my arms violently to get away, I shriek, "Let me go!"

"Hold still, Nina. Calm down."

Who the fuck is Nina and who is this guy? Where am I? Where's Carl?

"Get off me!" I wail through my burning screams. As soon as my arms are free, I bolt, leaping quickly off the bed only to be tackled down.

"Nina, breathe!" the man shouts as he pins me in his grip. I

287

struggle to fight my way off of his lap, but he keeps his firm hold on me from behind.

"Let go!"

"Breathe, baby. Please, just breathe."

He holds me tight as he continues to talk, slowly bringing me back into my body. The fog in my head filters out, and I begin to remember where I am. Finding my way out of the tunnel I felt I was just in, reality appears, and I realize I must have been hallucinating. The pounding of my heart shakes me, and when I look down, I'm covered in blood, sparking another spike of panic.

"Oh my God." My trembling voice is barely audible.

"It's okay, baby. You're okay," Declan soothes.

"There's blood."

"Shhh, baby. It's okay," he whispers. "Just breathe with me."

I slack into his arms, my back snug against his front, and focus on the rise and fall of his chest as I try to parallel my breathing with his. After a few moments, he lays me down as he sits over me.

I lie here, embarrassed about what just happened and the fact that Declan saw it. He reaches over to pull a blanket up, covering my exposed body. His eyes are heavy with worry as he looks over me. He takes my wrists in his hands, and that's when I notice the source of all the blood.

"We should clean you up." His words come out gentle. "There's a first aid kit in the bathroom," he tells me, and when I nod, he gets up to retrieve it.

I sit up, leaning my back against the headboard, wondering what the hell just happened. I used to have panic attacks like that back when I was a teenager, after I had run away. But that was so long ago. I feel numb, like I'm in a daze. Declan will surely question me about this, but I'm too disoriented to even stress about it.

He returns, sitting in front of me, and starts cleaning the blood from my hands and arms with a warm towel.

"Does it hurt?" he asks and I keep my focus on his hands as they tend to my abrasions.

I give a shake of my head, not wanting to speak right now, as he continues to clean and then bandage the cuts with a little gauze. Once he's done, he sets everything aside and moves to sit next to me, cradling me against his chest.

He holds me for a few minutes before asking, "What happened?"

"I'm sorry."

"Fuck, I'm the one who needs to be apologizing, not you. I should have never left you alone like that."

"Where did you go?" I ask.

"To lock the door out to the cockpit," he tells me, and then draws back to look down at me, running his hand through my hair, combing it back. "Tell me why you panicked."

Taking a deep breath, I decide to just be honest with him aside from a few details. "I'm claustrophobic. I guess with the blindfold and not being able to move, I just . . . I felt like I was suffocating."

"You looked at me as if you didn't know who I was though."

I close my eyes and sink back into his chest. "I don't know. I felt like I was hallucinating."

He kisses the top of my head, and when I look up at him, he plants another kiss on my forehead. The scruff on his face pricks my skin, and for a split second, it feels like my father. I close my eyes again, overwhelmed with the emotions that keep stacking up on me, and freely reveal, "Your stubble reminds me of my dad."

He cuddles me up tighter as words start to fall from my lips without much thought as I tell him, "He used to always kiss my forehead the same way you do." A few moments pass before I add, "I like that you do that."

"Were the two of you close?"

The tightening of my throat makes it hurt to speak when I simply breathe out a trembling, "Yeah."

I choke back the tears that threaten as he rests his cheek on the top of my head. Time is idle between us, and when I feel the wave of sadness creep away, I finally ask Declan, "Why do you do it?"

"Do what?"

"Tie me up. Have you always done that to women?"

He moves his head from mine when I look up to see his face. He gives a nod and then turns his eyes to me.

"Why?"

"Control."

"Will you talk to me about it?" I quietly ask, and his vulnerable words take me back when he admits, "I've never talked to anyone about it before."

"Why not?"

"Because it's painful." And I can see it written in the lines of his face.

I run my hand along his jaw, urging him to look at me

when I ask, "Do you think you could tell me? Help me understand you better."

The green in his eyes is bright, brighter than usual, a sign of the unshed tears that threaten him.

"Come closer to me," he says and I do, nuzzling my head in the dip of the center of his chest. I listen to his heartbeat for a few seconds before he starts to speak. "My father used to travel a lot when I was younger. He always made sure I knew I was the man of the house and that it was my job as a man to take care of my mum. I always did. When I was fifteen, my dad had come here to the States on business. My mother was in the den, reading, while I was watching a movie in my parents' room. The door was open, so I was able to see her curled up in my father's old, leather chair he liked so much. She would always complain about how hideous it looked, but when he'd leave, it's where she would always sit and read. She loved it but for some reason got a kick out of nagging my father about it."

I laugh under my breath, and murmur, "Funny."

"She was," he responds. "She had so much life in her and never let the stresses get her down." He takes a pause, and I can feel the muscles in his arms flex around me before he continues. "That night, I had fallen asleep on their bed when I heard a loud commotion that woke me up. My mother's screams were terrifying, and when I lifted my head to look out into the den, I saw a man with a gun pointed to her head."

That was the last thing I ever expected him to say, and when I look up, his jaw grinds down. Declan lowers his head to look at me, and I see the shame in his eyes as he says, "I was a coward."

Shaking my head, I ask, "Why?"

"Because when I saw that gun, I crawled and hid under the bed."

"Declan . . ."

"I could still see them though. My mum was crying and begging for her life while I did nothing to protect her. I didn't even try to help her," he reveals as tears rim his eyes. "I just laid there like a pussy, too scared to move, and watched as that man pulled the trigger and shot my mother in the head."

"Jesus."

Declan's face is tight as he tries to keep his pain under control, but the glimmer of a tear finds its way down his face. I reach up and run my thumb along the wet trail as he watches me, and then out of nowhere, I feel the heat of my own tear as it falls. I realize in that moment that we share a similar pain. Both of our parents were murdered, taken away from us, and we never had a choice in the matter.

"I'm so sorry," my heart whispers, because I genuinely feel his ache.

"That was my mum," his voice cracks, "and I did nothing."

"You were just a kid."

He shakes his head, unwilling to accept that as an excuse, and I know enough to realize that no one would be able to convince him otherwise, so I don't try.

"My father blames me for her death. He always has."

"That's ridiculous."

"Is it?"

"Yes," I state firmly. "What if you had run to protect her and you were the one who got shot? Your mother would have suffered, mourning the loss of her only child. It's a morbid thought, I know, but which would you prefer? A life of mourning or a quick death?"

He cradles my face in his hands, and I see his throat flex as he takes a hard swallow before he finally speaks, his voice holding only notes of seriousness, "I need control. I need to know that I hold the power so that nothing happens without my say. And with you, I've never felt like I needed that control more."

I slip my hands over his as they remain on my face. "Things are going to happen, Declan. That's the shit part of life, that we don't get a say in anything." The reality of these words prick at my heart, knowing the ugly truth all too well. "The world will never ask us what we want. It doesn't care what we want. Bad things are going to happen, but it'll never stop this world from spinning. And what happened to your mother . . . that had nothing to do with you."

"I can rationalize that, but it feels like a lie," he tells me.

"And what about your dad?"

"He reminds me every chance he gets that I'll never be enough. That I failed as a man. So I've spent my whole life busting my ass to prove him wrong. But you were right."

"About what?"

"What you said at the hotel that night. That I hate the name that owns me. You're right. The fact that I fell right into my father's business and didn't create my own success, it's just another piece of arson for him to use on me."

"But Lotus is all yours. Your father doesn't have a hand in it," I remind him.

"He doesn't need his hand in it to own entitlement. It shares the McKinnon name."

"I need to tell you something," I say, wanting him to be privy to the information I just found out about his dad. "Your father is looking to possibly invest with my husband's company. Bennett is going to New York to meet with him and I'm going too."

"When?"

"Later next week."

I can tell that he's pissed with the idea of mixing business with Bennett, and understandably so. He pulls me into his arms, tucking my head under his chin as he sits back, and lets go of a heavy sigh. "I want you far away from that man," he grits.

"I know, but I also know him and what he's capable of."

His arms are tense around me as I nestle my head against his hard chest. "It fucking kills me to sit at home and wonder if he's laying a hand on you. Do you have any idea what that does to me? I feel like a worthless bastard for sending you back to him."

"Don't. You're not."

He takes my hand and pulls it up to his lips and kisses the bandage around my wrist, before looking at me, saying, "I'm a bastard for *this*."

"I should have told you when you blindfolded me that I was feeling panicky."

"I need you to always be honest with me, especially during sex. It worries me that I could be hurting you."

When I nod my head, he leans down and gives me a tender kiss, sucking gently on my bottom lip before pulling away. He keeps his head close, nose against mine, and with my eyes still closed, he breathes in a low rasp, "I love you."

The tremolo of my heart excites me, to know that he's

feeling this way, but it also hurts, because he's become someone I like. I hate that I'm about to destroy this person for my own benefit, but it needs to be done. I almost feel guilty knowing that he's having these feelings for me that I don't share, but that's part of the game. That's part of revenge. I've never felt bad for Bennett, but Declan is a good guy. It's a shame that I have to do this to him, but I do.

I open my eyes and look into his, running my fingers behind his neck and up into his hair, giving the sentiment in return, only mine is laced in candied poison when I say, "I love you too."

twenty-eight

(PRESENT)

THE ABRASIONS ON my wrists healed quickly. Luckily Bennett had left for Miami the morning after my freak out, so I was able to hide my wrists from him for that one night by simply wearing one of his long-sleeved t-shirts and telling him that I was feeling sick. We always have sex before he goes out of town, but because he thought I wasn't feeling well, I was able to keep the scabs hidden from him as we just cuddled together in bed.

I spent the few days he was gone with Declan. He continues to grow closer to me, opening up more and telling me about what it was like for him to grow up after his mother had died. His father treated him like a piece of shit, always belittling him, giving him a sense of worthlessness that he now overcompensates for in his aggressions.

I've met Cal on several occasions and have always thought him bastardly. But with everything Declan has told me, it makes my stomach turn knowing that I have to put on my good graces while in his company tonight. We arrived in New York two days ago, and even though Bennett has had a couple meetings with him, I haven't been present.

Tonight, Cal has invited us to his home for dinner. So while Bennett was in meetings today, I spent my time shopping for a new dress to wear this evening. Nothing fancy, just a feminine, navy shift dress with a lace overlay that I have paired with nude pumps. Bennett looks his usual, wearing a tailored suit and tie, and when the door opens, a woman who can't be much older than me greets us.

"Welcome," she says warmly, looking polished in her ivory slacks and purple, silk top, the color making me cringe. Her raven hair is pulled back into a bun at the nape of her neck. "You must be Bennett and Nina. Thank you for joining us for dinner. Cal speaks highly of the both of you. I'm Camilla, by the way."

Bennett shakes her hand and greets her with a kiss on the cheek before she extends her hand to me, which I take in a polite shake as we exchange pleasantries.

"This is a lovely home, Camilla," I remark as we step into the foyer.

"Thank you. We just finished a remodel. For the past few months we've been living in a construction site," she says in playful displeasure.

I snicker at her mock exasperation, and she turns to me with a smile and adds, "You have no idea how many filthy ass cracks I had to look at during the process."

We both laugh at her crass words as she leads us through the impressive house.

"Cal, the Vanderwals are here," she announces as we walk

into a large home office which looks to double as a library as well, but I immediately stumble when I see Declan standing next to his father in front of the large, wood-burning fireplace.

"Bennett," Cal calls out as he walks over to us, but my eyes remain locked on Declan.

What the fuck is he doing here?

My neck heats in anxiety, almost instantly, as I stand arm in arm with my husband. Declan's eyes are dark as he looks at me with Bennett, and I give him the best *"What the hell are you doing here?"* look I can muster without drawing attention to myself.

"Nina," Cal greets, snapping me out of my nonverbal exchange with his son, and when I turn my attention to the silver-haired man, I smile.

"Mr. McKinnon, it's so good to see you again. It's been far too long."

"Enough formalities. Call me Cal and do an old man a favor," he says, opening his arms to me for an embrace. As I give him a hug, I look over his shoulder to Declan who is taking a long sip out of his brandy glass. When Cal draws back with a pleased grin, he looks to Bennett, saying, "You're one lucky man."

"I couldn't agree with you more," Bennett remarks. "She's stunning."

My eyes turn to Declan as my husband speaks his doting words. His face has a hard set to it as he begins to walk over, and in a powerful tone, he speaks to Bennett with his eyes remaining on me, "Entirely stunning. Yet somehow she married you."

I narrow my eyes at him before he looks to Bennett. His jealousy, if he doesn't get it under wraps, could ignite danger in this delicate situation, but Bennett takes it as manly banter and responds, "Indeed. Maybe it was a moment of weakness when she said yes to my proposal, which is why we married within months. I couldn't risk losing her when she finally came to her senses."

As awkward as it is, I have to keep the jig up as his wife, so I turn to him, laughing in false amusement, giving him a taste of the sass he enjoys so much. "Please, I had already figured you for another helpless man in need of a woman's influence before we ever said our 'I do's.'"

"And yet you still married me," he laughs.

"Smart woman," Cal boasts.

"And why's that?" I ask slyly.

"Well," he starts as he steps towards Bennett, clapping his hand on to my husband's shoulder, "most men only strive to be half of what he has become, and they still fail. I can only admire a man who works hard for everything he has. No handouts taken."

I note the underlying passive aggressive statement. That he's implying Declan is of the latter. His remark irritates me, and the need to speak up and defend the guy I feel is becoming a friend of mine pangs at me, so I snap in haste, "If nobody took those handouts, Cal, then everything would simply be left to die. Is that what you want to see? The death of everything you've worked so hard for? Or rather, you could take pride in the person who gives a shit enough to step in to ensure your dream continues to thrive. Seems you've got priorities a tad misappropriated and you should start respecting those that don't follow in your macho *do-for-yourself* attitude."

The look on Cal's face is of priceless shock that I would

speak so bluntly to him. The two of us just look at each other when Bennett finally speaks. "Honey—"

"Don't," I snap, interrupting him. "Don't defend his way of thinking. It's sophomoric."

"You'll have to excuse her. She's a feisty one," he remarks, trying to lighten the tension I just created.

When I look over to Declan, the air suddenly feels a little too thick to breathe.

"I can appreciate fire," Cal responds, giving me a wink, which irks me.

"Camilla," I say, turning my attention to her while she stands stoically at Cal's side, keeping a tight lip this whole time. "Could you show me to the powder room?"

After she gives me directions to the restroom, I excuse myself from the group for a much needed breather. Closing the door behind me, I lean against it and drop my head. I'm not sure what I was thinking, making a fool out of myself back there for a guy that's nothing more than a con to me.

"He's more than a con," the voice inside my head tells me. But the fact is, no matter how I identify with Declan, he is, at the end of the day, a con that I'm working. The fact that I can relate to him on certain levels isn't ideal, but it doesn't change the bottom line either. I need to pull my shit together, be the loving wife right now, and deal with Declan later. Preferably back in Chicago.

The turning of the door handle against my back causes me to startle and jump away.

"What the hell are you doing?" I seethe under my breath when Declan steps in, closing and locking the door behind him. "Why are you even here?"

He completely ignores my questioning and starts on his own, asking, "Why do you look at him like you do?"

"What?"

We keep our voices to a minimal whisper even though we are both hostile with inflection.

"The way you look at him, Nina. Don't fucking pretend with me."

"Declan, let me make this clear. He's. My. Husband."

He steps forward, caging me against the wall with his hands, eyes menacing, as he hisses through his Scottish brogue that's growing heavier the more irate he becomes, "Don't feed me shit right now. Tell me, how can you look at him like you do? That cocksucker fucking hits you."

"Because if I treat him like shit, what the hell do you think is going to be my punishment?" And in my moment of rage, I spit out my next words, "I'll give you a hint, the same thing you do when you punish me."

And the dreadful look of remorse that takes over his face makes me instantly regret saying that. For implying that Declan would be a man of such a vile nature.

"I'm sorry," I quickly recant, softening my tone. "I didn't mean th—"

He covers my mouth with his hand, stopping my words, and I feel like shit for what I just inferred. He's never touched me out of hate. I know Declan honestly cares about me, and I care about him. So when guilt fills his eyes, I grab his wrist and pull his hand away, whispering, "That was unjust. You're nothing like him. I know that. I was just caught up and angry."

"You're right."

"No, Declan. I'm wrong. You punish me out of love. It's

not the same. I'm sorry I implied it was," I tell him. "You don't hurt me like he does. With him, it's nothing but fear, but with you . . . when I'm with you, it's the only time I ever truly feel safe."

"My mind is fucking with me here. Especially when I see the way you look at him. When I see the way he touches you. Do you have any idea what that shit does to me when all I want is *you*?"

Taking his face in my hands, I affirm with fervor, "I love you, Declan. You. Not him. He's not a choice for me, you are."

"Say it again."

"I love you," I lie. "Only you."

"This can't last forever, you know? Me on the side while I sit at home knowing you're fucking that piece of shit."

"I know. But right now . . . Declan, he's in the other room. We have to go back. We can talk about this back in Chicago. He leaves for Dubai in a couple days."

His lips collide with mine, taking me in an instant, filling my mouth with his tongue. He's urgent and needy, hands on my tits, groping them firmly. I grip his shoulders when he presses his hips into me.

"You feel that? What you do to me?"

"Yes," I breathe as he grinds his erection against me.

"Hike it up," he demands, and I quickly grab the hem of my dress, pulling it up as he swiftly undoes his pants. With his hands firmly on my ass, he hoists me up against the wall, reaches between us, and yanks my panties to the side before thrusting his cock urgently inside of me. "So wet, baby. Always ready for me," he grunts, and the truth of his words hurts as I wonder why my body betrays me like it does for him.

His overwhelming aura has my mind losing focus as he pounds into me, a beautifully brutal display of his love. With my arms tightly wrapped around his shoulders, I hang on, burying my head in the crook of his neck while he fucks me mercilessly against the wall. The small room is filled with our labored breaths and the familiar smell of our sex.

This is Declan's arcane display of his primal need to mark me before sending me back to my husband. He's possessive and makes no apologies about it.

"Put your fingers in my mouth and then touch yourself," he instructs and I do, pushing two of my fingers past his lips so he can wet them for me before I slip my hand between us and start rubbing my already slick bundle of nerves.

"Ohh, God," I exhale.

"That's it. Make yourself cream all over my cock."

"Declan . . ."

"Do it," he commands as he hungrily slams inside of me, hitting me just right that I fall into a suspended reality.

My pussy pulses in waves of pleasure around his cock as I lose my breath in release.

"Fuck, yeah," he growls as he shoots his hot cum inside of me, claiming me as his. He drops his head to my chest as he begins to slow but still pumping small thrusts inside of me.

I let my head fall back against the wall, and when he looks up at me, his request is clear when he says, "Give it to me," and I slip my fingers back into his mouth so he can taste my arousal.

When he lowers me back down, holding on to me as I steady myself on my feet, his cum slowly seeps out of me, wetting my panties as I slip them back in place. We don't speak as we rush to pull ourselves together. I check myself in the mirror, swipe my fingers under my eyes, and then run them through my hair in an attempt to smooth it down. When Declan has his pants back on, he wraps his arms around me from behind and kisses me tenderly under my ear, moving his lips along the delicate skin, telling me, "I love you. So fucking much."

My heart is racing, not just from the abrupt sex, but also from the fear of knowing Bennett is in the other room. I turn in his arms, slightly out of breath, and soothe him the best that I can before I walk out of here and return to my husband.

"I love you too. If I had my way, I'd hide away with you in here forever."

He presses his lips into my neck, and then unlocks the door. "You go ahead. Give me a few minutes."

I run my hand along his jaw, taking in the feel of his whiskers and giving him a soft smile before leaving.

"There you are. I was about to come looking for you," Bennett says when I walk back to where I had left him.

I walk over to where he sits on the couch and take a seat next to him. "I'm sorry. Just needed a moment."

"Everything okay?"

"Yes," I say, and then turn to Cal, who's sitting with Camilla on the adjacent couch. "I apologize for my uncouth outburst. I don't know what came over me."

"No need to apologize. You have a spicy bite to you, nothing wrong with that," he says and then nods to Camilla, adding, "You should hear this one when she gets a fire under her ass."

"Calum!" she squeals, slapping his knee as he starts to laugh.

Bennett and I join the amusement in their exchange when Declan walks in. He quickly glances my way, scowling when he sees Bennett's arm wrapped around me as I'm cuddled up next to him.

"There you are, son. Where the hell have you been?" Cal questions in annoyance.

"Had to take a call," he answers. "I hate to do this, but I'm going to have to call it a night here. Father, it was good seeing you," he says as he walks over to say his goodbyes to Cal and Camilla before turning in my direction. Bennett stands to shake Declan's hand, totally unaware that he was just inside of me. I stand, nervously, next to Bennett, and when the two are finished saying their quick and stale goodbye, Declan takes my hand in his, bringing it up to his lips for a chaste kiss.

"Nina, always a pleasure."

"Likewise," I respond as casually as I can, and when he drops my hand, I watch as he turns to leave.

The rest of the evening passes by easily, but I can't help but wonder about Declan. I shouldn't be wasting my time worrying about how he's feeling, but I can't shake it off. After we leave and get back to the hotel, I pull out my phone and open up the text app that he had installed on my phone while Bennett showers.

Where are you?

His response comes quick.

Out.

His clipped text agitates me, but at the same time hurts me to know I've upset him.

I'm so sorry about tonight.

It was my mistake for being there.

I stare at the screen, not sure what I should type next, but it soon vibrates with another message from him.

Are you okay?

No. I miss you.

I miss you too, darling.

When I hear the water to the shower turn off, I quickly type out my next text.

I have to go. I love you though. I need you to know that.

I do know. I love you too.

I shut off my phone after I read his last text and slip it back inside of my purse. When Bennett comes to bed, his hands are all over me. And even though I was just with Declan, I don't deny Bennett. So as we have sex, I numb myself to him. I act out the motions as I always do, but inside, I turn every part of me off. The only thought I allow to float through my head is one that brings me a dark sense of satisfaction, knowing that this man I hate so much has his dick covered in another man's cum as he fucks me.

twenty-nine
(PRESENT)

"Not my face this time."

"Why?"

"Because Bennett will be back in a week. I can't have any leftover bruises that are on my face," I tell Pike.

"Okay, yeah. Your back then?"

With a nod, I nervously agree.

"You scared?" he asks.

"A little. My face hurt for a couple days after what we did. I'm okay though," I tell him. "Just do it." I turn away from Pike and tense up, waiting for the blow, but I'm greeted first by his caring touch as he runs his hands soothingly up and down my arms. But the waiting is just causing my anxiety to escalate. "Please, Pike. Now."

The knuckles of his fist hammer into me along my shoulder blade in a puncture of violent pain that shoots down the length of my arm. The force of the blow knocks me forward, and I fall to my knees, catching myself on my hands as I cringe against the pain.

Pike quickly instructs, "On your side," I immediately lie down when he strikes again.

"Ooow!" I scream as he kicks his booted foot into the same shoulder blade, followed by another excruciating blow, and then another. "PIKE!" I shriek in utter agony as I arch my back and roll on the floor, heaving through my breathless cries.

Pike drops beside me and brushes the hair away from my face as I writhe against the throbbing pain. He scoops me into his lap and holds me firmly against him while he whispers in my ear, "Just breathe. Calm down and just breathe," over and over as he rocks me in a lulling sway.

"It hurts to breathe," I strain. It hurts to talk too, like someone is stepping on my lungs.

"Talk to me."

"There's so much pressure in my chest and back."

He picks me up off the floor and carries me in his arms to his bed where he lays me down on my back.

"Take slow, deep breaths, okay?" he says, and I try to steady my trembling breathing into smooth inhales and exhales. "That's it. Just try to relax."

I lie here for quite a while until the pain starts to dull into a continuous heated ache. After I take a few Tylenol, I shift to my side, bringing my shoulder off the bed to relieve some of the pressure. Pike spoons in behind me and lifts my top to bare my shoulder.

"Fuck," he murmurs.

"What?"

"This looks really bad."

"That's the point, right?" I groan.

"Yeah," he says. "This just already looks nasty."

He gently plants a few kisses around my back where I hurt, and then drags his hand over my side and up my stomach. I push his hand away when he runs it over my breast.

"Not tonight," I tell him.

"What's going on?" he questions. I never turn down sex with Pike. It's always been something I've needed. He's my painkiller, taking away the ick in me, but for some reason, I don't feel like I need it this time.

"I don't know," I tell him honestly. "I just . . . I'm okay. I don't know why I feel this way, but I do."

"Come here," he says as he gently helps me roll over to face him. "What's going on?"

I see the confusion in him, but I feel it too. I've always been transparent with Pike, so I shrug and try to explain, "I don't know. Everything has just been so crazy lately. Maybe I'm just distracted, but I feel like I'm okay to not have sex with you right now."

"Are you sure? Because I worry about you. *This* worries me about you."

"I'm okay," I try to assure him.

"You've always needed me."

"I still need you, Pike. I'm always going to need you," I tell him and then give him a kiss.

We both linger in it for a moment before he pulls back and asks, "So how much longer do you think?"

"He's pretty firm on having me to himself," I explain. "He despises Bennett, so I don't think this will stretch out too long. It's hard to say though, but he's really intense. I think if he's triggered at just the right moment, he would snap."

"So you think he has it in him to kill Bennett?"

Swallowing hard, I think about what I know about Declan and answer honestly, "Yeah." But the thought makes my gut twist, knowing that I'm about to ruin this man's life by luring him into becoming a murderer. Pike and I always agreed from the start that we would make sure the blame lies elsewhere. It's the only way to ensure we remain safe and can move on to our new life of wealth and satisfaction. With Bennett alone, this was so easy, but now having Declan involved has made it a little difficult for me to keep my focus.

IT'S BEEN HALF an hour since Declan went up to the rooftop deck. When I got here and he was helping me take my coat off, I flinched in pain. He'd demanded to see my back and when I showed him the black and purple bruises that cover most of my upper back, he lost his shit. I've never seen him so furious before. He then apologized and said he needed some space to calm down. He grabbed his coat and went up to his private deck and has been there ever since, leaving me here on his couch waiting for him. But the temperatures are in the negatives, and I'm worried.

I go ahead and shrug my coat on before walking up the stairs to the door that leads outside. I spot him through the window, sitting on one of the wicker chairs. He has his face hidden in his hands, leaning over with his elbows resting on his knees as the snow falls over him.

I feel like shit.

What the fuck is wrong with me?

Pull your shit together; you've got a job to do.

My guilty conscience doesn't abate. I care about Declan, and I don't want to hurt him, but I have to. I have to make him feel this to drive him to kill Bennett. I just wasn't prepared to feel this way. When I notice his shivering hands, I open the door and walk over to him. He doesn't move as I kneel down in front of him, bracing my hands on his knees.

"Declan." My voice is soft as I speak to him. "It's freezing out here. You're going to make yourself sick."

He lifts his head and moves his hands to my face. "I'm already sick. Seeing what he did to you was all it took."

"Don't let him ruin our time together," I tell him and then stand up, taking his hands in mine. "Come inside with me."

We go back in and head downstairs to his bedroom. Declan doesn't speak as he walks into his closet to strip out of his cold, damp clothes and returns to me wearing nothing but long pajama bottoms. He lies down on the bed, slipping under the covers.

"Take your clothes off and come to me," he says.

I stand in front of him as he watches me undress. The expression on his face is difficult to read as I drop my clothes to the floor. When I slip my panties off, I pull the sheets back and crawl in next to him.

We hold each other close, his body freezing against my warm skin.

"You feel so good," he murmurs into my hair while his deft hands roam over my naked body.

The need to comfort him is strong, so I wrap myself

around him to warm him up. When he shifts me on top of him, I lay my chest against his, skin against skin, and he's instantly hard. Without thinking, our bodies begin to slowly move together, and I lift my head to kiss him. I want to take his pain away. The pain I inflicted. His soft lips feather against mine in light brushing kisses—sensual kisses—taking our time to simply feel each other.

He lifts my head with his hands, and I look down into the honesty of his green eyes. He doesn't say anything—he doesn't even need to—I can hear him clearly in the solitude of silence between us. He really does love me. I nod my head, letting him know that I know his thoughts, that I'm here with him.

The way he's touching me right now and with the stillness of the room, it would be so easy for me to escape, but I don't want to. I want to be here. Be in the moment—with him. I let myself drift to a place I've never been. Lost in Declan as he sits up and gently nips the bud of my nipple, hardening it to a peak before moving to the next to show the same loving attention. He savors me, and I like it.

"You're so beautiful," he whispers over my breasts.

Gripping fistfuls of his hair in my hands, I hold him close to me while he lifts his hips and shifts his pants down, and I don't even want to wait. I rise up on my knees as he holds himself beneath me and descend down over heat of his rock hard cock. Our moans blend as he fills me completely, his arms banded around my waist, hugging me, his cheek to my breast.

Neither one of us moves for a while as we hold each other, and when he eventually loosens his arms, he lays back and looks up at me. "I want to watch you take me."

Declan, giving up control and handing it over to me. So

with his words, I slowly rise up along his cock, and when I feel the ridge of the tip slip out, I take my time and fall back down over him, sucking him inside of my warmth. It's like my body just naturally craves him, needing him. I place my hands on his chest and continue to work the length of him while he watches me. He runs his hands up my thighs and over my stomach to my tits, handling me gently, caressing me.

I move my hands to his wrists and hold on to them as my eyes fall shut. I've never felt this with any other man. But it's not just now in this moment, it's every single time I'm with him. He always has a way of keeping me connected to him, never allowing my mind to drift, never allowing my body to go numb. I used to fight for that with him. But now? Now I don't even try.

Declan begins to move his hips beneath me, our bodies so in sync. There's a pressure in my chest, a foreign ache inside of me, and it begins to swell. My emotions swarm in confusion. Questions fill my head; each of them hitting the softest parts of me, parts I'm just now realizing exist within me.

Why doesn't this feel dirty?

Why am I not trying to escape?

Why do I let him see the weak in me?

Why do I hurt?

Why am I suddenly doubting everything I thought I knew?

Why can't I breathe?

And when my eyes open, I feel everything I never thought I was worthy of.

I love him.

A hard hit to my heart and I feel like I'm choking.

I really love him.

I see it, a shooting star above, exploding into a million

flittering pieces of diamond dust. Shimmering flecks trickling over me, and when I look down, I see them landing on Declan's golden chest. A splattering of crystals, each holding their own prism of sparkles as they glitter against his skin, and then he reaches his hand up to my cheek. Still holding on to his wrists, he wipes my damp cheek.

"Baby," he whispers, but I don't speak. The ache in my chest is too restricting. We don't stop moving as my tears continue to drop to his chest. And when it becomes too much, the realization that I'm falling in love with the one person I should have remained disconnected from, I choke out a painful sob.

Declan quickly pulls me down to him and I break, weeping into his neck as he hugs me against him. This has never felt okay—exposing this vulnerability that has always hidden itself inside of me—but until Declan, I never felt safe enough to expose it. I've always been safe with him. How could I've been so blind to not see what's been happening between us?

He's still deep inside of me, but we're no longer moving as he pets me. His hands gently running the length of my back, his fingers combing through my hair, while I find myself completely overcome with emotions I've never felt before. A deep connection with someone I should have kept at a distance, but somehow, he found his way inside of me.

"Talk to me," he says, and I slightly lift my head to look at him when I say the words I've said so many times, but this time, I truly mean them.

"I love you, Declan."

"I know, darling."

Dropping my forehead to his, I run my hand along his

stubbled jaw, needing the soothing prickles against my hand. "I mean . . . I *really* love you."

My confession causes his heart to pick up. I can feel it pounding against my chest. He kisses me slow and deep, tasting me, before he pulls back to speak. "This is what I've been waiting for."

"What?"

Sliding his hand between our bodies, he presses it against my chest, over my rapidly beating heart. "*This.*"

"You have it. It's been yours."

"I haven't truly felt it until right now," he says, and then I move my hand between us and rest it over his heart as well. It thumps into my palm as he tells me, "All I want is you. I'll do whatever it takes, but I need you to know that you're completely safe with me. I'll never hurt you; I only want to love you."

Knowing the web of lies I've created, I know that this will never come forth to culmination with him the way I want it to. I've created a hopeless situation in a place I never expected to find hope. But I did, and it rests inside of this man—a man I've allowed my heart to fall for. The realness is too much, knowing that all I'll come out of this with is all I've ever had—the heartbreak of life's cruel hand. And yet I don't want to fight it anymore, because I feel the same way he does.

He carefully rolls me onto my back and pushes himself deep inside of me, being gentle to not hurt my bruised back.

"Tell me you feel that," he says as he looks down at me and I nod. He pulls back, sliding his thick cock out of me before thrusting inside of me even deeper. "Tell me you feel how much I love you."

"I feel it."

He continues to fuck me with a powerful, slow force, each penetration going deeper and deeper. I grab on to his arms for support, his muscles flexing as his body tenses up with every intense stroke of our bare flesh as my body begins to climb with his.

When the heat ripples through me, I begin to shudder beneath him. He drops his head to mine, his cock grows even harder, thickening inside of me, pressing against my walls as they begin to constrict around his shaft, and I come hard.

"Oh, fuck," he growls, losing control of himself as he pounds into me.

My moans grow louder with each pulse of sheer euphoria that shoots through me. I wrap my legs around his hips, clamping my pussy around him, milking his cock, craving every drop of his sperm that fills me up. I've never felt so loved, but it consumes me in this moment as I surrender everything that I am and hand it over to Declan. I need him to spread his feral scent all over me as he takes me as his to do with as he likes, because I want to be a part of him.

He pins his eyes on me, and I know he can see the hunger in me when he starts fucking me even harder, refusing to stop even though he just came. His pupils are dilated black, flaring in possessive need when he hisses, "You're mine."

"Yes."

Thrust. Thrust.

"I own you."

Thrust.

"Completely," I breathe in submission.

Thrust.

"My property."

Thrust.

"Yes," I mewl in ecstasy as I come again, spiraling away into shrills of sensuous pleasure. He's a beast on top of me, and when he spreads my legs wide open, pressing my knees into the mattress, he slams his hips down, burying his cock inside of me to the root. With a carnal groan, I feel a warm stream of fluid flood inside of me and spill out between our connected bodies.

"Declan," I release on a faint breath—shocked as he fills me with his urine—claiming and marking me as his in the most animalistic way.

He releases my knees and quickly slips his arms under my back, holding me close before rolling us to our sides. My breathing is staggered as we stare at each other. Maybe I should be disgusted by what he just did, considering the things Carl used to do to me, but I'm not. I'm safe—safe enough to hand myself over to him entirely and know that he will take care of me—never hurt me. I love him, and I feel this intrinsic need to be as intimately close to him as I can possibly get.

"You belong to me," he eventually says as our bodies calm down, still connected, and bathed in his scent.

"Yes."

He threads his fingers through my hair, asking, "Your back? Did I hurt you?"

I shake my head slightly, responding, "You settled me. Everything you want from me is exactly what I want to give you. You don't even have to take it. Just have it because it's yours." I give my sincere words and watch as he digests them. His face softens peacefully, and when it does, I take his lips in the most loving kiss I've ever given.

Without selfishness.

Without expectations.

Without malicious undertones.

I give him the purest piece of my heart that I have remaining and hand it over in the most honest way I can despite all the evil that surrounds me. In this moment of time that I have with him, I want to love him and give him the best parts of me I can find. I want to feel this—the part of life that's good, the part of life I never thought I'd feel. I want to give every last bit of what I'm feeling right now to Declan because somehow, in some magical way, he makes life feel like it's worth living.

thirty

(PRESENT)

A RICH, INTOXICATING fragrance fills my senses as I stir awake. Rolling over in Declan's bed, I'm alone, aside from the dozens of pure white lotus flowers that are spread over the bed and myself. Containing my smile would be a feat, so I don't even bother. The heady mixture of fruit, rain, and earth wafts through the room as I take in the beauty of the delicate blooms—Declan's favorite flower.

Turning my head, I see a folded piece of paper sitting on his nightstand. I reach out and sit up, unfolding the paper to read his hand-written note.

> *Nina,*
>
> *I tried to shower you in something that was just as pure and beautiful as you, but I fell short. The lotus was the best I could do, but they don't even come close to the perfection I see every time I look at you. I know I said we'd*

spend the day together, but I have to run into the office for a little while. Call me when you wake up. I miss your sweet voice already.

No one could possibly love you more.

-D

The phone is already ringing by the time I finish reading as I wait for him to answer.

"Good morning," he says.

"When did you do this?"

"Secrets, darling," he teases, and I can picture his smile now, lines crinkling at the corners of his eyes.

"Keep your secrets then, as long as I continue to benefit," I joke right back.

"I adore you."

"When are you coming home?" I ask and his responding growl makes me laugh. "What's that all about?"

"Fucking makes me hard that you call my place *home.*"

"You're bad," I giggle.

"You have no idea."

"I think I do."

"No," he says and then pauses before he continues, "I don't think you could ever know how deep you run through me."

It's been nearly two weeks since I finally allowed myself to recognize that I love Declan. I spend every moment I can with him, and even with Bennett in the picture, we've connected in a way I didn't think two people ever could.

"Finish up your work and come home. I want you to show me how deep you can run through *me.*"

"Christ. You're not helping my dick by saying shit like that. I'm going to be walking around with a semi and blue balls for the rest of the day."

I laugh, telling him, "Good. Motivation for you to hurry up and get back here."

"I'll call you when I leave. I want you naked and on your knees, waiting for me. I'll let you pick out the belt because I'm going to have my way with you," he demands in a low voice, causing a delightful ache between my legs.

"I want the one you're wearing so that every time you look at it today, you'll think about me naked and on my knees," I say, flirting with mild laughter.

"Bad girl."

"I love you."

"Love you," he says before we hang up.

I lie back down in the sheets, staring at the flowers and dreading tomorrow when Bennett comes back and I have to go to my other home. I love being here with Declan. For the first time, I feel happy.

Truly happy.

Truth is, I'm confused.

Really confused.

Happy and confused.

I hate what I've done here with Declan—lying and manipulating. I want to be honest with him about who I am. I want him to know me, Elizabeth, not Nina. But there's no way to do that. I've set the ball in motion, and I'm not sure how to stop it. I don't think it can be, but I want it to be. I just want to freeze time, cast a spell and make the past disappear so that I can start fresh with Declan. Give him the real me.

But I fucked myself. Life has fucked me—it always has. And now I must forsake the one thing I want to be greedy with because what I want most of all is just more time with him.

I pick up one of the white flowers known for their birth in muddy waters only to grow and bloom into a flawless spread of purity. I wish for a moment that this flower could resemble me. That maybe I could be one of the lucky ones to truly get a new beginning. I've never felt as clean as I do with Declan. Not even Pike can clean me the way Declan does. But the reality is, my new beginning will still be filled with rot. Destroying the life of two men—one innocent and one who deserves the destruction—to live a life of retribution. Only that retribution will forever be tainted by the memory of what this will undoubtedly do to Declan.

I brush the soft petals along my lips, close my eyes, and picture my dad. My purity. My salvation. My prince. I wonder if my father sent Declan to me. If this is his gift to me. The good after all the bad. Declan used to scare me. He used to remind me of Carl with his forceful nature, his leather belts, and his affinity for tying me up. But when I started to see beyond that to the core of who he is, he reminds me of my dad. Because I can now look at Declan and see that, he too, is my purity, my salvation, my prince. Even down to the creases in the corners of his eyes when he smiles and the stubble along his face. My dad used to sing to me, and now I have Declan who hums gently into my ear when I'm scared or sad. The ways he soothes me is reminiscent of the things my father used to do.

I try not to think about having to go back to sharing a bed with Bennett. This whole thing with Declan, and the knowing that I can never truly have him, is just another reason to hate Bennett even more.

Needing to move and distract myself, I gather all the flowers and take them to the kitchen. Grabbing a stack of white bowls from the cabinet, I fill them with water and place the blooms down in them to float aimlessly and scatter the bowls throughout the loft.

Their scent envelops every room by the time I have taken a shower and gotten cleaned up and dressed for the day. I decide to go ahead and call Bennett since it's after five o'clock there and he should be heading back to his hotel with Baldwin. Our call is the typical, and after we talk for almost an hour, we hang up.

Things are going to get tricky for a while because Bennett informs me that his schedule is about to free up on his travel, meaning he's going to be home on a more steady basis. The thought of having to leave Declan's bed to spend the nights with Bennett is depressing. I didn't know I needed the comfort as much as I do, and Declan gives it to me perfectly and in a way that Pike could never completely fill for me.

Not wanting to dwell on having to leave tomorrow, I busy myself and decide to surprise Declan by attempting to cook for him. I go to the office and start surfing the internet for an easy, burn-proof recipe. His scent is encased within his leather chair, and I can't fight the sadness that finds my heart as I sit at his desk, in his office, surrounded by everything Declan. I find a pasta dish that seems like something I can manage and quickly print it off so that I can get out of here because I desperately need some fresh air.

I bundle up and make my way to the market. Needing the assistance of one of the workers to find a few of the ingredients,

I check my list, and when everything I need is in my basket, I make my purchases and head out.

"Surprised to see you on this side of town," I hear a familiar voice call out, and when I close the trunk, I'm greeted by Richard's snide smile. My heart jumps, and being caught off guard ignites a fire up my neck. Thank God for winter and concealing scarves.

I quickly collect myself, going into my well-crafted act, saying, "Richard. I could say the same about you. What brings you to River North, or, better yet, a grocery store of all places?" turning the question around on him.

"My attorney's office is here. Had a meeting I just got out of and needed to pick up some formula for the baby."

"Aren't you supposed to be in Dubai with Bennett?"

"Had to come back early," he snips before going back to his original question, "What are you doing here?"

"I've been cooped up for far too many days and needed a drive, so I thought I'd spend a few hours roaming some of the galleries," I tell him, figuring it was a good enough lie considering River North is known for its trendy array of art galleries.

"And yet here you are, buying groceries," he snarks. "Finally figuring out what it means to be a housewife?"

God, he's such a womanizing dick.

"As if any of my doings are your business, but since you seem so concerned with my takings on of wifely duties, yes, I thought I'd try my hand at cooking since I'm growing tired of Clara's freezer meals."

"Hmph," he remarks, eyeing me suspiciously.

His doubting look pisses me off, and when I move to walk

around him and open up the car door, I ask, "Is there anything else you'd like to question me about?"

"Jacqueline said she's stopped by your building a couple times since Bennett's been gone. Said you haven't been around much."

"Tell Jacqueline that I have a life and things to do, and if she'd like to schedule time together, then she best call or text me instead of making random drop-ins only to find that I have other obligations that call me away from home," I snap, trying to cover for my lack of presence on my side of town.

He nods with a look of spite before commenting, "I'll be sure to relay your friendly message."

"You do that, Richard."

Getting into the car and closing the door, my heart pounds with anxiety, wondering what the fuck Richard is really doing on this side of town, because I already know that we share the same attorney, and he isn't located in River North.

I drive back towards Declan's loft, all the while looking in my rearview mirror to make sure Richard hasn't followed me. When I'm sure that no one is watching, I turn into the parking garage and park in one of Declan's assigned spots. Turning the car off, I lean my head back, pissed at myself for being so careless. But that quickly morphs into being pissed that I have to be so guarded. That I've created such elaborate lies that they can't simply be washed away. I'm in way too deep for any possibility of that.

I think about Pike and everything he's sacrificed for me. Everything he's given up for the past few years while I work this con. And as I sit here and start to doubt what we're doing, the guilt of what that would do to Pike surfaces. I can't pull out of

this that easily anyway. I'm married. If I walked away—
disappeared—Bennett would come looking for me. He loves me
too much and it would devastate him to lose me. But it's not
Bennett that I care about—it's Declan. And how do I find my
way out of this without revealing all of my wicked deceit to him.
No one would be able to look past it or forgive me for what I
have already done. The only option I see right now is to keep
doing what I'm doing and cherish every last second I have with
him before Pike and I flee.

I GIVE THE sauce a quick stir after Declan calls to let me know
he's on his way. So far, I've managed not to set the smoke alarm
off in my quest to cook dinner. I walk over to the wine cage and
select a nice white to go with dinner and place it in the fridge to
chill.

When Declan arrives a while later, I laugh at the shocked
expression on his face as he enters the loft and sees me in the
kitchen.

"What are you up to?" he says inquisitively.

"What does it look like?"

"Well, you should be naked and on your knees, but instead,
you're cooking. Which I hope you've alerted the fire department
to be on standby," he chuckles as he rounds the bar, moving
close to give me a hug.

I swat his arm, saying, "I'll have you know that I've yet to
burn anything."

"Is that so?" he mocks as he grabs my wrist and yanks me

with force against his chest, giving me a sexy smirk.

"Yes. That's so."

His mouth instantly finds my neck, licking its way up to my ear where he gently nibbles on the lobe, causing a rush of goosebumps along my arms. I shiver in his hold, and he growls in pride at my body's response to him. I sling my arms around his broad shoulders when he reaches behind my thighs and lifts me up, setting me on top of the counter. With my legs wrapped around him, I feel his cock harden against me as he stands between my legs.

"Just know, next time I say I want you on your knees, you better be on your knees. I won't punish you for your disobedience though, because I love that you cooked for me," he says after kissing me thoroughly.

"Do you?"

He begins to laugh against my lips before saying, "Clearly my cock approves and is eager to thank you," which causes me to burst out laughing right along with him.

"You're such a dork."

"A dork, huh?"

"Yeah."

"No one has called me that since the fifth grade," he teases, and I giggle when I respond, "Well, maybe not to your face."

He buries his head in my neck, biting me and growling at my snarky remark, but it only turns me on. With my ankles crossed behind him, I urge his hips into me, needing the friction against my heat.

"Needy," he remarks.

"You have no idea."

He leans over, flipping off all the switches on the stove, and then hikes up the skirt of my dress. Leaning down between my legs, I hear him inhale deeply through his nose, scenting me.

"Fuck, I love the way you smell when your body readies itself for me," he says before violently ripping my panties right off of me, the lacy fabric shredded as they hang from my one thigh.

My hands take fistfuls of Declan's hair as he kneels before me, spreading my legs wider. I look down at him as he takes in the sight of me.

"You're so fucking beautiful," he says as he flicks his eyes up to mine. He then takes his fingers and sinks them between the lips of my already wet pussy, adding, "This . . ."

"Mmmm."

"This is so fucking beautiful," he says before plunging a finger inside of me.

My hands tighten around the locks of his hair as I release a heady moan. He keeps his eyes on mine while he slowly fucks me with his finger, peering up at me in raging heat.

"You like having me inside of you?"

"Yes," I answer.

"This is mine."

I moan in approval when he takes his thumb and starts pressing smooth circles over my swollen clit. He then crooks his finger to reach the most sensitive spot inside of me, causing my body to lose control as he sparks the live wire that's burning in me. But it's when his hot mouth covers me that I come undone, allowing him to possess me however he chooses.

With the flat pad of his tongue, he massages my clit in tender strokes before baring his teeth and with their razor edge, clamps down and bites me.

"Shit," I hiss as my body jerks away in pain, but he grabs my hips and keeps me in his mouth with a forceful grip. He quickly replaces his teeth with his tongue again, soothing the infliction, blurring the lines between pleasure and pain.

The gentleness that follows the torture makes me crave more of the loving abuse, and he knows it when he pulls away, urging, "Tell me you want it."

"Give it to me."

"Tell me what you want."

"You know what I want."

"Say it," he commands.

"Bite me."

"Ask me," he says. "Beg for it."

Pushing my hips towards his face, I nearly whimper in the desire that flushes through my veins, "Please, Declan. Bite me, and then take the pain away. I wanna feel it."

With a low groan, he's pleased with my request, approving, "Good girl," before unzipping his pants to free his massive erection, solid and hard.

"Your girl," I breathe as he takes me in his mouth again.

I can't keep my eyes off of him, watching him beat off while he blissfully fucks me with his tongue.

thirty-one

(PRESENT)

BENNETT HAS BEEN home for a couple of weeks now, making it difficult for me to see Declan. I have to come up with random excuses to get away and go to him. So I lie, telling him that Chicago Magazine wants another piece from me and that I've been meeting my editor for coffee and office meetings to discuss article topics, or that I'm spending the day at the spa, or going shopping. Whatever I can come up with, I tell him. Declan and I have been spending most of our time on his yacht. When I'm with him, nothing else exists—I'm happy and content. I know I've made a huge mistake and the more time I spend with him leaving my heart unguarded, the deeper I'm falling in love. But I can't help myself. He's intense, overwhelming, addictive, and utterly all-consuming. When I'm not with him, I want to be. These days, I can barely go an hour without wanting to talk to him. That's how much I crave him.

I've been putting off seeing Pike for these very reasons. I'm scared to tell him the truth about what's going on between Declan and me, so for the first time, I'm going to have to lie to him. It's been almost a month since I last saw him, so while Bennett is at work, and Declan is in meetings all day to discuss acquiring a piece of land in London for new construction, I take a risk and drive out to Justice to touch base with Pike. I normally wait until Bennett is out of town, but under the circumstances, I feel like I need to check in.

The place smells of his clove cigarettes, a scent that is so familiar to me, one that I find comfort in. But the smell that brings me the most comfort now is one of sweet, earthy rain— the smell of lotus blooms.

"Four weeks, Elizabeth," Pike's monotone voice says as he sits on the couch. His irritation doesn't come as a surprise as I walk over and sit down next to him.

"I'm sorry. Bennett's been home. He's not traveling as much right now," I try explaining, but he doesn't seem to be in any mood to hear my excuses.

"Just tell me what's going on."

"Pike."

"Tell me you're making progress with that guy."

"His name's Declan, and I'm trying. It's just taking a little longer than I expected," I tell him, lying because the only reason it's taking longer is because I want more time with him.

He looks over at me, fed up, asking, "What the hell does that mean? Last I saw you, you said he was in deep and didn't seem to have much doubt about this taking up a whole lot of time."

"I don't know," I say. "I think I was just wound up with excitement, but I don't feel like he's ready yet."

"How did he react to the last bruises I gave you?"

"He was pissed. I wound up staying with him the whole time Bennett was away."

He nods, stubbing out his cigarette. "So what do you think it's gonna take?"

"I'm not sure."

"How long is Bennett gone this time?" he asks.

"He's not. He's still here in town. It's just been a while since I saw you."

"So you needed me to take care of you," he says, wrapping his arm around my shoulder, assuming I came for sex. But I don't need that from him anymore. And as screwed up as it sounds, considering I'm married, the thought of having sex with Pike would make me feel like I was being unfaithful to Declan. It's a fucked up idea, but the feeling is there regardless.

"No. I just wanted to check in. I didn't want you worrying," I tell him and watch as his eyes narrow.

"What the fuck is going on? What aren't you telling me?" he snaps.

"Nothing."

"For nearly sixteen years you've always needed me for sex, and now, all of a sudden, you don't."

"Nobody said that I don't still need you, Pike."

"You didn't need me the last time you were here, and now today," he says suspiciously as he pulls his arm away from me. I don't speak as he stands up and takes a few steps across the room before turning back to face me. "You say you think Declan needs more time, that he's not ready. But now you've got me wondering if it's you that's not ready."

I stand up, defending instantly, "You don't think I'm ready to see Bennett dead? To see that asshole buried six feet under where he belongs?"

"I'm not talking about Bennett. I don't doubt that you want those things. I'm talking about Declan."

I try covering my nervousness with irritation when I cross my arms and bite my words, "Stop goading me and just say whatever it is you want to say."

He takes a moment, looking at me intently as if he's trying to read me, and then questions in a condescending tone, "You don't love the guy, do you?"

"What?! No!" I blurt out, but I know he doesn't buy it when he cocks his head.

"Then tell me why you don't need me."

"Pike. Don't."

"You're just fooling yourself, you know?" he says. "Don't forget, you're nothing but a lie to him."

But I don't need Pike to tell me what I already know.

"Stop."

But he doesn't. He just keeps talking, saying, "So when he says that he loves you, he doesn't really mean it. He's only in love with this fictional character you've created, *Nina*."

"Pike, I'm serious," I yell, losing my temper. "Cut the shit!"

"You and I both know that if he truly knew you, he wouldn't be saying those words."

"Fuck you!"

"No! Fuck you!" he shouts in hate. "We had a fucking plan here. And here you are, falling for the goddamn con!"

His words stab me, throwing the truth I want to deny in my face. Wishing that his words were nothing but lies, but they're not, and it pisses me off, so I shout back at him, "I'm not like you! I have cracks, and I can't always shut off my feelings like you do, settling for the life you were given. Don't forget I was given this life too!"

He flinches when I sling my words at him, and I'm taken aback by the softer tone of his voice when he responds, "So that's what you really think? That I don't feel? That I don't mourn the loss of the life I should've had? That I don't wonder about or miss the parents I never knew?" He takes a slow step towards me, his jaw flexing, hardening his voice as he continues, "You had a dad that you knew. You had it all. I never had a goddamn thing. But that's why people like you and me fight, because it gives us something to live for when we have nothing left. I thought we shared that."

The look on his face and the pain in his voice cut me deeply. I love Pike. I always have, and to see him hurt, because of me, isn't an easy thing to witness.

I move closer to him, telling him, "We do share that."

He cups my cheeks in his hands, assuring me, "We can do this. You and I can do this together. Don't let go of that because some guy makes you feel something. The real question you need to be asking yourself is: what does Elizabeth make him feel?"

He's right. Declan says he loves me, but what he loves isn't real. Not completely anyway. I allow him to see the real emotions in me, but he thinks I'm Nina, the girl from Kansas. If he knew Elizabeth, there's no way he would feel the same way about me. There's no denying how I feel about him, but Pike is right, I don't truly have the confirmation of how he feels about me—the real me.

I can't speak as I stand here and soak in his words, but he

soon breaks the silence, pleading softly, "Don't leave me alone in this."

I wrap my arms around his waist, wanting to comfort him. Pike rarely exposes himself like this to me, so when he does, it's hard for me to deal with. Pike is my rock. My backbone when I feel weak. We stand here and hold each other when I tell him, "I'll never leave you, Pike."

"When I tell you that I love you, I mean it. I love *you— Elizabeth*," he says. "That's something you will never have to question."

And I believe him, but Pike has always loved me in a way I don't share. His love has always bordered on an intimate level, whereas I love him like a brother. But when you grow up like we have, in a world where there is no black and white, it's hard to clearly distinguish the grey, and right and wrong no longer exist. I've never questioned him about his feelings towards me, he makes it clear, and I've never corrected his assumption of my feelings. But the feelings I know he wants from me aren't for him; they're for a man who believes I'm real, only I'm not. I'm nothing more than his poison paradise.

THE MOMENT I see Declan, all of Pike's words from earlier disappear. I watch Declan as he fixes my cup of tea in the galley of his boat, and after he adds a tiny splash of milk, he turns to hand me the mug.

"I've been wanting to ask you something," he says as he leads me down into his stateroom. I crawl up onto his bed, folding my legs in front of me and cradling the hot mug, and when he sprawls out, resting his back against the headboard, he reaches out, saying, "Give me your hand."

I offer him one of my hands and he turns it over, dragging a finger over my wrist. "These," he whispers, referring to the faint white lines that mar the inside of my wrist. They're barely even visible anymore, so I'm a little surprised that he's noticed them. Not even Bennett has.

Declan brings my wrist to his lips and presses them against the tiny reminders of being tied up and locked away as a child. The touch is soft, a sweetness that melts me. "Tell me how you got these?" he asks, and I want to tell him. For some reason, I want him to know the ugliness in me. Instead, I avoid because I don't want to lie to him if I don't have to.

I slowly shake my head, letting him know that I don't want to tell him, so instead he asks, "Did it hurt to get them?"

I don't answer right away as I look into his eyes, eyes that show his concern for me, his love and his caring nature that he's made me privy to.

"Yes," I eventually respond, and he kisses the scars again.

"Can I talk to you about something?"

"What's that?" I question before taking a sip of my hot tea.

"I want you to leave Bennett," he states matter-of-factly.

"Declan, I told you, I can't."

"I have an estate in Scotland," he reveals, "in the countryside of Edinburgh. Come with me. We can disappear."

"He'll find me."

"I'll hire security to watch his moves. We'll know if he purchases a plane ticket. We'll know everything he does. I won't let him get close to you."

The lengths this man is willing to go to for me are tempting. Bennett might try to find me, but he'd never hurt me like I've led Declan to believe. I immediately start thinking about what it would be like to run away with him. To leave everything behind and start a new life with Declan, far from my past. He'd never need to know because there'd be nothing to threaten the truth from revealing itself. But then I think of Pike. I can't disappear on him. He's my family. It's a nice fantasy, but it isn't reality.

"I can't just vanish," I tell him.

He takes my mug and sets it on the bedside table before taking both my hands in his. "Why not?"

"Because . . ." I shake my head, feigning my overwhelming reaction to his offer. "I mean, you're asking me to leave behind everything I know. To walk away and never look back."

"What is there that you'd want to look back for?"

"I don't . . . I don't know."

"We could have a life," he says softly.

"But . . . what about your job?"

"I own the hotel; I don't run it. This was simply a home base for me while it was under construction. Soon, if the deal goes through, I'll be working on the London property."

I hesitate, dropping my head with a defeated sigh. "I don't know."

"You love me, right?"

Lifting my eyes to meet his, I nod, answering, "Completely."

"Look, I know what I'm asking of you. And get that you're scared, but I know what I want, and that's a life with you. I'll do whatever it takes to get that." He moves his hands to my hips and pulls me onto his, my legs straddled on either side of him as he looks up at me. "I never thought I could love anyone the way I love you, but it's painful, knowing I can't keep you safe when you aren't with me. It makes me feel like a piece of worthless shit when I send you home to that bastard."

"You're not worthless," I tell him as I run my hands through his hair. "But what you're asking is a lot for me."

"I know."

"I want what you want, but it all comes with a price."

"I'll do anything to have you. I'll risk it all."

His words should make me happy, but instead, they hurt. I could easily lie to him right now, tell him that Bennett rapes me or some other fucked up shit, and I know Declan would lose his temper and kill the son of a bitch right now, but I don't. I don't want to lose him even though I know I will. It's inevitable, but I feel like I'm a little child, clinging to what makes me happy, desperate not to lose it.

My thoughts rake at my heart, pricking tears that begin to puddle in my eyes.

"Baby, don't cry."

The pressure inside my chest causes an ache throughout my body. I'm grieving the loss of what's sitting in front of me, and it cuts through me allowing the misery to bleed out. Tears fall as Declan watches in silence. He bands his arms around me while my body heaves in breathless cries.

"Tell me what you're feeling," he urges, and when I open my mouth to speak, the words tumble effortlessly from my lips.

"I hate this. I hate every moment I'm not with you. You're all that I want, and I hate life for not being fair to us. And I'm scared. I'm scared of everything, but I'm mostly scared of losing you. You're the one good thing that's ever come along for me. Somehow, in this fucked up world, you have a way of making all the ugly disappear."

"You're not going to lose me," he states in a stern voice.

"Then why does it feel like it's slipping away?" I weep.

"It's not. I promise you, it's not. You're just scared, but you have me now. I'll take all that fear away, every piece of it that you carry around. I'll take it away. I'll give you everything you deserve from this life. I'll do what I can to make up for all your suffering."

I let his words soak into the darkest parts of me, the parts that no longer believe in hope, but somehow, his words awaken what was once lost. If walking away from Bennett, leaving the plan behind and sparing his life, would mean a life with Declan, I'd do it. But I'm so torn up about where that would leave Pike. I feel like I'm in a no-win situation. No matter what I do, someone will get hurt. I want to be selfish. I want to keep Declan as my own. I want the fairytale, but once again, I'm having to face the fact that those are simply saved for books. Sometimes, for some people, there's no such thing as a happily-ever-after.

Through the tears, I kiss him, needing the closeness. Like a wound, I need Declan to kiss it away and dry my tears. I don't let up as our lips tangle in a turbulent desire for healing, a desire that we're both seeking in this very moment. He flips me over onto my back, pinning my wrists above my head with his strong hands. Kneeing my legs apart, he pulls his tongue out of my mouth long enough for me to give him my obedient words of submission.

"Take me, Declan. However you want me, you can have

me. I just need you inside of me right now."

And with that, he flips me on my stomach, ties my arms painfully behind my back, and with my ass in the air, he fucks me in a rage of fire. He's rough and in control, pulling my hair, slapping my ass and thighs, and then, like all the times before, holds my hands tightly in his as my body peaks and explodes into a violent orgasm that only he's been able to do for me. But he doesn't stop there. After he unties me, he rolls me to my back, drapes my legs over his shoulders, and feasts on my pussy with slow, loving ease, taking his time as he works my body to perfection until I come for him again. And when I'm done, he sits up on his knees and jerks off, spurting his cum all over my chest, covering me in his scent.

When my heart settles, I grow tired as I lie safely in Declan's strong embrace. The warmth of his chest and his arms around my body soothe me into a lull, and I release a sleepy hum as I begin to drift. Declan then shifts to his side, adjusting us so that we're lying face to face.

"I'm so tired," I murmur while Declan lazily strokes his fingers up and down the length of my spine, soothing me into a near tranquil state.

"Tell me what you dream about," he asks, looking at me as we lie together.

"Why do you want to know what I dream about?"

"Because you're beautiful when you sleep. It's the only time you look truly peaceful."

I release a soft hum when he urges, "Tell me."

"Carnegie." The truth slips out before I even think about it. "What?"

I take a second, and then decide to give him this piece of

the real me, revealing, "He's a caterpillar who lives in a magical forest. Well, actually, he's a prince, but his father had the kingdom's sorcerer turn him into a caterpillar."

"And why's that?" he asks, brushing a lock of my hair behind my shoulder.

"Because the king was upset that his son kept sneaking out of bed at night to steal juice from the kitchen."

"Is that so?" he teasingly questions, but when I don't give him any hint of a smile in return, he drops it as he scans my face.

"I'm a caterpillar too; Carnegie's my friend." The words hurt coming out as I begin fighting the razor of pain that's carving its way through my heart, exposing the blood through my eyes.

"Why are you crying?" he asks as he watches the tears slip out.

"Because it's a lie."

"What is?"

"Dreams. They're nothing but lies trying to trick me into believing life could really be like that."

"Sounds more like a fairytale than a lie."

"*Fairytale* is nothing but a fancy word for a lie used to deceive little kids," I tell him. "A false perception of reality used to give them hope in a hopeless world."

The look in his eyes causes me to close mine so I don't have to see the sadness he's feeling for me. Reality is a fucked-up head-trip that I've numbed myself to, but my dad, I've never been able to control the emotion when it comes to him. He's always been my one and only soft spot—until now—until Declan.

"Do you wish you were a caterpillar?" he asks as I feel the warmth of his thumb dragging across my cheekbones, collecting my tears.

"Yes."

Declan's arms envelop me, and I curl into him when he whispers, "Then go to sleep, darling," before kissing the top of my head and tucking it under his chin. "Go be a caterpillar."

thirty-two
(PRESENT)

ANOTHER THREE WEEKS have gone by since I've seen Pike. Bennett has been home for the most part, and whenever I can find time to slip away, I'm with Declan. I've been skirting around giving him a definitive answer on going to Scotland with him, but he's starting to grow irritated with my avoidance.

The bitter cold of snowy winter has finally let up, even though the city never seems to get above fifty, even on a good day. A gust of wind picks up, nearly blowing the door right out of my hand as I open it up and head inside the building where Dr. Leemont's office is located.

I've suffered from excruciatingly painful periods for around ten years; they are what led me to seek medical help, which resulted in my endometriosis diagnosis. About six months ago, I decided to try hormone therapy again to help with the pain but had to quit after a few months due to complications with side effects. Since December, the pain has been much more tolerable but the past few days have been nothing but razor sharp aches and pain, rendering me bed-ridden, practically unable to move.

Bennett's been a worried mess, taking off work to stay home, doing whatever he can to comfort me. The soonest I could get in to see the doctor was this morning, which really upset him because he had to go to Miami for business. He was supposed to head out a few days ago, but he refused to leave my side and pushed back all of his meetings, but he couldn't delay the trip any longer and wound up leaving late last night.

After signing in, leaving a urine sample for the nurse, and giving blood for the lab, I strip down, covering myself with the provided robe, and wait on the exam table for the doctor. As soon as I told Bennett about my diagnosis, he found Dr. Leemont, ensuring she was the best gynecologist in the state. I've been seeing her for over three years now, and when she finally walks in and I see her familiar smile, I release a heavy sigh, hoping she can do something for this pain.

"Nina, it's good to see you, although I hear you are dealing with some discomfort," she says as she walks across the exam room with her electronic notepad and sits down on a stool by the desk.

"Yes," I respond. "For the past few days."

As she looks at her notepad, she says, "Okay, so I see it's been about four months since you came off the hormones, correct?"

"Yes. Around late November, if I recall correctly."

"That's what I'm showing here on your chart," she remarks and then looks up at me, asking, "Have you experienced any other pain or cramping since coming off the pills?"

"A little, but it's been minor. Nothing that a few painkillers can't take care of."

"And do you recall your last menstrual cycle?"

"Umm, well, it would have been right before I started on the hormones. So . . . back in August or September," I tell her.

"What you are probably experiencing is the last of the hormones leaving your system," she starts saying when a nurse walks in.

"I have Mrs. Vanderwal's labs."

They both step out of the room, and when Dr. Leemont returns, holding the papers, she walks over to the desk and leans against it. She shifts her eyes from the papers to me, saying in a hushed voice, "You're pregnant."

The deflating of my lungs turns me cold in incredulity. "What did you say?"

"According to the urine and blood sample, you're pregnant."

Disbelief—that's all that courses through me right now as I can't seem to generate any other thought or feeling. I sit here and stare at the doctor for a moment when fear and confusion start to filter in.

"How?" I ask while each thump of my heart pumps bursts of anxiety through my blood. "I mean, there has to be a mistake because I can't have kids. I can't get pregnant." My voice is almost unrecognizable as the words fall out of me in a trembling stagger.

Dr. Leemont hands me a tissue, and it's then that I realize I'm crying. She takes a seat on her stool and rolls over next to me, placing her hand on my knee. "I can't imagine the shock you must be feeling right now," she says as I look at her, utterly confused, shaking my head. "Sometimes these things have a way of happening. Is it rare and typically unheard of without having to undergo surgery to remove the lesions? Yes."

"But I haven't even had a period."

"Well, the first ovulation you must have had probably ended up being the time you got pregnant, resulting in the missed period and the absence of one since," she explains, and then the realization that I've been having sex with three different men sends me into a complete panic as I go completely numb and freeze up inside.

Holy fuck! What have I gotten myself into?

"I want to be upfront with you though," she says, her voice remaining calm and soothing, a perfect contradiction of the chaos running through my entire being right now. "Because of the lesions on your uterus, the likelihood of you carrying this baby to term might be lower. This will be a high-risk pregnancy because of that."

Another wave of confusion hits me when her words spark a swell of sadness in me.

What the hell is wrong with me? This should make me happy, right? I can't have a baby, so if my body naturally expels it, then problem solved. So why does the thought of that happening make me sad?

When I don't respond, she asks, "Do you need a moment?"

"A moment?"

She gives me a nod, saying, "Yes. I'd like to go ahead and run an ultrasound to see how far along you are and get a few measurements of the baby."

"Baby," I whisper, repeating her foreign word.

"But if you need a moment—"

"No. I'm fine," I say, interrupting her.

"Okay then. I'll have my nurse call one of the ultrasound techs. She has a mobile station, so you won't have to switch rooms."

Dr. Leemont adjusts the table, allowing me to lie down while we wait. My heart pounds hard against my chest and the sound is all I can hear as I try to sort this all out in my head. I can't grasp on to a single coherent thought as they all tumble into each other in a maniacal collision, aside from the one piece that remains untouched and clear as day: I'm pregnant.

The door opens and a young tech wheels in the large machine. She introduces herself, but I remain quiet as I watch her set everything up while she and Dr. Leemont go over my labs.

Once she's set up and I lie down, she opens the front of my gown and squirts a warm blob of gel on my stomach. Pressing the wand down, she tells me, "Since we don't know how far along you are, I'd like to see if we can get a good view of the baby externally. Normally we do an internal exam, but I'd like to try this out first."

"Okay," I breathe as I keep my eyes glued to the monitor screen.

She begins clicking away on her keyboard while she presses the wand firmly onto my lower abdomen, almost painfully, but then she says, "There we go," and my heart stops. "See that?" she asks as she points to the white peanut on the screen, and as soon as she makes the slightest adjustment to the wand, she freezes the screen.

"Oh my God."

"Let me get a couple measurements to see how far along you are," she says, but *holy shit*, I can clearly see a head and a belly. Not a tiny blip you often hear about that doesn't look like anything. I clearly see a baby: head, belly, and four tiny nubs for its arms and legs. She doesn't even need to dissect the image for me because it's unmistakable. Never has reality hit me so hard with a truth that's undeniable.

"Nine weeks, five days," she says, and then looks at me with a smile before she turns to look at her conception calendar on the monitor. "New Year's baby, it looks like."

I can't speak. All I can think right now is Bennett, Declan, and Pike. I haven't had sex with Pike in over a month, but nine weeks ago, I was having sex with all three of them. God, I'm a sick human being, carrying a baby that could belong to any one of them.

"I'm showing October tenth for a due date," she tells me, and then she presses a button and a loud *woosh woosh woosh woosh* comes through the speakers at a rapid rate.

"What's that?"

"Your baby's heartbeat."

"Oh my God," I whisper again. A heartbeat? It's so real. So alive. Hearing that fast heartbeat inside of me is almost too much as I lie here, trying not to completely lose it.

"Good and strong," she says before turning the sound off and when it disappears, I close my eyes and replay the soothing sound in my head. How is this happening?

When she's done, I sit up and cover myself back up with the gown while she prints me off a few photos and hands them to me, saying a happy, "Congratulations."

But knowing my situation, and knowing what Dr. Leemont said about me being high-risk, there's nothing to be congratulating me about. She hands me the pictures, and both she and the doctor step out of the room so that I can get dressed, but I don't. I just sit here and look down at one of the pictures, a picture that shows a top view: head, belly, and four nubs. A weird laugh slips out through my tears when I compare the baby to a marshmallow.

My hand goes to my belly. I wouldn't even believe it if I didn't just see it with my own two eyes.

A baby. My baby.

I never thought I wanted one. Never thought it was even a possibility. But now that I have one, I don't know how I feel because I'm feeling so much. I'm scared and ashamed, but under that, I feel an overwhelming sense of protectiveness for it. Never have I had anything that was solely mine, and knowing what a fucked up world this is, I'm comforted by the fact that this baby is safe inside of me.

After I'm dressed and have made my next appointment, I head outside. As soon as the cold air hits me, I'm scared to resume my life—resume the lies.

A baby.

What does this mean for me? Will it even survive to see a moment of this world? Do I want it to? The questions multiply as I stand here on the sidewalk, people moving about, cabs honking their horns, life. The wind kicks up and I begin to cry, exposing myself to these strangers around me, but nobody stops to notice. Turmoil is a dark cloud that finds its home over me right now.

I leave my car and walk. I don't know where I'm going, but I need to move. Time passes as I wander the streets of the loop, all the while, crying. Do I tell Bennett? Is this something I can hide from him? If he knew, he'd assume it was his. What if it is?

God, I can't have him in my life. But could I kill him? The father of our baby?

Yes. I could. I'd have to because the thought of having to share this with him makes me sick to my stomach. The thought of having to look at his face, the thought of giving him a baby, giving him happiness and joy, it's all sickening.

I desperately need someone to help me. To come and hold me, tell me it's going to be okay. Someone to take care of me, hold my hand, and take away all my anguish. I'm sick of always feeling so alone.

I step off the curb and start crossing the street when I hear a horn blasting. I startle and jerk my head around to see through my blurred vision, a car, heading straight towards me, and I freeze.

"NINA!" a man's voice screams in a panic.

I close my eyes, more tears falling down my cheeks when something crashes into me. I'm no longer on my feet, I'm being carried, and when I finally touch the ground, I know I'm safe by the smell.

Declan.

"Are you okay?" he asks as I open my eyes to look up at him and then at my surroundings. I'm in the lobby of his hotel.

"What happened?" I whisper as I look out of the glass doors to see the street, busy with cars.

"I was in my office when I happened to see you walking. I went outside to catch you when you stepped out into oncoming traffic. What the hell were you thinking?"

"I don't . . ." my voice trembles, and then, like a porcelain doll falling to its death, I shatter. Falling into his arms, the sobs begin ripping out of me.

He quickly scoops me off my feet, cradling me in his arms, as he rushes me out of the lobby and into the elevator. He doesn't say anything as I cry against him with my arms clinging around his neck. He holds me like a child and it comforts me in a way only he can do, whispering, "Shhh, baby. I've got you," softly in my ear.

The elevator opens and he carries me into his penthouse room and sets me down on the couch as he crouches down in front of me. When I drop my head into my hands, he pulls them away, and I can't stop the tears from falling as I look down at him. His face is covered in worry and I know there's no way I could keep this from him because I need him so badly right now. He's the one I want reassuring me. He's the only one I want—always. So when he asks, "Baby, what's wrong? You're scaring me," I don't hesitate for a single moment when I tell him, "I'm pregnant."

I watch as his face falls in a painful expression that breaks my heart. His eyes close, forehead creased in agony when he pleads, "Please tell me it isn't his." The crack in his voice matches the one in my heart, and I give him what I know he wants, what I want, what I wish for—the fairytale that never will be—saying, "It isn't his."

His eyes open and tears fall. "How do you know?"

"Because I had just started sleeping with you and had backed away from Bennett that month. He was out of town a lot, so he didn't question my avoidance." My words, complete lies.

"But I thought you couldn't get pregnant?"

"I know," I cry out. "This was never supposed to happen. It shouldn't have happened, but it did, and I'm so scared."

"Don't cry," he breathes as he moves to sit next to me on the couch and pulls me into his arms. "When did you find out?"

"Just now. I just left the doctor's office. That's why I was walking around. I just needed to walk."

"You scared the shit out of me. That car almost hit you."

"I'm sorry."

"I need you to talk to me. Explain how this happened."

I lean back, pulling away from his hold and let out a heavy breath before telling him, "I've been in a lot of pain the past few days, so I went to see my doctor. I had been testing out a hormone therapy to help with the pain, but had to stop. The doctor told me the pain is showing up because it takes a while for the hormones to leave the system."

"Why didn't you tell me you were having pains?" he questions.

"Because you worry easily, and I knew it was probably nothing more than what I've always dealt with."

"I worry because I love you. I want to know what's going on with you. I don't want you keeping anything from me," he says, facing me and taking my hands in his, resting them on his lap. "So what did the doctor say?"

"Nothing. She took a look at my labs and that's when she told me I was pregnant." My voice falters on that last word as I begin to cry again.

Declan takes my face in his hands and assures me, "It's going to be okay. I know you're scared right now, but I'm not going anywhere."

"She told me that the baby probably wouldn't make it through the pregnancy though."

"Why?"

"Because I have too many lesions. She said they would keep a close eye on me. I have another appointment in two weeks."

"I'll go with you."

"You can't, Declan," I tell him. "Bennett is the one that found me this doctor. She knows he's my husband."

He grinds his teeth, causing his jaw to flex before hissing his words, "That's my fucking baby, right?"

"Yes."

"Did you tell him you're pregnant?"

"No," I respond, and then drop my head, admitting, "I'm scared, Declan. I'm scared for him to know." I look up, trying to contain the new slew of tears that threaten when I say, "I can't tell him. He can't know."

"He's going to find out, but you're not telling him without me by your side," he says, and the reality of this situation is starting to really hit me. "I know you're scared, but you're going to have to leave him."

"Declan—"

"You're leaving him," he demands.

"Just give me a little time."

"Fuck, Nina. All I've been doing is giving you time."

"I know. I'm sorry, but it isn't that easy. I'll leave him; I will," I say, trying to convince him, but I can no longer distinguish between truth and lies. I don't know what the fuck I'm doing. I'm just panicking at this point when all I really want to do is run away with Declan. For us to go to Scotland, have a baby, and leave this nightmare of a life behind.

"I don't want him fucking touching you anymore, do you understand me? You have my baby inside of you now. That fucker's not going to touch you," he bites with gravel in his voice and I don't even flinch when I agree. "Did he leave yet?"

"Late last night," I tell him. "He's gone for the rest of this week."

He nods his head, and I let my body slack into his, resting the top of my head to his chest. His hands come around the back of my neck and into my hair as I mumble, "I really am scared, Declan."

"I know, darling. I'm going to take care of you though," he says, and when I draw back and lift my head, he places his hand on my flat stomach, adding, "I'm going to take care of both of you."

His words make me smile. I run my hand over his, and I want to believe with everything I have that this baby is his.

"I heard its heartbeat," I murmur and his voice is barely an audible whisper when he asks, "You did?"

"Yeah. It's fast," I tell him. "They gave me a picture too."

I reach over to my purse and pull out the marshmallow photo and hand it to Declan. He stares down at it, and I watch his eyes gloss over in tears. He doesn't try to hide his emotions as he gets lost in the image.

"I didn't think it would look this real, with arms and legs," he chokes out around his tears.

"I'm almost ten weeks, so we missed the stage of the baby looking like a blob," I say as I let go of a sad laugh.

"Ten weeks?"

"I'm due in October," I tell him, and he finally looks up from the photo. His cheeks are damp, and I move to my knees, cup my hands along his jaw, and in the same loving way he does with me, I gently lick his tears away.

thirty-three

TODAY IS THE last day I have with Declan before I have to leave. Bennett returns this evening and I've been a wreck all morning. I'm scared and nervous that Bennett will know I'm pregnant, that somehow he'll be able to tell. But I'm also sad, because for these past few days since telling Declan, I've allowed myself to believe that this baby is his and that we're going to make this work. It's all a lie though. I don't know what I'm going to do, but whatever it is, I want to do it with Declan. I don't even want to imagine going back to a life where he doesn't exist for me.

I've never come across anyone like him. His intensity is entirely consuming, and when I'm not with him, all I can think about are ways I can sneak around to get to him. It's like he's the oxygen I need to survive, and when he's gone I'm suffocating. I don't know if love is supposed to feel this way, but it's all I know, and it's all with him.

"How are you feeling, darling?" Declan asks as he walks into the bathroom.

"Better. The heating pad just can't do what a hot bath can."

"You've been in here a long time."

Sinking down into the hot water, I look up at Declan as he stands over me and admire him. His square jaw, covered in day old stubble, the hard lines of his chest that are noticeable through his shirt, the roped muscles of his shoulders and arms. He's a beautiful man, casual in his dark jeans and bare feet, and suddenly, I'm mourning the loss of him as he blurs on the other side of the tears that flood my eyes.

Squatting down on the balls of his feet, he crosses his arms over his knees, asking, "What's wrong?" softly, his brows pinching in worriment.

"I don't want to leave." My voice is a mere whisper as I close my eyes to shield the tears from falling. I've never exposed this vulnerable side to another person as I find myself doing with Declan. I've always prided myself on how well I can cast the iron around me. Stoic and poised; the envy of everyone. But with him? It took something I didn't think I had in me.

Trust.

Somehow . . . somewhere along the way, he got me to trust him, and in the wake of that, I let him in. He now occupies a part of me that I had only reserved for Pike, but Pike only filled parts of that for me. It's Declan who fills me entirely, breaking the elasticity, filling me completely and running over to occupy the other vacant pieces inside of me.

The water laps around me, and I open my eyes to see Declan, naked, stepping down into the large tub. I move forward as he situates himself behind me, wrapping me up in his arms as

I sink into his embrace. He slowly combs his fingers through my wet hair, and I release a faint hum in approval for the soothing touch. I run my hands down his strong legs that I'm tucked between and close my eyes again.

"Lean forward," he says, and when I do, he starts to gently massage my lower back. "How's that feel?"

"Really good," I tell him. I've been suffering from searing stomach and back cramps, the same cramps that led me to the doctor earlier this week. Declan became really concerned the other night when he woke up to find me sleeping in the bath tub, filled shallow with hot water. He made me call the doctor to see if she could prescribe painkillers, but since I'm pregnant there isn't anything that wouldn't be harmful to the baby. So I've been spending most of my time soaking in hot baths since it seems to be the only thing that gives me any real relief. The doctor said that this type of cramping is pretty common during an endometriosis pregnancy.

"I hate that you're leaving when you're hurting so much," he says while he kneads his fingers along my back.

"I don't want to go."

"Don't. Stay. I'm not going to be able to function knowing you're with him."

Drawing my knees to my chest, I wrap my arms around my legs, making my request, "Talk to me." I need him to do something to distract me from my sadness.

"What do you want me to tell you?"

"Tell me about your home in Scotland. What's it like there?"

He pulls me back against his chest, grabs a washcloth, and starts dipping it in the water and wringing it out over my shoulders and neck.

"It's rainy most of the time," he begins, and I close my eyes, resting my cheek on his pec and listen as he speaks. "But the green, sprawling hills make up for the lack of sunshine. The countryside is amazing."

"Is that where your house is? In the countryside?"

He drags the washcloth around my neck and down to my breasts, answering, "Yes. It's south of Edinburgh in the Galashiels."

"What does it look like?" I ask, my eyes closed while he continues to soothe me with his voice and touch.

"The estate is called Brunswickhill. It was built in the mid-late nineteenth century, a neo-classical Victorian mansion, but was completely renovated before I took ownership a few years ago."

"You were here though."

"I know."

"Have you ever stayed a night there?"

"No. I hired someone to furnish the place, but I've never actually stayed there yet," he tells me.

"So why did you buy it?" I ask.

"Because after my father sold his house to take permanent residence in New York, I felt I didn't have any more roots there aside from my mother," he tells me.

I open my eyes and look up at him when I ask, "Is that where she's buried?"

"Yeah, it is," he murmurs.

"You bought the place to stay connected to her?"

He nods as he looks down at me, and then kisses my forehead before he continues, "You'd love it there. It's on six acres, so it's peaceful and quiet with a great view of the Tweed River."

"Tell me more."

"There's a huge garden and a Victorian grotto built entirely out of clinker under this huge glazed dome."

"Are there lots of flowers?"

He drops the washcloth and bands his arms around me, tucking my head under his chin, sighing, "Yeah, darling. Tons of red and purple ones."

"Purple?" I question, my mind suddenly seeing the purple walls of my childhood.

"Mmm hmm."

"I don't like purple," I mutter softly, and he doesn't let a second pass before saying, "Then we'll rip them out."

I laugh under my breath and then he inquires, "You've never told me what your favorite flower is."

I take a moment even though I already know the answer, but the thought alone grips my throat, tightening it as I reveal to him, "Daisies. I like pink ones."

"Daisies?" he questions in surprise. "Such a simple flower. I would have thought something lavish."

"Why's that?"

"You just seem like a girl who likes nice things, that's all," he responds casually as he leans back, pulling me with him as we recline.

"Daisies are nice. Simple and nice, which is why I like them."

"I want to know everything you like."

"Is that so?" I lightly tease, and when he kisses my temple, he says, "Tell me a few things you like."

"Mmmm," I hum before revealing, "I like tea, and I like cupcakes with sprinkles. Apple juice, but only when it's in a small juice box. And I like daisies."

"Pink daisies," he clarifies, and I nod, repeating, "Pink daisies."

"What else do you like?"

I tilt my head to the side so that I can see him when I say, "I like the way your stubbled jaw feels when you kiss me."

"Why's that?"

"It makes me think of how a prince's kiss would feel."

His smile grows as he questions, "Aren't princes clean-shaven?"

Reaching up, I run my hand around the back of his neck, saying, "Not in my dreams," before pulling him down to kiss me. His lips move gently with mine, eventually taking his tongue to open me up, tasting me deeply. I savor the ice of his mouth, gliding my tongue along his.

He takes my hips and eases me around to slide over his lap, my legs straddled around him. His cock is instantly hard, and the need for closeness takes over, so I lift up, and with my hand on his massive erection, guide him inside of me. His eyes close as I slowly descend down around him and hold myself still. Neither of us moves as we cling to each other—hugging—flesh against flesh.

"Tell me what you want," he breathes against my breasts as he starts planting soft kisses down the swell and over my nipple, tightening it to a stiff peak.

"This."

"Tell me," he urges.

"Just this. I just need to feel you inside of me right now," I respond, giving him my honest words, because I desperately need to be as close to him as possible right now.

"I am inside of you," he says, loosening his arms and slipping his hand between our bodies, resting it on my stomach. "This is *me* inside of *you*."

My eyes well as I nod, needing to believe that it is a part of him growing inside of me and not Bennett or Pike. I want it to be him because all I want is simply *him*. My tears fall as I gaze into his beautiful, green eyes. Eyes filled with adoration for me and I adore him just as much. I love him. And now I'm doubting everything because all I can see are the rolling hills of Scotland, a nineteenth-century estate, and Declan with our baby in his arms.

The pain of what it would mean to destroy everything good in this man and turn him into a murderer for the sake of this sick game Pike and I schemed up shreds my heart. I tried to stay focused, I tried to shut myself off from feeling anything towards Declan, I tried to stick to the plan. But I can't do it. This isn't a game; this is a man's life. A good man's life. A man that I deeply love.

I can't ruin him and turn him into a monster. If sparing Bennett's life, even though I want him to suffer for what he did to my life, means that Declan's life won't be destroyed, I'll do it.

Killing Bennett isn't worth sacrificing Declan.

My tears grow, spilling over and down my face as I whisper, "I love you. All I want is you. You and me and this baby."

His cock thickens inside of me with each word I speak, but he doesn't urge me to move as we remain connected, locked together intimately. I know what I must do, and it won't be easy. Pike has given up so much these past few years while I've been married to Bennett. But I can't do it. I won't do that to Declan.

Truth is, I don't have to kill Bennett to get my fairytale—my second chance—because that fairytale is right here in my arms. This is the happiness I've been missing all my life.

So I'll go to Pike and tell him it's over. Tell him I'll play it out, divorce Bennett, and fold my cards. I'll live the rest of my life as Nina, the girl from Kansas, if that means I won't lose Declan. I'll bury my past.

"I want to own every part of you," he groans as his eyes flare in heat, his fingers pressing into my skin as he grips my ass.

"You already do."

"Grab my shoulders and move," he commands, and I obey, lifting up along the shaft of his cock before gliding back down.

I continue to work the length of him, my pussy snug around him, gripping him in needy ecstasy as the water laps around our bodies. He handles one of my breasts in his hand, tugging on my hardened nipple as he drags his tongue over my other breast before fiercely sucking me into his mouth. With his teeth bared, he scrapes them along the delicate skin and then bites down with force. Screaming out in a seething aura of pleasure and pain, I ride his cock, rolling my hips over him. The warm water swirls over my swollen clit with each of my thrusts, driving me towards my peak.

Declan continues to work my tits, laving me with his tongue, feasting like I'm his last meal and he needs me to survive. He then grabs my hips, jerking me to pound against him as he shoves his cock deeper inside of me, hitting that bundle of nerves that only he's done, and I can't hold on. Dropping my head back, he quickly finds my hand, interlacing our fingers and squeezing it tightly. I pulse and spasm around him as the colorless light of my exploding orgasm blinds me. When I writhe against him, he wraps his free arm around my waist and roughly pins my body down over his cock. He throbs inside of me, growing and contracting with each pump of cum he shoots inside of me.

"Fuck," he moans in a sensual brute as we both come together.

Holding me close to him, my body begins to tremble in fiery aftershocks. I'm wrapped all around Declan when he eventually pulls his head back. Our breaths are erratic and labored as we try to find our way back down.

In a staggered voice, Declan pants, "I want to make you into everything you've ever dreamed of being."

And with those words, I don't need any convincing.

Fuck Bennett.

Fuck the revenge.

Fuck it all.

I have everything I'll ever want right here inside of this beautiful man.

thirty-four

(PRESENT)

I HAVEN'T GONE to see Pike yet. I know I have to, but I've been afraid about how he's going to react to the news that I want out of this. Bennett has been back in town for the past few days, and I find myself caring less and less about playing his wife. For me, it's over, but I feel I can't walk out until I talk to Pike.

I've seen Declan every day since Bennett has returned, and to say he's growing impatient with me is a severe understatement. My excuses are wearing thin, so I finish getting ready to drive out and tell Pike the new plan—the plan that will, for the first time, leave him without me by his side.

The guilt is insurmountable at this point. How do you tell the man, who is probably in love with you, and the one who has been your protector for the past twenty years, that it's no longer the two of you? That you've fallen in love and want to be with that other person? Pike and I have always been together, always honest with each other, until now. I told him I didn't love

Declan, but I knew he could see right through me. See deeper than even I could at that point. I knew I cared for Declan, that he was a friend that I was being drawn to, but I hadn't yet realized that I had already fallen for him. Pike already knew though; that's how connected we are.

The house phone rings as I throw on my sweater, and when I answer, it's Manuel from downstairs.

"Mrs. Vanderwal, I'm sorry to disturb you, but there's a gentleman here saying he's a cousin of yours."

"What?" I question, wondering who the hell is down there, and then I hear the unmistakable voice of Pike, arguing, "Dude, just let me go up."

"Yes, please, Manuel," I quickly interject as rampant fear streaks through me. "Go ahead and send him up."

My nerves crash, confounded as to why the hell Pike would come here. Never has he come here. We agreed from the start that our paths would never cross outside of Justice, so as I pace the foyer, waiting for his knock, I try to grapple with my thoughts and compose myself, all the while knowing what I must tell him.

When the knock comes, I open the door, grab his arm, and yank him inside, snapping, "What the fuck are you doing here?"

But his eyes don't meet mine, instead they scan around the room, taking in my home of the past four years. "Holy shit," he murmurs. "So this is where you've been while I'm rotting away in that shit tank?"

"Pike, what are you doing here? Are you crazy? What if Bennett was home?"

"Relax, Elizabeth. I've been sitting outside all morning waiting for that shit-stain to leave," he says, walking past me and into the dining room. "So . . ." he starts, letting the word linger as he drags a finger down the length of the cherry wood dining table, ". . . where the fuck have you been for the past month?" His words scrape out in frustration.

"I-I'm sorry. I ju—"

"Cut the shit. You told me Bennett was going to be out of town this past week, yet you never once came by to see me. Why is that?"

"Pike, please," I say on a shaky voice as chills run down my trembling arms, scared shitless with what I'm about to reveal.

"Please? What the fuck is going on with you, Elizabeth?!" he shouts, his voice booming through the open space as he slams his fist against the table. "You used to run to me the second Bennett left, you used to beg for my dick, but now, when you do finally decide to show your face, you rush out the door."

"Why are you screaming at me?!" I yell.

"Because you've got a job to do and it isn't getting done!" He walks the edge of the table and back over to me, but when he gets close, I take a step back. "Why isn't it getting done?"

My pulse races as I stutter out the words I've been afraid to say to him. "B-Because . . ."

"Because why?" he hisses as he glares at me.

Swallowing hard, I force out the words, "Because I want out."

His jaw locks and he begins a rhythmic clenching and unclenching of his hands, fisting them at his sides. He takes a moment before he breaks the silence, seething, "What do you mean *you want out?*"

"Pike, please don't flip out on me," I say, trying to keep my voice calm.

"What do you mean *you want out?*"

"I can't . . . I can't do this anymore." My face grows hot with the tears that threaten.

"It's Declan, isn't it?"

"I'm so sorry, Pike. I never thought—"

"You're nothing to him but an illusion, Elizabeth," he says, cutting me off.

"I love him."

My confession sparks a fury in his eyes, and when he takes another step towards me, I take another back, pissing him off.

"So, what now? You think he loves you back?"

"Yes," I breathe.

"You're full of shit. You have no idea what you're saying. You're so wrapped up in this lie that you're buying into this false reality. But it's *false*, Elizabeth. It's not real."

"It is."

"It isn't. You are not Nina. Can't you see that?"

"And what's Elizabeth? Huh? I mean . . . who is she really? Is she me?" I question as the levies break and the tears fall down my cheeks. "Because she doesn't feel like me. Because she was never supposed to be me!" My words now cries, pleading cries. "She only existed because of Bennett!"

"That's right, Elizabeth!!" he barks furiously. "Bennett! Feel that fucking hate! He's the reason for all of this! Don't lose sight of what he did to your life! To your father's life!"

And my fury parallels his, except that fury is robed in a mass of sadness and desperation when I shriek, "I know! God, I know, but I can't do it. I can't destroy Declan like that."

"Fuck Declan! He's the pawn. He's always been the pawn, and you, the queen."

"But sometimes the queen falls."

"Not you," he says sternly as his hands grip my shoulders that tremor under my emotions. "I'm not gonna let you fall."

"I already fell, Pike. I want out. I'll finish this; I'll divorce Bennett, and no one will ever have to know about this."

His fingers tighten around my shoulders, painfully. "You don't love him," he whispers, and I hear every morsel of pain he's trying to hide, but I can't lie.

"I do love him," I say under my breath, and as soon as he drops his head, he lifts it right back up. The look in his eyes turns to cold stone, and he takes a couple steps back, releasing his hands from me.

His sudden shift in demeanor rattles me as I watch him start to subtly shake his head before questioning, "Are you not telling me something?"

"What do you mean?"

"I mean the fact that your hand hasn't left your stomach for the past few minutes," he says, and when I look down, I see that I've got my hand right where he said it was—an unconscious act of protecting what's inside—and suddenly, all the blood drains out of me, leaving me utterly terrified as I watch the viperous hate surface in his eyes.

You've heard of Newton's first law of motion, right? The one that states that an object in motion will remain in motion unless acted upon by an unbalanced force? It's a science that can't be negated, and with the game in full speed, I'm about to learn the catastrophic consequences of that law.

"Pike," I soothe, needing him to calm down.

"Tell me that I'm losing my mind right now. That I'm not thinking clearly. That I'm not—"

Holding my hand up in front of me, I try coaxing my words

as I speak slowly, "Please, Pike. I need you to just—"

And then he loses it, exploding like a grenade, screaming in sulfur, "Tell me you are not fucking pregnant!!"

"Pike!" I yell as he grabs my arms violently.

His face—raging red, spitting his words, "What the fuck have you done?"

"Nothing! Let go of me," I yell, panicked, jerking to break free of his hold on me.

"Tell me!"

"Yes!" I immediately shout back, and he releases his grip.

He turns away from me, raking his hands angrily through his hair, as I stand here, nervously awaiting his next move. He keeps his back to me when he continues to talk, "You're fucking pregnant. Jesus Christ. And it can't be mine because you haven't been fucking me."

I don't correct him because he assumes that I'm not as far along as I actually am. This baby could very well be his.

He turns back, and the look in his eyes scares the living shit out of me. I don't see Pike behind them, only a monstrous version of what could be my brother. And when he starts moving towards me—body tense—the shrill of horror stabs me.

"This is over right now. I've spent too many years for you to fuck this up."

"What do you mean?" I ask as I start backing away from him.

And then my world goes into a paradox of raging fast slow motion.

His arm rises with a tight fist.

My arms wrap around my stomach.

Fist barreling down.

My eyes squeezing shut and coiling away.

A collision of knuckles against jaw.

Blow after blow, he's relentless as I fall lifelessly to the ground. The light begins to fade as my screams lull me into the blackness. My lungs cave with every fatal kick to my stomach, and there's nothing I can do as I lie here defenseless to this monster above me. A beating fire of pain ruptures inside, paralyzing me to a corpse as I feel everything breaking inside of me. My screams turn breathless and everything vanishes as Pike grunts like a wild beast, hammering his booted foot over and over and over into the womb that carries the purest part of me.

Black ink bleeds over me as I drift into nothingness. I'm a hollow tomb. Looking up, I see a dark sky, flickering with diamonds. Thousands of them. There's no more pain—there's nothing in this solitude of pure, deathly silence as I lie here and stare into the endless black hole.

Wishes.

I could make an infinite amount of them with all the stars that shine down upon me. But I'm not lying on the ground. I don't feel anything as I float in negative space.

Where am I?

How did I get here?

And then I see him. My old friend. He never changes and that constant nurtures the despair that has always followed me. His green and yellow accordion body slinks over to me, and it's then that I realize how small I am because he appears to be the same size as me.

"I've missed you," he says in his eloquent English accent.

"I've missed you too, Carnegie."

"Where have you been?"

"In hell."

"Is that why you came back?" he asks.

"I don't even know how I got here," I tell him, and he smiles, saying, "Maybe someone knew you needed a little break from hell," as he gives a nod up to the heavens.

"Maybe," I whisper and roll over onto my belly. It's then I see where I am. Large, green blades of grass standing high above the mass of earth beneath. Gigantic trees that border a sea of dark water. Brilliantly massive blooms are illuminated by the full moon above, casting its glow on the array of colorful, exotic flowers; pink, orange, yellow—but no purple in sight. And when my eyes shift down, I take in a breath of awe when I realize why Carnegie doesn't look so tiny. My body, a tube, roped in pink and black, and when I look back at Carnegie, he laughs, "It's spectacular, isn't it?"

"I'm a caterpillar!" I say in wonderment. "Carnegie, do you see this?!"

"I do."

And then it all comes together. I finally made it. I'm here . . . in the magical forest . . . and I'm a caterpillar, floating in a pond that seems like an ocean because I'm so tiny. I begin laughing as we float on our lily pad raft.

"It's good to see you smiling," he says as I scoot around the large, green leaf, reveling in my new form.

Meandering around, I respond, "It's been a while since I've felt this free."

"May I ask you a question?"

Giggling after I round my body into a ball, discovering I can roll, I take a few seconds to play around before acknowledging his request, answering, "Of course," as I straighten my body and inch over towards him.

"Why do you feel like you're in hell?"

His question dulls my zealousness, and when I flatten my body against the lily pad, I tell him, "It's always been hell, Carnegie. But lately, it's become overwhelming."

"What happened?"

"It's a long story."

"Look around," he says. "I've got nothing but time."

"I'm sure, but to relive everything isn't something I wish to do."

"Then tell me what happened last."

I blink and then look up at the black sky, glittered in stars, and tell him, "I fell in love."

"Ahh, love," he says as if he's wise in that spectrum, so I ask, "You ever been in love?"

"Me?" he questions and looks out over the water. "No. I was turned into a caterpillar before ever having the chance to experience such an emotion. But I wonder why it's hell you feel."

"The love is the only part of this story that isn't hell."

"Tell me what it feels like. Love."

A few fireflies above catch my attention, and as I watch them making skittering dashes of swirling light, I answer, "Amazing. It's like an urgency that can never be sated because you can't get enough. One day, you're walking through life, thinking you're satisfied, well, as satisfied as you can be, and then, when you finally feel the click and get your first taste of love, you realize you've been starving your whole life but never knew it. And that one person is all you need to truly feel alive."

"And you found that?"

Giving Carnegie my attention again, I reply, "Yeah. I never knew what it felt like to breathe until I met him."

"So what's hell?" he asks.

"The man I'm married to."

"The one who allows you to breathe?"

"No, the one who slipped the noose around my throat and caused me a life of suffering," I tell him as his beady eyes widen.

"I'm confused."

"I married my enemy," I begin to explain. "And the man I wound up falling in love with was someone who I was supposed to trick into killing my husband."

"Why do you want your husband dead?"

"Because when I was five, I was ripped away from my dad. He was arrested and went to prison where he was eventually murdered, and I went to a horrendous foster home."

"What does your husband have to do with that?"

"Everything," I say as we continue to float around the smooth water. Releasing a deep breath, I begin telling him the story of my father's arrest and how Pike was determined to find answers for me when we were older.

"It took a while, but after going through my father's police records and Pike blackmailing his old caseworker for my file, we finally found out that it all started with a child abuse claim. We kept digging because my father was the kindest man I knew and had never laid a hand on me. And then we found it. A call was made to DCFS from the Vanderwal family."

"Who are they?"

"I'll give you one clue," I say. "When I married my husband, Bennett, I took his name."

"Vanderwal," he concludes. "But why go after him if it was his parents who made the claim?"

"Because in that file was an interview. The interview was with Bennett."

"It was *his* claim?"

"Yes," I reply as I feel the hate begin to boil inside of me.

"What did it say?"

"He had been walking home from a friend's house one afternoon, and when he passed my house, he heard fighting and screaming coming from inside. He saw my dad through the window hitting someone, but he couldn't see the other person. He assumed it was me that was getting hit, so he went home, told his parents, and the call to DCFS was made."

"Who was it that your father was hitting?"

"I couldn't have been home that afternoon because I would have heard it. I was probably still at preschool or something. But looking back, with the information I have now, it was most likely someone he was doing business with. Maybe a deal gone bad; who knows?" I tell him. "The thing is, the state did their investigation. but they couldn't find any signs of abuse or neglect. However, it was noted that the caseworker noticed *suspicious activity* at the house while performing random drive-by's, so a request for further investigation was handed over to the police department who uncovered the gun trafficking. And that was it, he was arrested, and I never saw him again."

Those last words choke me up, the pain of that last image of my father. It's never faded for me; my father, on his knees, the tears running down his cheeks, his words, trying to convince me that everything would be okay.

When Carnegie begins to move closer to me, finding a new

spot on the lily pad, I'm pulled from the sad memory, and he questions, "So why did you marry him?"

"I felt this burning desire to avenge my father's murder, to make Bennett pay for all the abuse I suffered in foster care, for everything that was stolen from me.

My innocence.

My faith.

My childhood.

My trust.

My father.

My future.

Everything.

"Bennett is the reason there was a magnifying glass put on my father. It was Bennett who opened his mouth, made a false claim, and destroyed two lives, yet he goes on, happy, healthy, making his life into a glorious success. That was supposed to be my life. But because of him, he took it all away from me and I wound up being raped, molested, bound up in a closet, left for days to shit and piss all over myself. That's the life Bennett gave me.

"I wanted to make him pay for what he did. I wanted revenge."

"But you fell in love," he states, and I whisper my confirmation, "I fell in love."

"And now?"

"And now all I want is to spare destroying Declan. I still want to kill Bennett. I still want to make him pay, but not if it costs the good soul of the man I love."

"Let me ask you something. How old was Bennett when he told his parents he thought you were being abused?"

"Eleven."

Carnegie takes a moment before saying, "Just a kid. A young, innocent kid who saw something that probably scared him, thinking you were the one being hit, and his first reaction was to help."

"But he didn't help, and my dad wound up dead," I defend.

"He was just a kid trying to do the right thing," he counters, but instead of growing frustrated, the tranquility of being in this place with Carnegie keeps my frustrations at bay. "Can I ask you something else?"

I nod.

"What responsibility does your father hold in all of this?"

"My father was a good man," I declare.

"I'm not taking that away from him. But everyone has two sides, and your father was a gun trafficker, was he not?"

Taking a moment, I concur, "Yeah. He was. But he never hurt anyone."

"But he knew the illegal guns would hurt someone. He may not have been the one to pull the actual trigger, but in a way, he *did* pull that trigger," he says before adding, "And it wouldn't have mattered what Bennett ever said, the fact is, if your dad hadn't been dealing in something illegal, Bennett's claim would have been dropped and nothing would have ever happened."

"I know what you're trying to do. You're trying to be the voice of reason, but I've never claimed to be a rational or reasonable person."

"Have you ever had a voice of reason?" he questions.

"I've only ever had Pike, and he's just as screwed up as I am, if not more. We're sick people; I know this. But when you grow up like we did, you can't expect sanity," I say. "My father

377

was good. He didn't deserve the life that was dealt to him after what Bennett did. I didn't deserve it either. The thing is, there will always be someone next in line after my father. The gun trafficking doesn't stop, so what's the point? The world isn't suddenly good now that my father isn't here."

"So you plot to kill?"

"I used to fantasize about what it would feel like to kill when I was a kid," I admit. "The thought brought me a sense of satisfaction and elated me. Relief. Freedom. Peace. To eliminate the *truly* bad, removing it so that you no longer have to exist in a world where it does."

"You can't live like that. Killing and holding on to the past."

"I'm not holding on to it, I'm trying to let it go."

"You haven't let it go. Instead, you married it, and now it's controlling every aspect of your life. You met a man you love, but Bennett has power over that because he's your husband and you were forced to fill this other man with lies . . . because of Bennett—because of the past you are refusing to let go of."

His words hit me hard. But how do you let go of a wound that is cut so deep there's no chance of it ever healing, at least not without an ugly scar to remind you of it? So I simply ask, "How do I let go?"

"It's easy, really. You find what makes you happy, and you walk towards it, leaving the past behind," he tells me. "So what you need to ask yourself is, *what makes you happy?*"

"Declan." My answer comes without any second thought or hesitation.

"Then go to him. Go find him and don't look back. Soon the happiness will be enough to weaken the control the past has on you, and it won't hurt as badly as it does right now."

"But I'm here. How do I get back?" I ask and watch as he makes his way to the edge of the leaf, and when we pass a log floating in the water, he slides onto it when the bark meets the lily pad.

"Carnegie, wait! How do I get back?" I ask as I begin to drift away from the log.

"There are signs everywhere. You just have to look for them," he tells me. "Come back and visit me, okay?"

"I do. Every night in my dreams."

"Those are dreams though."

"Is this not a dream?" I ask, suddenly very confused about what this is, and his response doesn't help when he says, "This is your awakening," before scooting his spiraled body down the length of the log and eventually disappearing into the forest.

I continue to float aimlessly around the pond, staring up into the sky, thinking about everything Carnegie said to me. He's right; I need to walk away from my past if I don't want it to follow me.

Hours pass as I enjoy the serene tranquility of my surroundings, and when I see the shimmer of the sun rising through the trees in the distance, its sparkling rays light up the murky water. It's then that I see my sign. Green bulbs that stick out of the water begin to open, hundreds of them. One by one, lotus flowers bloom, spreading their pure white petals over the muddled water. They're beautiful, and when I float into the blooms, I have to squint against the bright light that the sun's glow is creating in this fragrant, white paradise.

thirty-five
(PRESENT)

DARKNESS.

Nothing but black as I lie here awake, although I'm not awake. I can feel a warm hand stroking my arm as I inhale a familiar smell.

Bennett.

My body aches, throbbing in a dulled pain, but when I try to move, I can't. When I try to open my eyes, I can't. But I can feel Bennett's touch. I can smell him. I can hear the steady beeping of a machine that alerts me to the fact that I'm in a hospital.

The last thing I remember is lying helplessly on my dining room floor while Pike threw kick after violent kick to my stomach.

My stomach!

My baby!

I can't wake up. But do I even want to? I already miss

Carnegie. Do I really want to wake up to find the horror that's waiting for me? What happened with Pike? Why did he do it?

"Mr. Vanderwal," a soft, female voice says, but I can't see anything as I lie here in my comatose state.

"Finally," he says with an urgency to his voice. "What's going on? Is she going to be okay?"

"She's stabilized, but she had a lot of internal bleeding. Unfortunately, there was a fetomaternal hemorrhage and by the time she arrived here by ambulance, she had already lost the baby."

No! God, no!

With all the strength I have, I try to move, I try to do anything, but nothing happens. I'm stuck, unable to get out a cry, a scream, a movement, something to release the torment that is beginning to flood inside of me.

"Baby?" Bennett questions. "What baby?"

Oh, God.

"Your wife was pregnant."

"No. There must be some mistake. My wife has endometriosis. She can't get pregnant," he refutes.

"I'm so sorry. I know this is a difficult time, but according to her OB/GYN file that was faxed over, it seems the pregnancy was confirmed last week. I have noted that an ultrasound was performed, indicating at that time, she was nearly ten weeks pregnant."

I don't hear a response from Bennett, and I can only imagine his shock right now.

Bennett, speak. Say something.

"I'll give you some time," she says. "I'll be back to check in. If you need anything, just hit the call button, okay?"

"Yeah," he responds on a breath, and when I hear the door click, he removes his hand from my arm, and the room is silent.

I can't even think about Bennett, all I can think about is my baby. The baby that Pike took away from me. The baby that Pike killed. He knew exactly what he was doing, beating my stomach as violently as he did.

I hate him.

I thrash around like a maniac inside, trying to free myself, but my body doesn't respond. I'm paralyzed in this bed.

"She's in the hospital," Bennett says, but I don't hear anyone else in the room.

"I need you to get here now," he demands. "Bring everything you have on her."

He has to be on the phone, but what the hell is he talking about? Who is he talking to and what do they have on me? *Fuck*. What's going on? I need to get out of here. I need to find Declan. I can't breathe. Oh my God, I'm panicking and I can't breathe. Machines start to go off, filling the room with loud beeps.

"Nurse!" Bennett yells, and moments later, a cold fluid swims through my veins and I drift out peacefully.

"WHAT THE HELL happened?" I hear a man's voice say. It sounds familiar, but my head is so fuzzy as I come out of a deep sleep.

"I got a call from Clara. She had come to the penthouse and found Nina beaten and unconscious. I don't know what happened. I've spoken to the police and they're investigating," Bennett says. "Tell me what you know."

"You wanna do this here?" the man questions.

"Yeah."

"Her name's not Nina."

Oh no. No, no, no, no.

"What are you talking about?" Bennett asks.

"Her name is Elizabeth Archer. A runaway foster kid," he reveals. "It's all in the file."

"Archer? Sounds familiar."

It should, you asshole.

"Her father was arrested for international gun trafficking," the man says.

"I know her."

"Looks like she came straight for you. Piece of advice . . . call your lawyer."

"As soon as you can, I want surveillance set up," Bennett demands, but there's no need. I'm done with him, and the only thing I'm guilty of is identity theft.

"The affair you originally suspected, she's having one. Name is Declan McKinnon."

"Fuck," he hisses. "What is she up to?"

"Here's the file. Everything's in it." There's a long pause before the guy speaks again, saying, "I'll get security set up. Everything should be in place tomorrow or the next day."

The door clicks and I know I'm alone with Bennett, and that freaks me out, because I no longer have control. He's not a stupid man. If he hasn't already figured it out, it won't be long before he does.

Fuck! Why can't I wake up?

"Elizabeth," he whispers, and I can tell it just clicked by his acknowledging tone. "I always wondered what happened to you."

Bullshit.

"Rick," he says, speaking our attorney's name. "Things could be better. Look, I have something that can't wait. When can you see me?"

What's he going to do? Shit. As much as I hate Pike right now, I need him.

"No, that works. I'll leave right now."

I listen to the movements around the room when a female voice says, "I need to change a couple of her bandages."

"That's fine. I was just leaving," Bennett responds. "Here's my card. I want you to call me the second she wakes up, and I mean *the second.*"

He leaves, and I continue to lie here in my comatose state, unable to react to anything. I don't know what I'm doing or what's going to happen to me. I need to run, to go find Pike. I hate that I still need him, but things are headed south, and fast.

I KNOW HE'S here. I can smell lotus blooms, and with that alone, the pinching angst that's been festering relents and I feel safe. His hand is on my belly, another combing through my hair, and I will myself to open my eyes. To move, to do anything to let him know I can feel him. My body hurts so badly as my muscles start to flex and shift.

That's it. Come on; wake up. Wake up.

"Nina?" he says, his voice is sad, but I need to hear it. I need that voice to pull me out of this darkness.

"Can you hear me?" he asks, grabbing my hand, and finally, I can feel my fingers move. "Baby, please wake up. Just open your eyes. Show me you're still with me."

I cling to his words, and light finally filters in. My eyes blink, responding to my body's request.

"Thank God," he sighs in relief as my blurred vision begins to clear. He leans over me, kissing my forehead, and I reach up, grabbing for any part of him.

"I'm here, darling," he assure as I clench on to his shirt, and his hand covers mine. "I'm here," he continues to soothe, and when I try to speak, I gag. "Shh, relax. You have a breathing tube down your throat. Just relax, okay?"

I nod, taking in a few deep breaths, allowing his soft, whispered accent to calm me, and notice the single, white lotus flower that's lying on the bed beside me.

"I'm sorry I wasn't here sooner. When I didn't hear from you, I called all over until I found you here."

I reach up and touch the tube coming out of my mouth and shake my head, needing to tell him that when I leave here, I'm going home with him. I need him to know it's over with Bennett and that it's him I want, but he takes my hand away, reading me well, saying, "It's fine. You don't need to say anything." His eyes are hard and serious when he says, "You'll never go back to that bastard again. You're coming home with me. I should have never let you leave my place the other night."

I nod, agreeing with everything he's saying.

"He's never going to touch you again."

I place my hand over the one he still has on my belly and the emptiness is too much as I begin to cry. He keeps his eyes on my stomach, fisting my hospital gown in his hand. His face pinches, as if he's trying to brace himself for the worst when he finally asks, his voice coming out hoarse, "Please tell me our baby is okay."

And when he finally brings his eyes to mine, I can already feel the salts eating away at my flesh as they spill out. He drops his head and releases a God-awful sob, and I do what I can to give him comfort as I run my fingers deep into his hair, gripping it tightly in my hand as he rests his head on my stomach. Seeing him in this much pain, this strong man who is always in so much control, is unbearable.

His shoulders hunch over and heave as he silently breaks. I want to be swallowed up by anything, just to be taken far away from this life, but I want to take Declan with me. I'll always want him with me, and when he lifts his head, I notice the blackness of his eyes. His jaw grinds and I watch the muscles along his arms constricting. I begin to shake my head as I witness his transformation—the one I had been leading him to make. My heart slams against my broken ribs, and when I grab ahold of his wrists, he snaps, "I'm going to kill that motherfucker."

No, no, no!

I shake my head, and he moves quickly to kiss the corner of my mouth, looking me in the eyes, forcing his words deep inside of me, saying, "That was our baby. My baby."

Frantically, I cling my arms around him, needing him to stay with me, but he pulls back, telling me, "I'm not losing you. I love you too much, but that fucker is going to pay."

I start clawing at the tube in my mouth, yanking it out of

my throat, but begin gagging and choking as I watch him walk out of the room.

Declan, NO! You're not a monster; don't do this! Come back!

I thrash my body up, and I shriek through my gagging when the pain from my broken ribs shoots through me like a virulent fire. The machines are going wild, beeping and flashing, and two nurses rush into the room as I try ripping the tubes and wires away from me.

DECLAN!!!

"Hold still. You need to calm down," the nurse scolds, but I can't. He's going to kill him. He can't kill him.

He can't.

Choking against the breathing tube, I'm pinned down as the one nurse removes it, and once it's out, I wail in utter pain, scratching out a dreadful cry, "Declan!! NO! Stop him!"

"Who?"

"Please!" I belt out, but I'm still pinned down, and when I see the syringe, I freak. "No! Don't! Please!!"

And in an instant, I'm a boulder, sinking like a thousand pounds, deep into the bed. I fight the drifting and weep, body and voice growing weaker with every passing second. I cry, powerless to stop what is bound to happen. I can't lose the Declan I know, the Declan I love, because if he does this, he'll never be the same. And in the end, I'll have no one to blame but myself.

What have I done?

When I can't hang on any longer, I slip under into a desolate sedation.

Alone.

thirty-six
(PRESENT)

When I woke from my sedation, only a few hours had passed. And when the police came to inform me that my husband had been murdered in our home—shot two times in the head—I needed to be sedated again. Knowing what Declan had done—for me—pushed me over the edge.

Guilt . . .

I haven't heard from him or seen him. I miss him. I worry about him. I'm scared for him. I haven't called him because I'm scared to draw any attention, but I've texted him using the app on my phone that he gave me. There's been no response though. Pike has been missing too. So here I am, having no idea what to do, and I'm all alone in a life I no longer want.

I couldn't go home when I was discharged from the hospital this morning; I was too scared of what I would see. The police told me that one of the building's residents made the call to 911 after hearing gunshots. There was no sign of forced entry though, and the police confiscated Bennett's computer and files, among other things, as they move forward in the investigation.

So now I sit here in a hotel room, staring out the window, looking down on a city full of people, but I've never felt so isolated.

Where's Declan? Why hasn't he come for me?

I've been doing nothing but crying. People assume I'm mourning the loss of Bennett, but I'm not. The sick part of me is content with his death. My tears are for my baby and Declan. Never have I been so close to my fairytale ending, and now I hang by a thread while I wait for any type of contact from Declan. I've been looking for signs, signs that Carnegie told me were everywhere, but I can't see beyond the pain of what I have lost so far and the birth of hatred for my brother. The one who promised me that he would always protect me and would fight forever to give me happiness. And then the moment I come within reach of that, he rips it away. I don't know if I could ever forgive him for what he did, because now, all I can do is wish for his death. At the same time, a part of me needs him. To know I still have someone here on this Earth.

What if I lost it all? What if nobody comes for me?

The misery that thought produces overpowers all the aches my body feels from Pike's beating. I couldn't believe what he did to me when I finally saw my reflection in the mirror. My first instinct was to cover my face, but then I realized I have no one to hide from. It's only me.

A pounding on the door startles me, and when I rush over

to look through the peephole, my stomach sinks and coils in fear but also relief.

"Pike," I breathe when I open the door and wrap my arms around him, crying hard for all the fucked up emotions I feel for him. Love and hate, it's a bitter mixture.

He kicks the door closed and holds me close before pulling back. His face is white in horror, hands shaking as he runs them through his hair.

"What's going on? How did you find me?"

"I went to see you at the hospital, but you weren't there, and when you weren't at home, I started calling everywhere looking for Nina Vanderwal." His voice is panicked as he speaks. "We have a huge problem."

"What do you mean?"

Pike paces back and forth like a maniac, telling me, "Declan knows."

"Knows what?"

He turns to face me, on the verge of completely losing it, when he says, "About you. He knows your name. He's knows you're Elizabeth."

"What?! How?" I go stiff, and my first thought is that I've already lost him. Pike doesn't give me much time to think though as he continues.

"I don't know, but when I was driving home earlier this morning, that fucker was waiting for me at the trailer."

"Shit! What did he say?"

"Nothing. I saw him, knew exactly who it was, and drove off, never stopping. I went straight to Matt's place and he said that some guy with an accent had called him the day before asking questions about you and me."

"Oh my God," I say, unable to catch my breath. "How does he know?"

"Don't know, but you've gotta get rid of him. He knows too much. He could already be on his way to the police."

"No," I blurt out, trying to scramble my thoughts together. "He wouldn't do that, would he? I mean, he's the one who killed Bennett."

"Are you willing to put your trust in a man you've only known for a few months, a man you conned, a man you drove to murder someone? This is no joke. You could go to prison if this got uncovered."

The rampant fear running through me causes me to go lightheaded and I have to sit down. I can't even think straight as I stare at the floor, trying to think of all the ways he could've found out. But the dagger here is how I deceived him and what he must be thinking, coming to the realization that he probably just killed a man for nothing but a lie—because that's exactly what he just did.

"Elizabeth, you can't sit here and wait. You have to go find him."

"And do what?" I question as I look up at him.

He stands next to the couch where I sit, and with determination in his eyes, he says, "You have to kill him."

"No." I snap, jumping off the couch, and the pain from my ribs twinges and causes me to stumble. Pike just stands there, unmoving as he watches me. And with my hand clenched around my side, I argue, "No. I'm not doing that."

"You don't have a choice! Are you not hearing me? He knows about us."

"I can't kill him, Pike. I won't do it."

"Cut the shit and wake up! You're not understanding what this could do to you," he shouts.

"I love him."

"You don't. And in the end, you're gonna see that you just got caught up in this fantasy. A fantasy that you and I both created for you. But it's not your life."

"It was my life! And then you came in and took it all away!" I yell, losing my cool and letting my emotions take over. "I do love him, and he loves me. I was finally going to have everything I've ever wanted. We were making plans for us, for our baby, and you destroyed it all! I hate you! I fucking hate you, Pike!"

He doesn't flinch at my words as he stands here. "We had a plan and that plan affected both of us. Bennett needed to die— for you! If I didn't do what I did, to push Declan over the edge, Bennett would still be alive and you'd never be able to forgive yourself for letting him go without any consequences for what he did to you." He takes a step towards me, and his condescending tone on his next words do nothing but fuel my hate, not only for him, but for everything my life is. "Do I need to remind you about how Carl would rape you, piss on that mattress, and force you to lay in it while he pounded his filthy dick inside of you?"

"Fuck you!" I shriek as I start throwing fists into him, frantically beating him in the swarm of pure, seething fire.

He quickly grabs my wrists, forcing me down to the couch, and with his face in mine, hisses, "Either you kill him or I will."

"Pike, no! Maybe he won't do anything at all. Maybe he's scared and will keep his mouth shut," my words tumbling out, giving him weak reason after weak reason, but I'm desperate.

"A scared man wouldn't have shown up to my place alone,"

he says before letting go of me and walking to the door.

I lurch off the couch and throw my body against him, trying to knock him down, but in a flash, he turns and strikes his fist against my already battered face. The force of his punch sends me stumbling back and falling down. By the time I can get up on my feet, he's gone.

"Shit!"

Adrenaline pumps its fury into my system, numbing all of my body's pains as I run to the bedroom and grab my keys. Running out of the room, I waste no time with the elevator as I make a mad dash down the stairs, flight after flight after flight, until I finally make it to the lobby. My throat burns with each breath as I run to my car. Pike is nowhere in sight, and when I pull out of the garage, I have two choices: Lotus or River North. I make the quick decision to try Declan's loft first, praying to anyone who will listen to me that he's there and Pike isn't. I fly through the busy streets, running stop signs and ignoring the red lights I hit.

"Fuck!" I bite out when I drive by Pike's car parked a block down from Declan's building.

Slamming on my brakes when I reach the front of the building, pain pierces my battered body as I run like hell, fumbling with the keycard Declan gave me, and when the elevator opens, I pound the button for his floor over and over as my body quakes in dread and anxiety.

"Come on, come on, come on. COME THE FUCK ON!" I scream with each floor we pass, and as soon as I hit the top floor, two rapid gunshots fire, echoing as the doors slide open.

Speaking isn't even a possibility as I run out and into Declan's living room where I see Pike charging through the loft and then look down at a massive puddle of blood pooling underneath the lifeless body of my prince.

A disgustingly vulgar shriek rips straight from the core of my heart as I run to Declan, falling to my knees in his blood. Touching his face, I try to take in the beauty of this perfectly sculpted man as I wail painfully over him.

"I've got it," I hear Pike say as he rushes back into the room, shoving a file inside of his jacket. Pike's hands are on me quick, pulling me back as I fight against him, screaming and crying. "We have to go!" he urges in a panic.

But I can't speak; the agony is choking me into screeching cries filled with sharp gravel.

"Come on! We have to go. NOW!"

I cover Delcan's body with mine, sealing my lips to his in a breathless kiss as the life drains out of him.

And then . . .

The touch is lost.

Pike has his arms banded around my chest as he lifts me off the floor and starts running.

"Let me go!" I scream, wincing against the pain of my injuries, as I thrash my arms, kicking, trying helplessly to fight my way out of his grip.

"We have to go before the cops get here."

Pike slams through a door, and when we get into the stairwell, he sets me down and pins me against the wall, keeping his hands locked on me.

"Listen to me," he says in a whispered grunt. "Pull yourself together before we both wind up in prison."

"You killed him!" I cry, my words bleeding through the jagged fractures of my heart.

"To save us. I killed him to save us," he defends. "You need to calm down and focus. Look into my eyes and focus."

I do.

"You with me?" he asks.

I don't respond when he adds, "I need you with me, okay? I'm all you have. Listen to me. I need you to do exactly what I say." His words are frantically rushed. "Get in your car. Go home, pack a couple bags, and meet me at the trailer. Don't answer the phone. Don't speak to anyone. Got it?"

"What are we going to do?"

"We're running. Don't fuck around, Elizabeth. Now come on, we have to go!"

And he's right, if we don't get out of here now, our lives will be over. So in a mindless rush of fight or flight, I thoughtlessly fly down the stairs, covered in Declan's blood as I flee towards a freedom I'm not sure even exists.

But I run anyway.

My hands clench the steering wheel, covered in the crimson life of the one man I thought could save me from me. But maybe people like me aren't supposed to be saved. Maybe I'm just destined to bear the weight of the demons that lurk among the good.

When I arrive back at the penthouse, walking through the door as only one, no longer having my beacon of hope growing inside of me, I begin to wonder: *What's the point?* I couldn't even protect the baby that was supposed to be safe from this world. Life's cruel joke of finally giving me something pure and holy, just to have it ripped away from me in an instant.

I don't waste any time though, running straight to the bedroom, the smell of Bennett everywhere. I wonder if he's watching me right now, laughing at the downfall, enjoying my suffering. The bile rises, and I begin slinging clothes in a mad haze into a bag, not even paying attention to what I'm throwing in. Simply moving for the sake of moving, but the actions are entirely thoughtless as the bitterness of my tears leak out and eat through my skin, burning their way back into me. Like a metaphor, reminding me that no matter what I do, I won't ever escape this pain because the moment my body tries to release it, it soaks it right back up.

Fucking life. I hate you.

The world is nothing but a whirlwind of colors and flashing lights, swirling around me as I run back down to my car, not knowing what the next move is—where I go from here—what life holds for me now. Tossing my bag into the back of my car, I look over to the Rover next to it—Bennett's car. And I think, if Bennett is laughing at me right now, does he deserve to be?

Probably so.

I don't know how anyone could be more pathetic than I am right now.

Maybe I'll show him how pathetic I can be; give him another reason to laugh at me.

I punch the security code on the door panel keypad and unlock the car. Opening the passenger door, I flip down the glove box and pull out the pistol that is always kept in there. I lock everything back up and toss the gun in the seat next to me as I pull out and head to Justice.

My thoughts are only on Declan as I drive, swerving around cars to get to a future I'm not sure wants me anymore. All I see are vibrant, green eyes, his beautiful smile that reached them, creating a fan of wrinkles in the corners. The contours of

bang

his shoulders and arms, the shoulders I would cling to and the arms he would soothe me with. His touch was unlike any other. Strong, comforting, warm, healing. His soul giving me a hope that maybe I could find happiness, and when I finally realized I had, and that it all rested inside of his heart, albeit tortured itself, he was able to give me something no one else has ever been able to do—something to look forward to.

I pull up to Pike's trailer, a place I used to find solace because I knew he was always on the other side of that door. Now I fear what's waiting for me behind it. But maybe it's the fear I need to find my freedom.

Slipping the gun into the back waistband of my pants, I head inside.

"Finally. I was beginning to worry," he says as he walks over to the window and peers out. "Anyone see you or follow you?"

"No one saw me," I murmur as I fight the need to fall to the floor and sob like a baby. Instead I stand, mournfully numb.

"Why the fuck are you still covered in his blood?! For fuck's sake, Elizabeth! Go clean that shit off of you."

Looking down at my hands, they continue to shake; the life of Declan, crusted in now splintering pieces of browning carmine. I walk, almost robotically to the bathroom and close the door. My image, reflected in the mirror, is frightening. Bruises and a split lip remain from Pike's beating, but the ugliness is adorned with Declan's blood. It's smeared across my lips and chin, the remainders of our kiss. The kiss of death. Sticking out my tongue, I lick it off, getting one last taste of that life, of that death. My death.

I turn the faucet on, but I can't bring myself to wash off the blood. To take the lasting elements and watch them go down the drain of this filthy sink. Maybe I'm twisted, but the thought of licking every last drop of his dried blood off of me, like an animal, delights me. Taking him and making a home for him deep inside of me.

So I walk out, back into the living room where Pike has his bags tossed on the floor. He turns to look at me, cocking his head, and giving me a look of sympathy as he walks over to me.

"You can do this," he says softly, taking his hands and stroking my upper arms. I'm not sure how I'm even breathing at this point with the noose that's strangling me, slowly inching its way up, and any second, my neck will snap with a delicious sound, taking me to Wonderland.

"I love you. You know that, right?" he says gently.

"Yeah," I sigh. I know he does. But Pike is a vile human, just like me, and the love we have for each other is infected with a sickness that only we know. "I love you too."

"I need you to clean yourself before we leave."

"I don't want to," I whimper like a child.

"I know. But it's over. And we don't have time to think about how it feels right now. More than ever, I need you to shut yourself off long enough to get the hell out of here."

"Where are we going?"

"Out of the country. I don't know. But we have to go somewhere long enough for us to figure this shit out."

I shake my head, dropping it, feeling the tears drip off my cheeks. They sink down into the dirty carpet by my feet, and I know I can't go on like this.

"I can't do this, Pike. I can't."

"You can. You're just scared. We've gotten through so much, and we will get through this. Just trust me."

A tingle runs up my arms and drifts slowly down into my chest as I awaken. "I don't know if I can do that anymore."

Pike steps back, dropping his hands, saying, "What does that mean?"

"I don't want to run."

He paces across the room, and I feel it. The end. And it fucking kills me because I do love Pike. I always have.

"They'll come after you, you know?" he threatens.

"No, they won't. I didn't do anything," I refute. "You did it all."

"Is that what you think? That your hands are the ones that are clean in this?" he says, growing irritated with me as his eyes turn to daggers. "I'm the invisible link here. It's you that they'll be after. The wife. The *unfaithful* wife. You had a motive too."

"And what's that?"

He pauses, taking a moment while a sly grin starts to spread across his face. "Your baby."

The mere mention causes a physical reaction inside of me as my heart picks up its pace, rapidly beating inside of me.

"That's right. The police probably already know. The lies you told will become truths because it's what you led everyone to believe."

"Why are you doing this to me?"

"You're doing this. You're the selfish one who's willing to drop everything because you can't do it anymore. What about me? You wanna leave me?"

"I don't know what it is I want because you took all those choices away from me."

"I'm not letting you leave me," he demands. "I've given you too much."

"All you've been doing is taking."

"I gave you my goddamn life!" he screams, clenching his fist and punching it right through the paneled wall. My body trembles in fear when he bores his eyes into me, seething, "I gave you everything. I love you. I always have."

And this is it. My moment of clarity. I'll never get that new beginning because you can't start a new life—a new beginning—when the past is right beside you. And Pike? He's not going anywhere. He'll never leave me, and he'll never let me leave. But I'm not sure I could ever truly walk away from him because when you cut through all the shit, I love him. I love my brother so much.

"I love you, Elizabeth," he says, lowering his voice, almost pleading.

"I know you do."

"You can't leave me. You know I hold too much over you," he threatens.

"I know," I weep, the tears flooding over and down my face as I reach behind me and welcome the feel of ice, cold steel in the palm of my hand.

"Elizabeth, please. Don't give up on me—on us."

"I'm so sorry, Pike. We'll never be apart from each other. Our hearts will always be linked."

And when the look of desperation in his eyes morphs into horror, widening as he watches me bring my arm around, he panics, "What are you doing?"

bang

I release a breathless cry.

"I love you, Pike."

(bang)

from the author

The stories I write are so close to me, they feel like the blood of my heart. Thank you for allowing me to expose that—it's beyond freeing!

acknowledgements

SO MUCH WORK was put into this book before I ever sat down and wrote the first word. The planning and plotting took months and months, and to see how this story morphed into what it is now is an amazing thing. The people involved with the creation of this book have been absolutely wonderful even though they have repeatedly questioned my sanity along the way.

Gina, you were the first person I ever told about the idea of this story that I was calling "Bang" because I just didn't know what else to call it. We laughed at the name so many times as we worked closely together creating the cast of characters. I must thank you for Declan; the idea of him was brilliant, and you gave me a great base to build on. Thank you for spending hours on the phone with me, listening to one crazy idea after another. You are my partner in crime, and I love that I can continue to shock you.

Cathy, how can I possibly thank you properly? The hours we spent nailing down the details of this story, the plotting, creating, planning, and developing. You are a priceless asset to me that I do not take for granted. I know I gave you a few moments were you probably thought I was crazy, but you cheered me on nonetheless. You are my ever-constant support and everything a parent and friend should be, and I love you beyond what you could ever imagine. I look forward to working on the following books in this series with you!

Lisa, my editor, thank you for taking my words and making them shine. You are tough on me, but I will forever run to you because it's the toughness I need. I truly feel like I have hit the jackpot with you. I don't know how any other editor could do what you do for me with each and every book. Thank you for caring about not only my words and my story, but for caring about me. I love you; there's nothing more I can say.

My husband, your undying support is beyond amazing and allows me to keep doing what I love. I don't know how to thank you enough, love.

Luna, my bright moon in the dark sky above, my motivator, my cheerleader, my fighter, my friend. Working on this book together and the conversations that it sparked between us have been quite interesting. We have gone from laughing to crying, all the while forming a friendship along the way. Thank you for opening yourself up to this story, for the hard discussions we had while I was writing, for all of your words of encouragement. But above all, thank you for your honesty, even when you knew the words would be hard for me to hear. You are the fire I need by my side.

V, I love our early morning conversations and the way you

laugh at me when I tell you my darkest ideas. Discussing my characters with you is always fun for me. You can always find a way to put a smile on my face no matter how discouraged I may be. Thank you for being my best friend through all these years.

My fans, I owe it all to you. For each and every one of you who read my stories, thank you. Bloggers, there are too many of you to mention, but I cannot thank you enough for all the time you spend reading, reviewing, and promoting my work. Your dedication means the world to me. My betas, thank you for all of your hard work. I absolutely couldn't do this without you.

Ways To Connect
www.ekblair.com
Facebook: https://www.facebook.com/EKBlairAuthor
Twitter: @EK_Blair_Author

Coming Soon
in
The Black Lotus Series
Echo
(book 2)
Hush
(book 3)

Other Titles by E.K. Blair

USA Today Bestseller

THE
FADING
SERIES

"Heart-wrenching, jaw-dropping, and absolutely beautiful."
-Aleatha Romig, *New York Times* bestselling author

"One of the most incredible, breathtaking stories I have ever read."
-Word

"Beautifully written and emotionally charged."
-Vilma Gonzalez, *USA Today* HEA blog

CPSIA information can be obtained at www.ICGtesting.com
Printed in the USA
BVOW08s2009110916

461685BV00018B/14/P

9 780578 141800